twenty years, trained as a nurse and a health visitor. Scarlet now works in public health and lives on the West Coast of Scotland with her fiancé and their two sons. Writing medical romances and contemporary romances is a dream come true for her.

Sophie Pembroke has been dreaming, reading and writing about romance ever since she read her first Mills & Boon as part of her English Literature degree at Lancaster University, so getting to write romantic fiction for a living really is a dream come true! Born in Abu Dhabi, Sophie grew up in Wales and now lives in a little Hertfordshire market town with her scientist husband, her incredibly imaginative and creative daughter and her adventurous, adorable little boy. In Sophie's world, happy is for ever after, everything stops for tea, and there's always time for one more page…

Wedding Belles

Wedding Belles: Summer Weddings

JESSICA GILMORE

SCARLET WILSON

SOPHIE PEMBROKE

MILLS & BOON

First Published in Great Britain 2021
By Mills & Boon, an imprint of HarperCollins*Publishers,* Ltd
1 London Bridge Street, London, SE1 9GF

www.harpercollins.co.uk

HarperCollins*Publishers*
1st Floor, Watermarque Building,
Ringsend Road, Dublin 4, Ireland

WEDDING BELLES: SUMMER WEDDINGS © 2021 Harlequin Books S.A.

Expecting the Earl's Baby © 2015 Jessica Gilmore
A Bride for the Runaway Groom © 2015 Scarlet Wilson
Falling for the Bridesmaid © 2015 Sophie Pembroke

ISBN: 978-0-263-30044-4

MIX
Paper from
responsible sources
FSC® C007454

This book is produced from independently certified FSC™ paper
to ensure responsible forest management.

For more information visit: www.harpercollins.co.uk/green

Printed and bound in Spain
by CPI, Barcelona

EXPECTING THE EARL'S BABY

JESSICA GILMORE

For Carla

A book about sisters, for my sister

Love Jessica x

PROLOGUE

'OH, NO!'

Daisy Huntingdon-Cross skidded to a halt on the icy surface and regarded her car with dismay.

No, dismay was for a dropped coffee or spilling red wine on a white T-shirt. Her chest began to thump as panic escalated. *This*, Daisy thought as she stared at the wall of snow surrounding her suddenly flimsy-seeming tyres, *this* was a catastrophe.

The snow, which had fallen all afternoon and evening, might have made a picturesque background for the wedding photos she had spent the past twelve hours taking, but it had begun to drift—and right now it was packed in tightly around her tyres. Her lovely, bright, quirky little city car, perfect for zooming around London in, was, she was rapidly realising, horribly vulnerable in heavy snow and icy conditions.

Daisy carefully shifted her heavy bag to her other shoulder and looked around. It was the only car in the car park.

In fact, she was the only person in the car park. No, scratch that, she was possibly the only person in the whole castle. A shiver ran down her spine, not entirely as a result of the increasing cold and the snow seeping through her very inadequate brogues. Hawksley Castle was a wonderfully romantic venue in daylight and when it was lit up at night. But when you were standing underneath the parapets, the great tower a craggy, shadowy silhouette looming above you and the only light a tepid glow from the lamp at the edge of the car park it wasn't so much romantic, more the setting for every horror film she had ever seen.

'Just don't go running into the woods.' She cast a nervous glance over her shoulder. The whole situation was bad enough without introducing the supernatural into it.

Besides it was Valentine's Day. Surely the only ghosts abroad today had to be those of lovers past?

Daisy shivered again as her feet made the painful transition from wet and cold to freezing. She stamped them with as much vigour as she could muster as she thought furiously.

Why had she stayed behind to photograph the departing guests, all happily packed into mini-buses at the castle gates and whisked off to the local village where hot toddies and roaring fires awaited them? She could have left three hours ago, after the first dance and long before the snow had changed from soft flakes to a whirling mass of icy white.

But, no, she always had to take it that step further, offer that bit more than her competitors—including the blog, complete with several photographs, that she'd promised would be ready to view by midnight.

Midnight wasn't that far away...

'Okay.' Her voice sounded very small in the empty darkness but talking aloud gave her a sense of normality. 'One, I can go into the village. It's only a couple of miles.' Surely the walking would warm up her feet? 'Two, I can try and scoop the worst of the snow off...' She cast a doubtful glance at the rest of the car park. The ever heavier snowfall had obliterated her footprints; it was like standing on a thick, very cold white carpet. An ankle-deep carpet. 'Three...' She was out of options. Walk or scoop, that was it.

'Three—I get you some snow chains.'

Daisy didn't quite manage to stifle a small screech as deep masculine tones broke in on her soliloquy. She turned, almost losing her footing in her haste, and skidded straight into a fleece-clad chest.

It was firm, warm, broad. Not a ghost. Probably not a werewolf. Or a vampire. Supernatural creatures didn't wear fleece as far as she knew.

'Where did you come from? You frightened the life out of me.' Daisy stepped back, scowling at her would-be rescuer. At least she hoped he was a rescuer.

'I was just locking up. I thought all the wedding guests were long gone.' His gaze swept over her. 'You're hardly dressed for this weather.'

'I was dressed for a wedding.' She tugged the hem of her silk dress down. 'I'm not a guest though, I'm the photographer.'

'Right.' His mouth quirked into a half smile. The gesture changed his rather severe face into something much warmer. Something much more attractive. He was tall—taller than Daisy who, at nearly six feet, was used to topping most men of her acquaintance—with scruffy dark hair falling over his face.

'Photographer or guest you probably don't want to be hanging around here all night so I'll get some chains and we'll try and get this tin can of yours on the road. You really should put on some winter tyres.'

'It's not a tin can and there's very little call for winter tyres in London.'

'You're not in London,' he pointed out silkily.

Daisy bit her lip. He had a point and she wasn't really in any position to argue. 'Thank you.'

'No worries, wouldn't want you to freeze to death on

the premises. Think of the paperwork. Talking of which, you're shivering. Come inside and warm up. I can lend you some socks and a coat. You can't drive home like that.'

Daisy opened her mouth to refuse and then closed it again. He didn't seem like an axe murderer and she was getting more and more chilled by the second. If it was a choice between freezing to death and taking her chances inside she was definitely veering towards the latter. Besides... 'What time is it?'

'About eleven, why?'

She'd never get home in time to post the blog. 'I don't suppose...' She tried her most winning smile, her cheeks aching with the cold. 'I don't suppose I can borrow your Wi-Fi first? There's something I really need to do.'

'At this time of night?'

'It's part of my job. It won't take long.' Daisy gazed up at him hoping her eyes portrayed beseeching and hopeful with a hint of professionalism, not freezing cold and pathetic. Their eyes snagged and the breath hitched in her throat.

'I suppose you can use it while you warm up.' The smile was still playing around his mouth and Daisy's blood began to heat at the expression in his eyes. If he turned it up a little more she wouldn't need a jumper and socks, her own internal system would have defrosted her quite nicely.

He held out a hand. 'Seb, I look after this place.'

Daisy took the outstretched hand, her heart skipping a beat as their fingers touched. 'I'm Daisy. Nice to meet you, Seb.'

He didn't answer, reaching out and taking her bag, shouldering it with ease as he turned and began to tread gracefully through the ever thickening snow.

'"Mark my footsteps, my good page,"' Daisy sang under

her breath as she took advantage of the pressed-down snow and hopped from one imprint to the other. Tall, dark, handsome and coming to her rescue on Valentine's Day? It was almost too good to be true.

CHAPTER ONE

Six weeks later...

DÉJÀ-VU RIPPLED DOWN Daisy's spine as she rounded the path. It was all so familiar and yet so different.

The last time she had been at Hawksley the castle and grounds had been covered in snow, a fantasy winter wonderland straight out of a historical film. Today the courtyard lawn was the pale green of spring, crocuses and primroses peeking out at the unseasonably warm sun. The old Norman keep rose majestically on her left, the thick grey stone buttresses looking much as they must have looked nearly one thousand years ago, a stark contrast to ye olde charm of the three-storey Tudor home attached to it at right angles.

And straight ahead of her the Georgian house.

Daisy swallowed, every instinct screaming at her to turn and run. She could wait a few weeks, try again then. Maybe try a letter instead. After all, it was still such early days...

But no. She straightened her shoulders. That was the coward's way out and she had been raised better than that. Confront your problems head-on, that was what her father always told her.

Besides, she really needed to talk to somebody. She

didn't want to face her family, not yet, and none of her friends would understand. He was the only person who this affected in the same way.

Or not. But she had to take the risk.

Decision made, smile plastered on and she was ready to go. If she could just find him that was...

The castle had a very closed-off air. The small ticket office was shut, a sign proclaiming that the grounds and keep wouldn't be open until Whitsun. Daisy swivelled trying to find signs of life.

Nobody.

There was a small grey door set at the end of the Georgian wing, which she recognised from her earlier visit. It was as good a place to start as any.

Daisy walked over, taking her time and breathing in the fresh spring air, the warm sun on her back giving her courage as she pushed at the door.

'Great.' It was firmly locked and there was no bell, 'You'd think they didn't want visitors,' she muttered. Well, want them or not she was here. Daisy knocked as hard as she could, her knuckles smarting at the impact, then stood back and waited, anticipation twisting her stomach.

The door swung open. Slowly. Daisy inhaled and held her breath. Would he remember her?

Would he believe her?

A figure appeared at the door. She exhaled, torn between disappointment and a secret shameful relief. Unless Seb had aged twenty-five years, lost six inches and changed gender this wasn't him.

Daisy pushed her trilby hat further back and gave the stern-looking woman guarding the door marked 'private' an appealing smile. 'Excuse me, can you tell me where I can find Seb?'

Her appeal was met with crossed arms and a gorgonish expression. 'Seb?' There was an incredulous tone to her voice.

The message was loud and clear; smiling wasn't going to cut it. On the other hand she hadn't been instantly turned to stone so it wasn't a total loss.

'Yes.' Daisy bit her lip in a sudden panic. She had got his name right, hadn't she? So much of that night was a blur...

'The handyman,' she added helpfully. *That* she remembered.

'We have an estate maintenance crew.' The gorgon sniffed. Actually *sniffed*. 'But none of them are named Seb. Maybe you have the wrong place?' She looked Daisy up and down in a manner that confirmed that, in her eyes, Daisy most definitely did have the wrong place.

Maybe it was the lipstick? Real Real Red wasn't a shade everyone liked. It was so very red after all but it usually made Daisy feel ready for anything. Even today.

It was like being back at school under her headmistress's disappointed eye. Daisy resisted the urge to tug her tailored shorts down to regulation knee length and to button up the vintage waistcoat she had thrown on over her white T-shirt.

She took a step back and straightened her shoulders, ready for war. She had replayed this morning over and over in her mind. At no point had she anticipated not actually seeing Seb. Or finding out he didn't exist.

What if he was a ghost after all?

Surely not. Daisy wasn't entirely certain what ectoplasm actually was but she was pretty sure it was cold and sticky. Ghosts weren't made of warm, solid muscle.

No, no dwelling on the muscles. Or the warmth. She pushed the thought out of her mind as firmly as she could and adopted her best, haughty public schoolgirl voice. 'This is Hawksley Castle, isn't it?'

Of course it was. Nowhere else had the utterly unique

blend of Norman keep, Tudor mansion and Georgian country home that ensured Hawksley remained top of the country's best-loved stately homes list—according to *Debutante* magazine anyway.

But Daisy wasn't interested in the historical significance of the perfectly preserved buildings. She simply wanted to gain access to the final third of the castle, the Georgian wing marked 'private'.

'Yes, this is Hawksley Castle and we are not open until Whitsun. So, I suggest, miss, that you return and purchase a ticket then.'

'Look.' Daisy was done with playing nice. 'I'm not here to sightsee. I was here six weeks ago for the Porter-Halstead wedding and got snowed in. Seb helped me and I need to see him. To say thank you,' she finished a little lamely but there was no way she was telling this woman her real motivation for visiting. She'd be turned to stone for sure.

The gorgon raised an eyebrow. 'Six weeks later?'

'I'm not here for a lesson in manners.' Daisy regretted the snap the second it left her mouth. 'I've been…busy. But better late than never. I thought he was the handyman. He certainly—' seemed good with his hands flashed through her mind and she coloured '—seemed to know his way around.' Oh, yes, that he did.

Nope. No better.

'But he definitely works here. He has an office. Tall, dark hair?' Melting dark green eyes, cheekbones she could have cut herself on and a firm mouth. A mouth he really knew how to use.

Daisy pulled her mind firmly back to the here and now. 'He had a shovel and snow chains, that's why I thought he was the handyman but maybe he's the estate manager?'

Unless he had been a wedding guest putting on a very good act? Had she made a terrible mistake? No, he hadn't been dressed like a wedding guest, had known his way around the confusing maze behind the baize door in the Georgian wing.

She was going to have to get tough. 'Listen,' she began then stopped as something wet and cold snuffled its way into her hand. Looking down, she saw a pair of mournful brown eyes gazing up at her. 'Monty!'

Proof! Proof that she wasn't going crazy and proof that Seb was here.

Crouching down to scratch behind the springer spaniel's floppy brown ears, Daisy broke into a croon. 'How are you, handsome boy? It's lovely to see you again. Now if you could just persuade this lady here that I need to see your master that will be brilliant.' She couldn't help throwing a triumphant glance over at her adversary.

'Monty! Here, boy! Monty! Here I say.' Peremptory tones rang across the courtyard and Daisy's heart began to speed up, blood rushing around her body in a giddying carousel. Slowly she got back up, leaving one hand on the spaniel's head, more for strength and warmth, and half turned, a smile on her face.

'Hi, Seb.'

It had been a long morning. It wasn't that Seb wasn't grateful for his expensive education, his academic credentials and his various doctorates but there were times when he wondered just what use being able to recite Latin verse and debate the use of cavalry at Thermopylae was.

Business studies, basic accountancy, and how to repair, heat and conserve an ancient money pit without whoring her out like a restoration actress would have been far more useful.

He needed a business plan. Dipping into what was left of the estate's capital would only get him so far. Somehow the castle needed to pay for itself—and soon.

And now his dog was being disobedient, making eyes at a blonde woman improbably dressed in shorts and a trilby hat teamed with a garish waistcoat. Shorts. In *March*. On the other hand… Seb's eyes raked the slender, long legs appreciably; his dog had good taste.

'Monty! I said here. I am so sorry…' His voice trailed off as the woman straightened and turned. Seb felt his breath whoosh out as he clocked the long blonde hair, blue eyes, tilted nose and a mouth that had haunted him for the last six weeks. 'Daisy?'

'Hello, Seb. You never call, you don't write.' An under-current of laughter lilted through her voice and he had to firm his mouth to stop a responsive smile creeping out. What on earth had brought the wedding photographer back to his door? For a few days afterwards he had wondered if she might get in touch. And what he would say if she did.

For six weeks afterwards he had considered getting in touch himself.

'Neither did you.'

'No.' Her eyelashes fluttered down and she looked oddly vulnerable despite the ridiculous hat tilted at a rak-ish angle and the bright lipstick. 'Seb, could we talk?'

She sounded serious and Seb tensed, his hands curling into apprehensive fists. 'Of course, come on in.' He ges-tured for her to precede him through the door. 'Thanks, Mrs Suffolk, I'll take it from here.' He smiled at his most faithful volunteer and she moved aside with a sniff of clear disapproval.

'I don't think she likes me,' Daisy whispered.

'She doesn't like anyone. Anyone under thirty and fe-male anyway.' He thought about the statement. 'Actually anyone under thirty *or* any female.'

Seb led the way through the narrow hallway, Monty at his heels. The courtyard entrance led directly into what had once been the servants' quarters, a warren of windy passageways, small rooms and back staircases designed to ensure the maids and footmen of long ago could go about their duties without intruding on the notice of the family they served.

Now it held the offices and workrooms necessary for running the vast estate. The few staff that lived in had cottages outside the castle walls and Seb slept alone in a castle that had once housed dozens.

It would make sense to convert a floor of unused bedrooms and offer overnight hospitality to those who booked the Tudor Hall for weddings rather than chucking them out into the nearby hotels and guest houses. But it wasn't just the expense that put him off. It was one thing having tourists wandering around the majestic keep, one thing to rent out the spectacular if dusty, chilly and impractical hall. The Georgian wing was his home. Huge, ancient, filled with antiques, ghosts and dusty corners. *Home.*

And walking beside him was the last person to have stayed there with him.

'Welcome back.' Seb noted how, despite her general air of insouciance, she was twisting her hands together nervously. 'Nice hat.'

'Thanks.' She lifted one hand and touched it self-consciously. 'Every outfit needs a hat.'

'I don't recall you wearing one last time.'

'I was dressed for work then.'

The words hung heavily in the air and Seb was instantly transported back. Back to the slide of a zip, the way her silky dress had slithered to the ground in one perfect movement.

Definitely no hat on that occasion, just glittering pins in her hair. It was a shame. He would have quite liked to have seen her wearing it when she had lain on his sofa, golden in the candlelight, eyes flushed from the champagne. Champagne and excitement. The hat and nothing else.

He inhaled, long and deep, trying to ignore the thrumming of his heart, the visceral desire the memory evoked.

Seb stopped and reconsidered his steps. The old estate office was an incongruous mix of antique desk, sofa and rug mixed with metal filing cabinets and shelves full of things no one wanted to throw away but didn't know what else to do with.

Now, with Daisy's reappearance, it was a room with ghosts of its own. Six-week-old ghosts with silken skin, low moans and soft, urgent cries. Taking her back there would be a mistake.

Instead he opened the discreet doors that led into the front of the house. 'Let's go to the library.' It wasn't cowardice that had made him reconsider. It was common sense. His mouth quirked at the corner. 'As you can probably tell, the house hasn't received the memo for the warmest spring in ten years and it takes several months for the chill to dissipate. The library is the warmest room in the whole place—probably because it's completely non-modernised. The velvet drapes may be dusty and dark but they keep the cold out.'

Daisy adjusted her hat again, her hands still nervous. 'Fine.'

He pushed the heavy wooden door open, standing aside to let her go in first. 'So, this is quite a surprise.'

She flushed, the colour high on her cheekbones. 'A nice one, I hope.' But she didn't meet his eye. He stilled, watching her. Something was going on, something way beyond a desire for his company.

Daisy walked into the oak-panelled room and stood, looking curiously about her. Seb leant against the door for a moment, seeing the room through her eyes; did she find it shabby? Intimidating? It was an odd mixture of both. The overflowing floor-to-ceiling bookshelves covered two of the walls; the dark oak panelling was hung with gloomy family portraits and hunting scenes. Even the fireplace was large enough to roast at least half an ox, the imposing grate flanked by a massive marble lintel. All that the library needed was an irascible old man to occupy one of the wing-back chairs and Little Lord Fauntleroy to come tripping in.

She wandered over to one of the shelves and pulled out a book, dust flying into the air. 'Good to see the owner's a keen reader.'

'Most of the English books have been read. That's the Latin section.'

She tilted her chin. 'Latin or not, they still need dusting.'

'I'll get the footmen right on it. Sit down.' He gestured to a chair. 'Would you like a drink?'

'Will a footman bring it?'

'No.' He allowed himself a smile. 'There's a kettle in that corner. It's a long way from here to the kitchen.'

'Practical. Tea, please. Do you have Earl Grey?'

'Lemon or milk?'

Seating herself gingerly in one of the velvet chairs, the dusty book still in her hand, she raised an elegantly arched eyebrow. 'Lemon? How civilised. Could I just have hot water and lemon, please?'

'Of course.'

It only took a minute to make the drinks but the time out was needed. It was unsettling, having her here in his private space, the light floral scent of her, the long legs, the red, red lipstick drawing attention to her wide, full mouth. The problem with burying yourself with work twenty-four-seven, Seb reflected as he sliced the lemon, was that it left you ill prepared for any human interaction. Especially the feminine kind.

Which was rather the point.

'A proper cup and saucer. You have been well brought

up.' She held up the delicately patterned porcelain as he handed it to her and examined it. 'Wedgwood?'

'Probably.'

Seb seated himself opposite, as if about to interview her, and sat back, doing his best to look as if he were at his ease, as if her unexpected reappearance hadn't totally thrown him. 'How's peddling ridiculous dreams and overblown fantasies going?'

Daisy took a sip of her drink, wincing at the heat. 'Business is good, thanks. Busy.'

'I'm not surprised.' He eyed her critically. 'Engagement shoots, fifteen-hour days, blogs. When you work out your hourly rate you're probably barely making minimum wage.' Not that he was one to talk.

'It's expected.' Her tone was defensive. 'Anyone can get a mate to point a camera nowadays. Wedding photographers need to provide more, to look into the soul of the couple. To make sure there isn't one second of their special day left undocumented.'

Seb shook his head. 'Weddings! What happened to simple and heartfelt? Not that I'm complaining. We are already booked up for the next two years. It's crazy. So much money on just one day.'

'But it's the happiest day of their lives.'

'I sincerely hope not. It's just the first day, not the marriage,' he corrected her. 'Romantic fantasies like that are the biggest disservice to marriage. People pour all their energy and money into just one day—they should be thinking about their lives together. Planning that.'

'You make it sound so businesslike.'

'It *is* businesslike,' he corrected her. 'Marriage is like anything else. It's only successful if the participants share goals. Know exactly what they are signing up for. Mark my words, a couple who go into marriage with a small ceremony and a robust life plan will last a lot longer than fools who get into debt with one over-the-top day.'

'No, you're wrong.' Daisy leant forward, her eyes lit up. 'Two people finding each other, plighting their troth in front of all their friends and family, what could be more romantic than that?' Her voice trailed off, the blue eyes wistful.

Seb tried not to let his mouth quirk into a smile but the temptation was too much. 'Did you just say plight your troth? Is that what you write in your blogs?'

'My couples say my blogs are one of the most romantic parts of their special day.' Her colour was high. 'That's why I do the engagement shoots, to get to know each couple individually, know what makes them tick. And no.' She glared at him. 'Even with the extras I still make well over the minimum wage and no one ever complains. In fact, one couple have just asked me to come back to document their pregnancy and take the first photographs of their baby.'

'Of course they did.' He couldn't keep the sarcasm out of his voice. 'The only thing guaranteed to waste more money than a wedding is a baby.'

Her already creamy skin paled, her lips nearly blue. 'Then you probably don't want to hear that you're going to be a father. I'm pregnant, Seb. That's what I came here to say.'

As soon as she blurted the words out she regretted it. It wasn't how she'd planned to tell him; her carefully prepared lead up to the announcement abandoned in the heat of the moment. At least she had shaken him out of the cool complacency; Seb had shot upright, the green eyes hard, his mouth set firm.

'Are you sure?'

Oh, yes. She was sure. Two tests a day for the past week sure. 'I have a test in my bag, I can take it here and now if you like.' It wasn't the kind of thing she'd usually offer to an almost stranger but the whole situation was embarrassing enough, another step into mortification alley wouldn't hurt.

'No, that won't be necessary.' He ran a hand through his hair. 'But we used... I mean, we were careful.'

It was almost funny—almost—that she and this man opposite could have spent a night being as intimate as two people could be. Had explored and tasted and touched. Had teased and caressed and been utterly uninhibited. And yet they didn't know each other at all. He couldn't even use the word 'condom' in front of her.

'We did.' Daisy summoned up all her poise and looked at him as coolly and directly as she could manage, trying to breathe her panicked pulse into submission, to still the telltale tremor in her hands. 'At least, we did the first and second time. I'm not sure we were thinking clearly after that.'

Not that they had been thinking clearly at all. Obviously. It was easy to blame the snowfall, the intimacy of being alone in the fairy-tale landscape, the champagne. That he had come to her rescue. But it still didn't add up. It had been the most incredible, the most intense and the most out-of-character night of Daisy's life.

A muscle was beating along the stubbled jawline; his eyes were still hard, unreadable. 'How do you know it's mine?'

She had been prepared for this question, it was totally reasonable for him to ask and yet a sharp stab of disappointment hit her. 'It has to be yours.' She lifted her chin and eyed him defiantly. 'There is no one else, there hasn't been, not for a long time. I usually only do long-term relationships and I split up from my last boyfriend nine months ago.' She needed to make him understand. 'That night, it wasn't usual. It wasn't how I normally behave.'

'Right.'

'You can check, have a test. Only not until after it's born. It's safer that way.'

His eyes locked onto hers. 'You're keeping it, then?'

Another reasonable question and yet one she hadn't even thought to ask herself. 'Yes. Look, Seb, you don't have to decide anything right now. I'm not here for answers or with demands. I just thought you should know but…'

'Hold on.' He stood up with a lithe grace, hand held out to cut her off. 'I need to think. Don't go anywhere, can you promise me that? I won't be long, I just, I just need some air. Come on, Monty.'

'Wait!' It was too late, he had whirled out of the door, the spaniel close to his heels. Daisy had half got up but sank back down into the deep-backed chair as the heavy oak door closed with a thud.

'That went better than I expected,' she murmured. She was still here and, okay, he hadn't fallen to his knees and pledged to love the baby for ever but neither had she been turned out barefoot onto his doorstep.

And wasn't his reaction more natural? Questioning disbelief? Maybe that should have been hers as well. Daisy slid her hand over her midriff, marvelling at the flat tautness, no visible clue that anything had changed. And yet she hadn't been shocked or upset or considered for even a nanosecond that she wouldn't have the baby.

Its conception might be an accident in most people's eyes but not in Daisy's. It was something else entirely. It was a miracle.

One hour later, more hot lemon and three pages of a beautiful old hardback edition of *Pride and Prejudice* read over and over again, Daisy admitted defeat. Wait, he had said. How long did he mean? She hadn't promised him anyway; he had disappeared before she could form the words.

But she couldn't leave without making sure he had a way of getting in touch. She hadn't thought last time, hadn't slipped her card into his hand or pocket with a smile and invitation. Had part of her hoped he would track her down anyway? Perform a modern-day quest in pursuit of her love. The hopeless romantic in her had. The hopeless romantic never learned.

But this wasn't about challenges. It was more important than that. Rummaging in her bag, Daisy pulled out one of her business cards. Stylish, swirling script and a daisy motif proclaimed 'Daisy Photos. Weddings, portraits and lifestyle.' Her number, website and Twitter handle listed clearly below. She paused for a second and then laid the card on the tea tray with a hand that only trembled a little. It was up to him now.

She closed her eyes for a moment, allowing her shoulders to sag under the weight of her disappointment. She had been prepared for anger, denial. Naively, she had hoped he might be a little excited. She hadn't expected him to just *leave*.

Her car was where she'd left it, parked at a slant just outside the imposing gates. If she had swallowed her pride and accepted the Range Rover her father had offered her then she wouldn't have been snowed in all those weeks ago.

Daisy shook her head trying to dislodge unwanted tears prickling the backs of her eyes. It had all seemed so perfect, like a scene from one of her favourite romantic comedies. When it was clear that she was stuck, Seb had ransacked the leftovers from the wedding buffet, bringing her a picnic of canapés and champagne. And she had curled up on the shabby sofa in his office as they talked and drank, and somehow she had found herself confiding in him, trusting him. Kissing him.

She raised her hands to her lips, remembering how soft his kiss had been. At first anyway...

Right. Standing here reliving kisses wasn't going to

change anything. Daisy unlocked her car, and took one last long look at the old castle keep, the grim battlements softened by the amber spring sun.

'Daisy!'

She paused for a moment and inhaled long and deep before swivelling round, trying to look as unconcerned as possible, and leaning back against her car.

Her heart began to thump. Loudly.

He wasn't her type at all. Her type was clean-shaven, their eyes didn't hold a sardonic gleam under quizzical eyebrows and look as if they were either laughing at you or criticising you. Her usual type didn't wear their dark hair an inch too long and completely unstyled and walk around in old mud-splattered jeans, although she had to admit they were worn in all the right places.

And Daisy Huntingdon-Cross had never as much as had a coffee with a man in a logoed fleece. The black garment might bear the Hawksley Castle crest but it was still a fleece.

So why had her pulse sped up, heat pooling in the pit of her stomach? Daisy allowed the car to take more of her weight, grateful for its support.

'Come back inside, we haven't finished talking yet.' It wasn't a request.

The heat melted away, replaced by a growing indignation. Daisy straightened up, folding her arms. 'We haven't *started* talking. I gave you an hour.'

'I know.' She had been hoping for penitent but he was totally matter-of-fact. 'I think better outside.'

'And?' Daisy wanted to grab the word back the second she uttered it. It sounded as if she had been on tenterhooks waiting for him to proclaim her fate. The kernel of truth in that thought made her squirm.

He ran a hand through his hair. The gesture was unexpectedly boyish and uncertain. 'This would be easier if we just went back inside.'

She raised her eyebrows. 'You think better outside.'

He smiled at that, his whole expression lightening. It changed him completely, the eyes softer, the slightly harsh expression warmer.

'Yes. But do you?'

'Me?'

'I have a proposition for you and you need to be thinking clearly. Are you?'

No. No, she wasn't. Daisy wasn't sure she'd had a clear thought since she had accepted that first glass of champagne, had hotly defended her livelihood as her rescuer had quizzed and teased her and had found herself laughing, absurdly delighted as the stern expression had melted into something altogether different.

But she wasn't going to admit that. Not to him, barely to herself.

'Completely clearly.'

He looked sceptical but nodded. 'Then, Daisy, I think you should marry me.'

CHAPTER TWO

SEB DIDN'T EXACTLY expect Daisy to throw herself at his feet in gratitude, not really. And it would have made him uncomfortable if she had. But he was expecting that she would be touched by his proposal. Grateful even.

The incredulous laugh that bubbled out of that rather enchanting mouth was, therefore, a bit of a shock. Almost a blow—not to his heart, obviously, but, he realised with a painful jolt of self-awareness, to his ego. 'Are we in a regency novel? Seb, you haven't besmirched my honour. There's no need to do the honourable thing.'

The emphasis on the last phrase was scathing. And misplaced. There was every need. 'So why did you come here? I thought you wanted my help. Or are you after money? Is that it?'

Maybe the whole situation was some kind of clever entrapment. His hands curled into fists and he inhaled, long and deep, trying not to let the burgeoning anger show on his face.

'Of course not.' Her indignation was convincing and the tightness in his chest eased a little. 'I thought you should know first, that was all. I didn't come here for money or marriage or anything.'

'I see, you're planning to do this alone. And you want me to what? Pop over on a Sunday and take the baby to the park? Sleepovers once a month?' Seb could hear the scathing scorn punctuating each of his words and Daisy paled, taking a nervous step away, her hand fumbling for the car handle.

'I haven't really thought that far ahead.'

Seb took another deep breath, doing his best to sound reasonable as he grabbed the slight advantage. 'You work what? Fifteen hours a day at weekends? Not just weekends. People get married every day of the week now. What are you going to do for childcare?'

'I'll work something out.' The words were defiant but her eyes were troubled as she twisted her hand around the handle, her knuckles white with tension.

He put as much conviction into his voice as possible. 'You don't need to. Marry me.'

Her eyes were wide with confusion. 'Why? Why on earth would you want to marry someone you barely know? Why would I agree to something so crazy?'

Seb gestured, a wide encompassing sweep of his arm taking in the lake, the woods and fields, the castle proudly overshadowing the landscape. 'Because that baby is my heir.'

Daisy stared at him. 'What?'

'The baby is my heir,' he repeated. 'Our baby. To Hawksley.'

'Don't be ridiculous. What has the castle got to do with the baby?'

'Not just the castle, the estate, the title, everything.'

'But—' she shook her head stubbornly '—you're the handyman, aren't you? You had a shovel and a fleece and that office.'

'The handyman?' He could see her point. If only his colleagues could see him now, it was all a long way from his quiet office tucked away in a corner of an Oxford college. 'In a way I guess I am—owner, handyman, manager, event-booker—running the estate is a hands-on job nowadays.'

'So that makes you what? A knight?'

'An earl. The Earl of Holgate.'

'An earl?' She laughed, slightly hysterically. 'Is this some kind of joke? Is there a camera recording this?' She twisted around, checking the fields behind them.

'My parents died six months ago. I inherited the castle then.' The castle and a huge amount of debt but there was no need to mention that right away. She was skittish enough as it was.

'You're being serious?' He could see realisation dawning, the understanding in her widened eyes even as she stubbornly shook her head. 'Titles don't mean anything, not any more.'

'They do to me, to the estate. Look, Daisy, you came here because you knew it was the right thing to do. Well, marrying me is the right thing to do. That baby could be the next Earl of Holgate. You want to deny him that right? Illegitimate children are barred from inheriting.'

'The baby could be a girl.' She wasn't giving in easily.

'It doesn't matter, with the royal line of succession no longer male primogeniture there's every chance the rest of the aristocracy will fall into line.' He held his hand out, coaxing. 'Daisy, come back inside, let's talk about this sensibly.'

She didn't answer for a long moment and he could sense her quivering, desperate need to run. He didn't move, just waited, hand held out towards her until she took a deep breath and nodded. 'I'll come inside. To talk about the baby. But I am not marrying you. I don't care whether you're an earl or a handyman. I don't know you.'

Seb took a deep breath, relief filling his lungs. All he needed was time. Time for her to hear him out, to give him a chance to convince her. 'Come on, then.'

Daisy pushed off the car and turned. Seb couldn't help taking a long appreciative look at her shapely rear as she bent slightly to relock the car. The tweed shorts fitted snugly, showing off her slender curves to perfection. He tore his eyes away, hurriedly focusing on the far hedge as she straightened and turned to join him, the blue eyes alight with curiosity.

'An earl,' she repeated. 'No wonder the gorgon was so reluctant to let me in.'

'Gorgon?' But he knew who she meant and his mouth quirked as she stared at him meaningfully. 'I don't think she's actually turned anyone to stone. Not yet. Mrs Suffolk's family have worked here for generations. She's a little protective.'

They reached the courtyard and Daisy started to make for the back door where Mrs Suffolk still stood guard, protecting the castle against day trippers and other invaders. Seb slipped a hand through Daisy's arm, guiding her round the side of the house and onto the sweeping driveway with its vista down to the wooded valley below.

'Front door and a fresh start,' he said as they reached the first step. 'Hello, I'm Sebastian Beresford, Earl of Holgate.'

'Sebastian Beresford?' Her eyes narrowed. 'I know that name. You're not an earl, you're that historian.'

'I'm both. Even earls have careers nowadays.' Although how he was going to continue his academic responsibilities with running Hawksley was a problem he had yet to solve.

He held out his hand. 'Welcome to my home.'

Daisy stared at his hand for a moment before placing her cool hand in his. 'Daisy Huntingdon-Cross, it's a pleasure to meet you.'

Who? There it was, that faint elusive memory sharpened into focus. 'Huntingdon-Cross? Rick Cross and Sherry Huntingdon's daughter?'

No wonder she looked familiar! Rock royalty on their father's side and pure county on their mother's, the Huntingdon-Cross sisters were as renowned for their blonde, leggy beauty as they were infamous for their lifestyle. Each of them had been splashed across the tabloids at some point in their varied careers—and their parents were legends; rich, talented and famously in love.

Seb's heart began to pound, painfully thumping against his chest, the breath knocked from his lungs in one blow. This was not the plan, the quiet, businesslike, private union he intended.

This was *trouble*.

If he married this girl then the tabloids would have a field day. A Beresford and a Huntingdon-Cross would be front-page fodder to rival anything his parents had managed to stir up in their wake. All the work he had done to remain out of the press would be undone faster than he could say, 'I do.'

But if he didn't marry her then he would be disinheriting the baby. He didn't have any choice.

Seb froze as he took her hand, recognition dawning in his eyes.

'Huntingdon-Cross,' he repeated and Daisy dropped his hand, recoiling from the horror in his voice.

For a moment she contemplated pretending she wasn't one of *those* Huntingdon-Crosses but a cousin, a far, far removed cousin. From the north. Of course, Seb didn't have to know that she didn't have any northern cousins.

But what was the point? He'd find out the truth soon enough and, besides, they might be wild and infuriating and infamous but they were hers. No matter how many titles or illustrious ancestors Seb had, he had no right to sneer at her family.

Daisy channelled her mother at her grandest, injecting as much froideur into her voice as she possibly could and tilting her chin haughtily. 'Yes. I'm the youngest. I believe the tabloids call me the former wild child if that helps.'

At this the green eyes softened and the corner of his mouth tilted; heat pooled in her stomach as her blood rushed in response. It was most unfair, the almost smile made him more human. More handsome.

More desirable.

'The one who got expelled from school?'

He had to bring that up. Daisy's face heated, the embarrassed flush spreading from her cheeks to her neck. He was an Oxford professor, he'd probably never met anyone who had been expelled before, let alone someone with barely an academic qualification to her name. 'I wasn't expelled exactly, they just asked me to leave.'

'Sounds like expulsion to me,' he murmured.

'It was ridiculously strict. It was almost impossible *not* to get expelled. Unless you were clever and studious like my sisters, that is.' Okay, it was eight years ago and Daisy had spent every minute of those eight years trying to prove her teachers wrong but it still rankled. Still hurt.

'The Mother Superior was always looking for a way to rid the school of the dullards like me. That way we didn't bring the exam average down.' She stared at him, daring him to react. He'd probably planned for the mother of his future children to have a batch of degrees to match his. His and her mortar boards.

'They expelled you for not being academic?'

'Well, not exactly. They expelled me for breaking bounds and going clubbing in London. But if I'd been predicted all As it would have been a slap on the wrist at the most. At least, probably,' she added, conscious she wasn't being entirely fair. 'There were pictures on the front page of *The Planet* and I think some of the parents were a little concerned.'

'A little?' Damn, the mouth was even more tilted now, the gleam intensifying in his eyes.

'I was sixteen. Most sixteen-year-old girls aren't locked away in stupid convent schools not even allowed to look at boys or wear anything but a hideous uniform. It isn't natural. But once front-page news, always front-page news. They hounded me for a bit until they realised how dull I really am. But I swear I could die at one hundred after a lifetime spent sewing smocks for orphaned lepers and my epitaph would read "Former wild child, Daisy, who was expelled from exclusive girls' school…"'

'Probably.' His voice was bleak again, the gleam gone as if it had never been there. 'Come on, let's go in. It's getting cold and one of us has unseasonably bare legs.'

Once the sun had started to set, the warmth quickly dissipated, the evening air tinted with a sharp breeze whipping around Daisy's legs. She shivered, the chill running up her arms and down her spine not entirely down to the cold. If she walked back into the castle everything would change.

But everything was changing anyway. Would it be easier if she didn't have to do this alone? It wasn't the proposal or the marriage of her dreams but maybe it was time to grow up. To accept that fairy tales were for children and that princes came in all shapes and sizes—as did earls.

Not that Seb's shape was an issue. She slid a glance over at him, allowing her eyes to run up his legs, the worn jeans clinging to his strong thighs and the slim hips, and up his torso, his lean muscled strength hidden by the shirt and fleece. But her body remembered the way he had picked her up without flinching, the play of his muscles under her hands.

No, his shape wasn't an issue.

But she had worked so hard to be independent. Not traded on her parents' names, not depended on their money.

Would marrying for support, albeit emotional not financial, be any different from accepting it from her family?

At least she knew they loved her. A marriage without love wasn't to be considered. Not for her. She needed to make that clear so that they could move on and decide what was best for the baby.

'Where's the cook? The faithful retainers? The maids' bobbing curtsies?' Daisy expected that they would return to the library but instead Seb had led her through the baize doors and back through the tangle of passages to the kitchen. She would need a ball of thread to find her way back.

The whole house was a restoration project waiting to happen and the kitchen no exception but Daisy quite liked the old wooden cabinets, the ancient Aga and Monty slumped in front of it with his tail beating a steady rhythm on the flagstone floor. It didn't take much imagination to see the ghosts of small scullery maids, scuttling out into the adjoining utility room, an apple-cheeked cook rolling out pastry on the marbled worktops. Automatically she framed it, her mind selecting the right filter and the focal point of the shot.

Any of Daisy's friends would strip out the cabinets, install islands and breakfast bars and folding doors opening out into the courtyard—undoubtedly creating something stunning. And yet the kitchen would lose its heart, its distinctive soul.

Seb gestured to a low chair by the Aga. 'Do you want to sit there? It's the warmest spot in the room. No, there's no one else, just me. A cleaner comes in daily but I live alone.' He had opened a door that led to a pantry bigger than Daisy's entire kitchen. 'Are you vegetarian?'

'For a term in Year Eleven.'

'Good. Anything you...erm...really want to eat?' He

sounded flustered and, as realisation dawned, her cheeks heated in tandem with his. It was going to be uncomfortable if neither of them could mention the pregnancy without embarrassment.

'Oh! You mean cravings? No, at least, not yet. But if I get a need for beetroot and coal risotto I'll make sure you're the first to know.'

The green eyes flashed. 'You do that.'

Daisy didn't want to admit it, even to herself, but she was tired. It had been a long week, excitement mixing with shock, happiness with worry and sleep had been elusive. It was soothing leaning back in the chair, the warmth from the Aga penetrating her bones. Monty rested his head on her feet as she watched Seb expertly chopping onions and grilling steaks.

'From the estate farm,' he said as he heated the oil. 'I'm pretty much self-sufficient, well, thanks to the tenant farmers I am.'

Neither of them mentioned the elephant in the room but the word was reverberating round and round her head. *Marriage.*

Was this what it would be like? Cosy evenings in the kitchen? Rocking in a chair by the fire while Seb cooked. Maybe she should take up knitting.

'Did you mean what you said earlier, in the library? That marriage is a business?'

He didn't turn round but she saw his shoulders set rigid, the careless grace gone as he continued to sauté the vegetables.

'Absolutely. It's the only way it works.'

'Why?'

Seb stopped stirring and shot her a quick glance.

'What do you mean?'

Daisy was leaning back in the chair, her eyes half closed. His eyes flickered over her. The bright waistcoat, the hat and the lipstick were at odd with her pallor; she was pale, paler than he would have expected even at the end of a long, cold winter and the shadows under her eyes were a deep blue-grey. She looked exhausted. A primal protectiveness as unexpected as it was fierce rose up in him, almost overwhelming in its intensity. It wasn't what he wanted, the path he had chosen, but this was his responsibility; she was his responsibility.

She probably deserved better, deserved more than he could offer. But this was all he had.

'Why do you think that?'

Seb took a moment before answering, quickly plating up the steaks and tipping the sautéed vegetables into a dish and putting it onto the table. He added a loaf of bread and a pat of butter and grabbed two steak knives and forks.

'Come and sit at the table,' he said. 'We can talk afterwards.'

It was like being on a first date. Worse, a blind date. A blind date where you suddenly lost all sense of speech, thought and taste. Was this his future? Sitting at a table with this woman, struggling for things to say?

'My grandparents ate every meal in the dining hall, even when it was just the two of them,' he said after a long, excruciating pause. 'Grandfather at the head of the table, grandmother at the foot. Even with the leaves taken out the table seats thirty.'

She put down her fork and stared at him. 'Could they hear each other?'

'They both had penetrating voices, although I don't know if they were natural or whether they developed them after fifty years of yelling at each other across fifteen foot of polished mahogany.' He half smiled, remembering their stubborn determination to keep to the ritual formality of their youth as the world changed around them.

'And what about your parents? Did they dispense with the rules and eat in here or did they like the distance?'

'Ah, my parents. It appears my parents spent most of their lives living wildly beyond their means. If I can't find a way to make Hawksley pay for itself within the next five years…' His voice trailed off. He couldn't articulate his worst fears: that he would be the Beresford who lost Hawksley Castle.

'Hence the handyman gig?'

'Hence the handyman gig. And the leave of absence from the university and hiring the hall out for weddings. It's a drop in the ocean but it's a start.'

'You need my sisters. Rose is in New York but she's a PR whizz and Violet is the most managing person I have ever met. I bet they could come up with a plan to save Hawksley.'

He needed more than a plan. He needed a miracle. 'My grandparents followed the rules all their lives. They looked after the estate, the people who lived on it. Lived up to their responsibilities. My parents were the opposite. They didn't spend much time here. Unless they were throwing a party. They preferred London, or the Caribbean. Hawksley was a giant piggy bank, not a responsibility.'

Her eyes softened. 'What happened?'

'You must have read about them?' He pushed his half-empty plate away, suddenly sickened. 'If your parents are famous for their rock-solid marriage, mine were famous for their wildness— drugs, affairs, exotic holidays. They were always on the front pages. They divorced twice, remarried twice, each time in some ridiculous extravagant way. The first time they made me a pageboy. The second time I refused to attend.' He took a swig of water, his mouth dry.

It was awful, the resentment mixed with grief. When would it stop being so corrosive?

'Yes, now I remember. I'm so sorry. It was a plane crash, wasn't it?'

'They had been told it wasn't safe but the rules didn't apply to them. Or so they thought.'

Daisy pushed her seat back and stood up, collecting up the plates and waving away his offer of help. 'No, you cooked, I'll clear.'

He sat for a moment and watched as she competently piled the dishes and saucepans up by the side of the sink, rinsing the plates. He had to make it clear to her, make sure she knew exactly what he was offering. 'Marriage is a business.'

Daisy carried on rinsing, running hot water into the old ceramic sink. 'Once, perhaps…'

'I have to marry, have children, there are no other direct heirs and there's a danger the title will go extinct if I don't. But I don't want…' He squeezed his eyes shut for a brief moment, willing his pulse to stay calm. 'I won't have all the emotional craziness that comes with romantic expectations.'

She put the dishcloth down and turned, leaning against the sink as she regarded him. 'Seb, your parents, they weren't normal, you do know that? That level of drama isn't usual.'

He laughed. 'They were extreme, sure. But abnormal? They just didn't hide it the way the rest of the world does. I look at my friends, their parents. Sure, it's all hearts and flowers and nicknames at the beginning but I've lost count of how many relationships, how many marriages turn into resentment and betrayal and anger. No, maybe my ancestors knew what they were doing with a businesslike arrangement—compatibility, rules, peace.'

'My parents love each other even more than they did when they got married.' A wistful smile curved Daisy's lips. 'Sometimes it's like it's just the two of them even when we're all there. They just look at each other and you can tell that at that moment it's like there's no one else in the room.'

'And how do you feel at those moments?'

Her eyelashes fluttered down. 'It can be a little lonely but…'

Exactly! Strengthened by her concession he carried on, his voice as persuasive as he could manage. 'Look, Daisy. There's no point me promising you romance because I don't believe in it. I can promise you respect, hopefully affection. I can promise that if we do this, become parents together, then I will love the baby and do my utmost to be the best parent I can.'

'I hope you will. But we don't need to be married to co-parent.'

'No,' he conceded.

'I've worked really hard to be my own person, build up my own business.' The blue eyes hardened. 'I don't depend on anyone.'

'But it's not just going to be you any more, is it?'

'I'll cope, I'll make sure I do. And not wanting to marry you doesn't mean that I don't want you in the baby's life. I'm here, aren't I?'

Seb sat back, a little nonplussed. His title and the castle had always meant he had enjoyed interest from a certain type of woman—and with his academic qualifications and the bestselling history books he was becomingly increasingly well known for appealed to a different type. To be honest he hadn't expected he'd have to convince anyone to marry him—he had, admittedly a little arrogantly, just expected that he would make his choice and that would be it.

Apparently Daisy hadn't got that memo.

Not that there was a reason for her to; she hadn't been raised to run a home like Hawksley, nor was she an academic type looking to become a college power couple.

'If you won't marry me then the baby will be illegitimate—I know.' He raised his hand as she opened her mouth to interrupt. 'I know that doesn't mean anything any more. But for me that's serious. I need an heir—and if the baby isn't legitimate it doesn't inherit. How will he or she feel, Daisy, if I marry someone else and they see a younger sibling inherit?'

Her face whitened. 'You'd do that?'

'If I had a younger brother then, no. But I'm the last of my family. I don't have any choice.'

'What if I can't do it?' Daisy was twisting her hands together. 'What if it's not enough for me?' She turned and picked the dishcloth back up. Her back was a little hunched, as if she were trying to keep her emotions in.

'It's a lot to give up, Seb. I always wanted what my parents have, to meet someone who completes me, who I complete.' She huffed out a short laugh. 'I know it's sentimental but when you grow up seeing that...'

'Just give it a go.' Seb was surprised by how much he wanted, needed her to say yes—and not just because of the child she carried, not just because she could solve the whole heir issue and provide the stability he needed to turn the castle's fortunes around.

But they were the important reasons and Seb ruthlessly pushed aside the memory of that night, the urge to reach out and touch her, to run a finger along those long, bare legs. 'If it doesn't work out or if you're unhappy I won't stop you leaving.'

'Divorce?' Her voice caught on the word and her back seemed to shrink inwards.

'Leave that.' He stood up and took the dishcloth from her unresisting hand, tilting her chin until she looked up at him, her eyes cloudy. 'If you wanted then yes, an amicable, friendly divorce. I hope you'll give it a real try though, promise me five years at least.'

That was a respectable amount of time; the family name had been dragged through the mud enough.

'I don't know.' She stepped back, away from his touch, and he dropped his empty hand, the silk of her skin imprinted on his fingertips. 'Getting married with a get-out clause seems wrong.'

'All marriages have a get-out clause. Look.' Seb clenched his hands. He was losing her. In a way he was impressed; he thought the title and castle was inducement enough for most women.

It was time for the big guns.

'This isn't about us. It's about our child. His future. We owe it to him to be responsible, to do the right thing for him.'

'Or her.'

'Or her.'

Thoughts were whirling around in Daisy's brain, a giant tangled skein of them. She was so tired, her limbs heavy, her shoulders slumping under the decision she was faced with.

But she was going to be a mother. What did she think that meant? All pushing swings and ice creams on the beach? She hadn't thought beyond the birth, hadn't got round to figuring out childcare and working long days on sleepless nights. It would be good to have someone else involved. Not someone she was dependent on but someone who was as invested in the baby as she was.

And if he didn't marry her he would marry elsewhere. That should make it easier to turn him down. But it showed how committed he was.

What would she tell people? That she'd messed up again? She'd worked so hard to put her past behind her. The thought of confessing the truth to her family sent her stomach into complicated knots. How could she admit to her adoring parents and indulgent sisters that she was pregnant after a one-night stand—but don't worry, she was getting married?

It wasn't the whirlwind marriage part that would send her parents into a tailspin. After all, they had known each other for less than forty-eight hours when they had walked into that Las Vegas chapel. It was the businesslike arrangement that they would disapprove of.

But maybe they didn't have to know…

'How would it work?'

He didn't hesitate. 'Family first, Hawksley second. Discretion always. I'm a private person, no magazines invited in to coo over our lovely home, no scandalous headlines.'

That made sense. A welcome kind of sense. Publicity ran through her family's veins; it would be nice to step away from that.

But her main question was still unvoiced, still unanswered. She steeled herself.

'What about intimacy?'

Seb went perfectly still apart from one muscle, beating in his cheek, his eyes darkening. Daisy took another step back, reaching for the chair as support as an answering beat pounded through her body.

'Intimacy?' His voice was low, as if the word was forced from him. 'That's up to you, Daisy. We worked—' he paused '—well together. It would be nice to have a full marriage. But that's up to you.'

Worked *well*? *Nice*? She had been thinking *spectacular*. Could she really do this? Marry someone who substituted rules for love, discretion for affection and thought respect was the pinnacle of success?

But in the circumstances how could she not? It wasn't as if she had an alternative plan.

Daisy swallowed, hard, a lump the size of a Kardashian engagement ring forming in her throat. This was so far from her dreams, her hopes.

'I have a condition.' Was that her voice? So confident?

Seb's eyes snapped onto hers with unblinking focus. 'Name it.'

'We don't tell anyone why we're marrying like this. If we do this then we pretend. We pretend that we are head over heels ridiculously besotted. If you can do that then yes. We have a deal.'

CHAPTER THREE

'HI.'

How did one greet one's fiancé when one was a) pregnant, b) entering a marriage of convenience and c) pretending to be in love?

It should be a kiss on the cheek. Daisy greeted everyone with a kiss on the cheek, from her mother to her clients, but her stomach tumbled at the thought of pressing her lips to that stubbled cheek, inhaling the scent of leather and outdoors and soap.

Instead she stood aside, holding the door half open, her knuckles white as she clung onto the door handle as if it anchored her to the safety of her old life. 'Come in, I'm nearly ready.'

Seb stepped through and then stopped still, his eyes narrowing as he looked around slowly.

A converted loft, all exposed brickwork and steel girders, one wall dominated by five floor-to-ceiling windows through which the midday sun came flooding in. A galley kitchen at one end, built-in shelves crammed with books, ornaments and knick-knacks running along the side wall and the rest of the ground-floor space bare except for an old blue velvet sofa, a small bistro table and chairs and the lamps she used to light her subjects. The bulk of her personal belongings were on the overhanging mezzanine, which doubled as her bedroom and relaxing space.

Daisy adored her light-filled spacious studio and yet, compared to Seb's home, steeped in history and stuffed with antiques, her flat felt sparse and achingly trendy.

'Nice.' Seb looked more at home than she had thought possible, maybe because he had ditched the fleece for a long-sleeved T-shirt in a soft grey cotton and newer, cleaner jeans. Maybe because he stood there confidently, unashamedly examining the room, looking at each one of the photos hung on every available bit of wall space. He turned, slowly, taking in every detail with that cool assessing gaze. 'Wedding photography must pay better than I realised.'

'It's not mine unfortunately. I rent it from a friend. An artist.' Daisy gestured over to the massive oil seascape dominating the far wall. 'I used to share with four other students on the floor above and it got a little cramped— physically *and* mentally, all those artistic temperaments in one open-plan space! It was such a relief when John decided to move to Cornwall and asked if I was interested in renting the studio from him.'

'Mates' rates?'

'Not quite.' Daisy tried to swallow back her defensiveness at the assumption. Her parents would have loved to set her up in style but she had been determined to go it alone, no matter how difficult it was to find a suitable yet affordable studio. John's offer had been the perfect solution. 'I do pay rent but John's turned into a bit of a hermit so I also handle all the London side of his business for him. It works well for us both.'

'Handy. Are you leaving all that?' He nodded towards the studio lights.

'I'll still use this as my workspace.' Daisy might have agreed to move in with Seb straight away but she wasn't ready to break her ties to her old life. Not yet, not until she knew how this new world would work out. 'It's only an hour's drive. I'm all packed up. It's over here.'

It wasn't much, less than her mother took for a weekend away. A case containing her favourite cameras and lenses. Her Mac. A couple of bags filled with clothes and cosmetics. If this worked out she could move the rest of her things later: the books, prints, artwork, favourite vases and bowls. Her hat collection. How they would look in the museum-like surroundings of Hawksley Castle she couldn't begin to imagine.

Seb cast a glance at the small pile. 'Are you sure this is all you want to take? I want you to feel at home. You can make any changes you want, redecorate, rearrange.'

'Even the library?'

His mouth quirked. 'As long as it stays warm.'

'Of course.' Daisy walked over to the hatstand at the foot of the mezzanine staircase and, after a moment's hesitation, picked up a dark pink cloche, accessorised with a diamanté brooch. It was one of her favourite hats, a car-boot-sale find. She settled it on top of her head and tugged it into place before turning to the mirror that hung behind it and coating her lips in a layer of her favourite red lipstick.

She was ready.

'First stop the registry office.' Seb had picked up both bags of clothes and Daisy swung her camera bag over her shoulder before picking up her laptop bag, her chest tight with apprehension.

She swivelled and looked back at the empty space. *You'll be back tomorrow*, she told herself, but stepping out of the front door still felt momentous, not just leaving her home but a huge step into the unknown.

Deep breath, don't cry and lock the door. Her stomach swooped as if it were dropping sixty storeys at the speed of light but she fought it, managing to stop her hand from trembling as she double-locked the door.

Did Seb have similar doubts? If so he hid them well; he was the epitome of calm as they exited the building and walked to the car. He had brought one of the estate Land Rovers ready to transport her stuff; it might be parked with the other North London four-by-fours but its mud-splattered bumpers and utilitarian inside proclaimed it country bumpkin. She doubted any of its gleaming, leather-interior neighbours ever saw anything but urban roads and motorways.

'Once we have registered we have to wait sixteen days. At least we don't have to worry about a venue. The Tudor hall is licensed and I don't allow weekday weddings so we can get married—' he pulled out his phone '—two weeks on Friday. Do you want to invite anyone?' He dropped his phone back into his pocket, opening the car door and hefting her bags into the boot.

Daisy was frozen, one arm protectively around her camera bag. How could he sound so matter-of-fact? They were talking about their wedding. About commitment and promises and joining together. Okay, they were practically strangers but it should still mean something.

'Can we make it three weeks? Just to make sure? Plus I want my parents and sisters there and I need to give Rose enough notice to get back from New York.'

'You want your whole family to come?' He held the door open for her, a faint look of surprise on his face.

Daisy put one foot on the step, hesitated and turned to face him. 'You promised we would at least pretend this was a real marriage. Of course my family needs to be there.' This was non-negotiable.

'Fine.'

Daisy's mouth had been open, ready to argue her point and she was taken aback at his one-word agreement, almost disappointed by his acquiescence. He was so calm about everything. What was going on underneath the surface? Maybe she'd never find out. She stood for a second, gaping, before closing her mouth with a snap and climbing into the passenger seat. Seb closed the door behind her and a moment later he swung himself into the driver's seat and started the engine.

Daisy wound her window down a little then leant back against the headrest watching as Seb navigated the narrow streets, taking her further and further from her home.

Married in just over three weeks. A whirlwind romance, that was what people would think; that was what she would tell them.

'That was a deep sigh.'

'Sorry, it's just…' She hesitated, pulling down the sun visor to check the angle of her hat, feeling oddly vulnerable at the thought of telling him something personal. 'I always knew exactly how I wanted my wedding to be. I know it's silly, that they were just daydreams…' With all the changes happening right now, mourning the loss of her ideal wedding seemed ridiculously self-indulgent.

'Beach at sunset? Swanky hotel? Westminster Abbey and Prince Harry in a dress uniform?'

'No, well, only sometimes.' She stole a glance at him. His eyes were focused on the road ahead and somehow the lack of eye contact made it easier to admit just how many plans she had made. She could picture it so clearly. 'My parents live just down the lane from the village church. I always thought I'd get married there, walk to my wedding surrounded by my family and then afterwards walk back hand in hand with my new husband and have a garden party. Nothing too fancy, although Dad's band would play, of course.'

'Of course.' But he was smiling.

Daisy bit her lip as the rest of her daydream slid through her mind like an internal movie. She would be in something lacy, straight, deceptively simple. The sun would shine casting a golden glow over the soft Cotswold stone. And she would be complete.

There had been a faint ache in her chest since the day before, a swelling as if her heart were bruised. As the familiar daydream slipped away the ache intensified, her heart hammering. She was doing the right thing. Wasn't she?

It's not just about you any more, she told herself as firmly as possible.

She just wished she had had a chance to talk her options over with someone else. But who?

Her sisters? They would immediately go into emergency-planning mode, try and take over, alternately scolding her and coddling her, reducing her back to a tiresome little girl in the process.

Her parents? But no, she still had her pride if nothing else. Daisy swallowed hard, wincing at the painful lump in her throat. She had worked so hard to make up for the mistakes of her past, worked so hard to be independent from her family, to show them that she was as capable as they were. How could she tell them that she was pregnant by a man she hardly knew?

Her parents would swing into damage-limitation mode. Want her to come back home, to buy her a house, to throw money at her as if that would make everything okay. And it would be so easy to let them.

Daisy sagged in her seat. She couldn't tell them, she wouldn't tell them, but all she wanted to hear was her dad's comforting drawl and step into her mother's embrace. She didn't allow herself that luxury very often.

'Actually, can we go to the registrar's tomorrow? I don't feel comfortable registering until we have told my parents. Would you mind if we visit them first?'

Daisy waited, her hands slippery with tense anticipation. It had been so long since she had consulted with someone else or needed consensus on any action.

'Of course.' Seb took his eyes from the road for one brief second, resting them appraisingly on her hands, twisting in her lap. 'But if we're going to tell your parents we're engaged we should probably stop at a jeweller's on the way. You need a ring.'

'Daisy! Darling, what a lovely surprise.'

It was strange being face to face with someone as familiar, as famous as Sherry Huntingdon: model, muse and sometime actress. Her tall willowy figure, as taut and slender at over fifty as it had been at twenty, the blonde hair sweeping down her back seemingly as natural as her daughter's.

'And who's this?' The famously sleepy blue eyes were turned onto Seb, an unexpectedly shrewdly appraising look in them. Maybe not that unexpected—you didn't stay at the top of your profession for over thirty years without brains as well as beauty.

'Sebastian Beresford.' He held his hand out and Daisy's mother took it, slanting a look at him from under long black lashes.

'What a treat.' Her voice was low, almost a purr. 'Daisy so seldom brings young men home. Come on in, the pair of you. Violet's around somewhere and Rick's in his studio— the Benefit Concert is creeping up on us again. Daisy, darling, you will be here to take some photos, won't you?'

'Wouldn't miss it.' Daisy linked her arm through her mother's as they walked along the meandering path that led from the driveway around the house. It was a beautiful ivy-covered house, large by any standards—unless one happened to live in a castle—dating back to William and Mary with two gracefully symmetrical wings flanking the three-storey main building.

Unlike Hawksley it had been sympathetically updated and restored and, as they rounded the corner, Seb could see tennis courts in the distance and a cluster of stable buildings and other outbuildings all evidently restored and in use.

An unexpected stab of nostalgic pain hit him. Hawksley should have been as well cared for but his grandfather had taken a perverse pride in the discomfort of the crumbling building—and as for Seb's father... He pushed the thought away, fists clenched with the unwanted anger that still flooded through him whenever he thought about his father's criminal negligence.

Sherry came to a stop as they reached a large paved terrace with steps leading upwards to the French doors at the back of the house. Comfortably padded wooden furniture was arranged to take the best advantage of the gorgeous views. 'I think it's warm enough to sit outside.' Sherry smiled at her daughter. 'I'll go get Rick. He'll be so happy to see you, Daisy. He was saying the other day we see more of Rose and she lives in New York. You two make yourselves at home. Then we can have a drink. Daisy, darling, let Vi know you're here, will you?'

'I'll text her.' Daisy perched on a bench as she pulled out her phone and, after a moment's hesitation, Seb joined her. Of course they would sit together. In fact, they should be holding hands. He looked at her long, slender fingers flying over the phone's surface and willed himself to casually reach over and slip his own fingers through hers.

Just one touch. And yet it felt more binding than the ring he had bought her and the vows he was prepared to make.

'That's Dad's studio.' Daisy slipped the phone back into her dress pocket and pointed at the largest of the outbuildings. 'The first thing he did was convert it into a sound-proofed, state-of-the-art recording studio—we were never allowed in unsupervised but it didn't stop us trying to make our own records. They weren't very good. None of us are particularly musical, much to Dad's disgust. The room next to it is used as rehearsal space and we turned the orangery into a pool and gym, otherwise we pretty much left the house as it was. It hasn't changed much since it was built.'

But it had. The paintwork was fresh, the soft furnishings and wallpaper new, the furniture chosen with care. New money in an old building. It was what Hawksley needed, if only his great-great-grandfather had married an American heiress.

'Have you lived here long?'

'Mum grew up here, her uncle is a baronet and somewhere along the family tree we descend from William Fourth, although not through the legitimate line. So, you see—' Daisy threw him a provocative smile '—you're not marrying beneath you.'

'I didn't think I was.' Seb knew very well that his blood was as red as anyone else's. It wasn't Daisy's ancestry that worried him, it was her upbringing. If she had been brought up in a place as lavishly luxurious as Huntingdon Hall how would she cope with the draughty inconveniences of his grand and ancient home?

'Daisy? You *are* alive. Rose was trying to persuade me to break into your apartment and recover your dead body. A whole week with no word from you?'

'Vi!' Daisy jumped to her feet, sprinting up the stone steps and flinging her arms around the speaker. 'What do you mean? I texted you both! Every day.'

'Texts, anyone can send a text that says I'm fine, talk soon. But—' she eyed Seb coolly over Daisy's shoulder '—I can see you've been busy.'

Seb stood and held out his hand. 'You must be Violet.' A meaningful glare from Daisy reminded him of his role. 'Daisy has told me so much about you.' He walked forward and slipped an arm around Daisy, ignoring the electricity that snaked up his arm from the exact spot where his fingers curled around her slender waist. Daisy started, just a little, at his touch before inhaling and leaning into him, her body pliant, moulding into his side as if she belonged there.

'Really? She hasn't mentioned you at all.' Violet took his outstretched hand in her cool grasp for a moment. 'She usually tells me everything.' Her eyes were narrowed as she assessed him. It was more than a little disconcerting to be so comprehensively overlooked even by such very blue eyes.

The family resemblance was striking. Violet was a little taller, a little curvier than her younger sister and her heart-shaped face gave nothing away, unlike Daisy's all too telling features, but she had the Huntingdon colouring, the high cheekbones and the same mane of golden hair.

That was as far as the resemblance went; Daisy was wearing a monochrome print dress, the bodice tight fitting and the skirt flaring out to just above her knees, a dark pink short cardigan slung over her shoulders and the carefully positioned hat finishing off the outfit with a quirky flourish. Violet, by contrast, was sensibly clad in jeans and a white shirt, her hair held back from her face by a large slide, her make-up understated and demure.

'Not everything.' Daisy flushed. 'I am twenty-four, you know. I do have some secrets.'

'Daisy-Waisy, you never managed to keep a secret in your whole life.' Violet grinned at her sister with obvious affection. Her eyes cooled as she returned to assessing Seb. 'And what is it that you do?'

For one, almost irresistible moment Seb had the urge to emulate his grandfather, draw himself up to his full six feet one, look down at Violet and drawl, 'Do? My good woman, I don't *do*. I am. Earl of Holgate to be precise,' just to shake her cool complacency. He didn't need Daisy's warning pinch to resist. 'I manage a large estate. That's where we met. Daisy was working there.'

'He came to my rescue.' The face upturned to his was so glowing Seb nearly forgot they were acting. 'I was snowed in and he rescued me. It was super romantic, Vi.'

'Words no father wants to hear.' Seb started at the deep American drawl and hurriedly turned.

'Dad.' Daisy tugged Seb down the steps, almost running. She slipped out of Seb's grasp and threw her arms around the slight man on the terrace.

'Missed you, Daisy girl. How's that camera of yours?'

'Busy, I already promised Mum I would cover the Benefit Concert but if you want some promo shots doing beforehand just ask. Formal, informal, you choose.'

'I'll ask Rose. She makes all those kinds of decisions. So who is this romantic knight you've brought home?' Rick Cross turned to Seb with an appraising gaze.

For the third time in five minutes Seb stood still as he was examined by keen eyes. Lucky Daisy, having such a loving, protective family. She didn't need to marry him at all; they would close ranks and take care of her. If he wanted to raise his heir he'd better keep his side of their strange bargain.

'Sebastian Beresford. It's an honour to meet you, sir.' Seb managed, just, not to blurt out that Rick Cross had made one of the first CDs he had ever bought. A CD he had listened to over and over again.

Daisy's father was so familiar it seemed odd that he was a stranger; the craggy face, wild hair and skinny frame were timeless. Rick Cross had burst onto the music scene at twenty and never left. Age had definitely not withered him; he still toured, released and dominated the headlines although these days it was philanthropy not wild antics that kept him there.

'Beresford? I've read your books. Good to meet you.'

Daisy slipped an arm around Seb and he obediently held her close as she beamed at her family. 'We've got some news. Mum, Dad, Vi. Seb and I are engaged. We're going to get married!'

It was exhausting, pretending. Hanging on Seb's arm, smiling, showing off the admittedly beautiful but somewhat soulless solitaire on her third finger as her family crowded around with congratulations and calls for champagne.

A glass of champagne Daisy pretended to sip. If her parents suspected for one single second the real reason for her marriage they would be so disappointed. Not in her, for her.

And she absolutely couldn't bear that. To let them down again.

They knew how much she wanted to fall in love, to be loved.

Vi hung back a little, her eyes suspicious even as her mouth smiled. Her sister had been so badly burned, it was hard for her to trust. And Daisy was lying after all.

'I'll call the vicar right away.' Her mother had swung into action with alarming haste. 'You'll want spring naturally, Daisy darling, next year or the year after? I think next year. A long engagement is so dreadfully dreary.'

Daisy looked at Seb for help but he had been drawn into a conversation with her father about guitar chords. Did Seb know anything about guitars or chords? She had no idea.

No idea what his favourite food was, his favourite memory, band, song, poem, book, film, TV programme. If he played a musical instrument, liked to run, watched football, rugby or both...

'Daisy, stop daydreaming,' her mother scolded as she had so many times before. 'Next year, darling?'

Daisy tugged her hat back into place. 'Sorry.' She put on her widest smile and did her best to look as if her heart weren't shattering into ever smaller fragments with every word. 'We're not getting married here.'

The rest of her family fell silent and Daisy could feel three sets of eyes boring into her. 'Not getting married here?'

'It's all you have ever wanted.'

'Don't be silly, Daisy girl. Where else would you get married?'

'It's my fault, I'm afraid.' Seb had stepped behind her and Daisy leant back into the lean, hard body with a hastily concealed sob of relief. 'I, ah, I own a licensed property and we rather thought we would get married there. I hope you're not too disappointed.'

'A licensed venue?' Vi, of course. 'Like a pub?'

'No, well, actually yes, there is a pub in the village. It's a tied village, so technically it belongs to me but I don't run it.'

So much for Seb rescuing her, although Daisy would bet her favourite lens that Mr Darcy would quail faced with her entire family. If Rose were here as well to complete the interrogation then Seb would be running for the hills, his precious heir forgotten.

'Seb owns Hawksley Castle, we're getting married there and it won't be next spring.' It was time to act as she had never acted before. Daisy nuzzled in closer to Seb, one arm around his neck, and kissed him. Just a short, quick kiss, his mouth hard under hers.

Heat shimmered through her, low and intense and she quivered, grabbing for words to hide behind, hoping Seb hadn't noticed how he had affected her. 'We're getting married this month, in just over three weeks. Excited?'

'Why the rush?' Vi's eyes flickered over Daisy's belly and she resisted the urge to breathe in.

'Why not?' Keeping her voice as light and insouciant as possible, Daisy pressed even closer to Seb, his arm tight around her. It might just be for show but she was grateful for the support both physically and mentally. 'After all, Mum and Dad, what do you always say? When you know, you know. You only knew each other for a weekend before you got married.'

'But, Daisy, darling that was the late seventies and we were in Vegas.'

'It's true though, honey.' Rick Cross's voice had softened to the besotted tones he still used whenever he spoke to his wife, the intimate voice that excluded everyone else, even their three daughters. 'We only needed that weekend to know we were meant to be. Maybe Daisy girl has been as lucky as we were?'

The ever-present ache intensified. 'I am, Dad. Be happy for me?'

'Of course we are. Hawksley, eh? I met your father once. Remember, Sherry? On Mustique. Now that was a man who liked to party. Talking of which, we've finished the champagne. Let's go in and get some more and toast this thing properly. I might have some photos of that holiday, Seb.'

Her parents bore Seb off up the steps, both talking nineteen to the dozen. Daisy stood for a moment, watching. In nearly every way this was the image from her dreams: a handsome, eligible man, her parents' approval.

A man she barely knew. A man who didn't love her. A man who might have a comforting embrace and a mouth she melted against but who wanted a businesslike, emotion-free marriage.

'You don't have to rush into this. How long have you known him?' Vi had also stayed behind. Her arms were folded as she waited for Daisy to answer.

'Six weeks.' This at least wasn't a lie. 'And I'm not rushing into anything. I want to do this, Vi. Be happy for me.' She smiled coaxingly at her sister.

'I want to be.' Vi stared at her, worry in her eyes. 'It's just, I heard rumours. Daisy, Hawksley Castle is beautiful but it's expensive and his parents spent a lot. More than a lot. Are you sure he's not...?' She paused.

'Not what?' But she knew. 'After my fortune? I don't have a fortune, Vi!'

'No, but Daddy does and you know it drives him mad we won't live off him. He'd do anything for you, Daise, even prop up a money pit like Hawksley.'

If Daisy knew anything about Seb it was this: she could hand on heart acquit him of any interest in her father's money. The shock in his eyes when he'd found out who she was had been utterly genuine. But Vi was right to be suspicious; they were deceiving her.

And yet anger was simmering, slow, hot, intense. 'Seb does not need my non-existent fortune or Daddy to bail him out. He's working every waking hour to turn Hawksley around his way and he'll do it too. So butt out, Vi. And no running to Rose either. Let her make her own mind up.'

Where had that come from?

Vi looked at her searchingly. 'Okay, Daise, calm down. I won't say anything. Let's go in and I'll get to know your Seb properly. My little sister's marrying an earl. You always did like to show off.'

'I didn't know he was an earl when I met him!' But Vi just laughed and pulled her up the steps and into the vast kitchen diner that dominated the back of the house.

'There you are, darling. Three weeks! That's no time at all to plan. We need to get started right now. How many people can you seat? There will be rooms at the castle for the family, I suppose? Colour scheme yellow and white, of course.'

'Great!' Violet scowled. 'So I get lumbered with light purple and Rose gets almost any colour she wants.'

'I could have called you Marigold, just think about

that,' her mother said. 'We need to go shopping right away, Daisy. And discuss menus, and cakes and do you think Grandpa will come?'

'The thing is, Mum…' Daisy took a deep breath. 'I don't need any of those things. It's going to be very small. Just us, and Rose, of course, if she can come. So no colour scheme needed. We could have cake though.'

'No!' Daisy jumped at the autocratic note in her mother's voice. It wasn't a note she heard often; her parents were indulgent to the point of spoiling their girls. Rose always said that was why they had sent them to such a strict boarding school, so that someone else would do the hard parts and they could just enjoy their daughters.

'No, Daisy. Not this time.'

This time? Daisy stared at her mother in confusion. 'I…'

She didn't get a chance to continue. Sherry's voice rose higher. 'You wanted to leave home in your teens? Your father and I respected that. We were both working at eighteen after all. You won't allow us to pay your rent or buy you a car or help you in any way? I don't like it but I accept it. You visit once in a blue moon? I tell myself that at least you text us and I can follow you on Twitter.'

The heat burned high on Daisy's cheeks. It hadn't really occurred to her that her parents would interpret her need to go it alone as rejection. She held up a hand, whether in defence or supplication she didn't know.

It made no difference; her mother had hit her stride. 'You want to get married in less than a month? Fine. You want to get married away from home? No problem. But you will *not* have a tiny wedding. I know you, you've dreamt of a big, beautiful wedding since you were tiny and that, my girl, is exactly what you are going to have. You are going to let me pay for it and, young lady, nobody—' the blue eyes flashed '—*nobody* is going to stop me organising it for you.'

CHAPTER FOUR

'I'M SO SORRY.' Daisy hadn't said much as they drove the sixty miles back to Hawksley Castle but she straightened once Seb turned the Land Rover down the track that led to the castle. 'I should have planned the visit—gone on my own, maybe. I know you don't want any fuss.'

Seb slid a gaze her way. She was pale, the red lipstick bitten away. 'We could just say no.' We. It felt odd saying the word, like putting on somebody else's sock.

'We could.' Daisy slumped further down into the seat and sighed. 'But then they'd know something was up. I may have mentioned my dream wedding plans once or twice.'

He'd bet she had, he already knew far too many details about Daisy's Dream Wedding. Details imparted by eager parents and a grim-faced sister all determined that she should have her Big Day. 'Tell them I'm allergic to the thought. Cold sweats, clammy hands and hives. Or that small is more romantic and they're lucky we're not eloping.'

She didn't respond and at her silence an unwelcome thought crept into his mind; was he being presumptuous? Starting off this unconventional marriage by trampling over his prospective wife's wishes. Great start. 'Unless you want this?'

'I thought I did.' Her voice was wistful. 'But that was before…'

A stab of something that felt uncomfortably like guilt pierced him. She hadn't sought this out. His carelessness had thrust it upon her—the least he could do was allow her to have her way on this one small thing, even if the thought of all that attention did make his stomach churn, his hands clammy on the steering wheel.

Seb inhaled. To make this work meant compromise on both sides. He needed to start somewhere. 'We could rearrange. Your house, your church, garden party—the whole shebang if it means that much to you.'

'Really?' Her face brightened for one second and then it was gone, as if the spark had never been. 'No, thank you for offering, I do really appreciate it but it's fine. That wedding was a dream, a romance. It would feel—' she hesitated '—even more fake if I made you go along with my silly dreams. Here will be much more appropriate. But would you mind, if we did accommodate Mum a little and allow her to help? I'll keep it under control, I promise.'

'Of course. This is your wedding and your home.' The words slid out easily even as his chest constricted. How would this pampered butterfly manage in a place as unwieldy and stately as Hawksley? But what choice did he have? Did either of them have? They had made their bed...

He braked as he slid the car into the parking space and turned to face her. 'Look, Daisy, I really think this can work. If we're honest with each other, if we keep communicating.'

She was staring down at her hands, her lashes dark as they shadowed her eyes. 'You don't think we are rushing into it?'

Seb couldn't help the corner of his mouth curving up. 'Not at all. I believe several of my ancestors only met their spouse on their wedding day. We'll have had at least two months between meeting and wedding—a shocking amount of time.'

There was no responsive smile. 'I still think there would be no harm in waiting until after we've had a scan and know more. It's still such early days. I haven't even been to the doctor's yet. If we marry and I am just ten weeks along there's still a chance something could go wrong. We'd be trapped in a marriage neither of us want with no baby! What would we do then?'

She made sense, every word made sense and the sensible side of Seb acknowledged the truth of it, welcomed the truth of it—and yet something in him recoiled.

'There are no certainties anywhere. If it goes wrong then we mourn. We mourn and regroup. Daisy...' He reached over and took one of her hands; it lay unresisting in his, the long slender fingers cold. 'I can't see into the future and, yes, in some ways you are right. We can wait, for the scan, wait till sixteen weeks or even thirty weeks. Or we can take a leap of faith. That's what marriage is. Ours is just a bigger leap.'

He thought about it for a moment. 'Or a shorter one. Our eyes are open after all.'

She looked straight at him, her eyes wide and troubled. 'I'm only agreeing to an early marriage so my family doesn't find out I'm pregnant, so they don't try and talk me out of it. They know how important marriage is to me, how important love is. What about you? Why don't you want to wait?'

Seb squeezed his eyes shut. He could still hear them, his parents' vicious arguments, their exuberant reconciliations. He thought about brushing her off but if he wanted this to work then he needed to be honest. Needed her to understand what he was offering—and what he could never give her.

'My mother didn't want a baby. She didn't want to ruin her figure with pregnancy, didn't want to stop partying, didn't want to go through labour. But she did want to be a countess and an heir was part of the deal. She told me once, when she was drunk, how happy she had been when they said I was a boy so that she didn't have to go through it all again. That if it was up to her she would have remained childless.'

I had you because I had no choice. It was the worst year of my life.

'Luckily there were grandparents, schools, nannies. She could at least pretend to be child-free—except when it suited her. I don't want our child to think that, to feel like a burden. I want to welcome him or her into the world with open arms and make sure he or she knows that they were wanted. Because we may not have planned it but I do want it—and you do too. That's why it matters, that they are born with all the ridiculous privileges this title gives them. That's why it matters that we marry.'

She didn't say anything for a long moment but her fingers closed over his, strength in her cool grasp. 'Okay,' she said finally. 'Three weeks on Friday it is. Let's go and see the registrar tomorrow morning and get booked in. I guess I should register with a doctor nearby as well.'

'Good.' He returned the pressure, relieved. At her acquiescence. At her silent understanding. 'Are you tired or do you want the full guided tour of your new home?'

'Are you kidding? A personal guided tour from the hot prof himself? Show me everything.'

'So this is the Norman keep. Family legend has it that a knight, Sir William Belleforde, came over with the invasion in 1066 and was granted these lands. During the next few centuries the name was anglicised and corrupted to Beresford. He built the keep.'

'Cosy.' Daisy pivoted, looking about her at the dark grey walls built out of blocks of grey stone, the narrow window slits. She pulled her cardigan closer as the wind whistled through the tower. 'Was this it?'

'There was a wooden castle attached but this was the main defensive base and would have been quite roomy. There were three floors inside here—look, there's the old staircase. There was also a fortified wall around the rest of the castle. When you visit the village you'll see that many of the older houses are built with the stone from the walls.'

Daisy tilted her head back, trying to imagine one thousand years away. 'Walls, battlements, arrow slits. Nothing says home like defensive buildings. Were there many battles here?'

Seb shook his head. 'There was very little fighting here even during the Wars of the Roses and the Civil War. My ancestors were too canny to get involved.'

'No Cavalier ghosts trailing along with their heads under their arms?' Obviously this was a relief and yet didn't a house like this deserve a few ghosts?

'Not a one. We changed our religion to suit the Tudors and the colour of our roses for the Plantagenets. You'll be glad to hear that an impetuous younger son did go to France with Charles II and when he inherited the title he was made first Earl of Holgate. Although some say that was because his wife was one of the King's many mistresses—with her Lord's consent.'

'Good to know she was doing her bit for the family's advancement. Is that still a requirement for the countess? I'm not sure I'm up to it if so!'

He shot her a wry smile. 'I'm glad to hear it. No, I'm more than happy with the earldom, no favours for advancements required. Of course by then the keep was abandoned as a home. It was already unused by the late fourteenth century and the Great Hall was built around one hundred years later.'

He led her out of the chill stone building and swung

open the huge oak door that led into the Tudor part of the castle.

Daisy had spent an entire day in this part of the castle, photographing a wedding. It had felt completely different with long tables set out, the dais at the far end filled with a top table, the candle-like iron chandeliers blazing with light. 'I can see why they moved in here. It may be large but it's a lot warmer. Having a working roof is a definite advantage. A floor is helpful too.'

'Especially when you let the place out,' he agreed. 'Brides can be a bit precious about things like dirt floors and holes in the roof.'

'It's in incredible condition.' She had taken so many photos of the details: the carvings on the panelling, the way the huge beams curved.

'It has to be. We couldn't hold events here if not. It may look untouched since Elizabethan times but there is electricity throughout, working toilets and a fully kitted-out kitchen through that door. In fact, this is more up to date than parts of the main house. It's always been used as a ballroom, which made the decision to hire it out a little easier.' He winced. 'My grandfather thought we had a duty to share the castle with the wider world, but not for profit.'

'Hence the restrictive opening hours?'

'Absolutely. I don't know what he would say if he saw the weddings. They're not making enough of a difference though, even though I charge an obscene amount. I'm trying to work out how to make the castle self-funding and yet keep it as a home. Keep the heart of it intact. It's not easy.'

'You're planning to stay here, then, not live in Oxford?'

'Now it's mine? Yes. I can stay in college if I need to, although it will be strange, commuting in after all these years. It's like being pulled constantly in two different directions, between the demands of my career and the demands of my home—they both need all of my time or so it seems. But a place like this? It's a privilege to own it, to be the one taking care of it.'

His eyes lit up with enthusiasm, the rather severe features relaxing as he pointed out another interesting architectural feature and recounted yet another bit of family history that Daisy was convinced he made up on the spot. Nobody could have such a scandalous family tree—rakes and highwaymen and runaway brides in every generation.

'You really love it, don't you?'

'How could I not? Growing up here, it was like living in my own time machine. I could be anybody from Robin Hood to Dick Turpin.'

'Always the outlaw?'

'They seemed to have the most fun. Had the horses, the adoration, got the girls.'

'All the important things in life.'

'Exactly.' He grinned; it made him look more boyish. More desirable. Daisy's breath hitched in her throat, her mouth suddenly dry.

Their gazes caught, snagged, and they stood there for a long moment, neither moving. His eyes darkened to an impenetrable green, a hint of something dangerous flickering at their core and awareness shivered down Daisy's spine. She moved backwards, just a few centimetres, almost propelled by the sheer force of his gaze until her back hit the wooden panelling. She leant against it, thankful for the support, her legs weak.

She was still caught in his gaze, warmth spreading out from her abdomen, along her limbs, her skin buzzing where his eyes rested on her, the memory of his touch skittering along her nerves. Nervous, she licked her lips, the heat in her body intensifying as she watched his eyes move to her mouth, recognised the hungry expression in them.

He wanted a working marriage. A full marriage.

Right now, that seemed like the only thing that made sense in this whole tangled mess.

He took a step closer. And another. Daisy stayed still, almost paralysed by the purposeful intent in his face, her pulse hammering an insistent beat of need, of want at every pressure point in her body, pressure, a sweet, aching swelling in her chest.

'Seb?' It was almost a plea, almost a sob, a cry for something, an end to the yearning that so suddenly and so fiercely gripped her.

He paused, his eyes still on her and then one last step. So close and yet still, still not touching even though her body was crying out for contact, pulled towards him by the magnetism of sheer need. He leant, just a little, a hand on either side of her, braced against the wall.

He still hadn't touched her.

They remained perfectly still, separated by mere millimetres, their eyes locked, heat flickering between them, the wait stoking it higher and higher. He had to kiss her, had to or she would spontaneously combust. He had to press that hard mouth against hers, allow those skilled hands to roam, to know her again. To fulfil her again. He had to.

Daisy jumped as a tune blared out from her pocket, a jaunty folk cover of one of her father's greatest hits. Seb's hands dropped and he retreated just a few steps as she fumbled for it, half ready to sob with frustration, half relieved. She hadn't even moved in yet and she was what? Begging him to kiss her?

Very businesslike.

Hands damp, she pulled out the phone and stared at the screen, unable to focus. Pressing the button, she held it shakily to her ear. 'Hello?'

'Daisy? You *are* alive, then?'

'Rose!' Daisy smiled apologetically at Seb and turned

slightly, as if not seeing him would give her some privacy, her heart still hammering.

'Vi said I had to call you right now. Where have you been? Not cool to go offline with no warning, little sis, not cool at all.'

It was what, four o'clock in the afternoon? It felt later, as if several days, not just a few hours, had passed since she had woken up in her own bed, in her own flat for the last time. It would still be morning in New York. She pictured her sister, feet on the desk, a coffee by her hand, an incorrigible mixture of efficiency, impatience and effortless style.

'Things have been a bit crazy.' Daisy knew she sounded breathless, welcomed it. Hopefully her sister would put it down to girlish excitement not a mixture of frustration and embarrassment. 'Rose, I have some news. I'm engaged!'

There was a long silence at the end of the phone. Then: 'But you're not even dating anyone. It's not Edwin, is it? I thought you said he was dull.'

'No, of course it's not Edwin!' Daisy could feel her cheeks heating. 'We split up months ago, and he's not dull exactly,' she added loyally. 'Just a little precise. It's Seb, Sebastian Beresford, you know, Rose, he wrote that book on Charles II's illegitimate children you loved so much.'

'The hot professor? England's answer to Indiana Jones?' The shriek was so loud that Daisy was convinced Seb could hear it through the phone. 'How on earth did you meet him, Daisy? What kind of parties are you going to nowadays? Dinner parties? Academic soirées?' Rose laughed.

There it was, unspoken but insinuated. How could silly little Daisy with barely a qualification to her name have anything in common with a lauded academic?

'Through work,' she said a little stiffly. 'He owns Hawksley Castle.'

'Of course,' her sister breathed. 'Didn't he just inherit a title? What is he, a baron?'

'An earl.' It sounded ludicrous just saying the words. She could feel Seb's sardonic gaze on her and turned around so her back was entirely towards him, wishing she had gone outside to have this awkward conversation.

'An earl?' Rose went off into another peal of laughter. Daisy held the phone away from her ear, waiting for her sister to calm down. 'Seriously? This isn't you and Vi winding me up?'

Was it that implausible? Daisy didn't want to hear the answer.

'It's true.'

'Well, I suppose I had better meet him if you're going to marry him. I'll be over for the Benefit Concert in about four weeks. There's only so much I can do this side of the Atlantic. With the tour on top of everything else I am completely snowed under. I can't cope with one more thing at the moment.' Rose was in charge of all their parents' PR as well as organising the annual Benefit Concert their father did for charity. His decision to take the band back on tour had added even more to her sister's already heavy workload.

So she was going to love the last-minute changes to her plan. 'Actually you're going to meet him sooner than that. We're getting married in three weeks and you have to be my bridesmaid, Rose. You will be there, won't you?'

'What? When? But why, Daisy? What's the rush?'

'No rush,' she replied, hating that she was lying to her family. 'We don't want to wait, that's all.'

There was a deep sigh at the other end of the telephone. 'Daise, you know what you're like. You always go all in at first. You thought you'd found The One at sixteen for goodness' sake, and again when you were at St Martin's. Then there was Edwin—you told me you were soulmates.

Then you wake up one day and realise that they're actually frogs, not your prince. Nice frogs—but still frogs. What makes this one different? Apart from the amazing looks, the keen brain and the title, of course.'

Daisy wanted to slide down onto the floor and stay there. Her family had always teased her about her impetuous romantic nature. But to have it recited back to her like that. It made her sound so young. So stupid.

But Rose was wrong. This wasn't like the others. She was under no illusions that Seb was her soulmate. She wasn't in love.

'This is different and when you meet him you'll understand.' She hoped she sounded convincing—it was the truth after all.

'Okay.' Rose sighed. 'If you say it's different this time then I believe you.'

What Rose actually meant was that she would phone Vi and get her opinion and then the two of them could close ranks and sit in judgement on Daisy. Just as they always did.

'You will be there though, won't you, Rosy Posy?' Daisy wheedled using the old pet name her sister affected to despise. 'I can't get married without you.' Her breath hitched and she heard the break in her voice. Her sisters might be bossy and annoying and have spent most of their childhood telling her to leave them alone but they were hers. And she needed them.

'Of course I'll be there, silly. I'll make the rings, my gift to you both. Send me his finger size, okay?'

'Okay.' Daisy clung onto the phone, wishing her sister were there, wishing she could tell her the truth.

'I have to go. There are a million and one things to do. Talk soon. Call me if you need anything.'

'I will. Bye.'

Daisy clicked the phone shut, oddly bereft as the connection cut. Rose had been abroad for so long—and when she did come home she worked.

'That was my other sister.'

Seb was leaning against the wall, arms folded, one ankle crossed over the other. 'I guessed.'

'She makes rings, as a hobby although she's so good she should do it professionally. She's offered to make ours so I need to send your finger size over.'

She half expected him to say he wasn't going to wear a ring and relief filled her as he nodded acquiescence. 'Why doesn't she—do it professionally?'

It was a good question. Why didn't she? Daisy struggled to find the right words. 'She's good at PR. Mummy and Daddy have always relied on her, and on Vi, to help them. They're so incredibly busy and it's easier to keep it in the family, with people they trust.' Her loving, indulgent, generous but curiously childlike parents.

'What about you? What do you do?'

'Me? I take photos. That's all I'm good for. They don't need me for anything else.' She couldn't keep the bitterness out of her voice.

He looked her curiously. 'That's not the impression I got today. They were bowled over to see you, all fatted calves and tears of joy.'

'That's because I don't go home enough.' The guilt gnawed away at her. 'I don't involve them in my life. It drives my mum crazy as you can probably tell. She doesn't trust me not to mess up without her.'

'Why not?'

Daisy looked at him sharply but the question seemed genuine enough. She sighed. 'It always took me twice as long as my sisters to do anything,' she admitted. 'I was a late talker, walker, reader. My handwriting was atrocious, I hated maths—I was always in trouble at school for talking or messing around.'

'You and half the population.'

'But half the population don't have Rose and Violet as older sisters,' she pointed out. 'I don't think I had a single teacher who didn't ask me why I couldn't be more like my sisters. Why my work wasn't the same standard, my manners as good. By the time I was expelled that narrative was set in stone. I was like the family kitten—cute enough but you couldn't expect much from me. Of course actually being expelled didn't help.'

'It must have been difficult.'

'It was humiliating.' Looking back, that was what she remembered most clearly. How utterly embarrassed she had been. 'It was all over the papers. People were commiserating with my parents as if my life was finished. At sixteen! So Mum and Dad tried to do what they do best. Spend money on me and paper over the cracks. They offered to send me to finishing school, or for Mum to set me up with her modelling agency. I could be a socialite or a model. I wasn't fit for anything else.'

'But you're not either of those things.'

'I refused.' She swallowed. 'I think the worst part was that the whole family treated the whole incident like a joke. They didn't once ask me how I felt, what I wanted to do. To be. I heard Dad say to Mum that I was never going to pass any exams anyway so did it really matter.' She paused, trying not to let that painful memory wind her the way it usually did.

It had hurt knowing that even her own parents didn't have faith in her.

'I didn't want them to fix it. I wanted to fix it myself. So I went to the local college and then art school. I left home properly in my first term and never went back. I needed to prove to them, to me, that they don't have to take care of me.' She laughed but there was no humour in her voice. 'Look how well that's turned out.'

'I think you do just fine by yourself.'

'Pregnant after a one-night stand?' She shook her head. 'Maybe they're right.'

'Pregnant? Yes. But you faced up to it, came here and told me, which was pretty damn brave. You're sacrificing your own dreams for the baby. I think that makes you rather extraordinary.'

'Oh, well.' She shrugged, uncomfortable with the compliments. 'I do get to be a countess and sleep with a king for social advantage after all.'

'There is that.' His eyes had darkened again. 'Where were we, when your sister phoned and interrupted us?'

Daisy felt it again, that slow sensual tug towards him, the hyper awareness of his every move, the tilt of his mouth, the gleam of his eye, the play of muscle in his shoulders.

'You were telling me about wanting to be an outlaw.' She felt it but she wasn't going there. Not today, not when she was in such an emotional tumult.

'Coward.' The word was soft, silky, full of promise. Then he straightened, the intentness gone. 'So I was. Ready to see the rest of your home? Let's zoom forward to the eighteenth century and start exploring the Georgian part. I'll warn you, there's a lot of it. I think we'll stick to the ground and first floors today. The second floor is largely empty and the attics have been untouched for years.'

'Attics?' A frisson of excitement shivered through her. As a child she had adored roaming through the attics at home, exploring chests filled with family treasures. Only there was nothing to discover in the recently renovated, perfectly decorated house. Photos sorted into date order? Yes. Tiaras dripping with diamonds or secret love letters? No. But here, in a house that epitomised history, she could find anything.

'Would you mind if one day I had a look? In the attics?'

Seb walked towards the door and stopped, his hand on the huge iron bolt. 'One day? I think you'll need to put aside at least six months. My family were hoarders—I would love to catalogue it all, although I suspect much of it is junk, but there's too much to do elsewhere. The whole house could do with some updating. I don't know if your talents run in that direction but please, feel free to make any changes you want. As long as they're in keeping with a grade one listed building,' he added quickly.

'And there I was, thinking I could paint the whole outside pink and add a concrete extension.' But she was strangely cheered. A house with twenty bedrooms and as many reception rooms—if you included the various billiard rooms, studies and galleries—was no small project. But taking it in hand gave her a purpose, a role here. Maybe, just maybe, she could make Hawksley Castle into a home. Into her home.

CHAPTER FIVE

'MORNING. HUNGRY?'

Seb half turned as Daisy slipped into the kitchen, tiptoe-ing as if she didn't want to offend him with her presence.

'Starving. I keep waiting for the nausea to start.' She was almost apologetic, as if he would accuse her of being a fraud if she wasn't doubled over with sickness. It would be easier, he admitted, if she were ill. He was after all taking it on trust that she was even pregnant in the first place, although she had offered him plenty of chances to wait for confirmation.

'You may be lucky and escape it altogether. How did you sleep?'

'Good, thanks. Turns out five-hundred-year-old beds are surprisingly comfy.'

The problem of where to put Daisy had haunted him since she had agreed to move in. To make this work, to fulfil her criteria as far as he could, meant he couldn't treat her like a guest and yet he wasn't ready to share his space with anyone.

Even though part of him couldn't help wondering what it would be like lying next to those long, silky limbs.

Luckily Georgian houses were built with this kind of di-lemma in mind. When he first took a leave of absence and returned to Hawksley six months ago to try and untangle the complicated mess his father had left, he'd moved into his grandparents' old rooms, not his own boyhood bedroom on the second floor.

There was a suite adjoining, the old countess' suite, a throwback to not so long ago when the married couple weren't expected to regularly share a bed, a room or a bathroom. The large bedroom, small study, dressing room and bathroom occupied a corner at the back of the house with views over the lake to the woods and fields beyond. The suite was rather faded, last decorated some time around the middle of the previous century and filled with furniture of much older heritage but charming for all that.

'There is a door here,' he had said, showing her a small door discreetly set into the wall near the bed. 'It leads into my room. You can lock it if you would rather, but I don't bother.'

The words had hung in the air. Were they an invitation? A warning? He wasn't entirely sure.

It was odd, he had never really noticed the door before yet last night it had loomed in his eyeline, the unwanted focal point of his own room. He had known she was on the other side, just one turn of the handle away. Seb's jaw tightened as he flipped the bacon. He could visualise it now as if it were set before him. Small, wooden, nondescript.

'Did you lock the door?'

'Bolted it.'

'Good, wouldn't want the ghost of a regency rake surprising you in the middle of the night.'

Daisy wandered over to the kettle and filled it. Such a normal everyday thing to do—and yet such a big step at the same time. 'I'm sure bolts are no barrier to any decent ghosts, not rakish-type ones anyway. Coffee?'

'All set, thanks.' He nodded at the large mug at his elbow. The scene was very domestic in a formal, polite kind of way.

Daisy sniffed the several herbal teas she had brought with her and pulled a face. 'I miss coffee. I don't mind giving up alcohol and I hate blue cheese anyway but waking up without a skinny latte is a cruel and unusual punishment.'

'We could get some decaf.' Seb grabbed two plates and spooned the eggs and bacon onto them.

'I think you're missing the whole point of coffee. I'll give liquorice a try.' She made the hot drink and carried the mug over to the table, eying up the heaped plate of food with much greater enthusiasm. 'This looks great, thanks.'

'I thought we might need sustenance for the day ahead. Registrar at ten and I booked you into the doctor's here for eleven. I hope that's okay. And then we'd better let the staff and volunteers know our news, begin to make some plans.'

'Fine.' A loud peal rang through the house causing a slight vibration, and Daisy jumped, the eggs piled up on her fork tumbling back onto the plate. 'What on earth is that?'

Seb pushed his chair back and tried not to look too longingly at his uneaten breakfast. It was a long way from the kitchen to the door, plenty of time for his breakfast to cool. 'Doorbell. It's a little dramatic admittedly but the house is so big it's the only way to know if there's a visitor—and it's less obtrusive than a butler. Cheaper too.'

'Is it the gorgon? If I get turned to stone I expect you to rescue me.'

He tried not to let his mouth quirk at the apt nickname. There was definitely a heart of gold buried deep somewhere underneath Mrs Suffolk's chilly exterior but it took a long time to find and appreciate it. 'The volunteers have a key for the back door—there's only two working doors between the offices and the main house and I lock them both at night.'

'Good to know. I don't fancy being petrified in my bed.'

Her words floated after him as he exited the kitchen and headed towards the front of the house.

Once, of course, the kitchen would have been part of the servants' quarters; it was still set discreetly behind a baize door, connected to the offices through a short passageway and one of the lockable doors that defined the partition between his personal space and the work space. But even his oh-so-formal grandparents had dispensed with live-in servants during the nineties and started to use the old kitchen themselves. For supper and breakfast at least.

His parents had brought their servants with them during the four years they had mismanaged Hawksley. Not that they had ever stayed at the castle for longer than a week.

The doorbell pealed again, the deep tone melodic.

'On my way.' Seb pulled back the three bolts and twisted the giant iron key, making a mental note to oil the creaking lock. He swung open the giant door to be confronted with the sight of his future mother-in-law, a huge and ominously full bag thrown over one shoulder, a newspaper in one hand and a bottle of champagne in the other.

Seb blinked. Then blinked again.

'Goodness, Seb, you look like you've seen a ghost.' She thrust the champagne and the newspaper at him, muttering cryptically, 'Page five, darling. Where is Daisy?'

'Good morning, Mrs Huntingdon…'

'Sherry.' She swept past him. '"Mrs" makes me feel so old. And we are going to be family after all.'

Family. Not something he knew huge amounts about but he was pretty sure the tall, glamorous woman opposite wasn't a typical mother-in-law. 'Right, yes. This way. She's just eating breakfast.'

He led the supermodel through the hallway, wincing as he noticed her assess every dusty cornice, every scrap of peeling paper. 'My grandparents rather let the place go.'

'It's like a museum. Apt for you in your job, I suppose.'
It didn't sound like a compliment.

They reached the kitchen and Sherry swept by him to
enfold a startled-looking Daisy in her arms. 'Bacon? Oh,
Daisy darling, the chances of you fitting sample sizes were
small anyway but you'll never do it if you eat fried food.
No, none for me, thank you. I don't eat breakfast.'

'Mum? What are you doing here?'

Seb couldn't help smiling at Daisy's face. She looked
exactly as he felt: surprise mixed with wariness and shock.

'Darling, we have a wedding to plan and no time at all.
Where else would I be? Now hurry up and eat that. We'll
get you some nice fruit while we're out. Page five, Seb.'

Seb glanced down at the tabloid newspaper Sherry had
handed him and opened it slowly, his heart hammering.
Surely not, not yet...

He dropped it on the table, a huge picture of Daisy and
himself smiling up from the smudged newsprint. 'Hot Prof
Earl and Wild Child to Wed' screamed the headline. He
stepped back, horror churning in the pit of his stomach,
his hands clammy.

'I knew it.' Daisy's outraged voice cut into his stupor.
'They mentioned the expulsion. Why not my first in photography or my successful business?'

'I expect they also mentioned my parents' divorces, re-
marriages, drinking, drug taking and untimely deaths.' He
knew he sounded cold, bitter and inhaled, trying to calm
the inner tumult.

'Yes.' Her voice sounded small and Seb breathed in
again, trying to calm the swirling anger. It wasn't her fault.

Although if she wasn't who she was then would they
be so interested?

'I'm sorry,' she added and he swallowed hard, forcing
himself to lay a hand upon her shoulder.

'Don't be silly, Daisy, of course they're interested. Seb

is just as big a draw as you, more so probably.' Sherry's blue eyes were sharp, assessing.

'Yes,' he agreed tonelessly. 'We knew there would be publicity. I just thought we would have more time.'

If Daisy hadn't gone to Huntingdon Hall, hadn't involved her parents…

'The best thing to do is ignore it. Come along, darling. Show me the wedding venue. I don't have all day.'

Daisy sat for a moment, her head still bowed, cheeks pale. 'We have appointments at ten, Mum, so I only have half an hour. If you'd warned us you were coming I could have told you this morning was already booked up.'

'You two head off, I'll be fine here. There's plenty to do, just show me the venue.'

'Honestly, Mum. I can organise this quite easily. I really don't need you to do it.' There was a hint of desperation in Daisy's voice as she attempted to reason with her mother.

'I know very well that you prefer to do everything alone, Daisy. You make that quite clear.'

Daisy pushed her half-eaten breakfast away and, with an apologetic glance at Seb, took her mother's arm. 'Okay, you win. Seb, I put your breakfast back in the pan to keep warm. Come along, Mother. I don't think even you can fault the Tudor Hall.'

Seb watched them go before sliding his gaze back to the open newspaper. He focused on the picture. He was driving and Daisy was looking back, smiling. It must have been snapped as they left the hall. How hadn't he noticed the photographer?

Was this how their lives would be from now on? Every step, every conversation, every outing watched, scrutinised and reported on.

With one vicious movement he grabbed the paper and tore the article from it, screwing it into a ball and dropping it in the bin, his breath coming in fast pants. He wouldn't, couldn't be hounded. Cameras trained on him, crowds waiting outside the gate, microphones thrust into his face. He had been five the first time, as motorcycles and cars chased them down the country lanes.

His father had driven faster, recklessly. His mother had laughed.

The tantalising aroma of cooking bacon wafted through the air, breaking into his thoughts. Seb walked over to the stove, his movements slow and stiff. The frying pan was covered, the heat set to low and inside, warmed through to perfection, was his breakfast. Saved, put aside and kept for him.

When was the last time someone had done something, anything for him that they weren't paid to do?

It was just some breakfast, food he had actually cooked, put aside. So why did his chest ache as he spooned it back onto his plate?

Daisy had to work hard to stop from laughing at the look on Seb's face. He stood in the Great Hall, staring about him as if he had been kidnapped by aliens and transported to an alternate universe.

And in some ways, he had.

Her mother had wasted no time in making herself at home, somehow rounding up two bemused if bedazzled volunteers to help her set up office in the Great Hall. Three tables in a U-shape and several chairs were flanked by a white board and a pin board on trestles with several sticky notes already attached to each. A seamstress's dummy stood to attention behind the biggest chair, a wreath of flowers on its head.

A carafe of water, a glass and a vase of flowers had been procured from somewhere and set upon the table and Sherry had proceeded to empty her huge bag in a Mary Poppins manner setting out two phones, a lever arch file already divided into labelled sections, a stack of wedding magazines and—Daisy groaned in horror—her own scrapbooks and what looked like her own Pinterest mood boards printed out and laminated.

So she planned weddings online? She was a wedding photographer! It was her job to get ideas and inspiration.

If Sherry Huntingdon ever turned her formidable mind towards something other than fashion then who knew what she'd achieve? World peace? An end to poverty? Daisy winced. That wasn't entirely fair; both her parents did a huge amount for charity, most of it anonymously. The Benefit Concert might be the most high-profile event but it was just the tip of the iceberg.

'There you are, Seb.' Sherry was pacing around the Great Hall, looking at the panelling and the other period details with approval. 'Before you whisk Daisy away I need a bit of information.'

'Whatever you need.' His eyes flickered towards the arsenal of paper, pens and planning materials set out with precision on the tables and a muscle began to beat in his stubbled jaw as his hands slowly clenched. 'Good to see that you've made yourself at home.'

'I think it's helpful to be right in the centre of things,' Sherry agreed, missing—or ignoring—his sarcastic undertone. 'Your nice man on the gate tells me that there are weddings booked in both weekends so I can't leave everything set up but we'll have the hall to ourselves for the four days before the wedding so I can make sure everything is perfect.'

Daisy noticed Seb's tense stance, the rigidity in his shoulders, and interrupted. 'It won't take four days to set up for a few family and friends—and it's such short notice I'm sure most people will have plans already.'

'Don't be ridiculous, of course they'll come. It'll be the wedding of the year—rock aristocracy to real aristocracy? They'll cancel whatever other plans they have, you mark my words. Now, the nice young man tells me the hall will seat two hundred so I'll need your list as soon as possible, Seb.'

'List?' The muscle was still beating. Daisy couldn't take her eyes off it. She wanted to walk over there, lay a hand on the tense shoulder and soothe the stress out of it, run a hand across his firm jawline and kiss the muscle into quiet acquiescence. She curled her fingers into her palms, allowing her nails to bite into her flesh, the sharp sting reminding her not to cross the line. To remain businesslike.

'I already did you a list, Daisy.' Of course she had. Numbly Daisy took the sheet of neatly typed names her mother handed her and scanned it expecting to see the usual mixture of relatives, her parents' friends and business associates and the group of people her age that her parents liked to socialise with: a few actors, singers and other cool, media-friendly twenty-somethings she had absolutely nothing in common with.

And yet… Daisy swallowed, heat burning the backs of her eyes. The names she read through rapidly blurring eyes were exactly—almost exactly—those she would have written herself. It was like a *This Is Your Life* recap: school friends, college friends, work associates, London friends plus of course the usual relatives and some of the older villagers, people she had known her entire life.

'This is perfect. How did you know?' Blinking furiously, Daisy forced back the threatening tears; all her life she had felt like the odd one out, the funny little addition at the end of the family, more a pampered plaything than a card-carrying, fully paid-up adult member of the family, a person who really mattered.

A person who they knew, who they understood. Maybe they understood her better than she had ever realised.

'Vi helped me.' Her mother's voice was a little gruff and there was a telltale sheen in her eyes. 'Is it right?'

'Almost perfect.' There were just a few amendments. Daisy swiftly added several new names, recent friends her family had yet to meet.

Seb moved, just a small rustle but enough to bring her back to the present, to the reality that was this wedding. What was she thinking?

Her hand shook a little bit as she reread the top lines. These were exactly the people she would want to share her wedding day with. Only...

'The thing is we did agree on a small wedding.' She tried to keep all emotion out of her voice, not wanting her mother to hear her disappointment or Seb to feel cornered. 'If we invited all these it would be a huge affair. I'll take a look at it and single out the most important friends. What do you think? Immediate family and maybe five extra guests each?' She looked around at the long hall, the vast timbered ceiling rearing overhead. They would rattle around in here like a Chihuahua in a Great Dane's pen.

But it was still a substantially larger affair than Seb wanted. Daisy allowed the piece of paper to float down onto the desk as if the thought of striking out the majority of the names didn't make her throat tighten.

Seb had moved, so silently she hadn't noticed, reaching over her shoulder to deftly catch the paper mid-fall. 'The problem is I don't actually have any immediate family.'

Daisy automatically opened her mouth to say something inane, something to smooth over the chasm his words opened up. Then she closed it again. What good were platitudes? But understanding shivered over her. No wonder this marriage was important to him. The baby was more than a potential heir; it would be all that he had. Responsibility crushed down on her. She had been so naïve, so happy at the thought of having a person in her life who needed her, depended on her. But the baby wasn't just hers. It was theirs.

'There are school friends.' He was scribbling away on the back of the list, his handwriting sure and firm. 'Other academics, publishing colleagues, staff and volunteers here and villagers I have known all my life. I think I will need eighty places including the plus ones but, if you agree, I propose a hog roast in a marquee in the courtyard in the evening and invite the whole village. Noblesse oblige I know but it's a tied village and expected.'

'Do you have a marquee?' Thank goodness her mother was on the ball because Daisy couldn't have spoken if her life had depended on it. He didn't want this, she knew that. People, publicity, fuss, photos and the inevitable press. The only answer, the only possible reason was that he was doing this for her.

She slipped her hand into his without thought or plan and his fingers curled around hers.

Maybe, just maybe this could work after all.

'Weddings here are all run and catered for by The Blue Boar, that's the village pub, and yes, they have several marquees of all sizes. Paul—' he smiled slightly, that devastating half-lift of his mouth '—the helpful man on the gate, he can give you all the details you need.'

'That is wonderful.' Her mother was rapidly taking notes. 'That gives me a lot to be getting on with. Rose will be doing the rings of course and Violet the flowers. You know what, Daisy, I think somehow we are going to be able to pull this wedding off.'

'We're going all the way into London?'

When she had left the day before Daisy had felt, fully aware of her own inner melodrama, as if she were being taken away from her beloved city for ever even though she knew full well that she would be returning for a studio shoot later that week. But it still felt slightly anticlimactic to be returning just over twenty-four hours later.

Her mother looked mildly surprised. 'Of course, we have a wedding dress to buy.' Her voice grew wistful. 'It was such a shame that Seb vetoed a Tudor theme. I think he would have carried off a doublet really well. And such an eminent historian, you would have thought he would have jumped at the chance to really live in the past.'

'So short-sighted.' Daisy couldn't suppress the gurgle of laughter that bubbled up as she remembered the utter horror on Seb's face when her mother had greeted them with her brilliant idea. 'I would have preferred regency though.'

'The building is all wrong but you were made to wear one of those high-waisted gowns. And breeches are possibly even better than doublet and hose.'

'Infinitely better.' Daisy settled herself into a more comfortable position, allowing her hand to move softly across her abdomen. All had been confirmed. She was definitely pregnant, close to seven weeks. Just as she had expected but it had been a relief to hear another human say it out loud.

A relief to give Seb the definitive tidings; backing out of the wedding now would have been awkward for both of them. It wasn't that she was actually beginning to enjoy the planning process, enjoy having her mother's undivided attention or even enjoy seeing Seb pulled so far out of his comfort zone he could barely formulate a sentence.

Except when the Tudor theme was mooted. He had been more than able to turn that idea down flat.

Once she had established where they were going Daisy took little notice of the route. It wasn't often she spent time alone with her mother.

Maybe if she had allowed her mother in a little more then there would have been more occasions like this but the price had always seemed too high. Her mother did have a tendency to try and take over, the wedding a perfect case in point.

But it came from a place of love; maybe she should have respected that more.

Daisy leant across and kissed her mother's still smooth and unlined cheek.

'Thank you,' she said. 'For helping.' It almost hurt, saying the words, but she felt a sense of relief when they were out, as if she had been holding onto them for a long, long time.

Her mother's blue eyes widened. 'Of course I want to help. My baby, getting married. And there is so much to do. Hawksley may be grand but I've seen more up-to-date ruins.'

'Part of it is ruined.' Daisy was surprised at how protective she felt towards the stately building.

Her mother gave her a wry glance. 'I mean the house part. Really, darling, it's a major project. Some of the rooms have been untouched for years.'

'I just wish you had checked with Seb before organising the cleaners.' Only her mother could get an army of cleaners, decorators and handymen organised in under two hours. It had been a shock to arrive back from their morning appointments to find the car park full of various trade vans, the house overrun by ladders, buckets and pine scents.

'Most of the family will be staying in the house after all. Updating and decorating are your preserve, darling, but cleaning and touching up before the big day is very much mine. Consider it my wedding present to you both.'

Daisy tried not to sigh. Seb employed one cleaner who was responsible for the offices as well as the house and she barely made a dent in the few areas he used. It would be nice to see the main house brought up to hygienic standards: the paintwork fresh, the wood polished and the sash windows gleaming. At the same time it was so typical of her mother to wave her magic wand with extravagant generosity, to think that money would solve the problem regardless of how it made the recipients feel.

There had been a bleak look on Seb's face when he surveyed the workers. He had withdrawn into his study pleading work and Daisy hadn't felt able to follow him in there.

The car drew up outside the iconic golden stone building that housed Rafferty's, London's premier designer store.

'It's simply too late for a gown to be made for you. I am owed a lot of favours but even I can't work miracles. But then I remembered what a fabulous collection Nina keeps here at Rafferty's. She has promised that she can have any gown altered to fit you in the timescale. Luckily I had my pick of the new spring/summer collections in Fashion Week last year so there will be something suitable for me.' Her mother sounded vaguely put upon, as if she were being expected to put an outfit together from a duster and an old feather boa, not premier one of the several haute couture outfits that had been made specifically for her.

Daisy felt the old shiver of excitement as they exited the car and walked into the famous domed entrance hall. It was once said you could buy anything and become anybody at Rafferty's—as long as you had the money. Would she become the bride of her dreams?

They were met at the door and whisked upstairs to the bridal department, an impressive gallery decorated in Rafferty's distinctive art deco style. The entrance to the department, reached through an archway, was open to the public and sold an array of bridal accessories including lingerie, shoes, tiaras and some ready-to-wear bride and bridesmaids dresses. But it was the room beyond, tactfully hidden behind a second, curtained arch, where the real magic lay. This room was accessed by appointment only. Today, Daisy and her mother were the only customers.

It needed little decoration and the walls were painted a warm blush white, the floor a polished mahogany. The sparkle and glamour came from the dresses themselves; every conceivable length, every shade of white from ice through to deep cream, a few richer colours dotted around: a daring red, rich gold, vibrant silver, pinks and rich brocades.

Daisy was glad of the cosy-looking love seats and chaises scattered about. So much choice was making her head whirl.

'Champagne?' Nina, the department manager who had been dressing the city's brides for nearly forty years, came over with a bottle of Dom Perignon, chilled and opened.

'No, thanks.' Daisy thought rapidly. 'I want a clear head. There's so much choice.'

'A large glass for me, please.' Violet walked in, slightly out of breath. 'I sense it's going to be a long afternoon. Rose says hi, don't make her wear frills and definitely not shiny satin.'

'They're all so beautiful.' Their mother was already halfway down a glass of champagne, a wistful look in her eyes as she fingered the heavy silks, slippery satins and intricate laces. 'Obviously I wouldn't have changed my wedding to your father for the world. It was very romantic, just us, in a tiny chapel. I was barefoot with flowers in my hair. But I did miss out on all this…' Her gaze encompassed the room. 'Which is why, Daisy darling, I am determined that no matter how whirlwind your wedding, no matter how little time we have, you are going to have the day you always dreamed of.'

CHAPTER SIX

'YOU LOOK TERRIBLE. What's wrong?'

Daisy, Seb had discovered in the week they had been living together, was just like him—an early bird. She usually appeared in the kitchen just a few moments after he did, already dressed, ready to moan about the lack of caffeine in her day while hopefully trying yet another of the seemingly endless array of herbal teas she had brought with her, hoping to discover the one to replace her beloved lattes.

Today she was dressed as usual, if a little more demure, in a grey skater-style dress with an embroidered yellow hem, a yellow knitted cap pulled back over her head. But there was no exaggerated groaning when she saw his coffee, no diving on the toast as if she hadn't eaten in at least a month. Instead she pulled out a chair and collapsed into it with a moan.

'Why, why, why did I agree to start work at nine?' She looked at the clock on the wall and slid further down her seat. 'It's going to take me well over an hour to get there. I'll need to set off in ten minutes.'

'Toast?' Seb pushed the plate towards her but she pushed it back with an exaggerated shudder.

'No, it's far too early for food.'

She hadn't said that yesterday at a very similar time. Between them they had demolished an entire loaf of bread.

'Is that a new brand of coffee?' Daisy was looking at his cup of coffee as if he had filled it with slurry from the cow sheds, her nose wrinkled in disgust.

'Nope, the usual.'

'It smells vile.'

Seb took another look. She was unusually pale, the violet shadows under her eyes pronounced despite powder, the bright lipstick a startling contrast to her pallor. 'Didn't you sleep well?'

'I could have slept for ever.' She sniffed again and went even paler. 'Are you sure that's the usual brand? Have you made it extra strong?' She pressed her hand to her stomach and winced.

'You look really ill. I think you should go back to bed.'

'I can't.' The wail was plaintive. 'I have a wedding to photograph. I'm due at the bride's house at nine for the family breakfast followed by the arrival of the bridesmaids and getting ready. I need to be at the groom's at half eleven for best man and ushers then back to the bride's for final departures, church at one and then the reception.'

'With a blog up by midnight and the first pictures available the next day?' His mouth folded into a thin line. It was a ridiculous schedule.

'That's what they pay me for.'

'There is no way you are going to be able to manage an eighteen-hour day on no breakfast.'

Daisy pushed her chair back and swayed, putting a hand onto the table to steady herself. 'I don't have any choice. I work for myself, Seb. I can't just call in sick. Besides, I'm not ill, I'm pregnant. This is self-inflicted, like a hangover. I just have to deal with it.'

'It's nothing like a hangover.' He stopped as she winced, a hand to her head. 'You need an assistant.'

'Possibly, but unless you can produce one out of one of the trunks in the attic that's not going to help with today.'

Seb regarded her helplessly. He wanted to march her back upstairs, tuck her in and make her soup. He was responsible for the slight green tinge to her skin and the shadows under her eyes.

But she was right, if she cried off a wedding on the day her reputation would be shattered. 'Can anyone cover for you?'

'Seb, this is morning sickness not a twenty-four-hour bug.' Her voice rose in exasperation. 'It could last for days, or weeks, or even months. What about Monday's engagement shoot? Or next Saturday's wedding? Or the baby photos on Wednesday? I can't just walk away from all my responsibilities.'

'No, but you can plan ahead.'

'But none of this *was* planned. Don't treat me like I'm some fluffy little girl without a brain cell.'

Woah, where had that come from?

'I didn't mean to offend you.' He knew he sounded stiff but this: histrionics, overreacting, unreasonable responses to reasonable points. It was everything he didn't want in his life.

To his surprise Daisy let out a huge sigh and slumped. 'I'm sorry, I am just so tired. You're right, I do need to start planning how I am going to cover my commitments over the next year.'

It was over, just like that. No escalation, no screaming, no smashing of crockery. Just an apology.

'I could have phrased it better.' It wasn't as full an apology as hers but it was all he could manage in his shock.

'I have been meaning to talk to Sophie. She was on my course and specialises in portraits, personal commissions mostly although she's been beginning to get some magazine work. Her studio rent was just doubled and now I'm not living in mine I thought we might join forces and she could cover weddings for me in lieu of rent, or at least give me a hand. But that doesn't solve today.'

No. It didn't.

Daisy took one dragging step towards the door and then another. Her laptop case, camera case and tripod were neatly piled up, waiting. How she was going to carry them he had no idea.

And she really needed to eat something.

'I'll come with you and help.'

She half turned, the first flicker of a smile on her face. 'You? Do you know when to use a fifty-millimetre, an eighty-five-millimetre or switch to a wide-angled lens?'

'No, I can barely use the camera on my phone,' Seb admitted. 'But I can fetch, carry, set up, organise groups, make sure you eat.'

A flicker of hope passed over her face. 'Don't you have a million and one things to do here?'

'Always.' Seb grimaced as he remembered the unfinished grant applications, the paperwork that seemed to grow bigger the more he did. Not to mention his real work, the research that seemed more and more impossible every day. The looming deadline for a book still in note form. 'Promise me you'll chat to Sophie tomorrow and at least sort out a willing apprentice for next week and I'll come and help.'

She was tempted, he could see. 'You really don't mind?'

'No, not at all. On the condition I drive and you try and eat something in the car.' The grant applications could wait, the paperwork could wait. He'd be worrying all day if he allowed her to walk out of the door and start a gruelling day on her feet without someone to watch out for her.

The sooner she got an assistant or partner, the better.

There were times when Seb wondered if all that sassy style and confidence was only skin deep. When he thought he saw a flash of vulnerability in the blue eyes. But not here. Not today.

If Daisy still felt sick she was hiding it well. She was all quiet control and ease as she snapped: candid shots, posed shots, detailed close-ups. Always polite, always professional but in complete control, whether it was putting the nervy mother of the bride at her ease or settling the exuberant best man and ushers down enough to take a series of carefully choreographed shots.

She was everywhere and yet she was totally discreet. Focused on the job at hand. Seb followed her with bags and the box of ginger biscuits, completely out of place in this world of flowers and silks and tears.

Even the groom had had tears in his eyes as the bride had finally—an entire twenty minutes late—walked down the aisle.

As for the mother of the bride, five tissues hadn't been enough to staunch her sobs. The whole thing was a hysterical nightmare. Leaving the church had been a huge relief and he had gulped in air like a drowning man.

But the ordeal wasn't over.

'I don't understand what else there is for you to do.' Daisy had directed him towards a woodland nearby and Seb was following her down the chipping-strewn path. 'You must have taken at least three hundred pictures already. How many group shots outside the church? His family, her family, his friends, her friends, his colleagues, her colleagues. The neighbours, passers-by…'

'Far more than three hundred.' She threw him a mischievous smile. 'Bored?'

'It just takes so long. No photos at our wedding, Daisy. Not like this.'

'No.' The smile was gone. 'But ours is different. We don't need to document every moment.'

'Just the obvious ones.' Perversely he was annoyed

she wasn't trying to talk him round. 'It would seem odd otherwise.'

'If you want.' She chewed her bottom lip as she looked at him thoughtfully. 'I think I'm going to change the order a little bit as you are here. If I put you in charge of the photo booth then there is some entertainment for the guests while I do the couple's portraits in the woods. Is that okay?'

Seb blinked. He was here to carry bags, not perform. 'The what? Do I have to do anything?'

'Smile. Tell them to say cheese. Press a button, four times. Can you manage that?'

Possibly. 'What do you mean by photo booth? Like a passport photo? At a wedding?'

She shot him an amused look. 'In a way, you know, teenagers sit in a photo booth and take silly pictures—or at least they did before selfies became ubiquitous.'

He shook his head. 'No, never did it. I've never taken a selfie either.'

Her mouth tilted into a smile. 'That doesn't surprise me. But you know what I mean? This is the same, only with props. And not a booth, just me with a camera—or in this case you. They put on silly accessories and then stand in front of a frame and try different poses. I print them up as a long strip of four pictures.'

Seb stared at her incredulously. 'Why on earth do you do that?'

'Because it's fun.' She rolled her eyes at him. 'I'll set the tripod up. All you need to do is explain they have three seconds to change pose and press the button. Honestly, Seb, it's fine. A monkey could do it.'

'And where will you be?'

'Portrait time. Followed by more group shots. And then candid evening and reception shots. Having fun yet?'

'Absolutely. The thought of wandering around these woods for hours carrying your cases is my idea of a perfect

day. Sure you know where you're going?' They seemed
to be going further into the woodland with no building
in sight.

'Yep, I did the engagement shoot here. Ah, here we go.'
She stopped, a hand to her mouth. 'Oh, Seb. Look at it.
Isn't it utterly perfect?'

Seb came to a halt and stared. Where was the hotel? Or
barn? A barn would be nice and cosy. Cosier than open
canvas at least. 'They must be crazy? An outdoor wedding in April?'

'It's not outdoors!'

'It's in a tent.'

'It's a tepee.'

'You say tent, I say tepee.'

Daisy ignored him as he hummed the words, a chill running through him as the next line of the song ran through
his head.

There was no calling the whole thing off now, not easily.
It had escalated far beyond his wildest imaginings: a guest
list of over two hundred not including the evening guests,
dresses, button holes, hog roasts, centrepieces, cravats—
Sherry's determination and vision taking it to a level neither Seb nor Daisy had wanted or sanctioned.

Did he want to call it off? He still wanted to marry
Daisy; it was still the most sensible solution. But this circus his life was becoming was out of control. His peaceful Oxford existence seemed further and further away.

Although that wasn't Daisy's fault. Running Hawksley
was more than a full-time job and not one he was finding it easy to delegate no matter how much he missed
his old life.

'Oh, that's perfect.' Daisy's voice broke in on his
thoughts and he pushed them to one side. He couldn't
change anything—including the wedding. He owed her
that much.

Daisy was lost in a world of her own. It was fascinating to watch her pace, focus, move again as she looked at the scene before her, crouching down to check angles and squinting against the light. No insouciance, no hesitation, just quietly in control.

Seb moved with her, trying to see with her, picture what she pictured. The path opened out into a woodland glade, which had been decorated with cheerful bunting and swaying glass lanterns. In the middle of the glade the huge canvas tepee stood opened up on three sides to the elements—although Daisy promised there were covers ready to be fastened on if April proved true to its name and christened the wedding with showers.

A wooden floor had been laid and trestle tables and benches ran down the sides, the middle left bare for dancing. A stage held the tables covered with food for the buffet; later food would be switched for the band. Two smaller tents were pitched to one side, one holding the bar and the other a chill-out area complete with beanbags.

On the other side a gazebo was pitched, the table inside heaped with a variety of wigs, hats, waistcoats and other props. A large frame hung from the tree beside it. This was to be Seb's workspace for his first—and hopefully last—foray into professional photography.

He had never been to a wedding like this before and something about its raw honesty unsettled him; it was a little Bohemian, a touch homespun with its carefully carefree vibe.

'Look at these colours. Their friends and family supplied the food in lieu of presents. Don't you think that's lovely? Everyone made something.' Daisy was over at the buffet table, camera out, focusing on a rich-looking salad of vibrant green leaves, red pomegranate seeds and juicy oranges.

'It depends on their cooking skills.' If Seb asked his

friends and colleagues to bring a dish they would buy something from a local deli, not spend time and love creating it themselves. He looked at a plate of slightly lumpy cakes, the icing uneven, and a hollow feeling opened up in his chest.

Someone had lavished care and attention on those cakes, making up with enthusiasm for what they lacked in skill. That was worth more than clicking on an item on a wedding list or writing a cheque.

Daisy looked up at a rustle and relaxed again as a bird rose out of a tree. 'Tell me as soon as you hear anybody. I want to capture their faces as they walk in.' The guests were being brought to the woodland by coach via a drinks reception at the local pub, the place where the bride and groom had first met.

'Shouldn't you be sitting down and maybe eating something while there's a lull?' But she didn't hear him, lost in a world of her own.

'Look, Seb,' she said softly, and he did, trying to see what she saw as she zoomed in on the brightly patterned bunting that bedecked the inside of the tent as well as the glade.

'These are the touches that make this wedding so special. Did you know that Ella and her friends made the bunting during her hen party? And look at these.' The camera moved to focus in on one of the paintings propped up on the small easels that were the centrepiece on each table. 'Rufus painted these, a different tree for each table—oak, laurel, ash, apple, all native species. Aren't they gorgeous?'

Studying one of the confident line drawings, Seb had to admit that they were. 'He's very talented.'

'Even the wedding favours are home-made. Ella spent her first day off work making the fudge, and her gran embroidered the bags. Look, they all have a name on. One for each guest.'

'It must have taken months.' Seb kept pace with her as she wandered.

'It did. This wedding is a real labour of love. Even the venue belongs to one of their friends.'

The contrast with their impending nuptials couldn't be starker.

But theirs wasn't a labour of love. It was a convenient compromise. Mutually beneficial. Maybe it was better to have the glitz and the glamour so lovingly lavished upon them by Sherry Huntingdon. Anything as heartfelt as this wedding, any one of the myriad tiny, loving, personal touches would be completely out of place at his wedding. Would be a lie.

'Admit it, you had fun.' Daisy threw herself into her favourite rocking chair, grateful for the warmth and the cushion supporting her aching back. She crooned to Monty as he padded over to lay his head in her lap. He was already her most faithful friend much to Seb's much-voiced disgust, possibly because she was not averse to sneaking him titbits from her plate.

'I'm not sure fun is the right word.' Seb filled the kettle and stifled a yawn. 'I always said your schedule was crazy but it's more than that, it's downright gruelling.' But there was respect in his voice and it warmed her. She was well aware of his opinion about her job.

And he was right, it *was* gruelling, somehow even more so in a small intimate setting like today's woodland scene. Gruelling and odd, being part of someone's wedding, integral to it and yet not connected. A stranger. As the afternoon faded to evening and the guests drank more, ate more, danced and the mood shifted into party atmosphere the gap between the help and the guests widened. There were times it was almost voyeuristic watching the interactions from the sidelines. It had been nice to have company today.

She really should get an assistant and not just because of her pregnancy.

'I would normally be the first to suggest you rest but don't you have a blog to write? If it's not up before midnight the world shifts on its axis and Cupid dies?' He held up a ginger teabag for her approval. Daisy considered it without enthusiasm before pulling a face and agreeing.

She shifted in the chair, pulling her feet under her, and began to pull at Monty's long, soft ears. He gave a small throaty groan and moved closer. 'Did it in the car. It's amazing, home before midnight and job done, for today at least.'

She looked over at her bag, the cameras loaded with images. 'Tomorrow however is most definitely another day. I promised them thirty images before they go away on honeymoon. Still, I feel much better than I thought I would. I don't suppose you would consider a permanent career as bag carrier and chauffeur—and photo-booth operator?' She smiled, a sly note creeping into her voice. 'You were quite a hit. Some of the women went back to have their photo taken again and again.'

'How do you know? I still can't believe it took an hour and a half to take those woodland shots. I think you went for a nap somewhere leaving me to do all the work.'

'Oh, I was. Curled up in a pile of leaves like Hansel and Gretel while woodland birds sang me to sleep and squirrels brought me nuts. And I know because the sexy photographer was quite the topic of conversation—and I don't think they meant me!'

'Jealous?'

Daisy didn't answer for a moment, focusing all her attention on Monty as she scratched behind his ears, the spaniel leaning against her blissfully. 'A little, actually.'

She still couldn't look at him as she chose her next words carefully. 'There was a little bit of me that wanted to tell them that you weren't available, that you were mine.' She looked up.

Seb froze, his eyes fixed on her.

The blood was pounding hard in her ears, like a river in full flood. What had she said that for? Not even married and already she was pushing too hard, wanting too much. 'Which is silly because you're not,' she back-pedalled, desperately wanting to make light of the words. 'Maybe it's pregnancy hormones not wanting my baby's hunter gatherer to shack up in someone else's cave.' She made herself hold his gaze, made herself smile although it felt unnatural.

'I have no intention of shacking up in anyone's cave.' She winced at the horror in his voice and his face softened. 'I promised you, Daisy, I promised you that if you married me I would be in this completely.' He paused and she held her breath, waiting for the inevitable caveat. 'As much as I can be.' There it was. Known, expected. Yet it still hurt.

And she didn't want to dwell on why. Maybe she was beginning to believe their fantasy a little too much, fool that she was.

'But there will be nobody else, you have no reason to worry on that score.'

'Thank you.' She exhaled, a low painful breath. 'It's just difficult, the difference between the public and the private. I know I asked you to pretend but I admit I didn't realise it would be so hard.'

'Why?' He hadn't moved.

'Why what?'

'Why are we pretending? Why don't you want to be honest?'

Her eyes flickered back to Monty and she focused

on the fuzzy top of his head, drawing each ear lovingly through her hands, trying to think of a way to explain that wouldn't make her sound too pathetic. 'It's a bit of a family joke, that I'm always falling in and out of love, that I'm a hopeless romantic. Even when I was a little girl I knew that I wanted to get married, to have children. But I wanted more than just settling down. I wanted what Mum and Dad have.'

'They're one in a million, Daisy.' Ouch, there it was. Pity.

'Maybe, but I know it's possible. It's not that they wouldn't understand us marrying for the baby, wouldn't be supportive. But they'd know I was giving up on my dream. I don't want to do that to them.' She paused then looked straight at him. 'As well as to myself.

'All my parents want is for me to be happy. They don't ask for anything more than that. When I was photographed and expelled they were disappointed, of course they were, although they didn't yell or punish me—but they weren't surprised either. They knew I'd mess up, somehow. And now I've messed up again. I was so determined to do it right, to show them I could cope on my own.'

'I think you are being hard on yourself—and on them,' he added unexpectedly. 'They adore you. Do you know how lucky you are to have that? People who care about you? Who only want you to be happy?'

All Daisy could do was stare at him in shock. 'I...' she began but he cut her off.

'I agree, lying to your family is wrong and I wish I had never agreed—but do you know what I fear? That you're right, that if you tell them the truth then they will stop you, they will show you that with a family like yours there is no way in hell you have to shackle yourself to me, that you and the baby will be fine, that you won't need me.'

'No, you're the baby's father and nothing will change

that. Of course the baby will need you.' There was so much she didn't know, so much that she feared—but of this she was convinced.

She could need him too. If she allowed herself. Today had been almost perfect: help, support, wordless communication. But she knew it was a one-off. She had to train herself to enjoy these days when they came—and to never expect them.

'I hope so.' His smile was crooked. 'As for the rest, Daisy, you messed up at sixteen. Big deal. At least you learned from it, got on with your life, made something of yourself. You're not the only member of your family—or mine—to have dominated the headlines. Both your sisters spent their time on the front covers and they were older than you.'

'I know.' Could she admit it to him? The guilt she never allowed herself to articulate to anyone? Not even herself. 'But Violet was set up. Horribly and cruelly and callously set up and betrayed—and I don't think it is a coincidence that it wasn't long after everything that happened to me. I often wondered.' She paused. 'I think it was because of me. I had dropped out of the headlines so they went after my sister. And they destroyed her.'

'It's because of who your parents are, simple as that. You're all wealthy and beautiful.' A shiver went through her at the desire in his eyes as he said the last word. 'You're connected. People love that stuff. That's why we have to be careful, not a breath of scandal. Or they'll never leave us alone.'

Daisy knew how deadly publicity could be, had experienced the painful sting firsthand, watched one sister flee the country and the other hide herself away. Had done her best to stay under the parapet for the last eight years. But she didn't have the visceral fear Seb had.

He was right, they couldn't allow their child to grow

up under the same cloud. Which meant she had to stick to their agreement. A civilised, businesslike, emotion-free marriage. She had to grow up.

'What are you thinking, Daisy?' His voice was low and the green eyes so dark they were almost black.

'That you're right. That I can do this.'

His mouth quirked into that devastating half smile and Daisy's breath hitched. 'Marriage is going to be a lot easier than I imagined if you're going to keep on thinking I'm right.'

Her chin tilted. 'This is a one-off, not carte blanche.'

His slow grin was a challenge. 'Just how right am I?'

'What do you mean?' But she knew. She knew by the way it was suddenly hard to get her breath. She knew by the way his voice had thickened. She knew by the way his eyes were fixed on hers. She knew by the heat swirling in her stomach, the anticipation fizzing along her skin.

She knew because they had been here before.

The memory of that night was impressed on each and every nerve ending and they heated up in anticipation, the knowledge of every kiss, every touch imprinted there, wanting, needing a replay.

'How in are you, Daisy?' His meaning was unmistakeable.

The heat was swirling round her entire body, a haze of need making it hard to think. They were going to get married, were going to raise a child, make a life together. They had every right to take that final step. Every need.

So he didn't love her? That hadn't mattered before, had it? A mutual attraction combined with champagne and the bittersweet comedown she always experienced after a wedding had been enough.

And it wasn't as if she were foolish enough to go falling in love with someone after just one week, someone who made it very, very clear that love was always going to be a step too far.

He didn't love her. But he wanted her. The rigidity of his pose, his hands curled into loose fists, the intensity of his gaze told her that. Every instinct told her that.

And, oh, she wanted him. She had tried to fight it, hide it, but she did. The line of his jaw, the way he held his hands, the dark hair brushed carelessly back, the amused glint that lit up the green eyes and softened the austere features.

The way each accidental touch burned through her, every look shot through to her core.

And, dear God, his mouth. Her eyes moved there and lingered. Well cut, firm, capable. She wanted to lick her way along the jaw, kiss the pulse in his neck and move up to nibble her way along his lips. She wanted to taste him. For him to taste her. To consume her.

The heat intensified, burning as her breasts ached and the pull in her body made the distance, any distance unbearable.

There was nothing to stop her. They were going to be married. It was practically her right to touch him. To be touched.

It was definitely her right to kiss him.

And just because she had been fixated on romance in the past didn't mean she had to be in the future. After all, look how quickly she tumbled out of love, disillusioned and disappointed.

There was a lot to be said for a businesslike, respectful marriage. Especially marriage with benefits.

She swallowed, desperate for moisture.

'Daisy?' It was more of a command than a question and she was tired. Tired of fighting the attraction that burned between them, tired of being afraid to take it on.

She stood up, slowly, allowing her body to stretch out,

knowing how his eyes lingered on her legs, up her body, rested on her breasts sharply outlined by her stretch. She saw him swallow.

'I'm going to bed,' she said, turning towards the door. She paused, looked back. 'Joining me?'

CHAPTER SEVEN

THE CUP TILTED as Seb nudged Daisy's door open and he hastily righted it before the lurid green mixture slopped onto the threadbare but valuable nineteenth-century runner. The tea was supposed to be completely natural but he'd never seen anything that resembled that particular green in nature.

He didn't wait for an answer but opened the door. 'Daisy? Tea.'

Luckily the nausea of last week had yet to grow into anything more debilitating but Daisy still found the first hour of the day difficult. A cup of something hot helped although replacing her beloved caffeine was still proving problematic. She was going to run out of new flavours of herbal tea to try soon.

'I'm in the bath.' A splashing sound proved her words.

'I'll just leave it here.' Seb tried to put the image of long, bubble-covered limbs and bare, wet torsos out of his mind as he placed the tea onto the small table by her window. He didn't have time for distractions, especially naked ones.

He turned and took in the bedroom properly. He hadn't set foot in here since Daisy had moved in two weeks ago. It had been the first suite tackled by her mother and, although the nineteen-fifties chintz flowery wallpaper still covered the walls, the furniture was still the heavy, stately mahogany and the carpet as threadbare as the landing's, the paintwork was fresh and white and the room smelled of a fresh mixture of beeswax, fresh air and Daisy's own light floral scent.

It wasn't just the aesthetic changes though. Daisy had somehow taken the room and made it hers from the scarves draped over the bedposts to the hat stand, commandeered from the hallway and now filled with a growing selection of her collection. Every time she went back to her studio she brought a few more. There were times when Seb feared the entire castle would be overtaken by hats.

Pictures of her parents and sisters were on one bedside table, a tower of stacked-up paperbacks on the second. A brief perusal showed an eclectic mix of nineteen-thirties detective novels, romances, two of last year's Booker Prize shortlist and a popular history book on Prince Rupert by one of Seb's colleagues and rivals.

Jealousy, as unwanted as it was sharp, shot through him. She did read history, just not his books it seemed.

'Get over yourself, Beresford,' he muttered, half amused, half alarmed by the instant reaction. It was professional jealousy sure, but still unwarranted. Unwanted.

A brief peek into the dressing room showed a similar colonisation. The dressing table bestrewn with pots and tubes, photos of herself and her sisters and friends he had yet to meet tucked into the mirror. The study was a little more austere, her laptop set up at the desk, her diary, open and filled with her scrawling handwriting, next to it.

Hawksley Castle had a new mistress.

Only the bed looked unrumpled. Daisy might bathe, dress and work in her rooms but she slept in his. Much as her nineteenth-century counterpart might have done she arrived in his bed cleansed, moisturised and already in the silky shorts and vest tops she liked to sleep in. Not a single personal item had migrated through the connecting door.

A buzz in his pocket signalled a message or a voice-mail. It was almost impossible to get a decent mobile signal this side of the castle. Seb quite liked not being wired in twenty-four hours a day.

He pulled his phone out and listened to the message, wincing as he did so.

'Problems?' Daisy appeared at the bathroom door clad in nothing but a towel.

'My agent.' He stuffed the phone back into his pocket, glancing at Daisy as he did so.

He drew in a long, deep breath. It was impossible to ignore the twinge of desire evoked by her creamy shoulders, the outline of her body swathed in the long creamy towel.

The towels were another of Sherry's luxurious little additions to the house. By the date of the wedding Hawksley would resemble a five-star hotel more than a run-down if stately family home.

There were fresh flowers, renewed every other day, in all the repainted, cleaned bedrooms as well as in the bigger salons and hallways. Every bathroom, cloakroom and loo was ornamented with expensive soaps, hand creams and bath salts. In one way the luxurious touches hid the signs of elegant decay, but Seb couldn't help calculate how the price of the flowers alone could be better spent on plumbing, on the roof, on the myriad neglected maintenance jobs that multiplied daily.

No matter. Seb would give Sherry her head until the wedding but after that, no more. He wouldn't accept a penny, not even from his bride-to-be's indulgent and very wealthy parents. Hawksley was his inheritance, his responsibility, his burden.

'What did she want on a Saturday?' Daisy sat herself at her dressing table and began to brush out her hair. Seb's eyes followed the brush as it fought its way through the tangled locks leaving smooth tresses in its wake.

'Just to finalise arrangements for this afternoon.' And to try and start another conversation about a television deal. He would shut that down pretty fast although the numbers must be good to make her this persistent.

'This afternoon?'

'I'm lecturing. Didn't I mention it? Talking of which...' He looked at his watch, blinking as he caught the time. 'What are you still doing sat in a towel? Shouldn't you be capturing a bride's breakfast? Or is this one a late-rising bride?'

She shook her head, the newly brushed hair lifting with the movement. 'I have the whole weekend off. Sophie's covering today's wedding for me as a trial. They didn't have the full engagement-shot package so I don't have a personal relationship with them. It seemed like a good place for her to try and see how it works. I do have a few interviews tomorrow with possible assistants but today I am completely free.' She pulled a face. 'That can't be right, can it? Whatever will I do?'

Seb looked at her critically. She still looked drawn and tired. 'You could do with a day off. Between wedding planning and work you never seem to stop.'

'Says the man who put in sixteen hours on the estate yesterday and still wanted to do research when he came home.'

'Technically I am on a research year, not an estate management year.' The ever-present fear crowded in. Could he do both? What if he had to give up his professorship? Swap academia for farming? He pushed it aside. That was a worry for another day.

'Besides, I'm not turning greener than that drink of yours every morning and growing another human being.

Why don't you book yourself into a spa or have a day shopping?'

She wrinkled her nose. 'Are those the only relaxing pursuits you can think of? I can't do most spa treatments and the last thing I want to do is shop, not after mother-zilla of the bride's efforts.'

Sherry had been keeping Daisy hard at it. Seb had barely seen her all week. She was either holed up in the Great Hall creating wedding favours, shopping for last-minute essential details or back in her studio, working.

Things would be much easier if she had a studio here. Would she want that? Moving her hats across was one thing, moving her professional persona another. Seb adored his library but there were times when he missed his college rooms with an almost physical pain. The peace, the lack of responsibility beyond his work, his students,

'My lecture's in Oxford. I doubt that would be relaxing or interesting. But maybe you could walk around some of the colleges, have lunch there.' His eyes flickered over to the book by her bed. 'Or you could come to the lecture.'

The blurring of professional and private had to happen at some point.

'What's the lecture on?'

'The history of England as reflected in a house like Hawksley.' His mouth twisted. 'It's the subject of my next book, luckily. It's hard enough finding time to work as it is, at least I'm on site. It's a paid popular lecture so not too highbrow. You might enjoy it.'

He could have kicked himself as soon as he uttered the words. Her face was emotionless but her eyes clouded. 'Not too highbrow? So even dullards like me have a chance of understanding it?'

'Daisy, there's nothing dull about you. Will you come? I'll take you out for dinner afterwards.'

There it was, more blurring. But he had promised respect and friendship. That was all this was.

'Well, if there's food.' But her eyes were still clouded, her face gave nothing away. 'What time do you want to leave? I'll meet you downstairs.'

'What an incredible place. I've never looked around the colleges before.' Daisy focused the lens onto the green rectangle of lawn, the golden columns framing it like a picture.

'Maybe it's because I knew I had no chance of actually coming here.' She clicked and then again, capturing the sun slanting through the columns, lighting up the soft stone in an unearthly glow.

'But you wouldn't have wanted to come here. You went to one of the best art colleges in the country. I doubt that they would have even let me through the door.' Daisy bit back a giggle. She had seen Seb's attempts to draw just once, when he was trying to show Sherry how the marquee connected to the hall. It was good to know there were some areas where she had him beat.

'You could pretend you were creating some kind of post-modern deconstruction of the creative process.' She followed the quadrangle round with her viewfinder. 'This place is ridiculously photogenic. I bet it would make a superb backdrop for wedding photos.'

'It's always about weddings with you, isn't it?' Seb slid a curious glance her way and she tried to keep her face blank. His scrutiny unnerved her. He always made her feel so exposed, as if he could see beyond the lipstick and the hats, beyond the carefully chosen outfits. She hoped not. She wasn't entirely sure that there was any substance underneath her style.

'It's my job.' She kept her voice light. 'You must walk in here and see the history in each and every stone. It's no different.'

He was still studying her intently and she tried not to squirm, swinging the camera around to focus on him. 'Smile!'

But his expression didn't change. It was as if he was trying to see through her, into the heart of her. She took a photo, and then another, playing with the focus and the light.

'Why photography? I would have thought you would have had enough of being on the other side of the lens?'

It was the million-dollar question. She lowered the camera and leant against one of the stone columns. Despite the sunlight dancing on it the stone was cold, the chill travelling through her dress. 'Truth is I didn't mind the attention as a kid,' she admitted, fiddling with her camera strap so she didn't have to look up and see judgement or pity in his eyes. 'We felt special. Mum and Dad were so adored, and there was no scandal, so all the publicity tended to be positive—glamorous red carpets at premieres or at-home photo shoots for charities. It wasn't until I was sixteen that I realised the press could bite as easily as it flattered.'

'Lucky you.' His voice was bleak. 'I was five when I was first bitten.'

She stole a look at him but his gaze was fixed unseeingly elsewhere. Poor little boy, a pawn in his parents' destructive lives. 'It was such a shock when it happened, seeing myself on the front pages. I felt so exposed. I know it wasn't clever.' She traced the brand name on her camera case, remembering, the need for freedom, the urge for excitement, the thrill of the illicit. 'But most sixteen-year-olds play hooky just once, try and get a drink underage somehow just once. They just don't do it under the public's condemning gaze.'

One set of photos, one drunken night, one kiss—the kind of intense kiss that only a sixteen-year-old falling in love could manage—and her reputation had been created, set in stone and destroyed.

'You couldn't have stuck to the local pub?'

He was so practical! She grinned, able to laugh at her youthful self now. 'Looking back, that was the flaw in my plan. But honestly, we were so naive we couldn't think where to go. The village landlord at home would have phoned Dad as soon as I stepped up to the bar. The pubs nearest school seemed to have some kind of convent schoolgirl sensor. We all knew there was no point trying there. Tana and I decided the only way we could be truly anonymous was in the middle of the city. We were spectacularly wrong.'

'Tana?'

'My best friend from school. I was going out with her brother and she was going out with his best mate. Teenage hormones, a bottle of vodka, an on-the-ball paparazzi and the rest is history. I don't even like vodka.'

'So as the camera flashes followed you down the street you thought, I know, I'd like to be on the other side?'

'At least I'm in control when I'm the one taking the photos.' The words hung in the air and she sucked in a breath. That hadn't been what she had intended to say— no matter that it was true.

She shifted her weight and carried on hurriedly. 'After school kicked me out I had no qualifications so I went to the local college where, as long as I took English and maths, I could amuse myself. So I did. I took all the art and craft classes I could. But it was photography I loved the most. I stayed on to do the art foundation course and then applied to St Martin's. When they accepted me it felt as if I had found my place at last.'

That moment when she looked through the viewfinder and focused and the whole world fell away. The clarity when the perfect shot happened after hours of waiting. The happiness she evoked with her pictures, when she took a special moment and documented it for eternity.

A chill ran through her and it wasn't just from the stone. She felt exposed, as if she had allowed him to see, to hear parts of her even her family were locked out of. She pushed off the column, covering her discomfort with brisk movements. 'What about you?' She turned the tables on her interrogator. 'When did you decide you wanted to stand in a lecture theatre and wear tweed?'

'I only wear tweed on special occasions.' That quirk of the mouth of his. It shocked her every time how one small muscle movement could speed her heart up, cause her pulse to start pounding. 'And my cap and gown, of course.'

'Of course.' Daisy tried not to dwell on the disparity in their education. Sure she had a degree, a degree she had worked very hard for, was very proud of. But it was in photography. Her academic qualifications were a little more lacking. She barely had any GCSEs although she had managed to scrape a pass in maths, something a little more respectable in English.

The man next to her had MAs and PhDs and honorary degrees. He had written books that both sold well and were acclaimed for their scholarship. He had students hanging on his every word, colleagues who respected him.

Daisy? She took photos. How could they ever be equal? How could she attend professional events at his side? Make conversation with academics? She would be an embarrassment.

'I don't think anyone grows up wanting to be a lecturer. I thought we already established that I wanted to be an outlaw when I was a child, preferably a highwayman.'

'Of course.' She kicked herself mentally at the repetition. Say something intelligent, at least something different.

'But growing up somewhere like Hawksley, surrounded

by history with literally every step, it was hard not to be enthused. I wanted to take those stories I heard growing up and make them resonate for other people the way they resonated with me. That's what inspires me. The story behind every stone, every picture, every artefact. My period is late medieval. That's where my research lies and what I teach but my books are far more wide ranging.'

'Like the one about Charles II's illegitimate children?' She had actually read his book a couple of years ago on Rose's recommendation. In fact, she'd also read his book on Richard III and his exposé of the myths surrounding Anne Boleyn, the book that had catapulted him into the bestseller lists. But she couldn't think how to tell him without exposing herself. What if he asked for her opinion and her answers exposed just how ignorant she really was?

Or what if he didn't think her capable of forming any opinion at all…?

'Exactly! Those children are actually utterly pivotal to our history. We all know about Henry VIII's desperate search for an heir and how that impacted on the country but Charles' story is much less well known beyond the plague and the fire and Nell Gwyn.' He was pacing now, lit up with enthusiasm. Several tourists stopped to watch, their faces captivated as they listened to him speak.

Daisy snapped him again. Gone was the slightly severe Seb, the stressed, tired Seb. This was a man in total control, a man utterly at home with himself.

'He actually fathered at least seventeen illegitimate children but not one single legitimate child. If he had the whole course of British History might have changed, no Hanoverians, no William of Orange. And of course the influence and wealth still wielded by the descendants of many of those children still permeate British society to this day.'

'Says the earl.'

It was a full-on smile this time, and her stomach tumbled. How had she forgotten the dimple at the corner of his mouth? 'I am fully aware of the irony.'

'Is it personal, your interest? Any chance your own line is descended through the compliant countess?'

'Officially, no. Unofficially, well, there is some familial dispute as to whether we can trace our descendants back to the Norman invasion or whether we are Stuarts. Obviously I always thought the latter, far more of an exciting story for an impressionable boy, the long-lost heir to the throne.'

He began walking along the quad and she followed him, brain whirling. 'A potential Stuart! You could be DNA tested? Although that might throw up some odd results. I wonder how many blue-blooded households actually trace their heritage back to a red-blooded stable boy?'

The glimmer in his eye matched hers. 'Now that would make an interesting piece of research. Not sure I'd get many willing participants though. Maybe the book after this, if I ever get this one finished.'

A book about Hawksley. Such a vivid setting. 'It would make a great TV show.'

'What? Live DNA testing of all the hereditary peers? You have an evil streak.'

'No.' She paused as he turned into a small passageway and began to climb a narrow winding staircase. Daisy looked about her in fascination, at the lead-paned windows and the heavy wooden doors leading off at each landing.

They reached the third landing and he stopped at a door, pulling a key out of his pocket. The discreet sign simply said Beresford. This was his world, even more foreign to her than a castle and a grand estate. Academia, ancient traditions, learning and study and words.

Daisy's breath hitched as he gestured for her to precede him into the room, a rectangular space with huge windows, every available piece of wall space taken up with book-shelves. A comfy and well-loved-looking leather chesterfield sofa was pulled up opposite the hearth and a dining table and six chairs occupied the centre of the room. His surprisingly tidy desk looked out over the quad.

She felt inadequate just standing in here. Out of place. Numb, she tried to grasp for something to say, something other than: 'Have you read all those books?' Or 'Doesn't your desk look tidy?'

She returned gratefully to their interrupted conversation. 'I was talking about Hawksley, of course. It's the answer to all your problems. Just think of the visitor numbers, although you'd have to rethink the ridiculous weekends only between Whitsun and August Bank Holiday opening times.'

'What's the answer?' His face had shuttered as if he knew what she was going to say and was already barricading himself off from it.

'Your book about Hawksley, how you can see England's history in it.'

He walked over to his desk and picked up the pile of letters and small parcels and began leafing through. 'The book I haven't actually written yet.' His tone was dismissive but she rushed on regardless.

'You should do it as a TV series. You would be an amazing presenter. Why aren't you? You're clever, photogenic, interesting. I'm amazed they haven't snapped you up.'

'Good God, Daisy.' There was no mistaking the look in his eyes now. Disgust, horror, revulsion. 'Despite everything you've been through that's your solution…' He paused and then resumed, his voice cutting. 'I suppose once a celebrity offspring, always a celebrity offspring. You don't think they've offered? That I haven't had a chance to sign myself and my life over? Do you know what it would mean, if I went on TV?'

She shook her head, too hurt by his response to speak.

'I'd be open game. For every paparazzi or blogger or

tabloid journalist. They could rake over my life with absolute impunity—and now your life too! Why would I want that? Why would you want that?'

Daisy could feel tears battling to escape and blinked them back. No emotion, that was the deal. And that included hurt. She wouldn't give him the satisfaction of seeing how much his contempt stung. But nor would she let him dismiss her. 'You need to make Hawksley pay and you said yourself land subsidies and a wedding every weekend won't do it. Besides, you write books—popular history books, not dull academic tomes. You don't mind the publicity for those.'

He paused and ran his hands through his hair. 'That's different.'

'Why?'

The question hung there.

She pressed on. 'Your books win prizes, have posters advertising them in bookshops, I've even seen adverts on bus shelters and billboards! You read in public, sign in public, give public lectures. How is that different from a TV series?'

At first she had sounded diffident, unsure of her argument but as she spoke Seb could hear the conviction in her voice. And he had to admit she was making sense. Unwelcome sense but still.

He fixed his eyes on her face, trying to read her. Every day he found out more about her; every day she surprised him. He had thought she was utterly transparent; sweet, a little flaky maybe, desirable sure but not a challenge. But there were hidden depths to Daisy Huntingdon-Cross. Depths he was only just beginning to discover.

'My books are educational.' He cringed inwardly at the pompous words.

She wasn't giving in. 'So is television, done right. More so, you would reach a far bigger audience, teach far more people, inspire more people. I'm not suggesting you pimp yourself on social media—though some historians do and they do it brilliantly. I'm not suggesting reality TV or magazine photoshoots. I'm talking about you, doing what you do anyway.'

Reach more people. Wasn't that his goal? He sighed. 'I didn't plan this.' Seb put down the pile of still-unopened post and wandered over to the window, staring out. 'I didn't think I'd write anything but articles for obscure journals and the kind of books only my peers would read. That's how I started. That's how academic reputations are made.'

'So what changed?'

'I got offered a book deal. It was luck really, an ex-student of mine went into publishing and the editor she was working for wanted a new popular history series. Stacey thought of me and set up a meeting.'

'She wouldn't have thought of you if you hadn't been an inspiring teacher. Not so much luck, more serendipity.' Daisy walked across the room and stood next to him. Without conscious intention he put his hand out and took hers, drawing her in close. Her hand was warm and yielding.

'Maybe.'

'It's just a suggestion, Seb. I know how you feel about courting publicity, I really do. But Dad always says that if you keep your head down and your life clean they'll lose interest. And he's right—just look at my parents. They were wild in their youth, real headline creators just like yours were. The difference is they settled down. They don't sleep around or take drugs or act like divas. They work hard and live quietly—in a crazy, luxurious bubble admittedly! But that's what we've agreed, isn't it? Quiet, discreet lives. If we live like that then there really is nothing to fear.'

Seb inhaled slowly, taking in her calm, reasonable words. Slowly he moved behind her, slipping an arm around her waist to rest on her still-flat stomach. 'They came after you though.' His voice was hoarse.

'We'll just teach the baby not to go out and get drunk in the middle of London when he or she is sixteen. And if it gets my beauty and your brains we should be okay as far as schooling goes.'

'The other way round works just as well. Stop putting yourself down, Daisy. Academic qualifications are meaningless. I think you might be one of the smartest people I know.'

Her hand came down to cover his, a slight tremor in the fingers grasping his. 'That's the nicest thing anyone has ever said to me.'

'I mean it.' The air around them had thickened, the usual smells he associated with his office, paper, leather and old stone, replaced by her light floral scent: sweet with richer undertones just like its wearer. Desire flooded him and he moved his other hand to her waist, caressing the subtle curve as he followed the line down to her hip.

Seb had no idea how this marriage was going to work in many ways but this he had no qualms about. They had been brought together by attraction and so far it continued to burn hot and deep. He leant forward, inhaling her as he ran a tongue over her soft earlobe, biting down gently as she moaned.

The hand covering his tightened and he could feel her breathing speed up. Reluctantly he left her hip, bringing his hand up to push the heavy fall of hair away from her neck so the creamy nape was exposed. She trembled as he moved in close to press a light kiss on her neck, then another, working his way around to the slim shoulder as his hand slid round to her ribs, splaying out until he felt the full underside of her breast underneath his thumb.

Her breaths were coming quicker as she leant against him, arching into his touch, into his kiss, holding on as she turned round to find his mouth with hers. Warm, inviting, intoxicating. 'Are we allowed to do this here?' she murmured against his mouth as he found the zip at the back of her dress and eased it down the line of her back. Her own hands were tugging at his shirt, moving up his back in a teasing, light caress.

'No one will come in,' he promised, slipping the dress from her shoulders, holding in a groan as one hand continued to tease his back, the other sliding round to his chest. 'We have over an hour before the lecture. Of course, I had promised you lunch...'

'Lunch is overrated.' She pressed a kiss to his throat, her tongue darting out to mark the most sensitive spot as her fingers worked on his shirt buttons.

'In that case, my lady—' he held onto her as she undid the final button, pushing his shirt off him with a triumphant smile '—desk, sofa or table?'

Daisy looked up at him, her eyes luminous with desire. 'Over an hour? Let's try for all three.'

Seb swung her warm, pliant body up. 'I was hoping you'd say that. Let's start over here. I think I need to do some very intensive research...'

CHAPTER EIGHT

'YOU WOULDN'T THINK you were publicity-shy, looking at those. My mother would kill to have that kind of exposure—and she doesn't get in front of a camera for less than twenty thousand a day.'

There were five large posters arrayed along the front of the lecture hall, each featuring the same black and white headshot of Seb. Daisy came to a halt and studied them, her head tilted critically. 'Not bad. Did they ask you to convey serious academic with a hint of smoking hot?'

'That was exactly the brief. Why, do you think I look like a serious academic?'

'I think you look smoking hot and—' she eyed the gaggle of giggling girls posing for selfies alongside the furthest poster '—so do they.'

Seb glanced towards the group and quickly turned away so his back was towards them. 'Just because they are a little dressed up doesn't mean they're not interested in the subject matter. They could be going out afterwards.'

'Sure they could.' Daisy patted his arm. 'And when I went to the very dull lectures on Greek vase painting it was because I thought knowing about classical figures on urns would be very helpful to my future career and not because I had a serious crush on the lecturer.'

She sighed. 'Six weeks of just sitting and staring into

those dark brown eyes and visualising our future children. Time very well spent. Of course he was happily married and never even looked twice at me.'

'This is Oxford, Daisy. People come here to learn.'

There was a reproving tone in his voice that hit her harder than she liked, a reminder that this was his world, not hers. 'I didn't say I didn't learn anything. You want to know anything about classical art, I'm your girl.'

'Seb!' Daisy breathed a sigh of relief as a smartly dressed woman came out of the stage door and headed straight for them, breaking up the suddenly fraught conversation. The woman greeted Seb with a kiss on both cheeks. 'I've been looking for you. You're late. How are you?'

Seb returned the embrace then put an arm around Daisy, propelling her forward. 'This is my fiancée, Daisy Huntingdon-Cross. I assume you've got the wedding invite? Daisy, this is Clarissa Winteringham, my agent.'

'So this is your mystery fiancée?' Daisy was aware that she was being well and truly sized up by a pair of shrewd brown eyes. 'Invite received and accepted with thanks. It's nice to meet you, Daisy.'

'Likewise.' Daisy held out her hand and it was folded into a tight grip, the other woman still looking at her intently.

'And what do you do, Daisy?'

Most people would probably have started with *congratulations*. Daisy smiled tightly. 'I'm a photographer.'

'Have you ever thought of writing a book?' The grip was still tight on her hand as Daisy shook her head. 'A photographer who gets propelled into the limelight as a model? Could work well for a young adult audience?'

'I don't think so.' Daisy managed to retrieve her hand. 'Thank you though.'

'I'm sure we could find someone else to write it. You would just need to collaborate on plot and lend your name to it. With *your* parents I'm sure I could get you a good deal.'

Of course Clarissa knew exactly who Daisy was, she wouldn't be much of an agent if she didn't, but it still felt uncomfortable, being so quickly and brutally summed up for her commercial value. 'Seb's the writer in the family and I don't think books about models are really his thing.'

'Shame, cheekbones like yours are wasted behind a camera. We could have done a nice tie-in, maybe a reality TV show. Get in touch if you change your mind. Now, Seb, they're waiting for you inside. Have *you* changed your mind about the BBC offer? You really should call me back when I leave messages.'

So she hadn't been the first person to mention TV? Seb didn't react with the same vehemence he'd shown Daisy earlier when she had made a similar suggestion, just shook his head, smiling, as Clarissa bore him off leaving Daisy to trail behind.

The lecture hall was crammed to capacity, an incongruous mixture of eager-looking students, serious intellectual types and several more groups of girls waving cameras and copies of Seb's latest books; pop culture meeting academia.

Daisy managed to find a seat at the end of a row next to an elderly man who commented loudly to his companion throughout the lecture but, despite the disruptions, the odd camera flashes and the over-enthusiastic laughter from Seb's youthful admirers every time he made any kind of joke, Daisy found that she enjoyed the lecture. Seb's enthusiasm for his subject and engaging manner were infectious.

It was funny how the sometimes diffident man, the private man, came alive in front of an audience, how he held them in the palm of his hand as he took them on a dizzying thousand-year tour of English history using his own family home as a guide. The hour-long talk was over far too quickly.

'He knows his stuff.' The old man turned to Daisy as the hall began to empty. Daisy had been planning to go straight to Seb, but he was surrounded immediately by a congratulatory crowd, including the girls she had seen earlier, all pressing in close, books in hand waiting to be signed.

Seb didn't look as if he minded at all. Hated publicity indeed!

'Yes, he was fascinating, wasn't he?' She'd seen her father perform in front of thousands, seen her mother's face blown up on a giant billboard but had never felt so full of awe. 'He's a great speaker.'

'Interesting theory as well. Do you subscribe to his school of thought on ornamental moats?'

Did she what? About what?

'I...'

'Of course the traditional Marxist interpretation would agree with him, but I wonder if that's too simplistic.'

'Yes, a little.' Daisy's hands were damp; she could feel her hair stick to the back of her neck with fear. *Please don't ask me to do anything but agree with you*, she prayed silently.

'Nevertheless he's a clever man, Beresford. I wonder what he'll do after this sabbatical.'

'Do? Isn't he planning to return here?' Seb hadn't discussed his future plans with her at all; he was far too focused on the castle.

'He says so but I think Harvard might snap him up. It would be a shame to lose him but these young academics can be so impatient, always moving on.'

Daisy sat immobile as the elderly man moved past her, her brain whirling with his words. *Harvard?* Okay, they hadn't discussed much in terms of the future, but surely if Seb was considering moving overseas he'd have mentioned it? She got to her feet, dimly aware that the large hall was emptying rapidly and that Seb was nowhere to be seen.

'There you are, Daisy.' Clarissa glided towards her accompanied by a tall man in his late fifties. 'This is Giles Buchanan, Seb's publisher. Giles, Daisy is Seb's mysterious fiancée. She's a photographer.'

'Creative type, eh? Landscapes or fashion?'

Daisy blinked. 'Er…neither, I photograph weddings.'

'Weddings?' Obviously not the kind of job he expected from Seb's fiancée judging by the look of surprise on his face. Daisy filled in the blanks: too commercial, not intellectual enough.

She'd wanted a chance to look inside Seb's world but now she was here she felt like Alice: too big or too small but either way not right. She stepped out onto the stairs. 'Excuse me, I need some air.'

How on earth was she going to fit in? Say the right things, do the right things, be the right kind of wife? She'd thought being a countess was crazy enough—being the wife of an academic looked like being infinitely worse.

Right now it didn't feel as if there was any chance at all. The gap between them was too wide and she had no idea if she even wanted to bridge it—let alone work out *how* to do it.

'Table decorations, seating plans, favours, flowers, outfits. We've done it all, Vi. There can't be anything left to plan.' Daisy tucked the phone between her ear and her chin as she continued to browse on her laptop. The wedding was feeling less and less real as it got nearer. It was one day, that was all.

And it felt increasingly irrelevant. The real issue was how the marriage was going to work, not whether Great-aunt Beryl was speaking to Great-uncle Stanley or what to feed the vegetarians during the hog roast.

Seb was right. The marriage was the thing. Not that she was going to tell him that, of course.

Less than a week to go. This was it. Was she prepared to spend the foreseeable part of her future with a man who was still in so many ways a complete stranger?

It wasn't that the nights weren't wonderful. Incredible actually. But was sex enough to base a marriage on?

But it wasn't just sex, was it? There was the baby too. The sex was a bonus and she needed to remember that. *Stop being greedy, stop wanting more.*

Seb definitely found her desirable. Had promised to respect her. That was a hell of a lot more than many women had at the start of their marriages. So she wasn't sure where she fitted in his professional life or at Hawksley? They didn't have to live in each other's pockets after all.

She was completely and utterly lucky—and that was before you factored in the fact she would be living in a castle and, improbable as it seemed, would be a countess. She just had to start feeling it and stop clinging onto the shattered remnants of her romantic dreams. Start carving out a place for herself at Hawksley, turn it into a home. Into her home.

If only she could help Seb work out how to make it pay. Other estates managed it, even without an eminent historian occupying the master bedroom…

Her sister's exasperated voice broke in on her thoughts. 'Daisy, Rose isn't getting here until the day of the wedding itself so as the only bridesmaid on the same continent it's down to me. I've hinted, Mum's hinted and you have been no help so I am asking you outright. Hen night. What are you wanting?'

Daisy straightened, the phone nearly falling out of her hand as she registered her sister's words. 'I forgot all about the hen night.'

'Sure you did.' Vi sounded sceptical. 'I've seen your scrapbooks, Daise, remember? And lived through twenty-four years of your birthday treats. You've left it too late for the Barcelona weekend or the spa in Ischia. So spa day near here? Night out clubbing in London? We could manage a night in Paris if we book today. You're cutting it awfully fine though. We should have gone yesterday.'

Daisy managed to interrupt her sister. 'Nothing, honestly, Vi. I'm not expecting anything.'

'Nothing?'

'Nope.'

'This isn't a test?' Vi sounded suspicious. 'Like the time you said you didn't want a birthday treat but we were supposed to know that you wanted us to surprise you with tickets to see Busted?'

'I was twelve!' Violet had to wheel that one out.

'Seriously, Daisy. Mum will be so disappointed. She's planned matching tracksuits with our names spelled out in diamanté.'

'Mother wouldn't be seen dead in matching tracksuits!'

'But she will be disappointed. You'll be telling me you're not going on some exotic honeymoon next!'

Daisy stopped dead. Honeymoon? She hadn't even thought about what would happen after the wedding and Seb hadn't mentioned it.

The Maldives, Venice, a small secluded island in the Caribbean, a chateau in the south of France; the destinations of the brides and grooms she had photographed over the last couple of years floated through her mind.

They all sounded perfect—for a couple in love.

It was probably a good thing they had forgotten all about it. A week or two holed up together would be excruciating. Wouldn't it? 'It's all been so quick, we haven't actually thought about a honeymoon yet.'

There was an incredulous pause. 'No hen night, no honeymoon. Daisy, what's going on?'

Daisy thought rapidly. She couldn't have a hen night. She couldn't be around her friends and family pretending to be crazy in love, she couldn't drink and her abstinence might have escaped their sharp eyes so far but nobody was going to believe that she wasn't going to indulge in at least one glass of champagne on her own hen night.

Her eyes fell on the copy of Seb's birth certificate lying on her desk; she'd put it in her bag after their visit to the register office and forgotten to return it to him. Name: Sebastian Adolphus Charles Beresford. How on earth had the Adolphus slipped past her attention? She hoped it wasn't a family name he'd want for their son.

Her eyes flickered on. Date of birth. April twentieth. Hang on…

Why hadn't he mentioned it? Right now she wasn't going to think about that. Not when salvation was lying right in front of her.

'The problem is, Vi, tomorrow's Seb's birthday and I've planned a surprise. And then it's just a few days before the wedding and I don't want a big night out before then. Besides,' she added with an element of truth, 'it wouldn't feel right without Rose. We can do something afterwards.'

'Wednesday night.' Vi wasn't giving up. 'That gives you two days before the wedding and we can do something small. Just you, me and Mum and Skype Rose in. Films and face masks and manicures at your studio?'

That sounded blissful. Dangerous but blissful. 'Okay. But low-key—and I won't be drinking. I'm on a pre wedding detox. For my skin.' That sounded plausible.

'Done. I'll source the girliest films and organise nibbles. Wholesome, vitamin filled, organic nibbles.'

'Thanks, Vi.' She meant it. An evening in with her mother and sister would be lovely. As long as she kept her guard up.

Meanwhile there was the small matter of Seb's birthday and the surprise she was supposed to be organising. Once she had decided just what the surprise actually was.

* * *

Something was up.

Daisy was going around with a suppressed air of excitement as if she were holding a huge balloon inside that was going to burst any second.

It should have been annoying. Actually it was a little bit endearing.

Seb stretched out in his old leather wingchair, the vibrant red of the curtains catching his eye. Sherry had not received the Keep Out of My Library vibe and his sanctuary was looking as polished and fresh as the rest of the house. It was actually quite nice not to sneeze every time he pulled out a book although he had preferred the curtains unlaundered. They had been less glaringly bright then.

It wasn't just Sherry. Daisy was quietly but firmly making changes as well: painting the kitchen, opening up the morning room and turning it into a cosy sitting room despite using little more than new curtains and cushions and replacing the rather macabre paintings of dead pheasants with some watercolour landscapes she had rescued from the attics. Although they still lived mainly in the kitchen or library, they had begun to spend their evenings in there reading, watching television or playing a long-running but vicious game of Monopoly.

It was almost homely.

But even as the castle began to take shape he was all too aware there still weren't enough hours in the day. It would be much easier if he brought in a professional to manage the estate, leaving Seb to his teaching and research.

It wasn't the Beresford way though. His grandfather had been very clear on that. A good owner managed his land, his people, his family and his home no matter what the sacrifice. And there had been many throughout the long centuries. There were times when Seb wondered if he would ever be able to return to Oxford and his real work.

Yet at the same time the pull of his ancestral home was so strong. He couldn't carry on juggling both the estate and academia but making a final decision was unthinkable.

He looked up at the sound of a soft tap on the door, relieved to take his eyes off the blank laptop screen. He had barely achieved anything yet again, he noted wryly. Worries and thoughts circling round and round; even his research wasn't distracting him the way it usually did. Money, Daisy, the baby, Hawksley, the book. In less than six months his whole life had turned upside down.

Although if he hadn't allowed himself to be so distracted by his career maybe Hawksley at least wouldn't be in such a state. He had his own culpability here.

The door opened and Daisy appeared bearing one of the massive silver tea trays. One mobile brow flew up as she looked at him. 'That's a terrifying scowl. Am I interrupting a crucial moment?'

'You're interrupting nothing but mental flailing and flagellation.' He tried to smile. 'Sorry if I scared you.'

'Mental flagellation? Sounds painful. Anything I can help with?' She carried the tray over to the table in the opposite corner and set it down with an audible thud.

'Not unless you have a time machine.'

Seb regretted the words as soon as he uttered them; he didn't need the flash of hurt to cross her face to show him how ill-judged they were. 'Not you, not the baby.' Not entirely. 'Goodness knows, Daisy, out of all the crazy tangled mess my life has become the baby is the one bright spot. No, I was just thinking if I'd acted sooner then things would be a hell of a lot easier now.'

'How so?'

He pushed his laptop away and sat back in the chair trying to straighten out his skein of thoughts and regrets. 'Kids are selfish, aren't they? I spent my holidays here, school and university—unless my mother was suffering one of her occasional fits of maternal solicitude, but I was so wrapped up in the past I never took an interest in the present. Never saw how Grandfather was struggling, never tried to help.' He suppressed a deep sigh of regret.

'History is all well and good but it's not very practical, is it? Grandfather suggested I go to the local agricultural college and do estate management, come and work here. I brushed him off, convinced I was destined for higher things.'

'You were right.' She was perched on the arm of the old leather chair, legs crossed, and his eyes ran appreciably up the long bare limbs. She was wearing the black tweed shorts, this time teamed with a bright floral shirt and her trademark hat was a cap pulled low over her forehead.

'Was I?' He had been sure then, sure throughout his glittering career. But the past few months had shown just how flawed his ambition had been. 'Hawksley needed new blood, Grandfather was struggling and my father was never going to step in. My grandfather was too proud to ask me directly and I was too busy to notice. But maybe I could have helped him turn things around—and been on the ground to stop my father's gross negligence.'

It was more than negligence. His father's wilful use of estate capital had been criminal.

'How could you have stopped it?'

'The money funding his extravagant lifestyle came from a family trust. It was never intended for private use, certainly not on his scale. Just one look at the accounts would have alerted me.' And he could have stepped in.

'I was far too busy chasing my own kind of fame.' The taste in his mouth was bitter.

She swung her legs down and hopped to her feet. 'Just because he suggested estate management doesn't mean he was desperate for you to live and work here. He was proud of you no matter which path you chose.'

'I wish I believed that.' His mouth twisted. 'I guess we'll never know.'

'I know.' She went over to one of the shelves, pulling a hardback book out. 'This is yours, isn't it? The first one? Look how well read it is, the spine is almost broken. So unless you spend your evenings reading your own words I think your grandparents must have read it. Several times.'

He took the book from her outstretched hands. He had given it to them, signed it and handed it over unsure if they would ever read it. The hardback was battered, corners turned, the pages well thumbed. A swell of pride rose inside him. Maybe they had been proud of his chosen career. He looked over at Daisy. 'Thank you.'

'I knew this library was all for show. If you ever looked at a book you'd have seen it for yourself,' but her eyes were bright and the corners of her full mouth upturned.

'Anyway—' she walked back to the tray '—I have a small bone to pick with you, my Lord. Why didn't you tell me it was your birthday?'

Seb gaped at her in shock. 'How did you know?'

'Incredible detective skills and a handy copy of your birth certificate. In my family birthdays are a very big deal.' She turned with a shy smile, her hands behind her back. 'And I must warn you I have very high expectations for mine, just ask my sisters, so if we are going to be a family—' the colour rose high on her cheeks and her eyes lowered as she said the words '—then your birthday has to be a big deal as well. So. Happy Birthday.'

With a flourish she pulled her arms from behind her back. One held a plate complete with a large cupcake, a lit candle on the top, the other a shiny silver envelope.

He stood, paralysed with surprise. 'What's this?'

'It's a card and cake. These are usual on birthdays.' Her colour was still high but her voice was light. 'You're supposed to blow the candle out.'

He just stood there, unable to move a muscle, to process what she was saying. 'I haven't had a birthday cake since I was ten. I was always at school, you see.'

Her eyes softened. 'The procedure hasn't changed. You blow, the flame goes out, I clap and then we eat it. Simple.'

He made a huge effort to reach out and took the plate of cake, holding it gingerly as if it were a bomb about to explode. The small flame danced before his eyes. He didn't want to blow it out; he wanted to watch it twist and turn for ever. 'And the card?'

'That you open. And then we get changed. I have a surprise for you. And I am quite convinced it is going to blow your socks off.'

CHAPTER NINE

'HOW DID YOU KNOW that this is my favourite band?' Seb, Daisy was learning, was not a huge one for words. If someone arranged a surprise for Daisy she found it hard to sit back and wait; instead she would be peppering them with questions, trying to guess where they were going, slightly anxious it wasn't going to live up to her own fevered imaginings.

Seb had just looked bemused, as if the concept of a surprise trip was completely alien to him. Which was ridiculous. He might not want high emotions or romance but he'd had girlfriends before—had none of them ever organised a day out? To a special library or a site of special historical significance?

But even his slightly annoying calm and collected manner had disappeared when the taxi pulled into the concert venue.

'Seriously, Daisy. You must be some kind of witch.' His hand sought hers and squeezed, his touch tingling. For a brief moment she allowed herself to fantasise that this was real, that she was on a night out with someone she was mad about, with someone who was mad about her.

'Yes, I am. My spells include listening to the music that people play and reading the labels on CD collections.' She couldn't help it, music had been such a huge part of her childhood she subconsciously noticed whatever music was playing although she didn't play an instrument herself and rarely listened to music for pleasure, preferring silence as she worked.

But Seb liked background noise whether in the kitchen, his study or driving around and when she had been searching the internet, trying to find something to do tonight, the name had jumped out at her—it had been the CD he was playing that very first night. One call to her father later and VIP seats had been procured.

But it had evidently been the perfect gift. Daisy was torn between shame that all she had managed was a last-minute, hastily organised event and a sneaking fear that maybe she knew him better than she had realised, than she wanted to admit.

Knew exactly what would make him happy. That would involve caring. Was that part of their deal?

Seb was evidently not having any deep thoughts or misgivings. It was fun to see him enjoying every moment like a child set free in a toy shop as they were led through the plush VIP area. 'A box? Seriously?'

'You may have the title but I am rock aristocracy and this is how we experience concerts,' she told him as they took their seats. 'If you would prefer to stand on the beer-covered floor with all the other sweaty people then you can. Your wristband allows you access.'

She could tell he was tempted. Daisy had never understood the allure of the mosh pit herself.

'Maybe later. You wouldn't mind?'

She shook her head. 'Knock yourself out.'

He looked around in fascination and Daisy tried to see it through his eyes, not her own jaded viewpoint. They were the only occupants of a box directly opposite the stage. Behind them was a private room complete with bar and cloakroom. The entire row was taken up with similar boxes for celebrities and friends and family of the band; corporates were restricted to the row above. Access to their coveted seats was strictly controlled.

'This is crazy.' Seb was staring at the aging rock star and his much-younger girlfriend enthusiastically making out in the next-door box. Daisy sat back; she hoped the rock star hadn't seen her. She'd been flower girl at his third wedding—and his new girlfriend looked younger than Daisy herself. 'I've been to plenty of events, literary events, historical conferences, Oxford balls but never anything like this.

'But I would have been just as happy on the beer-soaked floor with the other sweaty people,' he said. He meant it too.

'I'm spoiled,' she admitted. 'Dad gets tickets to everything and always took us along. I'd been to more concerts than films by the time I was ten. He drew the line at boy bands though. That's probably why they remain my own guilty pleasure. But I haven't done anything like this for ages.'

'Why not? If I had free access to gigs I'd go to everything!'

He wouldn't. Not with the high price tag. 'I don't usually like to ask for favours. Mum can get me anything, the new must-have bag or coat or dress—but the deal is you get photographed wearing it. If, like me, you want a quiet life then the price for a freebie is far too high. But tickets for this sold out months ago so it was best seats in the house or nothing!'

Daisy crossed her fingers, hoping that they weren't papped while they were here. There were far more gossip-worthy couples out in force; hopefully the spotlight would be far from them.

'Well, if we must sit in luxury while free drinks and

food are pressed on us then I suppose we must. Seriously, Daisy. Thank you. This is incredibly thoughtful.'

Daisy shifted uncomfortably, guilt clamping her stomach. Not so much thoughtful as expedient. She hurriedly changed the subject. 'I'm going to spend Wednesday night at the studio. Vi was insistent that I have some kind of hen night. Obviously I didn't want anything big so it's going to be a family-only films and pampering night. I've told her I'm not drinking for the sake of my skin. I must be more of a demanding bride than I realised. She completely bought it. I might stay there Thursday night too. It's meant to be bad luck to spend the night before together.'

'I guess we need all the luck we can get.' His voice was dry.

'Are you going to have a stag night?'

The shock on his face was almost comical. 'It hadn't even occurred to me! Maybe I should go to the local pub for a couple of drinks—just to add convincing detail to the wedding.'

'What a method actor you are.' But the rest of her conversation with Violet was running through her mind. 'Vi also asked about the honeymoon.'

Seb froze; she could see his knuckles turn white and hurried on. 'I said that we were planning something later on and were too busy right now. I don't think she's wholly convinced but when I tell them about the baby I'm sure they'll forget all about whether we did or did not go away.'

'Do you want a honeymoon?'

To her horror Daisy felt her mouth quiver. She gulped down an unexpected sob as it tried to force its way out. She had told herself so many times that she was at peace with her decision, that she was almost happy with her situation—and then she'd be derailed and have to start convincing herself all over again. 'Of course not.' She could hear the shakiness of her voice. 'I think we're doing brilliantly under the circumstances but a honeymoon might be a bit too much pressure.'

'Are you sure?'

She nodded, hoping he wasn't looking too closely. That he didn't see the suspicious shine in her eyes as she blinked back tears. 'Besides, I'm pregnant. No cocktails on the beach or exotic climates for me.'

'Is that what you would want?'

Yes. Of course it was. That was what people did, wasn't it? Flew to beautiful islands and drank rum and snorkelled in the sun, making love all night in a tangle of white sheets on mahogany beds.

Lovely in theory. Would the reality live up? 'Actually, I think I would want something a little less clichéd. Amazing scenery I could photograph, good food. History. The Alps maybe, Greece, the Italian coast.'

'A friend of mine has a villa on Lake Garda, right on the water's edge. I could see if it's free?'

For one moment she wavered. The Italian lakes. A private villa overlooking the lake sounded sublime. But they would still be pretending and without their work, without the routine of their everyday lives, how would they manage? 'No.' Her voice was stronger. 'Honestly. I'm absolutely fine.'

To her relief as she said the words the lights went down and Seb leaned forward, all his attention on the stage in front, leaving Daisy free to imagine a different kind of honeymoon. One where both parties wanted to be there, were so wrapped up in each other that they didn't need anyone or anything else. The kind of honeymoon she had always dreamed of and now knew she would never have.

It just wasn't adding up.

The Georgian part of the castle needed a new roof, ideally rewiring and, with the baby due before Christmas,

Seb really should sort out some of the ancient plumbing problems as well.

The work he had been doing on the estate land was already paying dividends and the farms and forests were looking healthy. It was just the castle.

Just. Just one thousand years of history, family pride and heritage. No big deal.

Seb tried to avoid his grandfather's eye, staring balefully out of a portrait on the far wall. He knew how much his grandfather had hated the idea of using the castle for profit—but surely he would have hated it falling around his ears much more.

But how far could Seb go? He was allowing a location agency to put the castle on their books, ready to hire it out for films and TV sets. It felt like a momentous step.

But not a big enough one.

Meanwhile there was the book to finish researching—and he was already halfway through his sabbatical. Just returning to Oxford for a day had reminded him how time consuming his teaching and administrative duties were.

Something was going to have to give and soon. It wasn't an easy decision.

'Seb, darling?' Sherry had materialised by his side. How on earth was the woman so dammed soft-footed? It was most unnerving.

Seb gripped the edge of his desk and took a deep breath, trying not to show his irritation. There were still three days to go until the wedding and he hadn't had ten uninterrupted minutes since breakfast. 'I have no idea, ask Daisy.' Whatever the question she was bound to know the answer.

'I haven't seen Daisy all morning.' Sherry frowned. 'Really, Seb. It would be helpful if one of you took an interest. These details may seem unimportant but they matter. A high bow at the top of the chair can be smart but rather showy. A lower one is classier maybe but can be lost. Especially with the pale yellow you've chosen.'

He'd chosen? Things might have changed at an alarming speed but there was one thing Seb knew for sure—he had had nothing whatsoever to do with choosing the colour of ribbons for the backs of chairs.

'Let's go for classy.' He rubbed his eyes. If anyone had suggested a month ago that he would be sitting in his library discussing bows with a supermodel he would have poured them a stiff brandy and suggested a lie-down. Yet here he was—and this particular supermodel wasn't going anywhere until he gave her the answer she wanted.

'You're probably right.' She reached over and ruffled his hair in a maternal way, incongrous coming from the glamorous Sherry Huntingdon. 'Classy is always best. Less is more, as I told the girls when they were growing up.'

'Wise advice.' But something she had said earlier was nagging at him. 'Where's Daisy gone?'

'I have no idea. She said she was tired after last night and wandered off. She did look peaky. There's a lovely picture of you two on the *Chronicle Online*. You do scrub up nicely, Seb. It's good to see you make an effort. There's no need to take the absent-minded-academic thing quite so seriously, you know.' Sherry gave his old worn shirt a pointed look.

'Hmm?' But he had already reached for the phone she was holding out, stomach lurching as he scrolled through the *Chronicle*'s long list of celebrity sightings and pictures. There they were entering the concert venue last night: Daisy long-legged in black shorts and a red T-shirt, her lipstick as bright as her top and her favourite trilby pushed back on her head. Seb had been unsure what to wear and had plumped for black trousers and a charcoal-grey shirt. Daisy's arm was linked through his and she was laughing.

To a casual observer—and to the headline writer—they looked very much the happy couple.

He thrust the phone back at Sherry. 'Why are they even interested? So we go to a concert, what's the big deal?'

'You have to admit it's a fairy-tale romance, rock star's daughter marrying an earl after just a few weeks.' Her voice was calm but the sharp gleam in her eyes showed her own curiosity. 'Of course they're interested. It'll die down.'

'Will it?' He could hear the bitter note in his voice and made an effort to speak more normally. 'I hope so.'

With in-laws like the ones he would shortly be acquiring, any chance of anonymity seemed very far away.

Sherry drifted away, her long list wafting from one elegant hand, and Seb tried to turn his attention back to his laptop. But once again his attention wandered. Where *was* Daisy?

She had slept in her own room last night citing tiredness. His own bed had seemed so huge, empty. Cold. At one point he had rolled over, ready to pull her into his arms—only she hadn't been there. It was odd how her absence had loomed through the long, almost sleepless night.

Odd how quickly he had grown accustomed to her presence; the low, even breathing, the warmth of her. The way she woke up spooned into him, the long hair spread over both pillows.

Odd how right it felt.

She hadn't shown up for breakfast either. Seb drummed his fingers on the desktop, the leather soft under his persistent touch. She had looked so vibrant in the photo but at some point in the evening her usual exuberance had dimmed and she had hardly said a word on the way back to Hawksley.

He cast his mind back, trying to remember the conversation of the night before. What had they talked about?

Had it been the mention of the honeymoon? The honeymoon she didn't want.

The honeymoon she didn't want to take with him.

Maybe she was wrong. Maybe they needed this, time away from the pressures of work and family, time away from putting on their best manners and working hard to fit their lives together—maybe it was time to find out how they operated as a couple. He would discuss it again with her.

Only… His fingers drummed a little harder as he thought. She had surprised him last night and it had been one of the most thoughtful things anyone had ever done for him. Maybe it was time for Seb to return the favour.

He pulled the laptop towards him, not allowing himself time to think things through and change his mind, quickly typing in Gianni's email address. Subject heading 'Lake Garda'.

He might not be her dream fiancé but Daisy deserved the perfect honeymoon and he was going to make sure she had it. It was the least he could do.

He had expected to find her in the kitchen. Daisy had been forbidden from doing any of the actual sanding herself. Seb was pretty sure all the dust wasn't good for the baby, but it didn't stop her superintending every job. Under her instructions the walls had been repainted a creamy white, the sanded and restored cupboards, cabinets and dresser a pale grey. He'd been sceptical about the colour but, walking into the warm, soothing space, he had to admit she was right.

The estate joiner had been hard at work planing and oiling wood from one of the old oaks that had fallen in the winter storms, creating counter tops from the venerable old tree. It seemed fitting that a tree that had stood sentry in the grounds for so many generations should be brought inside and used for the changing of the guard.

Daisy had found an old clothes rack in one of the outbuildings and had arranged for it to be suspended from the ceiling, hanging the old copper saucepans from it. She had unearthed his great-grandmother's tea set from the attic and arranged it on the shelves, the old-fashioned forget-me-not pattern blending timelessly with the creams and greys. The overall effect was of useful comfort. A warm, family kitchen, a place for work and conversation. For sweet smells and savoury concoctions, for taking stock of the day while planning the next.

The kitchen had been changing day by day and yet he hadn't really taken in the scale of her efforts. It wasn't just that the kitchen was freshly restored, nor that it was scrupulously clean. It wasn't just the new details like the pictures on the wall, old landscapes of the grounds and the castle, the newly installed sofa by the Aga and the warm rug Monty had claimed for his own. It was the feeling. Of care, of love.

The same feeling that hit him when he walked into her rooms, cluttered, sweet-smelling and alive. The same feeling she had created in the morning room and in the library where she had removed some of the heavier furniture and covered the backs of his chairs with warm, bright throws, heaped the window seats high with cushions.

His home was metamorphosing under his eyes and yet he'd barely noticed.

He should tell her he liked the changes.

Seb poured himself a glass of water and sat at the table, thinking of all the places she could have disappeared to. He didn't blame her for wanting some breathing space before the wedding; but if even Sherry couldn't run her to earth Daisy must have chosen her hiding space with care.

Neatly piled on the tabletop were some of the old scrapbooks and pictures Sherry had printed out from Daisy's website and internet pin boards. Seb reached out curiously and began to leaf through them. He expected to see a little girl's fantasy, all meringues and Cinderella coaches.

Instead he was confronted by details: a single flower bound in ribbon, a close-up of an intricate piece of lace, an embellished candle. Simple, thoughtful yet with a quirky twist. Like Daisy herself.

A piece of paper fell out and he picked it up. It was a printed-out picture of a ring: twisted pieces of fine gold wire embellished with fiery stones. A million miles away from the classic solitaire he had presented her with.

A solitaire she rarely wore. She was worried she'd lose it, she said. But it wasn't just that; he could see it in her eyes.

He hadn't known her at all when he'd bought it for her. Picked out a generic ring, expensive, sure, flawless—but nothing special, nothing unique. He could have given that ring to anyone.

And Daisy was definitely not just anyone.

Seb leant back, the picture in his hand. He really should show her just how much he appreciated all that she had done.

She was so busy trying to fit in with him, to turn his old house into a home. It was time he gave something back. The wedding of her dreams, the honeymoon of her dreams.

The ring of her dreams.

It wasn't the full package, he was all too aware of that. But it was all he had, wasn't it? It would have to do.

He just hoped it would be enough.

CHAPTER TEN

THERE IT WAS. Daisy sucked in a long breath, forcing herself to stay low and remain still, remain quiet despite every nerve fizzing with excitement. Slowly, carefully, she focused the zoom lens.

Click.

The otter didn't know it was being photographed—much like Daisy herself last night. Would the otter feel as violated, as sick to its stomach if she published the shot on her website?

Had Seb seen it? Each time a photo of them appeared in the press he got a little colder, a little more withdrawn and she could feel herself wither with each snap too.

Was it the intrusion itself she minded—or the image portrayed in the pictures? They looked so happy last night, hands clasped, heads turned towards each other, as if they were wrapped up in their own world, totally complete together.

And they said the camera never lied…

Daisy shook off the thought, allowing her own camera to follow the sleek mammal as it swam up the river, turning giddy somersaults in the water, playing some game she longed to understand. Was it lonely, swimming all by itself? Maybe by the summer it would have cubs to play with. She hoped so.

Her mind drifted down to the new life inside her. Still so small, only perceptible by the swelling in her breasts and sensitivity to certain smells and yet strong, growing, alive. 'Will I be less lonely when you're here?' she whispered.

It was a terrible burden to put on a baby. Happiness and self-fulfilment. Daisy focused again on the gliding otter. She had her camera, her work, her family. That was enough. It had to be enough.

Only. What if it wasn't? She was trying so hard. Trying to be calm and sensible and fit in with the slow and steady pace of life at Hawksley she glimpsed between wedding preparations: Seb with his research, Seb out in the fields, talking to tenants, the weekend tourists herded around the small areas open to the public. It was as distant from her busy London life as the otter's life was from an urban fox's streetwise existence.

She was making a list of the most immediate refurbishments needed in the house and was happily delving deep into the crammed attics. But despite everything Seb said she didn't feel as if she had a right to start making changes; it felt as if she were playing at being the lady of the house. She was still a visitor, just a momentary imprint in the house's long history.

And although Seb hadn't gone into great detail she knew that money was tight, the trust set up to keep the castle depleted, ransacked in return for a jet-set existence. Seb had to wait for probate before he could start to sell off all the luxury items his parents had lavished their money on. Until they were sold it was impossible to know just how much she could draw on. Right now she was doing her best with things scavenged from the attic, materials she could turn into cushions or curtains, pictures that just needed a polish.

Hawksley needed far more work than easy cosmetic

fixes. How could she plan the renovations it needed when she knew full well the cost would be exorbitant?

It was hard to grasp how life would be afterwards. The wedding overshadowed everything, created buzz and fuss and work and life. Once Sherry left for good, the vows were said and the marquee tidied away what would be left for her? Would she find herself desperate to shout out loud, to stand in the middle of the courtyard and scream, to tear the calm curtain of civility open? To get some reaction somehow.

The wedding was just a day. She had the rest of her life here to navigate.

And there was nobody to discuss it with. Seb didn't want emotions in his life and she had agreed to respect that. This fear of loneliness, emotions stretching to breaking point, was exactly the kind of thing he abhorred.

And of course, where there wasn't emotion there couldn't be love. Could there?

Daisy got slowly to her feet, careful not to disturb the still-basking otter. Love? Where had that come from? She knew full well that love wasn't on offer in this pact of theirs. It was just…

There was passion behind that serious, intellectual face. She had known it that very first night. Had seen it again time after time. Not just in bed but in his work, his attachment to his home. And passion was emotion…

Seb might not think that he did emotion but he did. His books were bestsellers because they brought the past alive. No one could write with such sensual sensitivity about the lusts of the Stuart court without feeling the hunger himself.

There were times when the almost glacial green eyes heated up, darkened with need. Times when the measured voice grew deeper, huskier. Times when sense was tossed aside for immediacy. Seb desired her, she knew that. Desire was an emotion.

Of course he was capable of love! Just not for her. Maybe, if she hadn't interrupted the steady pace of his life, he would have met somebody suitable. Someone who shared his love for the past, who would have known how to overcome his fears, helped to heal his hurts.

He'd been robbed of his chance for love just as she had. They were in this together.

And so she wouldn't dwell on the way her stomach lurched every time he looked directly at her, on the way her skin fizzed at every causal touch. She wouldn't allow herself to think about how he made her feel smart as well as sexy. As if she counted.

Because that way lay madness and regret. That way led to revelations she wasn't ready to face. That way led to emotions and maybe Seb was right. Maybe emotions were too high a price to pay. Maybe stability was what mattered.

'Where have you been?' Daisy started as she heard the slightly irritable voice. She bit back a near hysterical giggle. Think of the devil and he will come.

'I've been looking everywhere. Your mother is worried. Says she hasn't seen you all morning and that you look tired.' His gaze was intent, as if he were searching out every shadow in her face. In her soul.

'I just couldn't face any more in-depth discussions about whether as Violet's best friend Will should count as her date, or if Vi and Rose should have the same hairstyle so I came out for some air.' It wasn't a total lie. The nearer the wedding got, the more she wanted to run. Funny to think that once she had planned for this, thought all these tiny details mattered.

Now she just wanted it over and done with.

'Some air?' Seb bit back a smile. 'You're almost at the edge of the estate. I couldn't believe it when Paul said he'd seen you walk this way.'

'I like it down here. It's peaceful.' The river wound

around the bottom of the wooded valley, Hawksley invisible on the other side of the hill. Here she was alone, away from the fears and the worries and the nerves.

'It used to be one of my favourite places when I was younger. There's a swimming spot just around that bend.'

'Shh! Look!' Daisy grabbed his arm and pointed. 'There's another one. Do you think they're mates? Do otters live in pairs?' She dropped his arm to pull her camera back up, focusing and clicking over and over.

'Not European otters.' Seb spoke in a low even tone as they watched the pair duck and dive, their sinewy bodies weaving round each other in an underwater dance. 'They're very territorial so I think we might be lucky enough to see a mating pair—in two months' time there could be cubs. They actually mate underwater.'

'It looks like she's trying to get away.'

'The dog otters often have to chase the females until she agrees.'

'Typical males!'

They stood there for a few minutes more, almost unable to breathe trying not to alert the couple to their presence until, at last, the female otter took off around the bend in the river doggedly pursued by the male and the pair were lost from sight.

'That was incredible.' Daisy turned to Seb. His eyes reflected her own awe and wonderment, the same incredulous excitement. 'I can't believe we were lucky enough to witness that.'

'Do you think he's caught her?'

She tossed her head. 'Only if she wants him to. But I hope she did. What a project that would make—documenting the mating dance right through to the cubs maturing.'

'I didn't know you were into nature photography?'

His words brought back the look of utter incomprehension on his publisher's face. Nature photography, high fashion, art—they were intellectual pursuits, worthy. Weddings, romance? They just didn't cut it.

'I'm into anything wonderful, anything beautiful.' She turned away, a mixture of vulnerability and anger replacing the excitement, then turned back again to face him, to challenge him. 'What, you thought I was too shallow to appreciate nature?'

He gripped her shoulders, turning her to face him, eyes sparkling with anger of his own. 'Don't put words into my mouth, Daisy.'

'But that's what you meant, wasn't it?' She twisted away from his touch, acidic rage, corrosive and damaging, churning her stomach. 'A nature photographer wife would be so much more fitting for you than a wedding photographer. So much more intellectual than silly, frivolous romance.'

'How on earth did you reach that crazy conclusion? This has nothing to do with me.' Seb dropped his hands, stepped back, mouth open in disbelief. 'It's to do with you. Why do you always do this? Assume everyone else thinks the worst of you? The only person who puts you down, Daisy Huntingdon-Cross, is you. Photograph babies or weddings or cats or otters. I don't care. But don't take all your insecurities and fasten them on me. I won't play.'

'Why? Because that would mean getting involved?' Daisy knew she was making no sense, knew she was stirring up emotions and feelings that didn't need to be disturbed. That she was almost creating conflict for the sake of it. But she couldn't stop. 'God forbid that the high and mighty Earl of Holgate actually feel something. Have an opinion on another person.'

Seb took another step back, his mouth set firm, his eyes hard. 'I won't do this, Daisy. Not here, not now, not ever. I told you, this is not how I will live. If you want to fight, go pick a quarrel with your mother but don't try and pick one with me.'

Daisy trembled, the effort of holding the words in almost too much. But through the tumult and silent rage another emotion churned. Shame. Because Seb was right. She was trying to pick a quarrel, trying to see if she could get him to react.

And he was right about something else. She was fastening her own insecurities on him. He was very upfront about her job; he mocked it, laughed at it but he *had* supported her when she'd needed it. And he might think weddings frivolous but he had commented on some of her photos, praised the composition.

'I was being unfair.' The words were so soft she wasn't sure if she had actually said them aloud. 'I don't know if it's the stress of the wedding or pregnancy hormones or lack of sleep. But I'm sorry. For trying to provoke you.'

He froze, a wary look on his face. 'You are?'

Her mouth curved into a half smile. 'I grew up with two sisters, you know. This is how we operated—attack first.'

'Sounds deadly.' But the hard look in his eyes had softened. 'Are you ready to walk back? If you're very lucky I'll show you where I used to build my den.'

Daisy recognised the conciliatory note for what it was and accepted the tacit peace offering. 'That sounds cool. We had treehouses but they were constructed for us, no makeshift dens for us.'

'I can imagine.' His tone was dry. Whatever he was imagining probably wouldn't be too far from the truth. They had each had their own, ornate balconied structures constructed around some of the grand old oaks in Huntingdon Hall's parkland.

They strode along, Seb pointing out objects of interest as Daisy zoomed in on some of the early signs of spring budding through the waking woodland. The conversation was calm, non-consequential, neither of them alluding to the brief altercation.

And yet, Daisy couldn't help thinking, he had been the first to react. Immediate and unmistakeable anger. In his eyes, in his voice, in the grip on her shoulders, in his words. She had got to him whether he admitted it or not. Was that a good thing? A breakthrough?

She had no idea. But it was proof that he felt something. What that actually was remained to be seen but right now she would take whatever she could get.

Because it meant hope.

'These are really good, Daisy.'

'Mmm.' But she sounded critical as she continued to swipe through the files. Seb had no idea why. Whether the pictures were colour or black and white she had completely captured the otters' essence. Watching the photos in their natural order was like being told a story.

She obviously felt about her photos the way he felt about his words—no matter how you tinkered and played and edited they could always be better.

Daisy pulled a face and deleted a close-up that looked perfect to him. 'What I need down there is a proper hide. Preferably one with cushions and a loo.'

It would be the perfect spot. 'I did consider putting in a nature trail, but it means more people coming onto the land.'

'And that's a problem, why?' She looked up from the laptop, her gaze questioning.

He bit back the surge of irritation, trying to keep his voice even. 'This is my home, Daisy. How would you like people traipsing all over Huntingdon Hall at all times of the day?'

She leant back, the blue eyes still fixed on him. 'We often open up the hall. Mum and Dad host charity galas and traditionally the hall is the venue for the village fete plus whatever else the village wants to celebrate—and there's always something. Besides, yes, they do own some parkland and the gardens are huge by nearly anyone else's standards but it doesn't even begin to compare to Hawksley. Don't you think you're a bit selfish keeping it locked up?'

Selfish? Words were Seb's trade—and right now he had lost his tools. All he could do was stare at her, utterly nonplussed. 'I let people look around the castle.'

She wrinkled her nose and quoted: '"Restricted areas of the house are available to members of the public from eleven a.m. until three p.m., weekends only between Whitsun and September the first."'

Okay, the hours were a *little* restrictive. 'I hire out the Great Hall.'

'Saturdays only. And you don't allow anyone else onto the estate apart from the villagers and your tenants.'

His defensive hackles rose as she continued. It was as if she had looked into all his worries and was gradually exhuming each one. 'That's how we've always done things.' An inadequate response, he knew, but until he made some difficult decisions it was all he had.

'I know.' She looked as if she wanted to continue but instead closed her mouth with a snap, continuing to flick through the photos.

'But?' he prompted.

'But things are different now. You need to start running the estate as a commercial enterprise, not as a gentleman's hobby.'

Ouch. 'What do you think I've been doing these last few months?' he demanded. 'Research? I have barely touched my book. I've been doing my damnedest to try and get all the farming grants I can...'

'That's not going to be enough.' She bit her lip and

looked down at her screen, clearly thinking hard about something. 'I didn't want to show you this until I had done more work on it. It's not ready yet.'

'Show me what?' Wariness skittered down his spine.

She clicked on the screen and swivelled the laptop round so he could see the screen.

Seb had expected a photo. Instead a formatted slide complete with bullet points faced him. He raised an eyebrow. 'PowerPoint?'

Daisy coloured. 'I know it's a little OTT but I couldn't think how else to order it.'

'Go on, then. Amaze me.' He knew he sounded dismissive but, honestly, what on earth could a wedding photographer who was expelled from school at sixteen contribute to the ongoing Hawksley struggle that he hadn't considered? But, he conceded, if this was going to be her home he should at least listen to whatever crackpot ideas she had dreamed up.

She chewed on her lip for a moment, looking at him doubtfully before taking a deep breath and pointing one slim finger at the screen.

'Okay.' She slid him a nervy glance. 'I want you to have an open mind, okay?'

He nodded curtly even as he felt his barriers go up.

'This is Chesterfield Manor. The house, grounds and estate are a similar size to Hawksley. Chesterfield Manor has been open to the public for the last fifteen years. They specialise in outdoor trails and natural play.' She sounded self-conscious, as if she were reading from a script.

'An insurance nightmare.'

'This one…' The slide showed a magnificent Tudor house. 'This is known for productions of plays, especially Shakespeare and they also do themed medieval banquets.'

'In costume? Tell me you aren't serious!'

Daisy didn't reply, just carried on showing him slide

after slide of stately homes spread throughout the UK ranging from a perfectly preserved Norman Castle to a nineteenth-century gothic folly, her manner relaxing as she settled into the presentation, pointing out all the various ways they attracted paying visitors.

Seb's heart picked up speed as he looked at each slide, hammering so hard it rivalled the tick of the old grandfather clock in the hallway.

Everything she was showing him he had considered. Every conclusion she had drawn he had already drawn—and rejected. Too risky, not in keeping. A betrayal of his grandfather's already squandered legacy.

Risks and spending money without thought of the consequences had almost broken Hawksley once.

Allowing the cameras into their home had just fuelled his parents' narcissism, and greed.

He couldn't go down that road. Didn't she understand that?

He had thought she understood.

He had obviously been very wrong...

Seb took in a deep breath, stilling his escalating pulse, and sat back and folded his arms. 'So people like stately homes.'

'Hawksley has two things none of these have.' She waited expectantly.

He sighed. 'Which are?'

'Its utterly unique appearance—and you. An eminent historian in situ right here. Look, I've been talking to Paul...'

His eyes narrowed. 'You have been busy.'

She lifted her chin. 'The farms pay for themselves, the village pays for itself—but the castle is in deficit. You can apply for as many grants as you like but that's not going to fix the roof and certainly won't replace the money your father squandered. The income from the trust used to pay for all the castle's bills and living expenses for the earl and his family—right now you'd find it hard to replace the toaster.'

It was an exaggeration but his gut tightened at her words. Did she think he didn't know this? Didn't lie awake night after night thinking of every which way he could solve it?

'But, Seb, there are so many ways we could use the castle to generate the income it needs. Start using the keep, as well as the hall, for weddings and parties too—erect a wooden and canvas inner structure inside the walls just like they did at Bexley. Hold plays, open all week Easter to September and weekends out of season. Have a Christmas open house.' She hesitated. 'Allow tours of the main house.'

Seb's chest tightened at the very thought of strangers wandering around his house. 'No!'

She hurried on. 'I don't mean open access but "pay in advance and reserve your place" tours. Put in a farm shop and nature trails and play parks. We could convert some of the outbuildings into holiday cottages and bridal accommodation.'

'With what?'

'There's some capital left.'

He stared. 'You want me to gamble what's left, finish what my father started?'

'Not gamble, invest.'

'Meanwhile I'm what? A performing earl, the public face of Hawksley, like some medieval lord of the manor...'

'You are the lord of the manor.'

'It's all about publicity with you, isn't it? You say you don't want it but you can't see any way but the obvious—photos and newspapers and the public.'

'No.' She was on her feet. 'But with a place like Hawksley the right kind of publicity is a blessing.'

'There is no such thing as the right publicity.'

She stared at him. 'Come on, Seb, you know that's not true. Look at your books!'

'They're work, this is my home.' His voice was tight.

Daisy bit her lip, her eyes troubled. 'You can't see past your fears. You are so determined to do things your way you won't even consider any alternatives!'

His mouth curled in disgust. 'Is this about those damned TV lectures?'

'They would be a great start.'

Bitterness coated his mouth. 'I thought you understood.'

'I do. But you want me to marry you, to give you an heir. An heir to what? To worry? To debt? To fear? Or to a thriving business and a home with history—and a roof that doesn't leak?'

He pushed his chair back and stumbled to his feet. 'Hawksley is mine, Daisy. Mine! I will sort this out and make it right.'

Her eyes were huge. 'I don't get any say?'

That wasn't what he meant and she knew it. 'Stop twisting my words and stop creating drama.'

But she wasn't backing down. He didn't know her eyes could burn so brightly. 'You can't just shut me down, Seb, every time we have a difference of opinion. That's not how life works, not how marriage works.'

'I'm not shutting you down.' He just didn't want to argue. What was wrong with that?

'You are! If we are going to do this then we have to be partners. I have to be able to contribute without you accusing me of picking fights. I have to be involved in your decisions and your life.'

He couldn't answer, didn't know what to say. He hadn't expected her to push him like this. He had underestimated her, that was clear. What had he expected? A compliant partner, someone to warm his bed and agree with him?

He could feel his heart speeding up, his palms slick

with sweat. He had obviously overestimated himself just as much. Pompous ass that he was.

'That's not what you want, is it?' Her voice was just a whisper. 'You're happy for me to redecorate some rooms but you don't want my input, not where it matters.' Her voice broke. 'You're right, what does a romantically inclined girl with no qualifications know anyway?'

'That's not what I said.'

'It's what you think though.'

He couldn't deny it.

The blue eyes were swimming. 'I know I said I could do this, Seb, but I'm not sure I'm the kind of woman who can warm your bed and raise your children and not be needed in your life.'

She could read him like a book. He wanted to say that he did need her but the words wouldn't come. 'You promised to try.'

'I have tried.' Her cry sounded torn from the heart. Half of him wanted to step forward and enfold her in his arms, promise her that it would be okay—the other half of him recoiled from the sheer emotion.

'So what are you saying? The wedding is off?'

She swallowed. 'I don't know. I know how important getting married is for the baby's sake but I have to think about me as well. I need some time, Seb. Some time on my own to figure things out. I'm sorry.'

And while he was still searching for the right words, the right sentiments, a way to make her stay she slipped out of the room and he knew that he'd lost her.

And he had no idea how to find her again.

CHAPTER ELEVEN

SHE'D LEFT HER favourite camera at Hawksley. She'd also left her favourite laptop and half of her hats but right now it was her camera she needed.

If she wasn't going to expose herself to her own merciless gaze then she needed to turn that gaze elsewhere. She needed to find a subject and lose herself in it.

Daisy stared mindlessly out of the windscreen. She had other cameras at her studio but returning there, right now, felt like a retreat. Worse, it felt like an admission of failure.

But she had failed, hadn't she?

She'd tried to change the rules.

They hadn't even managed the shotgun marriage part before she had started interfering. Demanding responses, pushing him, putting together PowerPoint presentations. Daisy leaned forward until her forehead knocked against the steering wheel.

She was a fool.

And yet…

Slowly Daisy straightened, her hands pressing tighter on the wheel. And yet she had felt more right than she had in a long, long time. As if she had finally burst out of her chrysalis.

She didn't know if she could willingly shut herself back in. She'd enjoyed the research, enjoyed finding conclusions—she'd even enjoyed figuring out PowerPoint in the end after she had emerged victorious after the first few scuffles. She'd never put together any kind of business plan before, never pushed herself.

Never allowed herself to broaden her horizons, to think she might be capable of achieving more. Hidden behind her camera just as Seb hid behind his qualifications.

She'd wanted to help him. Had seen how much he was struggling, torn between his career and his home, the expectations of his past and the worries of the present.

But he didn't want her help. Didn't need her.

Without conscious thought, just following her instinct, Daisy began to drive, following the road signs on autopilot until she turned down the long lane that led to her childhood home. She pulled the small car to a stop and turned off the engine, relief seeping through her bones. This was where she needed to be, right now.

It had been a long time since she had run home with her problems.

It was only a short walk along the lane and through the gates that led to the hall but with each step Daisy's burden lightened, just a little. Maybe asking for help wasn't a sign of weakness.

Maybe it was maturity.

Huntingdon Hall glowed a soft gold in the late afternoon light. Daisy paused, taking in its graceful lines, the long rows of windows, the perfectly symmetrical wings, the well-maintained and prosperous air of the house. It wasn't just smaller than Hawksley, newer than half of Hawksley—it was a family home. Loved, well cared for and welcoming.

But it wasn't her home any more, hadn't been for a long time. She shut her eyes for a moment, visualising the way the sun lit up the Norman keep, the thousand-year-old tower reflected in the water. When had Hawksley begun to feel like *her* home?

The kitchen doors stood ajar and she ran up the steps, inhaling gratefully the familiar scent of fresh flowers, beeswax and the spicy vanilla scent her mother favoured. Inside the kitchen was as immaculate as always, a huge open-plan cooking, eating and relaxing space, the back wall floor-to-ceiling glass doors bringing the outside inside no matter what the weather.

She'd walked away from all this comfort, luxury and love at eighteen so convinced she wouldn't be able to find herself here, convinced she was the family joke, the family outcast. Tears burned the backs of her eyes as she looked at the vast array of photographs hung on the walls; not her father's record covers or her mother's most famous shoots but the girls from bald, red-faced babies, through gap-toothed childhood to now. Interspersed and lovingly framed were some of Daisy's own photos including her degree shoot prints.

What must it have cost them to let her go? To allow her the freedom to make her own mistakes?

'Hey, Daisy girl.' Her father's rich American drawl remained unchanged despite three decades living in the UK. 'Is your mother with you?' He looked round for his wife, hope and affection lighting up his face. What must it be like, Daisy wondered with a wistful envy, to love someone else so much that your first thought was always of them?

'Nope, she's still browbeating the caterers and obsessing over hairstyles.' She leant gratefully into her father's skinny frame as he pulled her into a cuddle. How long was it since she had allowed herself to be held like this? For too long she had stopped after a peck and a squeeze of the shoulders. 'Hi, Dad.'

'It's good to see you, Daisy girl.' He pulled back to look

her over, a frown furrowing the famously craggy face. 'You look exhausted. Your mother working you too hard?'

'I think you and Mum had the right idea running away.' Daisy tried not to wriggle away from his scrutiny.

'It saved a lot of bother,' he agreed, but the keen eyes were full of concern. 'Drink?'

'Just water, please.' She accepted the ice-cold glass gratefully, carrying it over to the comfortable cluster of sofas grouped around the windows, sinking onto one with a sigh of relief.

She had begun to recreate this feeling in the kitchen at Hawksley, sanding back the old kitchen cupboards so that they could be repainted a soft grey and bringing in one of the better sofas from an unused salon to curl up on by the Aga. Slowly, step by step turning the few rooms she and Seb used into warm, comfortable places. Into a family home.

'I feel like I should be coming to you with words of advice and wisdom.' Rick sat down on the sofa opposite, a bottle of beer in one hand. 'After three daughters and three decades of marriage you'd think I'd know something. But all I know is don't go to bed angry, wake up counting your blessings and always try and see the other person's point of view. If you can manage that—' he raised his bottle to her '—then you should be okay.'

'Funny.' She smiled at him. 'Mum said something very similar.'

Rick took a swig of his beer. 'Well, your mother's a wise woman.'

Daisy swung her legs up onto the sofa, reclining against the solid arm and letting the cushions enfold her. She half closed her eyes, allowing the sounds and smells of her childhood home to comfort her. After a few moments Rick got up and she could hear him clattering about in the food preparation part of the kitchen. Her eyelids fluttered shut and she allowed herself to fall into a doze, feeling safe for the first time in a long while.

'Here you go.' She roused as a plate was set before her. 'I know it's fashionable for brides to waste away before their wedding but if you get any thinner, Daisy girl, I'll be having to hold you down as we walk down that aisle.'

'My favourite.' The all-too-ready tears pricked her eyelids as Daisy looked at the plate holding a grilled cheese and tomato sandwich and a bowl of tomato soup. Her childhood comfort food—not coincidentally also the limit of Rick Cross's cooking skills. 'Thanks, Dad.'

Her father didn't say another word while she ate; instead he picked up one of the seemingly endless supplies of guitars that lay in every room of the house and began to strum some chords. It had used to drive Daisy mad, his inability to stay quiet and still, but now she appreciated it for what it was. A safety blanket, just like her camera.

As always the slightly stodgy mix of white bread, melted cheese and sweet tomatoes slipped down easily and a full stomach made her feel infinitely better. Rick continued to strum as Daisy carried her empty dishes to the sink, the chords turning into a well-known marching song.

Rick began to croon the lyrics in the throaty tones that had made him a star. He looked up at his daughter, a twinkle in his eyes. 'Thought I might sing this instead of making a speech.'

She couldn't do it, couldn't lie to him a single moment longer. So she would slip back into being the problem daughter, the mistake-making disaster zone. Maybe she deserved it.

She could take it. She had to take it.

She was tired of doing it all alone. Tired of shutting her family out. Tired of always being strong, of putting her need to be independent before her family.

Maybe *this* was what being a grown-up meant. Not shutting yourself away but knowing when it was okay to accept help. When it was okay to lean on someone else. The day Seb had come to help her with the wedding had been one of the best days of her adult life. She'd come so close to relying on him.

Tension twisted her stomach as she fought to find the right words. But there were no right words. Just the facts.

Daisy turned, looked him straight in the eyes and readied herself. 'I'm pregnant. Dad, I'm pregnant and I don't know what to do.'

Her father didn't react straight away. His fingers fell off the guitar and he carefully put the instrument to one side, his face shuttered. Slowly he got to his feet, walking over to Daisy before pulling her in close, holding her as if he meant to never let her go.

The skinny shoulders were stronger than they looked. Daisy allowed herself to lean against them, to let her father bear her weight and finally, finally stopped fighting the tears she had swallowed back for so long, shudders shaking her whole body as the sobs tore out of her.

'It's okay, Daisy girl,' her father crooned, stroking her hair as if she were still his little girl. 'It's okay.'

But she couldn't stop, not yet, even though the great gusty sobs had turned into hiccups and the tears had soaked her father's shirt right through. The relief of finally not having to put on a brave face was too much and it was several minutes before her father could escort her back to the sofa, setting another glass of water and several tissues in front of her.

'Hold on,' he said. 'If living with a pack of women has taught me anything it's that there's a surefire remedy for this kind of situation.' He walked, with the catlike grace that made him such a hypnotic stage performer, to the fridge and, opening the freezer door, extracted a pint of ice cream. 'Here you go, Daisy girl,' he said, setting it down in front of her and handing her a spoon. 'Dig in.'

He didn't say anything for a while. Just sat there as Daisy scooped the creamy cold chocolatey goodness out of the carton, allowing it to melt on her tongue. She couldn't manage more than a couple of mouthfuls, the gesture of far more comfort than the actual ice cream.

'I take it this wasn't planned?' His voice was calm, completely non-judgemental.

Daisy shook her head. 'No.'

'How long have you known?'

She could feel the colour creeping over her cheeks, couldn't meet her father's eye. 'A month. I told Seb three weeks ago.'

'This is why you're getting married?'

Daisy nodded. 'It's because of Hawksley, and the title. If the baby isn't legitimate...' Her voice trailed off.

'Crazy Brits.' Her dad sat back. 'Do you love him, Daisy girl?'

Did she what? She liked him—sometimes. Desired him for sure. The way his hair fell over his forehead, a little too long and messy for fashion. The clear green of his eyes, the way they darkened with emotion. The lean strength of him, unexpected in an academic. The way he listened to her, asked her questions, respected her, made her feel that maybe she had something to contribute—until today.

She understood him, knew why he strived so hard to excel in everything he did, tried to keep himself aloof, the fear of being judged.

Her father's gaze intensified. 'It's not that hard a question, Daisy girl. When you know, you know.'

'Yes.' The knowledge hit her hard, almost winding her. 'Yes, I do. But he doesn't love me and that's why I don't know if I can do it. I don't know if I can marry him. If I can say those words to someone who doesn't want to hear them, for him to say them to me and not mean them.' That was it, she realised with a sharp clarity. She had been prepared to lie to everyone but she couldn't bear for him to lie to her. To make promises he didn't mean.

'Love means that much to you?' Her father's eyes were kind, knowing.

Daisy put her hand down to cradle her still-flat stomach. She wanted the baby; she already loved it. Which love meant more? Pulled at her more? What was worse? Depriving her baby of its heritage or bringing it up in an unequal, unhappy household?

'With your example before me? Of course it does. I want a husband who looks at me the way you look at Mum. That's what I've always wanted. But it's not just about me, not any more. Oh, Dad, what am I going to do?'

Her father put an arm around her and she sank into his embrace wishing for one moment that she were a little girl again and that there was nothing her dad couldn't fix. 'That's up to you, Daisy girl. Only you can decide. But we're all here for you, whatever happens. Remember that, darling. I know how independent you are but we're here. You're not alone.'

Loneliness had been such a constant friend for so many years he had barely noticed it leave.

Yet now it had returned it felt heavier than ever.

The primroses carpeted the woodland floor, their pale beauty a vivid reminder of the colour overtaking his home. Sherry liked a theme and had incorporated the yellow-and-white colour scheme into everything from the guest towels to the bunting already hung in the marquee. It was like living in a giant egg.

Apart from the rooms Daisy had been working on. She had kept her mother out of those, keeping them private, personal.

Creating a family space.

His throat closed tight. *Their* family space.

Normally Seb loved this time of year, watching the world bud, shaking off the sleepy austerity of winter. It wasn't as obvious in Oxford as it was here at Hawksley where every day signalled something new.

Oxford. It had been his focus for so long, his sole goal. To excel in his field. He had almost made it.

But suddenly it didn't seem that important, more like a remembered dream than a passion. His research? Yes. Digging into the past, feeling it come alive, transcribing it for a modern audience, that he missed. But college politics, hungover undergraduates, teaching, tourist-filled streets, the buzz of the city?

Seb breathed in the revelation. He didn't miss it at all.

He was home. This was where he belonged.

But not alone. He had been alone long enough.

Seb retraced his steps, anticipating the moment his steps would lead him out of the wood and over the hill, that first glimpse of Hawksley Castle standing, majestic, by the lake edge. The Norman keep, grey, watchful, looking out over the water flanked by the white plaster and timbered Tudor hall, picturesque with the light reflected off the lead-paned windows. Finally the house itself, a perfect example of neoclassical Georgian architecture.

Daisy was right: it would make a wonderful setting for a TV series.

Seb's heart twisted. Painfully.

What if she didn't come back? How would he explain her absence to her mother? The guests already beginning to arrive in the village and in neighbouring hotels? If the wedding was called off the resulting publicity would be incredible, every detail of his own parents' doomed marriage exhumed and re-examined over and over.

The usual nausea swirled, sweat beading at his forehead, but it wasn't at the prospect of the screaming head-lines and taunting comments. No, Seb realised. It was at the thought of the wedding being called off.

Slowly he wandered back towards the castle barely no-ticing the spring sunshine warming his shoulders. No wed-ding. It wasn't as if he had wanted this grand, showy affair anyway. It was a compromise he had had to make for the baby, wasn't it?

Or was it?

The truth was he hadn't hesitated. He'd taken one look at Daisy's face as she'd read through that long list of names and known he couldn't deny her the wedding of her dreams.

Truth was he couldn't deny her anything.

He wanted to give her everything—not that she'd take it, absurdly proud as she was.

She was hardworking, earnest and underestimated her-self so much she allowed everybody else to underestimate her too, hiding behind her red lipstick, her quirky style and her camera.

He knew how she put herself down, made light of her own perceived failures, preempting the judgement she was sure would come. What must it have taken to put that pre-sentation together, to show him her work—and yet he had thrown all her enthusiasm, all her help back in her face.

Shame washed over him, hot and tight. He hadn't wanted to listen, to accept that a fresh pair of eyes could ever see anything in Hawksley that he couldn't see. Hadn't wanted to accept that he was stuck on the wrong path.

He had spent so long ensuring he was nothing like his spoilt, immoral parents he had turned himself into his grandfather: upstanding sure, also rigid, a relic from a time long dead, refusing to accept the world had changed even as his staff and income shrank and his bills multiplied.

It seemed a long way back to the castle, weighted down

with guilt and shame. The truth was Daisy was right: he did need to make some changes and fast.

Starting with the estate. Much as he wanted to jump in his car, find her, beg her forgiveness he had to make the much-needed changes first. That way he could show her.

Show her that he had listened, show her that her work had value.

That he valued her.

Seb stood still, feeling his heart beat impossibly hard, impossibly loud.

Was this valuing her? This nausea, this knot of worry, this urge to do whatever it took to show her?

Or was it something more? Was it love?

It was messy and painful, just as he had feared, but it was more than that.

It was miraculous.

She made him a better person. It was up to him to repay that gift, even though it would take him the rest of his life.

The estate office was, as usual, a mess, cold and cluttered, an unattractive tangle of paperwork, old furniture, tools and filing cabinets. It felt unloved, impermanent. Seb sank down into the creaking old office chair and looked about at the utilitarian shelves, filled with broken bits of machinery and rusting tools. This was no way to run a place the size of Hawksley.

He picked up a notebook and flipped it open to a fresh white page. It mocked him with the unwritten possibilities and he sat for a moment, paralysed by how much he had to do, how sweeping the changes ahead.

But this wasn't about him, not any more. It was about his child, about his heritage, about the man he was—and the man he should be.

It was about his future wife.

The first thing he needed to do was admit he needed

some help, he couldn't do it all on his own no matter how much he wanted to.

He uncapped his fountain pen and began to write.

1. Resign from college

Seb sat back and looked at the words, waited to feel sad, resentful, to feel the weight of failure. He still had so much more to achieve; the visiting professorship at Harvard for one. Was he ready to give up his academic career? He could produce another ten bestselling books but without his college credentials they would mean nothing, not to his colleagues.

But the expected emotions didn't materialise; instead the burden on his shoulders lessened.

He leant forward again.

2. Employ a professional estate manager

Daisy was right, damn her. What use was he to anyone, sitting up late, scrutinising crop-rotation plans and cattle lists? He had done his best but he still knew less than an apprentice cattle man. If he put in an estate manager he could free his time up for writing—and for the house itself. Which led to the third thing. Admitting that Hawksley wasn't just his family home, it was a living legacy and he needed to start treating it as such.

3. Tidy and redecorate the offices to a professional standard

So that he could then…

4. Employ an events planner

*5. Talk to the solicitor about breaking into the trust
and investing in the estate*

What was it Daisy had suggested? An internal structure in the Norman keep. That could work, maintain the
integrity of the historical ruins while making it both safe
and comfortable for weddings and parties. Seb winced. It
looked as if the medieval-themed banquets might be un-
avoidable after all. As long as he wasn't expected to wear
tights and a jerkin…

What else? Holiday cottages, nature trails… He thought
back. It had only been this morning. How was it possible
that so few hours had passed? She had left her laptop behind. He needed to take a look, see what other ideas he
had dismissed. But there was definitely one more thing
to add to the list.

6. Tell my agent I am willing to consider TV ideas

Her room looked just as it always did, with no inkling that
its mistress had fled. The usual jumble of scarves, the ever-
increasing collection of hats. Seb stood at the door and inhaled the faint floral scent she always wore.

When had he begun to associate that smell with home?

He didn't want her hidden away behind the discreet
door, not any more. He wanted her with him; hats, scarves
and whatever else she needed to make herself at home. Her
rooms would make an incredible nursery.

If she would just come back.

He stepped past the neatly made bed and into the small
chamber Daisy used as an office. Her laptop still stood
open and, when he tentatively touched a key, it lit up, her
PowerPoint presentation still on the screen. Seb took it
back to the beginning and began to read.

Shame flared again. Searing as he flicked through the

slides. She had put a lot of time into this. For him. She had only looked at comparable estates in terms of size and had got as much useful information as she could including entrance prices, numbers of staff, opening hours and affiliations to member organisations. It was invaluable data, the beginnings of a business plan right here.

He closed the file down and sat back, his chest tight. How could he make it up to her?

Seb was about to switch the laptop off when a file caught his eye. Saved to her desktop, it was simply titled Hawksley. Was it more research? Curious, he double clicked.

More photos. Of course. A smile curved his mouth as he looked at his beloved home from Daisy's perspective: panoramic views, detailed close-ups, the volunteers at work, the farms. All the myriad details that made up Hawksley chronicled. She understood it as much as he did—possibly even more. She was so much more than the mother of his child, more than a fitting mistress for this huge, complicated and much-loved house.

She was perfect.

Another photo flashed up, black and white, grainy, an almost-sepia filter. It was Seb, sitting at his desk. His first instinct was to recoil, the way he always did when faced with a candid shot, the familiar churn of horror, of violation.

But then he looked again. He was reading, his forehead furrowed; he looked tired, a little stressed. It completely encapsulated the past few months, the toil they had taken on him.

Another image, Seb again, this one in full colour. He was outside, leaning against a tractor chatting to one of the tenant farmers. This time he looked relaxed, happy.

Another—Seb in Oxford, mid flow, gesticulating, eyes shining as he spoke. Another, another, another…

It wasn't just Hawksley she understood, had got to the heart of. It was Seb himself.

He closed the laptop lid and sat back, images whirling about his brain. Not the ones she had captured but those images firmly stuck in his memory. The tall, earnest girl stuck in the snow, desperate to fulfil her promise to a couple she didn't even know. That same girl later that night, eyes half closed in ecstasy, her long limbs wrapped around him.

The look in her eyes when she told him she was pregnant. Her reaction to his proposal. Her desperate plea for him to pretend he loved her. Her need to be loved. Wanted. Appreciated.

Did he love her enough? Want her enough? Appreciate her enough?

Did he deserve her?

Seb's hands curled into fists. He liked having her here. He liked waking up next to her, liked listening to her take on life, liked the way she brought fresh air and life into his ancient home.

He liked the way she used her camera as a shield, he liked how hard she worked, how seriously she took each and every wedding. He liked the way she focused in on the tiniest detail and made it special.

How she made him feel special.

He liked her dress sense, the vivid shade of red lipstick. He liked how long it took her to choose the hat of the day, how that hat evoked her mood. He liked her first thing in the morning, rosy-cheeked, make-up free, hair tousled.

He liked pretty much everything about her. He loved her.

They were supposed to be getting married in just a few days. Married. For him a business arrangement sealed with a soulless diamond solitaire. He was a fool.

He flipped open her laptop again, clicking onto her

email. He needed her sister Rose's email address. Maybe, just maybe, he could put this right. It might not be too late for him after all.

And then he would bring her home.

CHAPTER TWELVE

'Hi.'

It seemed such an inadequate word. Daisy's breath hitched as Seb came to a stop and looked at her. He was pale, his eyes looked bruised as if he hadn't slept at all and a small, shameful thrill of victory throbbed through her.

Only to ebb with the realisation that it probably wasn't Daisy herself he had spent the night tossing and turning over. The publicity that calling the wedding off would cause? Probably. Losing a legitimate heir? Most definitely.

'Hello.'

He took a step forward and stopped, as if she were a wild animal who might bolt.

It was chillier today and Daisy wrapped her arms around herself, inadequate protection against the sharp breeze blowing across the lawn.

'How did you know I was here?' Had her father called him?

'I didn't. I tried the studio first.'

That meant what? Three hours of driving? A small, unwanted shot of hope pulsed through her. 'I'm sorry for just taking off. I know how much you hate emotional scenes but I really needed some space.'

'I understand.' He swallowed, and her eyes were drawn to the strong lines of his throat. 'I've been thinking myself.'

'About what?'

'Us. Hawksley. My parents. My job. Everything really.'

'That's a lot of thinking.'

'Yes.' His mouth quirked. Daisy tried to look away but she couldn't, her eyes drawn to the firm lines of his jaw, the shape of his mouth.

'Does my mother know why I left?' Sherry had been sleeping at the castle the past week, dedicating every hour to her daughter's wedding. How could Daisy tell her it was all for nothing?

'No. I just said you needed some space,' His eyes were fixed on her with a painful intensity; she was stripped under his gaze. 'She and Violet have gone to your studio to decorate.'

'To what?' What day was it? Her stomach dropped at the realisation. 'Oh, no, the hen night. It's supposed to be low-key.'

'I got the sense that things may have evolved a little. Violet was very excited about buying in some special straws?'

'Straws?'

'Shaped straws…anatomically shaped straws.'

'Oh. Oh! Really? Vi has?'

'I didn't want to tell them they may not be needed, not until I'd spoken to you.' His mouth curved into the familiar half smile and Daisy had to curl her fingers into a fist to stop herself from reaching out to trace its line. 'And, well, it's always good to have a stock of penis straws in.'

'I'll bear that in mind.'

All the things she had planned to say to him had gone clear out of her mind. Daisy had been rehearsing speeches all night but in the end it was her father's words that echoed round and round in her mind. *When you know, you know.*

She knew she loved him. Just one look at him and she was weakening, wanted to hold him, feel his arms around her, allow him to kiss away her fears. But he wouldn't do that, would he? No. Kisses were strictly for the bedroom.

And wonderfully, toe-curlingly delicious as they were, that wasn't enough.

'Seb,' she began.

Another step and he was right before her. 'No hat.' His hand reached out and smoothed down her hair. 'No lipstick.' He ran it down the side of her cheek, drawing one finger along her bottom lip. Daisy's mouth parted at the caress, the tingle of his touch shivering through her.

'I didn't bring anything with me.' She had raided Violet's wardrobe first thing: jeans, a long-sleeved T-shirt. Ordinary, sensible clothes. She felt naked in them; there was nothing to hide behind.

'You're beautiful whatever you wear.' His voice was husky and her knees weakened as she looked up and saw the heat in his eyes.

Her mouth dried. All she wanted to do was press her mouth to his, forget herself, forget the wedding, the baby, her doubts in the surety of his kiss. 'I can't.' She put a hand out, warding him off.

'Daisy.' He swallowed and she steeled herself. Steeled herself against any entreaty. Steeled herself against the knowledge that whatever he told her, however he tried to convince her there were words he would never say no matter how much she yearned to hear them.

And steeled herself not to yield regardless.

'Will you come back with me? No—' As she began to shake her head. 'I don't mean for good. I mean now. There's something I want to show you.'

So much for all her good intentions. But she had to return at some point didn't she? To collect her things. To help dismantle the wedding her mother had spent three weeks lovingly putting together.

To start forgetting the jolt her heart gave as the car pulled over the hill and she saw Hawksley, proud in the distance.

Or to make up her mind to make the best of it, to keep her word, to put their baby first. Trouble was she still didn't know which way to turn.

To be true to her own heart or to be true to her child?

And in the end weren't they the same thing?

Daisy started walking, no destination in mind; she just had to keep moving. Seb fell into step beside her, not touching her, the inches between them a chasm as she rounded the corner past the stables.

'I was thinking that this end stable would make a great studio. They're not listed so you could do whatever you wanted for light—glass walls, anything. I know you want to carry on photographing weddings and that's fine but if you did want to exhibit your other work we could even add a gallery.'

Was this what he wanted to show her? A way of making her career more acceptable? Her heart plummeted. 'A gallery?'

'Only if you wanted to. I know how much you love weddings, but your other work is amazing too. It's up to you.'

'It would make a great space, it's just…' She faltered, unable to find the words.

'It's just an idea. This is your home too, Daisy. I just want you to know that I can support you too, whatever you need. The way you support me.' He sounded sincere enough.

Yesterday those words might even have been enough.

Her heart was so heavy it felt as if it had fallen out of her chest, shrivelled into a stone in the pit of her stomach. She had to keep moving, had to try and figure out the right thing to say. The right thing to do.

The marquee had been set up at the far end of the court-yard and curiosity pulled her there; she hadn't seen inside since it had been decorated.

'Wow.' Swathes of yellow and silk covered the ceiling, creating an exotic canopy over the hardwood dance floor. Buffet tables were set up at one end, covered in yellow cloths, and benches were set around the edges.

Daisy swivelled and walked back through the tent, try-ing to envision it full, to see it as it would be in just forty-eight hours filled with laughter and dancing—or would it be taken down unused?

A canvas canopy connected the marquee with the door to the Great Hall, a precaution against a rainy day. The heavy oak doors were open and she stepped through them, Seb still at her side. 'Oh,' she said softly as she looked around. 'Oh, it's beautiful.'

Daisy had seen the Great Hall in several guises. Empty save for the weight of history in each of the carved panels, the huge old oak beams. Set up for another wedding cer-emony and, later, a busy party venue. Her mother's work-space complete with whiteboards, elaborate floorplans and forelock-tugging minions.

But she had never seen it look as it did today.

The dais at the far end was simply furnished with a white desk and chairs for the registrar, flanked on both sides by tall white urns filled with Violet's unmistakeable flower arrangements: classy, elegant yet with a uniquely modern twist. A heavy tapestry hung from the back wall: Seb's coat of arms.

Facing the dais were rows of chairs, all covered in white, hand-sewn fabric daisy chains wound around their legs and backs.

A yellow carpet lay along the aisle ready for her to walk up, and more of the intricate woven daisy chains hung from the great beams.

'Mum has worked so hard,' she breathed.

'The poor staff have done three dummy runs to make sure they can get the tables set up perfectly in the hour and a half your mother has allowed for drinks, canapés and photographs—on the lawn if dry and warm enough, in the marquee if not. Everything is stacked in the back in perfect order—linens, table decorations, place settings, crockery. Your mother should really run the country,' Seb added, his mouth twisting into a half smile. 'Her organisational skills and, ah, persuasive skills are extraordinary.'

'We've always said that.' Daisy stared at the room perfectly set up for the perfect wedding. For her perfect wedding.

This was what she had always wanted—she had just never known who would be standing by her side. She had certainly never imagined a tall, slightly scruffy academic with penetrating green eyes, too-long dark hair and a title dating back four centuries.

Could she imagine it now? Standing up there making promises to Seb? Images swirled round and round, memories of the last three weeks: tender moments, passionate moments—and that remote, curt aloofness of his. Nausea rose as a stabbing pain shot through her temples; she swayed and he leapt forward, one arm around her shoulders, guiding her to a chair.

Daisy rubbed her head, willing the pain away. 'I'm okay. I forgot to eat breakfast.'

'Come with me, there's some croissants in the kitchen. And there's something I want to show you.'

The knot in her stomach was too big, too tight, food an impossibility until she spoke to him. But would a few more minutes of pretending that all this could be hers hurt?

'I told you I had been doing a lot of thinking,' he said as they stepped back into the courtyard. The wind was still sharp but the sun had come out, slanting through the grey clouds, shining onto the golden stone of the main house. Seb had a glimpse of a future, of children running in and out of the door, games in the courtyard, dens in the wood.

If he could just convince her to stay.

'I've resigned from the university.'

She came to an abrupt stop. 'You've what?'

'Resigned. I'll still write, of course. In fact, without my academic commitments I'll have more time to write, more time to explore other periods, other stories.'

'Why?'

'I'm needed here.' But that wasn't all of it. 'I love delving into the past, you know that. And I loved academia too. Because it was safe, there were rules. When I was a boy—' he inhaled, steady against the rush of memories '—I just wanted to keep my head down, to do the right thing. At school, as long as you worked hard, played hard and didn't tell tales then life was easy. I liked that. It was safe compared to the turbulence of my parents' existence. In a way I guess I never left school. Straight to university and then on an academic path. Everything was clear, easy. I knew exactly what I had to do, what was expected of me—until I inherited Hawksley.

'Until I met you.'

A quiver passed through her but she didn't speak as they walked around the house and in through the main door, towards the library, their steps in harmony. He pushed the library door open and stood there, in the entrance.

'I've made some other decisions too. I've spoken to my agent and asked her to investigate TV work, I've got an agency looking for suitable candidates to take over the estate management and kick-start an events programme and I've asked three architects to submit plans for converting the outbuildings.'

She did speak then, her voice soft. 'You've been very busy.'

'No.' He shook his head. 'I've been at a standstill. You were the one who was busy, busy looking into the future. I've just taken your ideas and made the next step. But I don't want to do it alone.'

She shook her head, tears swimming in her eyes. Tears were good, right? They meant she felt something. Meant she cared.

He needed to throw everything he had at her. Strip away the diffidence and fear and lay it all out. No matter how much it cost him to do it, the alternative was much worse.

'Daisy, I do need you. Not just physically, although my bed has been so empty the last two nights I couldn't sleep. But I need you to challenge me, to push me, to make me take my head out of the sand and face the future.'

'You'd have got there on your own, eventually.'

Would he? He doubted it.

'Seb, I can't live in fear. I don't like being in the papers but I accept it may happen. I can't hide just in case some bored person snaps me. And I can't not say what I think because you don't like emotional outbursts. Life isn't that tidy.'

'I thought it could be,' he admitted. 'I didn't see a middle way between the hysterical ups and downs of my parents' life and the formality of my grandparents. If it was a choice between sitting at opposite sides of a fifteen-foot table and making polite conversation or throwing plates and screaming then give me cold soup and a hoarse voice any day.'

'Most families aren't so extreme…'

'No. No, they're not. And I don't want either of those for the baby. I want it to grow up like you did, part of a happy, stable family. With two parents who love each other.'

Her eyes fell but not before he saw the hurt blaze in them. 'You don't have to say that. I don't want you to lie to make me feel better.'

'The only person I've been lying to was myself.' Seb took her chin and tilted it, trying to make her see the sincerity in his eyes.

'Love, it's complicated. It's messy and emotional and difficult. I wasn't ready for it. But then you came sauntering in with your hats and that mouth—' his eyes dropped to her mouth, lush and full even without its usual coating of slick red '—your camera and your absolute belief in love. Your belief in me and in Hawksley and you turned my world upside down. And not just because of the baby.'

Her eyes blazed blue with hope. 'Really?'

'I hadn't been able to stop thinking of you since that first night,' he told her frankly. It was all or nothing time. 'I asked the groom who you were the next morning and he sent me a link to your website. I must have clicked onto the contact me button a dozen times. But I was afraid. Nobody had ever got under my skin like that before. And then you came back…'

She laughed softly. 'You looked like you'd seen a ghost.'

Seb smiled back down at her, the warmth creeping back into her voice giving him a jolt of hope. 'I couldn't believe my luck. But I was terrified too. Of how you made me feel. How much I wanted you. There was nothing sensible about that. And the more I got to know you, Daisy, the more terrified I was.'

'I'm that scary?' A light had begun to shine in her eyes, the full mouth quivering.

'You are quite frankly the most terrifying woman I have ever met—and I am including your mother in that. And if you ever begin to believe in yourself, Daisy Huntingdon-Cross, then I don't think there is anything you won't achieve. Because—' he moved in slightly closer, emboldened by the curve of her smile '—you are definitely the smartest out of the two of us. It took you leaving for me to acknowledge how I felt about you. But now that I have I want to tell you every day. Every hour of every day. I love you, Daisy, and I really, really hope that you will marry me in two days.'

With those words the load he had been carrying for so long, the fear, the shame, finally broke free. Whatever her answer he would always be grateful to her for that—even if he had to spend the rest of his life proving the truth of his words to her.

'You love me? You think I'm smart?' Her voice broke and he dropped her chin to encircle her waist, pulling her in close. He inhaled the soft floral scent of her hair. It was like coming home.

'Ridiculously so.' Reluctantly he let her go, backing into the half-open door and pushing it open, taking her hand and pulling her inside.

'You're not the only one to see that the house needs changing, needs making into a home. I can't begin to match what you've achieved but I'm trying to make a start.'

Daisy stood stock-still, staring at the wall. Gone was the line of stern portraits; no more bewigged gentleman with terrifying eyebrows or stern Victorians with bristling moustaches. Even Seb's grandfather had been removed to a more fitting place in the long gallery.

Instead two huge canvas prints hung on the wall, sur-rounded by smaller black-and-white prints of Hawksley: the castle, the woods, the gardens. Her photos.

She looked up at the photos, eyes widening as she took in the photo of Seb. It was the one she'd taken of him in Oxford, the light behind him. It felt hubristic having such a large picture of himself on his own wall.

But it wasn't just his wall now.

Flanking him was another black-and-white photo, this time of Daisy—also at work. The trees framed her as she held the camera up to her face, her profile intent, her focus absolute.

'Where…?' She gaped up at the picture. 'Where on earth did you get that?'

'I took it.' Seb tried and failed to keep the pride out of his voice. 'I had a moment in between those photobooth shots and I turned around—and there you were. Lost in the moment. So I snapped it. I saved it onto my computer, thought you might want it for your website or something.'

'It's actually pretty good, nice composition.'

'Total and utter fluke,' he admitted. 'Daisy—' he took her hands in his '—I want the castle, every room, every decision we make to be about us. About you, me and the baby. I want to help you turn Hawksley into a family home. Into a house full of love and laughter. I asked you to marry me three weeks ago for all sorts of sensible reasons. I told you marriage was a business. I was a fool.

'I want to marry you because I love you and I hope you love me. Because I actually don't think I can live without you—and I know I can't survive without you. So, Daisy.' Seb let go of her hands and took out the ring. The ring that had miraculously arrived by overnight courier, the ring that Daisy's sister had somehow known to have ready.

Slowly, looking up into her face, he lowered himself onto one knee.

'Daisy Huntingdon-Cross. Will you please, please marry me?'

'Get up!' Daisy pulled him up, snaking her arms around his neck, smiling up at him, her eyes full of joy. 'Well, the guests *are* already invited.'

'They are.'

'It would be a shame to waste my mother's hard work.'

'A real shame.'

'And the chance to see my mother with a penis straw is not one to be passed up.'

Seb grimaced. 'I can personally live without that image, my love. But knock yourself out.'

'Say that again.'

'Knock yourself out?'

'No, the name you called me.'

'My love.' Seb's heart felt as if it might explode from his chest as he bent his head, ready to capture her mouth with his. 'My love.'

EPILOGUE

'READY, DAISY GIRL?'

Daisy pulled at the waist of her dress with nervous fingers before smiling up at her father.

'Ready, Dad.'

'Well, I'm not.' Rick Cross's eyes were suspiciously damp. 'I don't think I will ever be ready to walk you down that aisle and hand you over to another man.'

Violet rolled her eyes. 'It's the twenty-first century, Dad. Nobody gets handed over.'

'If anyone is in charge in this house, I'm sorry, I mean in this castle, it's Daisy. I've only been here a few hours and even I can see she's got that poor earl right under her thumb.'

Daisy stuck her tongue out at Rose. 'How I wish I had made you wear frills.'

Her sisters looked stunning in the simple silk dresses she had chosen. The sweetheart necklines and ruched bodices were white, flaring out into yellow knee-length skirts. Her dress had a similar bodice although instead of bare shoulders, hers were covered with a sheer lace and her floor-length skirt fell straight from the bust in a sweep of white silk to the floor.

'And I wish I had made that ring too large.' Rose nodded at the band made of twisted yellow gold, white gold petals alternating with small diamonds that adorned Daisy's left hand.

Daisy smiled down at the ring. 'I don't think you've ever made anything more lovely, Rose. I don't know how you knew to make it but thank you.'

'It goes better with your wedding ring,' Rose said, but her eyes, so like Daisy's own, were sparkling with pride. 'You look beautiful, Daisy.'

'Will Seb recognise you without a hat?' Violet tucked an errant curl behind Daisy's ear and tweaked the flowers that held her twist of hair back into place. 'There, perfect.'

'You picked a good dress.' Rose was looking her up and down. 'Your boobs are a little bit bigger but otherwise you don't look pregnant.'

'I'm not showing yet!' Daisy still couldn't mention the pregnancy without blushing. She'd told her mother and sisters during her hen night while Rose Skyped in; they had all been delighted. Especially as she hadn't needed to lie to them—they weren't just getting married because of the baby. They were getting married because they belonged together.

It was as simple and as wonderful as that.

Seb had expected to feel nervous. He was used to standing in front of large crowds, used to speaking in public. But when he taught or lectured he put on a persona. This was him, raw and exposed, in tails and a yellow cravat, ready to pledge his troth to the woman he loved.

He bit back a wry smile. He was even using her terminology now.

Sherry sat at the front, resplendent in something very structured and rigid. Seb knew very little about fashion but he was aware she was wearing something very expensive that mere mortals would never be able to carry off.

The buzz of voices came to a sudden stop as the band

struck up one of Rick's most famous tunes, a song he had composed soon after Daisy's birth. The familiar chords sounded even more poignant than ever as a violin picked up the vocal lines, soaring up into the beams as one of the twins, Seb had no idea which one, solemnly began to walk down the central aisle followed by the other.

And then his heart stopped as Daisy appeared. All in white except for her red lipstick and the bouquet of daisies, her eyes shining and a trembling smile on her lips. His fiancée, his bride, the mother of his baby.

Two months ago he was struggling on alone. Now he had a family, hope, joy. He had a future.

He smiled as a camera flashed from the back of the hall. Let them take photos, let them publish them everywhere and anywhere. He was the luckiest man alive and he was happy for the whole world to know.

* * * * *

A BRIDE FOR THE
RUNAWAY GROOM

SCARLET WILSON

For two gorgeous brides who are now two fabulous mummies,

Carissa Hyndman and Hayley Dickson.

And to my fellow authors, Jessica Gilmore and Sophie Pembroke,

for making this such fun!

CHAPTER ONE

Something wasn't right.

No, scratch that. Something was very, very wrong.

Everything should be perfect. Her sister's wedding yesterday had been beautiful. A picture-perfect day with a bride and groom that truly loved each other. It was a joy to be a part of a day like that.

But, by midnight, the days of jet lag that she'd been ignoring had finally caught up with her and she'd staggered to bed and collapsed in a heap, catching up on some much-needed sleep.

Her new brother-in-law, Seb, had a house to die for. Hawksley Castle, a home part Norman, part Tudor and part Georgian. The room she was in was sumptuous and spacious with the most comfortable bed in the world.

At least it would be—if she were in that bed alone.

She could hear breathing, heavy breathing, sometimes accompanied with a tiny noise resembling a snore.

Right now, she was afraid to move.

She hadn't drunk much at all yesterday—only two glasses of wine. Because of the jet lag they'd hit hard. But not so hard she'd invited someone into her bed.

She'd attended her sister's wedding alone. No plus-one for Rose.

There had been no flirtations, no alluring glances and

no invitations back to her room. And this definitely was *her* room. She opened her eyes just a little to check.

Yes, there was her bright blue suitcase in the corner of the room. Thank goodness. She hadn't been so tired that she'd stumbled into the wrong room. Seb's house was so big it might have happened.

But it hadn't.

So, who was heavy breathing in her bed?

She didn't want to move. Didn't want to alert the intruder to the fact that she was awake. She could feel the dip in the bed at her back. Turning around and coming face-to-face with a perfect stranger wasn't in her plans.

She needed to think about this carefully.

She edged her leg towards the side of the bed. Stealth mode. Then, cringed. No satin negligee. No pyjamas. Just the underwear she'd had on under her bridesmaid dress that was lying in a crumpled heap at the bottom of the bed. Brilliant. Just brilliant.

Her painted toenails mocked her. As did her obligatory fake tan. Vulnerable. That was how she felt. And Rose Huntingdon-Cross didn't take kindly to anyone who made her feel like that.

Just then the stranger moved. A hand slid over her skin around her hip and settled on her stomach. She stifled a yelp as her breath caught in her throat. Something resembling a comfortable moan came from behind her as the stranger decided to cuddle in closer. The sensation of an unidentified warm body next to hers was more than she could take.

She slid her legs and body as silently as possible out of the bed. The only thing close to hand that could resemble a weapon was a large pink vase. Her heart was thudding against her chest. How dared someone creep into bed with her and grope her?

She held her breath as her feet came into contact with the soft carpet and she automatically grasped the vase in both hands.

She spun around to face the intruder. In other circumstances, this would be comical. But, right now, it felt anything but comical. She was practically naked and a strange man had crept into bed beside her. How dared he?

Who on earth was he? She didn't recognise him at all. But the wedding of an earl and a celebrity couple's daughter was full of people she couldn't even take a guess at. Undoubtedly he was some hanger-on.

If her rational head were in place she would grab her clothes and run from the room, getting someone to come and help with the intruder.

But Rose hated being thought of as a shrinking violet. For once, she wanted to sort things for herself.

She padded around to the other side of the bed in her bare feet, hoisting the vase above her head just as the stranger gave a little contented moan.

It was all she needed to give her a burst of unforgiving adrenaline. The initial fear rapidly turned to anger and she brought the vase down without a second thought. 'Who do you think you are? What are you doing in my bed? How dare you touch me?' she screamed.

The vase shattered into a million pieces. The guy's eyes shot open and in one movement he was on his feet—fists raised and swaying.

He blinked for a few seconds—big, bright blue eyes with a darker rim that didn't look the least bit predatory, but a whole lot shell-shocked—then dropped his fists and clutched his head.

'Violet, what on earth are you doing? Are you crazy?' He groaned and swayed again, one of his hands reaching out to grab the wall—leaving a bloodstained mark on the expensive wallpaper.

She couldn't breathe. Her heart was thudding against her chest and her stomach was doing crazy flip-flops. 'What do you mean, *Violet*? I'm not Violet.'

This just wasn't possible. Okay, Violet was her identical twin. They didn't usually look so similar, but a few years stateside and not seeing each other on a daily basis meant she'd shown up with an identical hairstyle to her sister.

This clown actually thought he was in bed with her sister? What kind of a fool did that?

He was still shaking his head. It was almost as if his vision hadn't quite come into focus. 'But of course you're Violet,' he said.

'No. I'm not. And stop dripping blood on the carpet!'

They both stared down at the probably priceless carpet that had two large blood drips, and the remnants of the vase at his feet and across the bed.

He grabbed his shirt from the chair next to the bed and pressed it to his head. It was the first time she'd even noticed his clothes—discarded in the same manner as her yellow and white bridesmaid dress.

His eyes seemed to come into focus and he stepped forward, reaching one hand out to her shoulder. He squinted. 'Darn it. You're not Violet, are you? You haven't got her mole on your shoulder.'

His finger came into contact with her skin and she jumped back. One part of her knew that this 'intruder' wasn't any danger to her. But another part of her was still mad about being mistaken for her twin and being felt up by her twin's boyfriend. How on earth could this be explained? This guy was obviously another one of Violet's losers.

Violet burst through the door. 'What's going on? Rose,

are you okay?' Her eyes darted from one to the other. The guy, in his wrinkled boxer shorts and shirt pressed to his forehead, and Rose, in her bridesmaid underwear. The broken vase seemed to completely pass her by.

She wrinkled her nose in disgust and shook her head. 'Will? My sister? Oh, tell me you didn't?'

They didn't sound like words of jealousy—just words of pure exasperation.

She threw her hands in the air and spun around, muttering under her breath. 'Runaway groom my sister and I'll kill you.'

Rose was feeling decidedly exposed. The only thing she could find to hold in front of herself was her crumpled bridesmaid dress.

Whoever he was, he obviously wasn't Violet's boyfriend—not with that kind of reaction. But did that make things better or worse? She'd still been groped by an absolute stranger.

He wobbled again and sagged down into the chair strewn with his clothes, arching one eyebrow at her. 'So, crazy twin. Do you assault every man you meet?'

'Only every man who climbs into my bed uninvited and cops a feel!'

'Well, lucky them.' He sounded oh, so unimpressed. Then he frowned. 'Did I touch you? I'm sorry. I was sleeping. I didn't even realise I'd done that.'

The blood was starting to soak through his shirt. She cringed. Maybe the vase had been a bit over the top. And at least she'd got some kind of apology.

She stepped forward and took the shirt from his hand. 'Here, let me.' She pressed down firmly on his forehead.

'Youch! Take it easy.'

She shook her head. 'The forehead's a very vascular

area. It bleeds easily and needs a bit of pressure to get the bleeding to stop.'

'How on earth would you know that?'

'Friends with children who seem to bang their foreheads against every piece of furniture I own.'

He gave her half a smile. It was the first time she really noticed how handsome he was. There were no flabby abs here. Just a whole load of nicely defined muscles. With those killer blue eyes and thick dark hair he was probably quite a hit with the ladies.

A prickle flooded over her skin. In the cold light of day this guy seemed vaguely familiar.

'How do you know Violet?' she asked.

He winced as she pressed a little harder. 'She's my best friend.'

Rose sucked in a deep breath. Things were starting to fall into place for her. Because she'd been working in New York she hadn't met Violet's best friend for the last few years. But she had heard a lot about him.

She pulled her hand back from his forehead. Now she understood what Violet had said. '*You're* the Runaway Groom?' She was so shocked she dropped her dress.

A single dark red drop of blood snaked down his forehead as he looked at her in disgust.

'I hate that nickname.'

The Runaway Groom. No wonder he looked vaguely familiar. He'd been on the front page of just about every newspaper in the world. Self-made millionaire Will Carter had been famously engaged three—or was it four?—times. He'd even made it down the aisle once before turning on his heel and bolting.

The press should hate him. But they didn't. They loved him and ate it up every time he fell in love and got engaged again. Because Will was handsome. Will was charming. And Will was sitting semi-naked in front of her.

She was trying so hard not to look at the abs and the scattering of dark hair that seemed to lead the eye in one direction.

She gave herself a mental shake just as a heavy drop of blood slid past his eye and down the side of his face. She leaned over to catch it with the shirt, just as he lifted his hand to try and brush it away.

The contact of their skin sent a tingle straight up her arm, making her heart rate do a strange pitter-patter. All the little hairs on her arms stood on end and she automatically sucked in her stomach.

'Look, I'm sorry about your head. But I woke up and there was a strange man in bed with me—then you touched me and I was frightened.' And she hated saying those words out loud but since she'd caused bodily harm to her sister's best friend it seemed warranted. She raised her eyebrows. 'You're lucky it was only a vase.'

His gaze was still on her. 'So you're Rose?' It wasn't really a question—more an observation and it was obvious from his expression that a million thoughts were currently spinning through his brain. What on earth had Violet told him about her?

He looked at the fragments beneath his feet and gave a half-smile. A cute little dimple appeared in one cheek. 'Oh, you're definitely not going to be Seb's favourite sister-in-law. At a rough guess that's over two hundred years old.'

A sick feeling passed over her. Defence was her automatic position. 'Who puts a two-hundred-year-old vase in a guest bedroom? He must be out of his mind.'

He shrugged. 'Your sister obviously doesn't think so. She just married him.'

Daisy, Rose's youngest sister, was still floating happily along on cloud two hundred and nine. And Seb seemed a really sweet guy. Just as well since she'd told her sisters just before the wedding that two were about to become three. The first baby in the family for more than twenty years. Rose couldn't wait to meet her niece or nephew, and she was doing her best to ignore the vaguest flicker of jealousy she'd felt when Daisy had told her.

She frowned. How much did a two-hundred-year-old vase cost anyway? She lifted the shirt again and winced. 'Hmm.'

His eyebrows shot up. 'What's "hmm"?'

'*Hmm* means it's deeper than it originally looked and I think you might need stitches. Maybe I can get you a packet of frozen peas from the kitchen?' She paused and looked around. 'Do you even know where the kitchen is in here?' Even as she said the words she almost laughed out loud. Seb's kitchen would probably spontaneously combust if someone even said the words 'frozen peas' in it. Daisy really had moved into a whole different world here.

He shook his head and placed his hand over hers. His hand was nice and warm, whereas hers was cold and clammy. Another thing to annoy her. He wasn't nearly as worked up as she was. This was all just another day in the life of the Runaway Groom. How often did he wake up next to a strange woman?

'What were you playing at anyway? You might be Violet's best friend but why on earth would you be climbing into bed with my sister? It's obvious from Violet's reaction that there's nothing going on between you. What on earth were you doing?'

Will gestured his head towards her suitcase. 'If I'm going to need stitches why don't you get dressed? You'll need to take me to the hospital.'

He hadn't answered her question. Did he think she hadn't noticed? Of course she had.

And the assumption that she'd take him to the hospital made her skin bristle.

All of a sudden she was conscious of her distinct lack of clothes. She slid her hand out from under his and moved over to her suitcase, cursing herself when she remembered he'd just had a big view of her backside.

Still, if he sometimes bunked in with Violet, then he was used to being around her sister in a semi-naked state. She glanced backwards. He didn't seem to have even noticed. Was she relieved or mad? She couldn't work it out. Apart from a few freckles, moles and little scars—one of which he'd already noted—she and her sister were virtually identical. Maybe that was why he wasn't looking? He'd seen it all before.

She grabbed a summer dress from her case and pulled it over her head. A little rumpled and yesterday's underwear still in place. Not the best scenario. But she didn't fancy fishing through her smalls to find a new set while he sat and watched in his jersey boxer shorts that left nothing to the imagination.

'Don't you have a bride in waiting that can take you to hospital?'

He scowled at her. 'Not even funny, Rose. You work in PR, don't you? Surely you know better than to believe everything you read in the papers?'

His words were dripping with sarcasm. The nerve she'd apparently just touched ran deep.

She folded her arms across her chest. 'But I thought most of the time you sold those stories and worked them in your favour.'

'What made you think that?' he snapped.

'Oh, I don't know. The ten-page photo spreads in *Ex-*

clusive magazine. How many of them have you featured in now?'

He gritted his teeth together. '*Not* my idea.'

It was good to see him uncomfortable. Waking up with a strange guy in your bed was horribly intimidating. To say nothing of the discomfort and embarrassment. What if she snored—or made strange noises in her sleep?

And he still hadn't answered the question about sleeping with her sister. What exactly was the deal? His eyes were still fixed furiously on her and the blood was soaking through his shirt. She decided to give him a little leeway.

She gestured towards him. 'What about you? You can't wear that shirt. Where are your clothes?'

He wrinkled his nose. 'I'm not sure. I ran in here at the last minute yesterday. I think my bag might be in Violet's room.'

'Violet's room?' She said it bluntly, hoping he'd take the hint and decide he should go there. But if he did, he ignored it.

'Yeah, would you mind running along and grabbing something for me?' He had that smile on his face. The one that was usually plastered all over the front page of a magazine, or on his face when he was charming some reporter. It was almost as if someone had flicked a little switch and he'd just fallen into his default position. His voice and smile washed over her like a warm summer's day. Boy, this guy was good. But she was determined not to fall for his charms.

'I will. But only because I've probably scarred you for life. I'm not Violet. I'm not your best friend—or your bed buddy. Once I've taken you to the hospital, we're done. Are we clear?'

His Mediterranean-sea-blue eyes lost all their warmth.

'Crystal.' He waited until she'd reached the door before he added, 'And you're right. You're not Violet.'

He watched her retreating back as she stomped out of the door. His head was definitely muggy and he wasn't quite sure if it was from the alcohol last night or the head injury this morning.

Part of him felt guilty, part of him felt enraged and part of him was cringing.

Last night was a bit of a blur. He'd just made it to the wedding on time and hadn't eaten a thing beforehand. His charity commitments were hectic and he was anxious not to let people down, which meant he'd been pulling on his tie and jacket in the sprawling car park at Hawksley Castle. A business call had come in just as dinner had arrived so he'd missed most of that, too. Then the party had truly started. And Violet had mentioned something about staying in her room as she'd fluttered past in her yellow and white bridesmaid dress.

A bridesmaid dress he'd definitely seen on the floor as he'd stumbled into the room. She'd been sleeping peacefully with her back to him and he hadn't even thought to wake her. Actually, he knew better. If he'd shaken Violet awake to let her know he was there she would have killed him with her bare hands.

Maybe the sisters had more in common than he thought?

It was strange. He'd never once considered Violet in a romantic sense. They'd clicked as friends from the start. Good friends. Nothing more. Nothing less.

He trusted her. Which was a lot more than he could say of some people. She gave it to him straight. There was no flirting, nothing ambiguous. Just plenty of laughs, plenty of support and plenty of ear bashing.

But Violet's identical twin… Well, she was a whole different story.

It didn't matter they looked so similar it was scary. They were two totally different people. No wonder they got annoyed when people mixed them up. And you couldn't get much more of a blunder than the one he'd just made.

But it wasn't the blunder that was fixating in his head. It was that little missing mole on her left shoulder. The memory of her skin beneath the palm of his hand. And the site of her tanned skin and rounded backside when she'd turned to get dressed. They seemed to have imprinted on his brain. Every time he squeezed his eyes shut, that was the picture he saw inside his head.

He stood up and walked over to the en suite bathroom. He grimaced when he saw his face. It was hardly a spectacular sight. His shirt—worn once—was ruined. Not that he couldn't afford to buy another one. But he'd picked this one up especially for the wedding. Even millionaires didn't like waste.

He stuck his head back out of the bathroom door. Maybe he should put his trousers back on? Meeting someone for the first time dressed only in jersey boxers was a bit much—even for him. But every time he lifted his hand from his forehead the blood started gushing again. Struggling into a crumpled pair of trousers one-handed was more than he could think about.

He couldn't help but smile. He knew Violet well. Her sister Rose? He didn't know her at all. This was their first meeting. And she obviously wasn't bowled over by him.

Will wasn't used to that. Women normally loved him. And he normally loved women. This was a whole new experience for him.

There was more to Rose Huntingdon-Cross than met the eye. And he'd already seen more than his fair share.

He could even forgive the Runaway Groom comments. Violet said her sister was a PR genius and she'd handled the whole publicity for their father's upcoming tour and charity concert.

Maybe he should get to know Rose a little better?

Rose strode down the hall. She could feel the fury building in her chest. The audacity of the guy. Who did he think he was?

She pushed open the door of her sister's room. 'Violet? What on earth is going on? Why would the Runaway Groom be in bed with me—and think I was you? Why would you be in bed with that guy? And why would there be touching?'

Violet was leaning back on her bed drinking tea, eating chocolate and reading a celebrity magazine. She lifted her eyebrows at her sister and started laughing. 'You didn't hook up with Will?'

'No! I didn't hook up with Will! I woke up and he was lying next to me. He thought I was you!'

Violet folded her arms across her chest and looked highly amused. 'He doesn't like the Runaway Groom tag.'

Rose rolled her eyes. 'So I gathered.'

Violet grinned. 'Will copped a feel?'

Rose shivered and waved her hand. 'Don't even bring that up.'

Violet shrugged and continued to drink her tea. 'So, it was a simple mistake. I'd say send him back along the corridor, but…' she paused and raised her eyebrows, giving Rose that oh, so knowing smile '…I'm thinking this looks a whole lot more interesting than that.'

'What's that supposed to mean?' Rose was getting mad now. Neither Violet nor Will was really giving anything away about their relationship and she couldn't understand why it irked her so much.

'Violet, come and take your plaything back. I don't have time for this. I've got a hundred things to sort out for Dad's tour. Another set of wedding rings to make for a couple who are getting married in two weeks. And a runaway groom who needs his head stitched. Be a good sister and take him to the hospital for me?'

Violet shook her head and jumped off the bed. 'Not a chance, dear sister. You caused the injury. You can try and make it up to Will. He can be very good company, I'll have you know.'

She gave Rose a little nod of approval. 'By the way, Daisy and Seb's wedding rings? Probably the nicest I've ever seen. That's what you should be doing. You're wasting your talent running Dad's tours for him.'

Rose sighed and sat down on the edge of the bed. A little surge of pride rushed through her chest. Violet's opinion mattered to her. 'Making those rings was the best thing I've ever done, Vi. I know I've made lots of different pieces for people before. But making something for your sister?' She smiled and gave her head a little shake. 'And watching the person she loves with her whole heart give it to her and knowing that she'll wear it for a lifetime? You just can't beat that.'

A flicker of something passed over Violet's face. Not annoyance. Not frustration. Just…something.

'I'll make your wedding jewellery for you, too,' she added quickly.

Violet let out a laugh. 'I'll need to find a groom first. In fact, we both do. Our baby sister's gone and beat us to it.'

Rose leaned backwards on the bed, propping herself up with her elbows. 'I know.' She lifted one hand up. 'And she's done it in such style. Do we really need to call her

Lady Holgate now, or Countess? Because I can tell you right now—' she shook her head '—it's never, *ever* going to happen.'

The two of them laughed out loud and collapsed back onto the bed. 'Daisy Waisy it stays.'

Rose turned her head to look at her sister, leaning over and picking up a strand of her blonde hair. 'You know, Vi, we almost look like twins,' she said sarcastically. 'We'll have to do something about these hairdos.'

Violet sighed. 'I know. I couldn't believe it when I saw you the other day. Maybe I'll go back to curls.'

'Don't you dare. That frizzy perm was the worst thing I've ever seen.'

Violet laughed and shook her head. 'Oh, no, the worst thing *I've* ever seen was you kissing Cal Ellerslie at that party years ago.'

Rose's shoulders started shaking with laughter and she shuddered. 'Oh, yuck, don't remind me. I still feel sick at the thought of that. He was all tongue. The guy had no idea what he was doing.'

She turned on her side and rested her head on her hand. 'Is there anyone you've been kissing lately?'

Violet sighed again. 'You're joking. There are absolutely no decent men around.'

'What about Will—your runaway groom?' She was prying and she knew it. But she couldn't help but ask the question out loud. Violet had been talking about Will for months. Maybe Rose just hadn't been paying enough attention.

But Violet's eyes widened. 'Are you joking—Will?' She let out a snort. 'No way. I mean, I love him to bits—just not like that. Never like that. I trust Will. Completely. I've been in his company lots of times, sometimes even raging drunk. He's a gentleman through and through. He's the kind of guy that sees you home, puts you to bed and stays with you until morning.' She wrinkled her nose. 'In fact, I've done the same for him. We're good company for each other.' She smiled. 'And every time he gets engaged, I get to buy a new wedding outfit with matching shoes and bag. What more could a girl want? Even if they never get an airing.'

Rose rolled her eyes. She knew better than most that Violet couldn't care less about wedding outfits, shoes and handbags. She was much more down-to-earth than most celebrities. They all were. 'Yeah, right.'

But Violet had drifted off. Her eyes were fixed on the ornately decorated ceiling, carved with cherubs. 'There's just no spark between us, Posey. None. Not even a little zing, a little tingle.' She turned her head to face her sister on the bed. 'You know what I mean?'

Oh, boy, did she. She'd felt that little tingle shoot up her arm like an electric shock. She blinked. Her sister was looking at her with her identical big blue eyes. They were unyielding. Their bond was strong. She'd always been able to see inside Rose's head—even when Rose didn't want her to.

Rose shifted uncomfortably on the bed. But Violet blinked. For once, she was lost in her own little world. 'I mean, there's got to be someone out there.' She regained her focus. 'For both of us,' she added quickly.

Rose smiled. It was the first time she'd ever seen her sister actually contemplate a future partner. Maybe the fact their younger sister, Daisy, had beat them both up the aisle and was going to be a mother had made their biological clocks start to tick. It was an interesting concept. And one she wasn't quite sure she was ready to explore.

Coming back to England had been hard enough. Visiting in the last three years had been painful. Everything seemed to be a reminder of that dreadful night a few years ago. The one that was imprinted on her brain like a painful branding.

But sisters were sisters. She couldn't really stay away too long. She still spoke to, Skyped or emailed her sisters every day. Not even an ocean—or a tragic death—could come between them.

But now her father's tour was coming back to Britain. It was big news for the band. A relaunch after a few quiet years—with only an annual charity concert—followed by a brand-new album. And she had to be here, in England, to deal with the last few PR issues. Her quietly building wedding jewellery business would have to be pushed to the side for a few months. She needed time to focus on the final details of the tour.

The last thing she needed was any distractions. And that was exactly what the Runaway Groom was—a distraction. Even if he did make her arm tingle.

Rose rolled off the bed. She hated that little feeling at the pit of her stomach. The one that had given a little flutter when her sister had assured her there was nothing between her and Will.

Nothing at all. Funny how those words were so strangely satisfying.

CHAPTER TWO

THE FROZEN PEAS were a godsend. It appeared that Hawksley Castle did have some—even though Rose had doubted. The lump on his head wasn't quite so big and, as long as he kept them pressed to his head, the bleeding stopped.

He'd managed to struggle into the T-shirt and jeans that Rose had brought from his bag in Violet's room. But instead of leaving him alone to get dressed, she'd leaned against the wall with her arms folded.

'What, no privacy?'

'From the guy who was in my bed? You lost the privacy privilege a while ago, mister. Anyway, hurry up. I've got things to do today.'

'Really? I would have thought after your sister's wedding you might want to chill out a bit.'

She crossed the room as he slid his feet into his training shoes. 'I'd like to have time to chill out, but I don't. I've got the final touches to make to my dad's tour, then I need to finish some jewellery for another bride.'

He looked up. 'Ready. Do you know where the nearest hospital is?'

She nodded. 'I know this area well. Let's go.'

They walked down the corridor and out of the front doors of Hawksley Castle. She opened the door of a pale blue Rolls-Royce and nodded at him to get in the other side.

Will couldn't hide the smile on his face as he slid into the cream leather seat. 'Didn't take you for this kind of car,' he said in amusement.

She started the engine and frowned at him. 'What kind of car did you think I'd drive?'

'Something sporty. Something small. Probably something red.' He looked thoughtful for a second. 'Probably one of those new-style Minis.' He wasn't revealing that his identical Rolls-Royce was parked a few cars down in the car park.

She pulled out of the car park and down the sweeping mile-long driveway. 'This is my dad's. You forget, I've been in New York for the last three years. There isn't much point in me having a car here right now, so I just borrow one when I'm home.'

'And he lets you?' Rick Cross's car collection was legendary. 'How many does he actually have?'

She laughed. And it was the first genuine laugh he'd heard from her. It was beautiful. Light and frivolous. Two things that Rose didn't really emanate. 'You mean, how many does Mum think he has—or how many does he *actually* have?'

Now Will started laughing. 'Really? How does he manage that? Where on earth can he hide cars from her?'

She shrugged. 'He's a master. We've got more than one home. You'll have seen the garages at Huntingdon Hall. There are eighteen cars there. Four in New York. Three in Mustique. And—' she glanced over her shoulder as if to check if someone was there '—another twelve at an unspecified location in London.'

'Another twelve? You've got to be joking.'

'I never joke about my father.' She shrugged. 'What can I say? It's his money. He can spend it how he likes. Same with my mother. They have beautiful homes, there might even have been the odd nip and tuck here and there, and to the outside world they seem like a pretty frivolous couple.'

He could hear the edge in her voice. Just as he'd heard the same tone in Violet's voice on a few occasions. He'd met Rick and Sherry. They seemed like regular, nice folks. Polite, well-mannered, and they obviously loved their daughters.

'So, what's the problem?'

Her head whipped around. 'Who said there was a problem?'

'You did. Just now.'

'I did not.'

He sighed. 'You and Violet are more alike than you think. She does that, too—starts talking about your parents and then starts to say strange things.'

'She does?' Her voice was a little squeaky and her knuckles turned white on the steering wheel. It was nothing to do with her driving. And nothing to do with the car.

The Rolls-Royce was eating up the country roads with ease. It should be a pleasant enough drive. But Rose looked tense.

'You must deal with the press all the time. Why does it annoy you when they describe your parents as frivolous?'

'Because they're not really. Not at heart. Yes, they spend money. But they also give a lot away. Lots of celebrities do. My mum and dad both support lots of charities.'

He nodded. 'Yeah, I remember. I've seen her in the magazines and doing TV interviews.'

'That's what you see. What you don't see is all the work they don't let the public know about. My dad does a lot of work for one of the Alzheimer's charities. He doesn't tell anyone about it. My mum works on a helpline for children. She sometimes does a twelve-hour shift and then goes out to do her other charity work.'

'That sounds great. So, why are you annoyed?' He couldn't understand why either of the sisters would be unhappy about their mum and dad doing good work.

'Because they are so insistent that no one finds out. Sometimes I think they're working themselves into the ground. To the world they seem quite frivolous. But they're not like that in person.'

'I don't get it. Why the big secret? What's the big deal?' His arm was beginning to ache from holding it against his head. He might be a millionaire himself, but even he didn't want to risk bleeding all over the inside of Rick's precious car.

Rose turned the car onto a main road, following signs toward the hospital. 'Because they don't want people to know. My uncle—my dad's brother—has Alzheimer's. He developed it really early. It's in my dad's family and he says it's private. He doesn't want people knowing that part of his life and invading my uncle's privacy. Mum's the same. She says the calls from the kids are all confidential. If people knew she worked there, the phone line would probably get a whole host of crank calls that would jam the lines.'

He nodded. 'I get it. Then, the kids that needed to, couldn't get through.'

She pulled into the hospital car park. 'Exactly.'

'So, your parents do something good.' He waited while she pulled into a parking space. 'I can relate to that.'

'You can?' She seemed surprised.

'Yeah. I do a lot of work for one of the homeless charities. But it doesn't get a lot of good publicity. It's something I need to think about.' He gave her a smile. 'Maybe you could give me some advice? You do PR for your father? Maybe you could tell me what I should be doing to raise the profile of the charity.'

She gave the slightest shake of her head. 'Sorry, Will, but this is it for me. I've got a hundred and one things to do in the next few weeks. I don't even know how long I'll be staying. Once your head is stitched I need to get back to work.'

He climbed out of the car, still pressing the now unfrozen peas to his head. Rose was intriguing him. He could use someone to give him PR advice. Someone who knew how to try and spin the press. Maybe he should try and persuade her?

The woman behind the desk didn't even blink when he appeared at the desk. 'Name?'

'Will Carter.'

She lifted her eyebrows and gave a half-smile. 'Oh, it's you. Did one of those brides finally give you the smack you deserved?'

He couldn't help but smile. 'No. I'm all out of brides at the moment—have been for a little while.' He glanced towards Rose, who was looking distinctly uncomfortable. 'It was just a friend who did this.'

A nurse walked towards them and the receptionist handed her a card. 'Will Carter, the Runaway Groom. Head injury.' She rolled her eyes. 'What a surprise.'

The nurse gave a little grin and nodded her head. 'This way.'

'Come on.' He followed the nurse down the corridor and gestured to Rose to follow them.

Her footsteps faltered. It was obvious she didn't really want to come along. But Will had just been hit by a brainwave. And a perfect way to make it work.

'I'll just sit in the waiting room,' she said quickly. She'd no wish to see Will Carter getting his head stitched. Even the thought of it made her feel a bit queasy.

'No, you won't.' His voice was smooth as silk. 'I want you with me.'

The nurse's eyebrows rose just a little as she pulled back the cubicle curtains. 'Climb up on the trolley, Mr Carter, and I'll go and get some supplies to clean your wound.'

She disappeared for a second while Rose stood shifting self-consciously on her feet, not quite sure where to put herself.

'What's wrong, Rose? Don't like hospitals?'

'What? No, I don't mind them. I just would have preferred to sit in the waiting room.'

He lifted the peas from his head. 'Don't you want to see the damage you've done?'

Her face paled. 'But I didn't mean to. I mean, you know that. And what did you expect? You climbed into bed with a perfect stranger.'

The nurse cleared her throat loudly as she wheeled the dressing trolley into the cubicle.

Rose felt the colour flood into her cheeks. Twenty-seven years old and she was feeling around five. 'I didn't mean… I mean, nothing happened…' She was stumbling over her words, her brain so full of embarrassment that she couldn't make sense to herself, let alone to anyone else.

The nurse waved her hand as she walked to the sink and started scrubbing her hands. 'Everything's confidential here. My lips are sealed.'

'But there's nothing to—'

Will was laughing. He leaned over and grabbed her hand. 'Leave it, Rose. You're just making things worse.' As he relaxed back against the trolley, his hand tugged her a little closer. There was a gleam of amusement in his eyes. Mr Charming wasn't flustered at all and it irked her.

'I kind of like seeing you like this.' Even his voice sounded amused. She'd never wanted out of somewhere so badly. She could practically hear the waiting room calling her name.

'Seeing me like what?' she snapped. The nurse had finished washing her hands and was opening a sterile pack and some equipment on the dressing trolley. She couldn't wipe the smile from her face.

Will's dimple appeared. 'You know—babbling. Violet doesn't get like this at all. It's quite nice to see you flapping around.'

'I'm not flapping around. This is all your fault anyway—and you know it.'

The nurse lifted the peas from Will's head and deposited them in the bin. 'Youch,' she said, pulling a head lamp a little closer. 'It looks as though you might have a tiny fragment in your wound. What caused your injury?'

'She did.'

'A vase.'

Their voices came out in unison. Rose was horrified. He'd just told the nurse this was her fault. The nurse's eyes flickered from one to the other. Thank goodness she was bound by confidentiality, otherwise this would appear all over the national press.

But she was the ultimate professional. She picked up some swabs and dipped them in the solution on the dressing trolley, along with a pair of tweezers. 'Brace yourself, Mr Carter. This is going to sting a bit. I'm going to give this a clean, then try and pry out the little piece of vase that is embedded in your wound. Five or six stitches should close this up fine.'

'Five or six?' Rose was beginning to feel light-headed. 'Can't you just use that glue stuff?'

The nurse shook her head. 'Not for this kind of wound. It's very deep. Stitches will give the best result—and hopefully the least amount of scarring.' She pulled up some liq-

uid into a syringe. 'I'm just going to give you an injection
to numb the area before we start.' Her experience showed.
The injection was finished in a few seconds. 'It will tingle
for a bit,' she warned. Her gaze shot from one to the other.
'I'm obliged to ask, but I take it from your tone this was
an accidental injury?'

Rose felt her cheeks flame. 'Absolutely.' She couldn't
get the words out quickly enough.

Will was watching Rose with those dark blue-rimmed
eyes. She saw a flicker of something behind his eyes. He
looked at the nurse with a remarkable amount of sincerity. 'Rose wouldn't normally hurt a fly. There's nothing to
worry about. So, you said I'll definitely have a scar, then?'

'Yes.' She nodded as she cleaned the wound. 'Think of
yourself as Harry Potter.' She gave a little laugh. 'I hear
he gets all the girls.'

Was it hot in here? Or had she just forgotten to put de-
odorant on this morning? It was getting uncomfortably
warm. She pulled her dress away from her body for a few
seconds to let the air circulate.

Will was still watching her as he continued his conversation with the nurse. 'Will it be a bad scar?'

Rose shifted on her feet. Boy, he was laying it on thick.
Stop talking about the scar. Guilt was flooding through
her. She'd just scarred a man for life. And it seemed as if
he'd talk about it for ever.

The nurse bent forward with her tweezers, then pulled
back. 'Here it is!' She dropped the microscopic piece of
vase on the dressing trolley. How on earth had she even
seen it?

She gave Will's head a final clean, then picked up the
stitching kit. 'This won't take long. I'll give you some instructions for the next few days.' She glanced towards
Rose. 'When the vase hit you—were you knocked out?'

'No,' he said quickly. 'I was sleeping and, believe me, once the vase hit I was wide awake.'

Rose rolled her eyes and looked away. He was making a meal of this. It was clear the nurse was lapping up his Mr Charming act. And it was making her more than a little uncomfortable.

Because, like it or not, it was hard not to get pulled in. One look from those big eyes, along with the killer smile and dimple, was enough to make the average woman's knees turn to mush.

No wonder this guy got so much good press. Why on earth would he think he needed any help?

She fixed her eyes on the floor as the nurse started expertly stitching the wound. Will Carter, Runaway Groom would now have a scar above his left eyebrow. A scar that *she'd* caused. It was definitely making her feel a bit sick.

The stitches were over in a matter of minutes and then the nurse handed Will a set of head injury instructions. 'You shouldn't be on your own for the next twenty-four hours.' She gave Rose a smile. 'I'm assuming that won't be a problem?'

'What? You mean me? No. No, I can't. Will? I'm sure there must be someone who can keep you company for the next twenty-four hours.' A wave of panic was coming over her.

But Will shook his head, then lifted his hand towards his head. 'Ouch.'

The nurse moved forward again and looked back to Rose. 'This is why he really needs someone to be around him. There can be after-effects with a head injury. If you can't supervise he'll need to be admitted to hospital. Are you sure you can't help?'

Her tone was serious. It was obvious she was apportioning the blame at Rose's door. The words were stuck in her throat. And as the guilt swamped her she couldn't think of a single good reason to say no.

Will leaned forward a little. The tiniest movement. The nurse had her back to him with her hand on her hip. Will's face appeared through the gap at her elbow and he pointed to his head. 'Scarred for life,' he mouthed before giving her a wink.

The cheeky ratbag. He was trying to blackmail her. And she hated to admit it—but it was working.

'Fine.' She snatched the instructions from the nurse's hand. 'Anything else?'

The nurse switched on her automatic smile. 'Not at all.' She turned to Will. 'Pleasure to meet you, Mr Carter. Pay special attention to the instructions and—' she glanced at Rose '—I wish you well for the future.' She wheeled her dressing trolley out of the cubicle.

Rose was fuming. Half of her thought this was all his own fault, and half of her was wondering if the millionaire would sue her for personal damages. She'd heard of these things before. What if Will couldn't sell his next wedding to *Exclusive* magazine because of his scar?

What if he sold the story of how he got his scar instead? She groaned and leaned back against the wall.

'Rose, are you going to pass out? Sorry, I didn't think you were squeamish.'

She opened her eyes to face his broad chest. He'd made a miraculous recovery and was standing in front of her with his hand on her arm to steady her.

The irony wasn't lost on her. *She* was supposed to be looking after *him*—not the other way about.

He'd told her he needed help with publicity. Maybe she'd unwittingly played into his hands? Her brain started to spin.

Her head sagged back and hit against the cold hospital

wall. Her eyes sprang back open and he was staring right at her again.

How many women had he charmed with those blue eyes? And that killer dimple...

His arm slid around her shoulders. 'It's hot in here. Maybe you'll feel better if we get some fresh air.'

His body seemed to automatically steer hers along. Her feet walking in concordance with his, along the hospital corridor and back out to the car park. Her first reaction was to shake off his unwanted arm.

But something weird was happening. Her body seemed to enjoy being next to his. She seemed to fit well under his shoulder. In her simple sundress the touch of his arm across her shoulders was sending little currents to places that had been dormant for a while.

Twenty-four hours. That was how long she would have to be in his company.

Panic was starting to flood through her, pushing aside all the other confusing thoughts. This guy could charm the birds from the trees. She'd thought she'd be immune. But her body impulses were telling her differently.

As soon as the fresh air hit she wriggled free from under his arm. 'I'm fine.' She walked across the car park and jiggled her keys in her hand.

'We need to have some ground rules.'

He leaned against the Rolls-Royce. She could almost hear her father scream in her ear.

'What exactly might they be?' One eyebrow was raised. He probably couldn't raise the other. That part of his forehead would still be anaesthetised. Darn it. The guilty feelings were sneaking their way back in.

'I think when we get back to Hawksley Castle we should ask Violet to stay with you. After all, she knows you best. She'll know if you do anything out of character—like grope strange women.' She couldn't help but throw it in there. She waved the instructions at him. 'You know, anything that might mean you need to go back to hospital.' Now she was saying the words out loud they made perfect sense.

He waved his finger at her. 'Oh, no, you don't.'

'Don't what?'

'Try and get out of this.' He pointed to his forehead. 'You did this to me, Rose. It's your job to hang around to make sure I'm okay.'

He was so smooth. A mixture of treacle and syrup.

'Oh, stop it, Will. I'm not your typical girl. I'm not going to fall at your feet and expect a ring. And if you keep going the way you are I'll hit you again with the next vase I find. I've got things to do. I can't hang around Hawksley Castle.'

He smiled and opened the car door. 'Who said we were spending the next twenty-four hours at Hawksley Castle?'

She started as he climbed in. She pulled open the car door and slid in. 'What on earth do you mean? Of course we're going back to Hawksley Castle.'

He shook his head. 'I think both of us have overstayed our welcome. You've damaged one of Seb's precious heirlooms and I've probably put immovable stains on an ancient carpet and wall. I suggest we regroup and go somewhere else.'

She started the engine. 'Like where?'

'Like Gideon Hall.'

Gideon Hall. Will Carter's millionaire mansion. At least at Hawksley Castle she'd be surrounded by family and friends. There was safety in numbers. Being alone with Will Carter wasn't something she wanted to risk.

'Oh, no. I need to work, Will.'

'I can give you access to a phone and computer. What else do you need?'

'My jewellery equipment, my soldering iron, my casting machine. My yellow, white and rose gold. My precious stones. Do you have any of those at Gideon Hall?'

The confident grin fell from his face. 'You're serious about making the jewellery?'

His question annoyed her. 'Of course I am. Working for my dad is the day job. Working to make wedding jewellery? That's the job I actually want to do. I spend most of my nights working on jewellery for upcoming weddings. I have an order to make wedding rings for a bride and groom. I can't afford to take any time off.'

It was nice to see his unwavering confidence start to fail. It seemed Mr Charming hadn't thought of everything.

She sighed. 'If need be, we can collect our things from Seb's, then go back to my parents' place. If you've hung around with Violet long enough you must be familiar with it.'

He settled back in the chair. 'Do you have your equipment at your parents' house?'

She nodded. 'I have one set in New York, and one set here.'

'That's fine. We can move it to my house in the next hour. I'll get someone to help us.'

He pulled his phone from his pocket and started dialling. 'What? No. What on earth is wrong with you? I've said I'll hang around you for the next twenty-four hours. Isn't that enough?'

He turned to face her. 'Actually, no, it's not. I've got a meeting later on today with a potential investor for the homeless charity. It's taken for ever to set up and I don't want to miss it.'

'Can't you just change the venue?'

Will let out a long, slow puff of air and named a footballer her father had had a spat with a few months ago. 'How would your dad feel about him being in his house?'

She gulped. 'Wow. No. He'd probably blow a gasket. He hates the guy.' She frowned. 'Are you sure he's the right kind of guy to help your charity?' She was racking her brains. Her dad was a good judge of character. He could spot a fake at twenty paces and didn't hesitate to tell them. She was sure there was a good reason he didn't like this footballer—she just couldn't remember what it was.

Will still couldn't frown properly. It was kind of cute. 'I've no idea. I've never met him before. But he's well known and popular with sports fans. It's not so much about the money. It's the publicity I need help with. We need to get the homeless agenda on people's radars. They need to understand the reason people end up on the streets. It's not just because they're drunks, or drug addicts or can't hold down a job.'

She turned back into the grounds of Hawksley Castle. 'You're really serious about this, aren't you?'

'Of course I am. Why would you think I'm not?'

She bit her lip. 'What's in it for you? Why is a homeless charity your thing?'

It took him a few seconds to answer. 'I had a friend at university who ended up on the streets. I didn't know. He didn't ask anyone for help because he didn't want anyone to know the kind of trouble he was in. I found out later when someone tried to rob him and stabbed him in the process. The police found my details amongst his things.'

She pulled the car to a halt and turned to face him. 'Was he dead?'

Will shook his head. It was the first time she'd really seen complete sincerity on his face. No charm, no dimple, no killer smile. In a way, it made him all the more handsome even though she tried to push that thought from her brain.

'No. But Arral needed help. And there's a lot more people out there who need help, too.'

'So, you really want good PR to raise awareness and you think this footballer will give you it?'

He folded his arms across his chest. 'Is that scepticism I hear in your voice, Rose?'

She gave him a smile as she opened the door and took the key from the ignition. 'I just don't know if he's your best choice.'

Will climbed out next to her. 'Neither do I, but, right now, he's my only option. How long will it take you to grab your stuff?'

She shrugged. 'My clothes? Five minutes. What about my equipment?'

'I'll arrange for someone to go your parents' and pick it up. Do you want to drop by first?'

She nodded. 'It won't take long. Let me get my clothes and I'll meet you back here.'

Will was true to his word. There was a man with a van waiting outside her parents' house when they arrived. She took him around to her workshop and collected the things she'd need to start work later that night.

As she was collecting a few other items her father appeared. 'Oh, hi, Dad. I didn't expect you to be back yet. I thought you'd still be at Hawksley Castle.'

He smiled. 'Your mother and I came back an hour ago. We had a few things we wanted to discuss.'

Her mother appeared at her father's side, his arm slipping around her waist and resting on her hip. Sherry Huntingdon still had her model-girl looks and figure even though she was in her fifties.

Rose's father's face was a little more lived-in. Rock and roll did that to you. His hair was still longer than normal—he still loved the shaggy rock-star look.

Rose's stomach started to do little flip-flops. Her father's words were a bit ominous. He had a tendency to spring things on her. And it looked as if nothing was about to change.

Rick crossed the room and put his hand out towards Will. 'Will, aren't you hanging around with the wrong daughter?' There was an amused tone in his voice. 'And what happened to your head? Did one of those brides finally get you?' He threw back his head and let out a hearty laugh.

Rose cringed. How many times was Will going to hear those words?

But Will seemed unperturbed. 'Ask Rose—she was the one that socked me with a vase.'

'She what?' Rose's mother seemed shocked.

Rose waved her hand quickly. 'It was a misunderstanding. That's all. What did you come back to talk about, Dad?' She wanted to distract them before they asked too many questions.

Her mother and father turned and smiled at each other. There it was. That sappy look that they got sometimes. In a way it was nice. Still romantic. It was obvious to the world that they still loved each other.

It was just a tad embarrassing when it was your parents.

'Your mother and I have made a decision.'

'What kind of decision?' She had a bad feeling about this.

Both of them couldn't stop smiling and it was making her toes curl. She just knew this was going to be something big.

'After all the preparations for Daisy's wedding—and

the fact everything went so beautifully—your mother and I have decided to renew our wedding vows.'

'You have?' It was so not what she expected to hear.

Her mother put her hand on her father's chest. She was in that far-off place she went to when ideas started to float around her head. 'You know we never had a big wedding.' She turned to acknowledge Will. 'We ran away to Vegas and got married after only knowing each other for a weekend. I never really had the fancy dress, flowers or meal like Daisy had. So, we've decided to do it all again.'

Rick shrugged and smiled at Will. 'It might seem hasty, but believe me—' he smiled at his wife '—when you know, you just know.'

A thousand little centipedes had started to crawl over Rose's skin. She had a horrid feeling she knew exactly where this was going.

'It's a lovely idea. When were you thinking? Next year—after the tour is over?'

'Oh, no.' Rose's mother laughed. 'In a few weeks.'

'A few weeks!' She couldn't help but raise her voice. Will shot her a look, obviously trying to calm her. But he had no idea what was coming next. Rose did.

Sherry stepped forward. 'What's the problem? We have the perfect venue.' She spun around. 'Here. We just need a marquee for the grounds. And a caterer. And some flowers. And some dresses.' She turned to Rick and laughed. 'And a band!'

Rick stepped forward. 'It shouldn't be a problem. You can arrange all that in a few weeks, can't you, Rose? You do everything so perfectly. And you're just so organised. We couldn't possibly trust anyone else with something so important.' Her father stepped over and gave her a hug and dropped a kiss on her cheek. It was clear he was floating on the same love-swept cloud that her mother was.

'Me?' Her voice came out in a squeak as Will's eyes widened in shock.

Oh, now he understood. This was what she got for doing such a good job. She was the official PA for her father's band and her mother's career. With all the tour preparations she barely had time to sleep right now. But she loved her parents dearly so she let them think it was all effortless. Her parents had been so strong and so supportive when she'd needed them—even though she secretly felt she'd disappointed them. Their love and support was the only thing that had got her through. All she wanted to do was make them proud. If they were trusting her with something like this? It made her anxious to please them, to let them be confident in her choices, even if this was the last thing she needed.

Her father's voice was steady. 'You know just how hard your mother's been working recently. And what with planning Daisy's wedding, she's just exhausted. If you could do all this it would be a whole weight off our minds.'

The dopey smiles on her parents' faces were enough to melt her heart—even though it was fluttering frantically in her chest and her brain was going into overdrive.

Will seemed to pick up on her overwhelming sense of panic. He stepped forward. 'What a fantastic idea. But these things normally take a while to plan—don't you want to wait a while and get everything just right?'

It was a valiant attempt. But Rose knew exactly how this would go. Once her parents got an idea in their heads there was no changing their minds.

Rick gave a wave of his hand. 'Nonsense. It didn't take long to sort out Daisy's wedding, did it?' He gave Rose *that* look. The one he always did when she knew he meant business. Rick Cross had invented the word *determined*.

'I'm not sure, Dad. There's a lot to do, what with the tour and the charity concert and everything.'

His hand rested on her arm and he glanced in his wife's direction. 'Now, Rose. Let's give your mother the wedding she always deserved.'

The truth was he wasn't picking up her cues. He was too busy concentrating on the rapt expression on his wife's face. Anxiety was building in her stomach. If she could do this, maybe she could repay her parents for everything they'd done for her. When she'd been splashed over the press when her friend had died she couldn't have asked for better advocates or supporters. Family was everything.

She started to murmur out loud. 'But I know nothing about weddings. Receptions, marquees, dinners, dresses...'

Her mother smiled. 'Oh, honey. Leave the dress to me. I'm going to get the one I always wanted.' Her gaze locked with Rick's and it was clear they were lost in their own little world.

Rick waved his hand. 'Ask Daisy. She knows all about it.' He let out a little laugh. 'Or ask your friend. He's had his fair share of organising weddings.'

Her parents turned and drifted back out of the room, lost in conversation with each other. That was it. Decision made. And *everything* left to Rose.

Rose turned to face Will. Her tongue was stuck to the roof of her mouth. She'd kill for a cosmopolitan right now. Her mouth was so dry she couldn't even begin to form words. She'd been blindsided. By her parents.

Will was looking just as pale.

She lifted her hands. 'I... I...' But the words wouldn't come out. The only sound that did come out was a sob. All this work. Organising a wedding in a few weeks might be okay for some people. But some people weren't Rick Cross and Sherry Huntingdon. They'd have a spectacular guest list—who'd all come with their list of demands. Where on earth would she find the kind of caterer she'd need at short notice? Her parents were very picky about food.

And what was worse—already she wanted it to be perfect for them.

Her heart was thudding in her chest. The more she thought, the more she panicked. Her chest was tight. The air couldn't get in. It couldn't circulate. Tears sprang to her eyes.

Will stepped straight in front of her. 'Rose? Sit down. You're a terrible colour.' He pulled a chair over and pushed her down onto it, kneeling beside her. 'In fact, no. Put your head between your legs.'

The inside of his palm connected with the back of her head and pushed down. She didn't even have time to object.

The thudding started to slow. She wasn't quite so panicky. After a few seconds she finally managed to pull in a breath.

This was a nightmare. A big nightmare. She didn't have enough hours in the day to do what her parents wanted. But how on earth could she say no?

She lifted her head a little and a tear snaked down her cheek. She wiped it away quickly.

Will looked worried. 'There must be someone else who can organise this for them? What about your sisters? They can help? Or can't you hire someone?'

'To organise my own parents' renewal of vows? How, exactly, would that look?' She waved her hand. 'And Daisy might just have done it all but she's off on her honeymoon to Italy for the next two weeks. Violet knows as much about weddings as I do.' Her voice cracked as their gazes collided.

And something in her head went *ping*.

'Will, you have to help me.'

A furrow creased his brow. The anaesthetic had finally started to wear off. 'But isn't it supposed to be the other way? I wanted you to give me some advice about PR for my homeless charity.'

She straightened her shoulders and drew in a deep breath. Things were starting to clear in her head. She wasn't dumb. Only an hour ago Will Carter hadn't been above trying to blackmail her. Head injury or not—it was time for her to use the same tactics.

'Dad was right. You have the perfect skill set to help me out here. Help *us* out.'

Realisation started to dawn on him and he shook his head. 'Oh, no. Your dad wasn't being serious.' It was his turn to start to look panicked.

She smiled. This was starting to feel good. 'Oh, I think he was.'

She placed her hands on her hips as she stood up. Will was still kneeling by her chair. It was the first time she'd been head and shoulders above him. There was something empowering about this. She held out her hand towards him. This might be the only way out of this mess.

'Will Carter? If you want my help, then I want yours.' She could feel herself start to gain momentum.

'You can't be serious.'

'Oh, but I am. I help you and you help me.'

He stood up. 'Do what exactly?'

There was something good about the way he mirrored the same panicked expression she'd had a few minutes earlier.

She stretched her hand a little further. 'I help you with your PR. You help me with this crazy wedding renewal.'

He shook his head. 'I think you've got this all wrong. I only ever made it to one wedding. The rest never got anything like that far. Sure, I helped with some of the planning but that doesn't make me an expert. The label in the press—Runaway Groom—it doesn't really mean that. I've never even been a groom.' He was blustering, trying anything to get out of this. 'I don't even like weddings!' was his last try.

She pressed her lips together to stop herself from laughing out loud. She liked seeing him floundering around. Will Carter liked to be in control. Liked to be charming. She could almost feel the weight lift from her shoulders. This might even be the tiniest bit fun.

She smiled at him. 'Will Carter? I think you're about to be my new best friend.'

The Runaway Groom was starting to look a whole lot more interesting.

CHAPTER THREE

WILL WAS STARTING to freak.

What had started as a bit of flirting and curiosity was turning into something closely related to the things he normally fled from.

It didn't matter that this was someone else's wedding. Weddings were the *last* thing he wanted to get involved in.

Except, he'd said that before. Four times exactly.

And he always meant it. Right up until he met the next girl—the next love of his life—and things went spectacularly. The romance, the love, the inevitable engagement, the press and then the plans started.

Everything always started swimmingly. Beautiful, fairy-tale venues. Wonderful menus. Great bands.

Then, things started to get uncomfortable. Fights about meaningless crap. Colours, ties or cravats, kilts or suits. Sisters and mothers-in-law interfering in he didn't even know what.

Arguments about wedding vows, dresses—spectacular scenes about dresses having to be ordered eighteen months in advance and not arriving in time. Ridiculous costs for 'favours'—things that no one even cared about and everyone left lying on the dinner tables anyway.

Tantrums over cakes. Tantrums over cars.

And love dying somewhere along the process. But it

wasn't the wedding process that really did it for him. It was that feeling of *for ever*. That idea of being with one person for the rest of your life. Whenever his bride-to-be had started talking about wedding vows Will always felt an overwhelming sense of panic. And all of a sudden he wasn't so sure.

It didn't help that he knew his friend Arral's wife had walked out and left Arral when he'd lost his job. It had all contributed to Arral sinking into depression and ending up homeless. For better or worse. Someone to grow old with. The theory was great. But what if when the chips were down his potential bride-to-be decided she didn't want for ever any more?

He didn't really understand why, but as the wedding date drew nearer Will always had a massive case of cold feet. Actually, it wasn't cold feet. More like being encompassed by the iceberg that had sunk the *Titanic*.

The trouble with being a nice guy was that it was hard to realise when exactly to back out. Once, he'd got right to the main event, but had backed out in spectacular fashion, earning him the nickname the Runaway Groom.

Even now he winced and closed his eyes. His bride-to-be had sensed his doubts and made veiled threats about what she might do if he didn't turn up.

So, he'd turned up. And made sure when he left she was surrounded by family and friends—even if all the family and friends were about to do him a permanent injury.

Violet had a theory on all this. She said that he hadn't met the right girl yet. Once he had? Everything would fall into place. Everything would click and he wouldn't have any of these doubts and fears. But what did Violet know about all this?

'I'm not the guy for this,' he said quickly.

Rose seemed capable. From what Violet had told him

Rose ran her life like clockwork. She never missed a dead-line and made sure all those around her never missed one, too. He would only get in the way of someone like that.

Rose was standing in front of him. Her pale blue eyes fixed on his. 'Oh, yes, you are.' There was an edge to her voice. A determination he hadn't heard before.

But he recognised the trait. She was obviously her fa-ther's daughter.

'Oh, no, I'm not.'

Rose folded her arms across her chest. It was very un-fortunate. All it did was emphasise her breasts in her pale yellow sundress. He could hardly tear his eyes away.

'Will Carter, you are not going to leave me in this mess.'

It felt as if the room were crowding around him. The walls, slowly but surely pushing forward. Sort of the way he normally felt when he knew he had to run from a wed-ding. None of this was his making. None of this was his responsibility.

'This isn't anything to do with me, Rose. It's bad enough that you cracked me over the head and scarred me for life with some vase. Now, you're trying to force me to help with your parents' wedding plans. This is nothing to do with me. Nothing at all. I'm far too busy for this. I've got a hundred other things to do to get publicity for my homeless charity. That's where I need to focus my efforts right now. Not on some celebrity wedding.' He flicked his hand, and she narrowed her gaze.

She was mad. And not just a little.

'Don't you give me any of your crap.' She poked her finger into his chest. 'You slunk your way into my bed un-invited. You've forced me to be around you for the next twenty-four hours when I should be working. I'm good at my job, Will. I manage my commitments. But this? On top of everything else I've got to do? I know nothing about weddings. Nothing. Ask me to design the jewellery—fine. Ask me to do anything else? I don't have a clue.' She poked his chest again. 'Which is where you come in.'

She lifted her chin and gave him a smug smile. 'You want publicity for your homeless charity? Oh, I can get you publicity. I can get you publicity in ways you might never even have imagined. But it comes at a price.'

Boy, she could look fierce when she wanted to. He wondered whatever happened to any guy that crossed her. He could barely begin to imagine.

'Weddings give me cold sweats,' he said quickly.

'Weddings have you running for the hills,' she countered.

There was no way she was going to back down. He was beginning to regret virtually blackmailing her into coming back to his house for twenty-four hours. Somehow him doing the blackmailing didn't seem quite so bad as her doing it back.

That would teach him.

But something happened. Rose seemed to change tack. A smile appeared on her face and she reached over and rubbed his arm. 'This one won't require you to break out in a cold sweat, Will. You're safe. This is someone else's wedding you're organising—not your own.' The smile stayed fixed on her face. He had a sneaking suspicion she was used to getting her own way.

But something was burning away underneath. It didn't matter that the face was identical to his best friend's. The personality and actions were totally different. She even smelled different. And her scent was currently winding its way around his senses. Something fruity. Something raspberry.

She flicked her blonde hair over her shoulder and he got another waft. Shampoo. It must be her shampoo. Rose

Huntingdon-Cross was a knockout. And he was in danger of being bitten by her quirky charm. Her words had already captured his attention but the image in front of him and that enticing scent were in danger of doing much more.

He tried to focus. He needed PR for the homeless charity, he needed the rest of the world to understand why people ended up that way and help put in place things to prevent it.

'What exactly do you mean? Forget about the wedding stuff. Tell me about your PR ideas.'

She wagged her finger at him. 'Oh, no. Not yet. You have to earn the privilege of my PR expertise. You help me, and I'll help you.'

What mattered more to him? Giving some crazy recommendations for caterers or wedding cars—or raising the profile of the charity he supported? There was no question. Of course he could do this. It couldn't possibly take that long. Rose looked like the kind of girl who could make a decision quickly. With wedding planning that was half the battle. Maybe this wouldn't be as bad as he thought?

She was biting her lip now, obviously worried he wouldn't agree. Biting a pink, perfectly formed lip. Perfectly formed for kissing. It was the thing that finally tipped him. Rose looked vulnerable. And he was a sucker for damsels in distress. It had got him into a whole lot of trouble in the past and probably would in the future.

His impulses got the better of him. He reached forward and grabbed her hand. 'Right, you've got a deal. Now, let's go before your parents appear again and give you something else to do.'

'You'll help me? Really?' He could almost hear her sigh of relief. 'Fabulous!' She was practically skipping alongside him as they crossed the room.

What on earth was he getting into?

* * *

Her brain was spinning. The guys from Will's place had packed up her gear in their van. She'd run after her parents and tried to get them to answer a few basic questions—like a date. But that had been fruitless. Apparently everything was up to her. They just wanted to decide on the guests.

The journey in the car to Will's place had been brief while she'd scribbled frantic notes in her handy black planner. She didn't go anywhere without that baby. He'd spent most of his time on the phone talking business. Then they'd turned down a country road that seemed to go on and on for ever.

Then, all of a sudden they were driving alongside a dark blue lake with an island in the middle, all sitting in front of a huge country house. The driver pulled up outside and she turned to him as he pushed his phone back into his pocket.

'You own a lake? And an island?' Her jaw was practically bouncing off her knees. Rose had been lucky. She'd had a privileged background. She was used to country mansions and houses costing millions. Seb's castle had just about topped everything. But this place?

Wow. The house might not be so big. But the amount of land was enormous. Will Carter was sitting on a gold mine.

'You like?' He was smiling at her amazed expression as she climbed out of the car.

The wind had picked up a little and was making her dress flap around her. She stepped around the car and walked towards the lake. There was a wooden jetty with two expensive boats sitting next to it.

She shook her head. 'Violet never mentioned a lake, or an island.' She thought she knew her sister well. This was definitely the kind of thing she would normally mention.

Will walked up behind her, blocking the wind. Her first thought was relief. Her next was how close he was standing. The soft cotton of his T-shirt was brushing against her shoulder blades.

In any other set of circumstances she would step away. But for the first time in a long time, she didn't feel like that. She was comfortable around Will. They might have got off to a bad start but there was something safe about him. It didn't help that the driver had just magically disappeared.

And it was easier to think safe than sexy. Because that was the other thought circulating around in her brain.

Will Carter was more than a little handsome. He was tongue-hanging-out, drip-your-food-down-your-dress handsome.

'Violet was never that interested in the lake or the island. She wouldn't even let me take her over in the boat.' His deep voice, right next to her ear, made her start.

'Oh, sorry. Did I give you a fright?' His arm slid naturally to her hip, to stop her from swaying. And she didn't mind it there. She naturally turned her head towards his and gave her full attention to the dark blue rim around his paler blue eyes. It was unusual. It was almost mesmerising.

'No,' she murmured, giving the slightest shake of her head.

This was freaking her out. She could feel her heart miss a few beats as she made the association. Last time she'd paid this much attention to a man had been over three years ago.

Three years ago and a party. A party where she'd left her friend to her own devices—because she'd been distracted by that man. Her friend had made some bad decisions that night and paid the ultimate price. And Rose had spent the last three years in New York to get away from the fallout.

She'd still spoken to her sisters every day and had been back in England every year for their father's annual rock

concert, but she just hadn't stayed for long. It was easier
to avoid the same circle of friends and their whispers if
you weren't there to notice them.

But things were changing. It was looking as though a
move back to England was on the cards. The European
tour would need her close at hand. It would be just as easy
to do the rest of her work here as in New York. The annual rock concert was due to take place soon and as long
as she had equipment she could make her wedding jewellery anywhere.

'Rose?'

Will reached over and slid his hand in hers. 'Come on,
I'll take you over to the island.'

He gave her hand a little tug. Oh, no. There was a warm
feeling racing up her arm, making her heart rate do strange
things. Pitter-pattering and electric shock kind of things.

She was trying to be cool. She was trying so hard to
be cool. But his touch brought a natural smile to her face.
She couldn't stop the little edges of her mouth turning upwards. 'Sure,' she said as he pulled her towards the boat.

It was one of two moored on a little wooden jetty and
it certainly wasn't your old-fashioned rowing boat. It was
white and sleek with a small compact engine on the back.

He jumped down and held out his hand towards her
as the boat wobbled on the rippling surface of the water.

She leaned forward and hesitated a little. The step to the
boat was a little broader than normal; chances were she
would have to pull up her dress to make it across.

But it was almost as if Will read her mind. He reached
forward with his long arms, circled her waist and lifted
her across. He did it so quickly she didn't even have time
to think. Her feet touched the base of the boat as the momentum made it sway a little more.

'Sorry.' He smiled. 'Forgot about your dress. Don't want

to get a glimpse of anything I shouldn't.' He had that twinkle in his eye again—knowing full well he'd more or less glimpsed the full package this morning. *As had she.*

She sat down on one of the comfortable leather seats in the boat and shook her head. 'My grandmother would love you—but you're just full of it, aren't you? I often wondered if Mr Charming might be a journalist's daydream. I always wondered how you managed to stay on the good side of the media. But you're just every mother's dream, aren't you?'

He started the engine and laughed. 'I think I can name at least four mothers who don't like me that much at all.'

The boat moved easily across the peaceful lake. It really was perfect. A few swans were gathered at the other side and a few ducks squawked from the edges amongst the reeds.

Rose couldn't help but shake her head. 'I don't get it. I just don't. You must have known you didn't want to marry those girls. Why on earth would you leave it to the last minute? Who does that?'

He sat down next to her as he steered the boat. He wasn't as defensive as before. Maybe because they'd been around each other a bit longer. He'd seen the fix her parents had just left her with.

He sighed as the boat chugged across the water. 'I know. It's awful. And I don't mean to—I never do. And, to be fair, I've had bad press. I've only *actually* done it on the day once. It's just much more fun for the press to label me the Runaway Groom on every occasion. My problem is I always start to have doubts. Doubts that you can't say out loud without hurting the person you're with. The would-she-still-love-me-if-I'm-bankrupt? kind of doubts. Then, you start planning the wedding and the lovely woman you've fallen in love with is replaced by a raging, seething perfectionist.'

Rose laughed. 'What's wrong with that? Doesn't every bride want her day to be perfect? And don't most people have a few doubts in the lead-up to a wedding?'

But Will looked sad. 'But why does it all have to be about the details? Shouldn't it just be about two people in love getting married? Why does the wedding planning always turn into "this wedding has to be better than such and such's wedding"? I hate that.'

The words sent a little chill over her skin. He was right. More than he could ever know. She couldn't believe that the man the press called the Runaway Groom actually felt the same way she did.

'Why do you have doubts?' she asked quickly.

He paused and shrugged his shoulders. 'I'm not always sure. What I can tell you is that I don't regret calling off any of my weddings. I just regret the one time of being an actual runaway groom. At least two of my exes have since agreed that we should never have got married. They've met their perfect person and are happy now.'

Rose gave a sad kind of smile. 'Not every wedding is a disaster. Some couples are meant to be together. Daisy's wedding was fast, but she did plan everything she wanted. I might have been in New York but she emailed every day.' The island was getting closer, giving little hints of what lay beneath the copse of trees. She gave a little shudder. 'I'm not a fan of big weddings. I like small things. And I like the idea of two people, alone, agreeing to spend the rest of their lives together. Let's face it. That's what it's all about.' She smiled at Will. 'Just as well I'm not the bride. If it was a big, flamboyant wedding maybe I would steal your thunder and be the Runaway Bride?'

He leaned back a little in the boat as they neared the island's jetty. 'Really? A woman that wants a quiet wedding? Even after all the splendour of Daisy's?' He raised his eyebrows in disbelief. 'You don't want a little of that for yourself?'

'Absolutely not.' Her answer was definite.

He paused for a second. 'It really wasn't about the weddings. It was about the relationships. Once the initial happy buzz of being engaged vanished I started trying to picture myself growing old with that person. And no matter how hard I tried, I could never see it. I realised I didn't love them the way I should. The way a husband should love a wife—like your mum and dad.' He was gazing off onto the island and he suddenly realised what he'd said. Will Carter had probably revealed much more than he wanted to. He gave a little start and tried to change the subject quickly. 'Anyway, I don't believe you. I bet you want the big wedding just like every other girl.'

He stood up as the boat bumped the jetty and tied the mooring line securely. He jumped onto the wooden platform and she held out her hand to his. But Will seemed to think they'd set a precedent. He reached both arms down and caught her around the waist, lifting her up alongside him.

Her feet connected with the wooden structure but his hands didn't move from her waist. She was facing his chest, his head just above hers. Her hands lifted naturally to rest on his muscled biceps. The only noise was the quacking ducks and rippling water. She'd seen a little glimpse of the real Will Carter. Not the one in the media. Not Mr Charming. And she actually liked it. She would never admit it to anyone but he intrigued her. She smiled. 'No, I don't want any of that. What's more, I bet I could outrun you, Will Carter.' Her voice was quiet, almost a whisper. It was just the two of them. And their position was so close it seemed almost intimate. She could feel his fingers spread a little on her waist—as if he were expanding his grip to stop her getting away.

The perfect smile appeared, quickly followed by his dimple. It was all she could do not to reach out and touch it. 'The Runaway Bride and the Runaway Groom? We could be quite a pair.' He left his words hanging in the air. Leaving them both to contemplate them.

Her breath was caught in her throat. Never. She was too young. Too stupid. She had too many plans. There was no room for someone like Will Carter in her life right now. Especially when she found it so hard to trust her instincts. Her stomach flipped over. He was joking. They both were. But she couldn't help but feel a little surge of confidence that he'd even suggested it.

She stepped back, breathing deeply and breaking the intimate atmosphere between them. 'What's on this island anyway?'

Something flitted across his eyes. Disappointment? She felt a tiny surge of annoyance. She'd no intention of being his next passing fling. He'd already admitted he fell in love too easily. Rose didn't have that problem. She'd never fallen in love at all.

Ever the gentleman, he gestured with his hand to the path ahead leading through some trees. She walked ahead of him and looked around. The thick, dark trees were deceiving. They were hiding more than she could ever have imagined.

Her hand came up to her mouth as they stepped out from the path to a red-brick stone church with a huge stained-glass window.

'A hidden church? You have got to be joking.'

'No.' He walked over and swung open the thick wooden door, flicking a switch. The sun was shining down through the dark copse of trees. The church was tiny, the window

almost taking up one whole wall. Only around twenty
people could fit in here along the four benches on each
side of the aisle.

The late afternoon sun was streaming through the window, sending a beautiful array of colours lighting up the
white walls. There was a dark wooden altar table at the
front. Nothing else.

'This place is amazing. You own a church?'

He nodded. 'There's an equally tiny cottage behind the
church. Both were ruins when I bought the place. I had
the church rebuilt and the stained-glass window put in.
The cottage was just refurbished.'

She spun around in the rainbow of lights. 'I love this
place. What was it originally?'

'No one really knows for sure. I think it was some kind
of retreat. There used to be a monastery on these grounds
right up until the dissolution of the monasteries in the fif-
teen-hundreds. This is the only thing that was left.'

Rose took a deep breath and walked over and touched
the white wall. 'Think of all the history here. Think of
all the things that could have happened between these
four walls over the centuries.' She walked over and gently
touched one of the pieces of stained red glass as she swept
her eyes over the scene in the window. 'What is this? Was
there something like this already here?'

'It's inspired by Troyes Cathedral in France. They have
some of the oldest medieval stained-glass windows. This is
two of the prophets, Moses and David.' He seemed genuinely interested in what he was telling her. It was obvious
a lot of thought—and a lot of expense—had gone into the
restoration work.

'You should get a grant of approval to do wedding cer-
emonies here.'

He shook his head. 'What? And have the bride fall out

of the boat on the way over? This lake might look pretty, but, I can assure you, it's dark and murky at the bottom.'

She laughed and stepped closer. 'Words from a man that sounds like he fell in.'

'I did. I came out like a creature from the black lagoon.'

She held out her hands. 'So what do you use this place for?' She finally felt as if she was getting to know Will a little better. He might be Mr Charming for the press but he was also a nice guy. He was easier to be around than she'd first experienced. Violet wasn't known for her poor judgement. She should have trusted her sister.

He waved her forward. 'Come and I'll show you.'

They walked outside and behind the church to a white-washed cottage with black paint around the windows and a black door. He pushed it open and showed her inside.

It was tiny, but spectacular. Almost every part was in view. An open modern kitchen at one end, a sitting area in the middle and a platform with a king-sized bed. There was even a smoky glass bricked wall, which hid the wash-hand basin and toilet, but the roll-top bath was placed in front of one of the two windows.

'You bathe at the window!' Rose's mouth dropped open.

Will grinned. 'It's all private. If someone is staying here, the island is all theirs. No one else can set foot on the place. Total privacy. People like that.'

It was just the way he said the words. They were happy, nonchalant. But as they left his mouth she tried to picture who would want to get away from everything. There was no obvious TV, no phone and she doubted there would be an Internet signal.

'Who comes here, Will? Do you hire it out?'

He shook his head. 'Never. This place is for friends. For people who need a little time, a little space.'

She tilted her head to the side. She'd heard of places

like this. One of the members of her dad's band had taken himself off to a mountain retreat a few years ago after numerous visits to rehab clinics. She sucked in a breath. Was this the kind of place she should have gone three years ago after her friend had died from the drug overdose?

This place was a sanctuary. A private hideaway from the world outside. It was perfect.

'Like your friend who was homeless?'

He was fighting an internal battle that played out on his tightly composed features. He gave a brief nod.

'I love it,' she whispered. 'I hope the people that come here find what they need.'

Will's hands appeared at her waist. She hadn't even realised he'd moved close to her. He exhaled sharply and she could feel his muscles relax behind her. 'That's so nice to hear you say. And it's why I don't bring people here—don't advertise the fact there's anything on this island.'

He was trusting her. He was trusting her not to say anything to the world outside. Something inside her chest fluttered.

All of a sudden she had a real awareness of the big bed on the platform behind her. It looked sumptuous. It looked inviting. They were here alone, on an island that no one else could reach. They wouldn't be disturbed.

'You don't bring people here?'

He shook his head. 'Never.' His voice was low, husky. It was sending blood racing through her veins.

Her head was swimming. She was crazy. She'd just met this guy. He might be her sister's best friend but she hardly knew him at all. Trouble was, everything she did know she liked.

Her hands rested on the warm skin of his muscled arms again, feeling the tickle of tiny hairs under the palms of her hands.

'Then why me?' Her throat felt scratchy. She was almost afraid to breathe.

Before she knew what she was doing she lifted one hand and touched his rumpled, slightly too long hair. With his dimple and killer blue eyes all he needed was a white coat and he could easily replace that actor from the lastest TV hospital show.

His head tilted slightly towards her hand as she ran her fingers through his hair, holding her breath. What on earth was she doing?

Her mouth was dry and she had a strong urge for some of the leftover wine from her sister's wedding. Last night she'd just been too exhausted to have even more than two glasses.

Will didn't seem to object to her touch. He responded instantly, stepping forward and firming his gentle grip on her waist. His face was only inches from hers. She could feel his breath on her cheek. She could see the tiny, almost invisible freckles on the bridge of his nose, the tiny lines around his eyes. Her mouth was wet and she ran her tongue across her lips. They tingled. All the pores of her skin lifted up in a soft carpet of goosebumps, each hair on her body standing up and tingling at the roots. She'd never experienced anything like this before.

He didn't bring people here—but he'd brought her. What did that mean? She had absolutely no idea.

'I thought you might like it. Might appreciate it the way others wouldn't. I was right.'

Her head was telling her to back away, to break their gaze and step out of his hold. Her brain was befuddled. She'd learned not to trust her instincts. She'd learned to question everything. But Will moved forward, the hard planes of his chest and abdomen pressing against her breasts, his hands sliding downward and tilting her pelvis towards his.

His words were like a drug. As an independent woman Rose had never craved a man's approval before. But suddenly Will Carter liking her, respecting her, seemed like the most important thing on earth.

This was it. Enough. It was time to step away. This man had led enough women on a merry dance. She wasn't about to be the next.

But her body wasn't listening to her brain.

Neither of them had spoken for the last few seconds. Any minute now he'd step away and she'd feel like a fool. She was sleep deprived—that was what was wrong.

Even though she'd gone to bed at midnight and slept soundly until this morning she was still on New York time. It was making her do strange things. It was making her act in ways that she wouldn't normally.

Will blinked. His gaze was hypnotic. She couldn't pull herself away. She didn't want to—no matter what her brain said.

'I don't just like it,' she whispered. 'I love it.' It was true. This place felt safe. Felt private. Like a complete and utter haven where two people could suspend disbelief and do anything they wanted.

She moistened her lips as his gaze lowered to her mouth.

He reached up a finger and brushed a strand of hair away from her face. His touch like butterfly wings on her skin. She bit her swollen lips. As he moved forward his scent enveloped her. Pure and utter pheromones. She couldn't get enough of them.

It was her last thought as Will Carter's lips came into contact with hers.

CHAPTER FOUR

FOR A FEW seconds he was lost. Lost in the smell of her. Lost in the taste of her. And lost in the surge of hormones that were rushing around his body.

He was engulfed in the wave of restless energy floating through the air between them, colliding like seismic waves. Someplace, somewhere the Richter scale was measuring the magnitude between them.

It was great. *She* was great. His hands skirted over her curves, his fingers brushing against her silky skin. A groan escaped from the back of his throat as every body part acted accordingly.

Then, from out of nowhere, a voice echoed in his head. *Runaway groom my sister and I'll kill you.*

It brought him back to his senses, back to reality. Violet would kill him. There was no doubt.

He stepped back, leaving Rose's lips mid-kiss and her eyes still shut. She was frozen for the tiniest of seconds in that position before her startled eyes opened.

He was trying to catch his ragged breath. Trying not to still taste her on his lips.

Their gazes collided and he saw a million things flash through her eyes. Confusion. Embarrassment. Lust.

He lifted his hands and shook his head. 'Rose, I'm so sorry. I should never have done that. I just...I just...'

He couldn't find the words—probably because his brain was completely scrambled. He walked over to the edge of the bed and sat down, running his fingers through his hair. The same motion that she'd been doing only seconds earlier.

Bad idea. Very bad idea. She looked even more confused now. He threw up his hands. 'It's this place. Here, and the church.' She still hadn't said a word. But the expression on her face was killing him. Violet really would kill him if her sister told her about this.

'I never meant for this to happen. I didn't plan it.'

'Obviously.' It was her first word and it was as cold as ice. The beautiful ambient temperature had just dropped by about twenty degrees.

'No. That's not what I mean. You're beautiful. You're more than beautiful. And your smell. And your curves. I just…'

The initial glare disappeared and the corners of her mouth started to turn upwards. His babbling must be amusing her. But he couldn't help it. He always got like this when he'd blundered. Why say three words when you could say twenty?

She stepped forward so that the fabric of her dress was almost touching his nose. It was swaying gently. He was trying not to think what was underneath. Or about the feel of her skin.

She sighed. 'Will, do I make you nervous?' He couldn't miss the hint of amusement in her voice.

He looked up. She was close, oh, so close. Her scent was there again.

'Yes…I mean no. Well, maybe.'

She folded her arms across her chest. 'How about we just file this away somewhere? You're Violet's best friend and…' she raised her eyebrows '…you have just about the worst reputation on the planet. I'm never going to get involved with a guy like you.'

'You're not?' He couldn't help it. Defence was the instant reaction to her words. What was so wrong with him anyway? Okay, he might have been engaged a few times but he was a good guy. Really, he was.

She was definitely smiling now. He should be relieved. He should be thankful. So why was he feeling a little insulted?

'No. I'm definitely not.' She turned and walked over to the window. 'Why don't we just chalk this up to a moment of madness? I need you to help me with the wedding stuff. You need me to help with your publicity. We can do this, can't we? We can spend the next few weeks around each other and forget that this ever happened.'

It wasn't a question. It was a statement of fact. She was right. He knew she was right. But Will had never had problems getting a woman before. Rose telling him outright *no* was a bit of a revelation for him.

He stood up and touched his head. She was trying to brush this off. The easiest thing in the world to do was let her. 'Why don't we just pin it down to my head injury?' He was teasing her. Hinting that she'd caused the whole thing.

But Rose was far too quick for him. She laughed. 'Are you trying to make out I've taken advantage of the person I'm supposed to be looking after? What does that make me?'

'A ruthless businesswoman.'

She smiled. She seemed to like that, then something flitted across her eyes and she glanced at her watch. 'Will? Weren't you supposed to have a business meeting this afternoon?'

Recognition flooded through him. 'Oh, no. What time is it? Darn it.'

She shook her head and opened the door. 'We've got five minutes. We can make it in that time, can't we?'

'Let's run.' He grabbed her hand as he jogged past and pulled the door closed behind them. It only took a minute to run along the path to the boat and he started the engine quickly. Rose didn't wait to be helped into the boat. She lifted her skirt up, giving him a complete flash of her bronzed legs as she jumped over the gap between the jetty and the boat. The boat rocked furiously as she landed and he grabbed her around the waist and pushed her into one of the seats.

The boat crossed the water in a few minutes. This meeting was important. He had to make it on time. But his eyes kept skimming across to Rose. Her blonde hair was streaking behind her in the wind and her yellow dress outlined her curves again.

He groaned. How on earth was he going to manage the next few weeks?

The football player was every bit as sleazy as she remembered. He'd practically sneered once Will had introduced her and he'd clicked about who her father was. But Rose couldn't have cared less. She'd work to do.

Her jewellery equipment had arrived and with the help of two of Will's staff she'd set it up quickly and spent a few hours putting the finishing touches to the two wedding rings.

'Rose, are you in here?'

She looked up from giving the rings a final polish. Will crossed the room in a few steps, smiling as usual. 'I see you managed to get things set up. How's it going?'

She held up the rings encased in their black velvet boxes. 'I've just finished. The courier will be here to pick them up in the next hour. What do you think?'

He bent forward and moved her Anglepoise light to get a better look at the intricate mix of rose and yellow gold for the bride's ring, and solid white gold for the groom's. She could see the flicker of surprise on his face.

'Rose, these are beautiful. You made these from scratch? Yourself? How on earth did you know where to start?'

She sighed and leaned back. 'Did you think I was pretending to make jewellery?'

He shook his head, obviously realising his mistake. 'No, I didn't mean it like that, it's just…' Then he stopped. And smiled. And sat down next to her.

'How do you do that to me?'

She couldn't help but grin. She knew exactly what was coming but she put on her most innocent expression. 'Do what, exactly?'

He shrugged his shoulders. 'Make me start babbling like some teenage boy. I always seem to say the wrong thing around you, then can't find the words to straighten things out.'

She raised her eyebrows. 'I thought you said I didn't make you nervous.'

He frowned. 'Well, you don't. But then—you do.' He flung up his hands. 'See, I don't know.'

She laughed. 'How did your business meeting go with El Creepo?'

His mouth fell open and his shoulders started shaking. 'El Creepo? That's what you're calling him?'

She nodded sombrely and folded her arms. 'I think it suits him.'

'I think you might be right.' He ran his fingers through his hair, carefully avoiding his stitched forehead. Guilt surged through her again. It had to be sore, but he hadn't complained at all. 'But at the moment he's the best bet I've got. You're right. There's just something about him I can't put my finger on. But if it's the only way to raise publicity then what choice do I have?'

Sitting in such close proximity to Will, she could see the tiny lines around his eyes and on his forehead. He was genuinely worried about this. He was genuinely trying to do some good. How far would he go?

She bit her lip. 'I might have some alternative ideas about that.'

'For the publicity?'

'Yes.' She rubbed her hands on her dress. It was warm in this room. Her soldering equipment gave out a lot of heat, which only made it worse. And she couldn't wait to actually hit the shower and change her clothes.

'Tell me more.'

She shook her head. 'Not yet, and you still have to hold your side of the bargain.' She stood up. 'I want to get changed and have a shower but I don't have any of my things.'

He looked a little sheepish. 'Actually you do. Violet sent your bright blue case over. I take it you'll have everything you need in there? Why don't you freshen up and we can have some dinner?'

Violet had sent her case over? Just like that? Just wait until she spoke to her sister. She'd better not be trying to matchmake.

She gave a little nod of her head just as Will's eyes twinkled and his smile broadened to reveal his dimples. Darn it. Those were the last things she needed to see right now.

'Now, I'm only showing you to a room in my house if you promise not to cause any damage.'

He was waiting for her at the door. 'Do you keep any ancient vases in your rooms?' she quipped.

'Not in yours,' he countered.

'Any unidentified men crawling into bed with perfect strangers?'

His gaze met hers. 'Only if requested.'

Her breath caught in her throat as her skin prickled involuntarily. Oh, boy, he was good. She had to keep remembering just how many times this guy had been attached. Still, dinner at Gideon Hall might actually be quite nice. Rose was as nosey as the next person and always liked to see around beautiful homes.

Will led her up the large curved staircase and along a corridor. Everything was sparkling. Everything was clean. Everything was cream.

He swung open the door of one room and she stepped inside. Finally, a tiny bit of colour. Pale yellow to complement the cream. It was gorgeous. She couldn't help but walk straight across to touch the ornate curtains. Curtains and soft furnishings had always been her weakness. It was like something from one of those classy house magazines. An enormous bed with soft bedding and cushions that just invited you to dive in, pale yellow wallpaper with tiny flowers, a pale yellow carpet and light-coloured furniture all leading to large windows looking over the gardens.

'These are beautiful. The whole place is beautiful.' She smiled wickedly. 'Which one of your brides-to-be helped you decorate?'

'Actually, some of it I chose myself. Others, I had some help from professionals.' He straightened a little more and his chest puffed out. He was obviously pleased with the backhanded compliment.

'Really?' She was surprised. She'd just imagined that he'd waved his hand and asked someone else to sort all this out for him.

'Yes, really. Why does that seem strange?'

'It just does, that's all.'

'It's strange that a guy is interested in how his home looks?'

She paused. When he said it out loud it didn't seem so strange. She just couldn't imagine Will Carter sitting with a dozen sample books and picking wallpaper and soft furnishings.

She walked over and stuck her head into the white bathroom with pale yellow towels. Everything matching perfectly. 'Okay, maybe not.'

He gave a little nod. As if he was pleased he'd won the argument. 'How about I leave you to freshen up and we meet downstairs later for dinner?' He hesitated. 'Is there anything you don't like? Any allergies?'

She shook her head. 'I'll let you into a secret. I'm a simple girl. Chicken is my favourite no matter what you do to it.'

He looked relieved. 'I can definitely do chicken.' He glanced towards the window again. 'How do you feel about sitting outside? We could have dinner on the patio overlooking the gardens and the lake.'

Her insides gave a little flutter. This was starting to sound a lot more like a date than a business meeting. And even though it was wrong—even though she'd already told Will he would never be for her—it was still flattering.

The last few years had been hard. She wasn't the party girl she'd been before. She'd been used to flirting and high-speed dating. As soon as she'd bored of one guy, she'd moved on to the next—none of them serious.

But everything had changed after Autumn's death. They'd been friends for a few years and had liked socialising together. When Rose had left the party with the man of the moment she'd assumed Autumn was fine, too. An assumption that was completely wrong. She'd been foolish. And partly to blame. Even though Rose had never dabbled with drugs herself she'd known that Autumn did so on occasion. But Autumn was independent and strong-willed. Telling her not to do something was practically impossible. But the guilt Rose felt was still overwhelming. If she'd been there, she would have noticed Autumn was unwell. Her friend wouldn't have been found slumped in a corner and not breathing. She could have called an ambulance and intervened.

Instead a few hours later she'd heard her dad's scratchy voice on the phone demanding to know where she was and if she was okay. Rose had known straight away something was wrong. Her parents were very liberal and once the girls had reached the age of twenty-one they could pretty much do what they wanted. By the grand old age of twenty-four she should have known so much better. She'd never forgotten the look on his face as she'd pulled up in a taxi outside Huntingdon Hall. He'd been standing in the doorway watching for her while her mother was sitting inside waiting to tell her the news.

Drug deaths were always good media fodder. And Rose had found herself the unwitting angle for every story.

Pop star's daughter at drug party.

Wild child Rose Huntingdon-Cross's friend dies of drug overdose.

After the funeral she hadn't been able to get out of the country quick enough. Dealing with PR was the last thing she'd wanted to do. But it went hand in hand with the job for her dad's band. She'd learned who to talk to, who to ignore and who to threaten to sue. All valuable skills in this life.

Skills she was going to exploit to help Will Carter get what he wanted. She only hoped he'd listen to reason when she explained what she wanted to do. She smiled at him. 'Dinner outside would be lovely. Thanks. Give me an hour to get changed.'

He gave a little nod of his head and walked out, closing

the door behind him. Leaving Rose staring out over the lake towards the island. She ran her hands up and down her arms. There was something about that place. Something magical. Something mystical. And there was no way she was ever setting foot there again with Will Carter.

Violet's sister. Violet's sister. He muttered the words under his breath all along the length of the corridor. If he kept reminding himself that he'd put the relationship with his best friend at risk if he ventured too near, he might actually convince himself.

He had to do something, because right now his head was full of *that kiss.*

The softness of her hair, the silkiness of her skin, the taste of her lips. Enough.

He had to stop this. Violet had warned him, and she almost knew him better than he knew himself. She knew he fell head over heels with the next beautiful woman to come along—suitable or not. And Rose was definitely *not* suitable.

But Rose wasn't like any of the others. He'd never felt compelled to take any of his fiancées to the island—none of them had ever shown much interest.

And none of them had ever had the same expression in their eyes that Rose had when he'd shown her into her room. It wasn't anything to do with wealth or prosperity; it was to do with making a house a home. Rose appreciated that. And he appreciated her because of it.

He walked down the wide staircase and into the kitchen where Judy, his housekeeper and chef all rolled into one, was waiting. 'What'll it be?' She smiled.

'Chicken. Do whatever you like with it, as long as it's chicken.'

She nodded. 'Well, that's easy. Do you want some dessert, too?'

Darn it. He hadn't even thought to ask. But Judy was used to him.

'How about some fresh fruit pavlova? I made some earlier for that grump of a football player but he didn't want any.'

Will gave a sigh of relief. 'Perfect.' He took a quick look around the kitchen. As usual everything was gleaming. The staff who worked here really took their jobs seriously. He was lucky to have them.

Judy started pulling ingredients from the huge fridge. 'So, who is our guest, then? Anybody I should know?'

He shook his head quickly. 'It's nobody. It's just Violet's sister.'

Judy looked interested. 'Rose? I've heard Violet talk about her a lot but I've never met her before. Are they alike?'

He paused, not quite sure how to answer. Violet had never made the blood race back through his veins as Rose had. 'They look alike, but they're totally different people,' he said quickly. It seemed the simplest enough answer.

Judy gave a little nod of her head as she started slicing vegetables on a wooden board. 'I'll look forward to meeting her, then. Dinner will be ready in about forty minutes. Just give me a shout when you're ready.' She gave Will a little wink and he cringed. She always did that.

It was almost as if she could read his mind and see what he was really thinking.

Business. That was what this was. And if he kept that in his head he'd do fine. Weddings. He tried to stop the shiver going down his spine at the mere thought of it. He could write a list. That was what he'd do. He'd change his shirt, then write a list for Rose of the things she'd need to plan.

Anything to keep him on track.

* * *

Rose was used to luxury. Their family home certainly didn't scrimp on anything. Hawksley Castle had been something else entirely. But this place—Gideon Hall— added a whole new dimension.

It wasn't quite as big as Huntingdon Hall but it had more land—more space. And Will's taste was surprisingly good. The furnishings were comfortable but stylish. It had a show-home look about it, while still giving that you-could-actually-live-here feel.

She finished drying her hair and opened her suitcase to find some more clothes. It didn't take long. Clean underwear and a bright blue knee-length jersey dress. Even though the sun wasn't quite so high in the sky it was still hot outside and the last thing she wanted to do round about Will Carter was feel hot and bothered.

She gave a quick squirt of perfume, spent two minutes putting on some make-up and stuck on some flat, comfortable gold sandals. Done.

By the time she walked down the main staircase at Gideon Hall she was feeling like a new woman. It was amazing what a shower and change of clothes could do for a girl. Will was standing at the door to the huge kitchen. 'Rose, come and meet Judy. She's made dinner for us.'

Rose came into the kitchen and held her hand out towards Judy. 'It's a pleasure to meet you. I hope you haven't gone to too much trouble for us.'

Judy beamed and shook her hand swiftly. 'You're so much like your sister. It's amazing. Do you ever get mistaken for each other?'

Will could see the tiniest flicker of something in Rose's face. She'd probably heard this for the best part of her twenty-seven years. And from most of the pictures he'd seen of Violet and Rose they normally tried to look a bit different—a bit more individual.

Rose touched her long, straight hair. 'We look alike more by default than anything deliberate. I've been in the States for the last few years. Violet and I always tried something different. I would be shorter, she would be longer. I would go lighter, she'd go darker. I'd be curls, she'd be straight. You get the picture.' She shrugged her shoulders. She fingered a lock of her blonde hair. 'I'll really need to do something with this.'

'Don't you dare.' The words were out before he knew it and both heads turned towards him with startled expressions on their faces. He gulped and let out his best attempt at a laugh. 'Oh, I was just joking. Will we have some wine? What would you prefer—white or red?'

'White, sparkling if you have any.' Both women exchanged an amused glance as Will felt himself bluster around the kitchen. Where was the darn sparkling wine when he needed it?

Judy pulled the chicken from the oven and the smell of bubbling chicken stock, tomatoes and spicy peppers swamped the kitchen. 'That smells great,' said Rose. 'Is there anything I can do to help?'

Judy waved her hand. 'Not at all. Give me two minutes and I'll plate up for you, then you can take it outside. The cutlery and napkins are already there.'

He finally managed to find a chilled bottle of wine and popped the cork before grabbing a couple of glasses. Rose stood waiting with two plates of piping hot food in her hands. 'Lead the way, Mr Carter, and I hope you're prepared for this business meeting we're about to have.'

He couldn't help but smile as he led her through the house and out through the wide open doors at the dining room. The table was positioned on the patio overlooking the gardens and lake. It only took a few moments to pour the wine and he sat across from her and raised his glass.

'To interesting bed companions.'

She grinned and clinked his glass. 'To things that go bump in the morning.'

This was such a bad idea. She knew it from the second they clinked glasses and she let the cold sparkling wine slide down her throat. How many times had he done this before? Had a woman sit with him overlooking the gardens for dinner? The house was spectacular. Judy's cooking was brilliant. And Will was looking at her with that twinkle in his eyes...

He pulled out a piece of paper from his back pocket. 'Here. I've made you a list.'

'A list of what?' She spun the paper around and looked at the printed list with the bold heading of Wedding Arrangements. She bit the inside of her cheek to stop herself from laughing. 'What? You have a ready-made template just sitting, waiting for use?'

His brow wrinkled and he waved his fork at her. 'Enough. If you want my help, you're going to have to stop with all the wedding jokes. I thought you might want it for that black planner of yours.'

She tilted her head to one side as she lifted her glass towards him. 'You're such a spoilsport.'

He lifted his hand to his head and feigned a flinch. 'I think I've already suffered quite enough at your hands.'

'How long are you going to keep this up?'

He couldn't hide his smirk. 'Let's see. Stitches come out in seven days—at least that long.'

'If I find another vase, I'm hitting you again.'

He leaned across the table towards her and hit her with his million-watt grin. 'Oh, go on, Rose, play fair.'

She couldn't help but laugh. Even when he was annoying, Will Carter was still alarmingly cute. And handsome. And sexy.

She took a final bite of the chicken and glanced down at the list. 'Why do some of these have ticks?'

Will leaned back in his chair and started counting off on his fingers. 'Rose, you've no idea how easy you've got it. The biggest thing—the venue. Your parents have already said they want to do it at Huntingdon Hall. Easy.' He gave a little shrug. 'You really need to check numbers though. You'll need to ensure you get a big enough marquee for the grounds.'

She gulped. A marquee. Where on earth was she going to find one of those, big enough to accommodate wedding guests and available in less than four weeks just as they were coming into summer? She lifted her glass. 'I think I'm going to need some more wine. What else?'

He kept counting on his fingers. 'Wedding photographer you've got. Why would you use anyone but Daisy?'

She nodded. 'But what about the pics we want Daisy to be in?'

'Doesn't she have an assistant?'

Rose racked her brain. 'I'm not sure. I'll need to ask.'

Will continued. 'As for the flowers, it goes without saying that Violet will do them. Even if it does mean getting up to go to some flower market at three a.m.'

Rose nodded. Violet would be able to conjure up whatever concoction her mother wanted for the day. Sherry had a tendency to like beautiful, bright and exotic flowers rather than the quiet-style flowers she'd named her daughters after.

'So what does that leave?'

Will took a sip of wine. 'Band, celebrant—or whoever they want to say their vows to—caterers, décor, wedding favours, drinks and bar.' He wrinkled his nose. 'Will you need a children's entertainer? Or a nanny for the guests' kids? Cars?' He waved his hand. 'No, they're getting married at home.'

Rose felt her stomach start to lurch. He was saying this was easy, but it sounded anything but. 'I have a horrible feeling that both Mum and Dad will want to make an entrance. They'll probably leave by the back door and come back up the drive for the wedding in front of the guests.'

'So you will need cars?'

She picked up the pen sitting on the table and drew a thick black line through the word *Cars*. 'Absolutely not. With what I know is sitting in Dad's garages? Between what Mum knows about, and what she doesn't, there will definitely be enough for her to pick something she likes to come up the driveway in. Surely it's not that big a deal?'

Will let out a laugh. 'Oh, you've got so much to learn in so little time.' His hand came casually across the table and touched hers. 'Are you really ready for this?'

In an instant her tongue was sticking to the roof of her mouth, the inside so dry a camel could be marching through it. A dozen little centipedes had just invaded her body and were racing their way up the inside of her arm and directly to her fluttering heart. It was a warm evening. She wasn't the least bit cold. But the heat currently shooting up her arm could light up this whole mansion house.

What on earth was wrong with her? She'd been on lots of dates. She'd had a few relationships. But she'd never felt any of the old thunderbolts and lightning. She'd always thought that was nonsense.

But it seemed as if her body was trying to tell her something else entirely.

When she'd got ready earlier she hadn't really been that concerned about what she was wearing or how she looked.

But all of a sudden it felt as if her dress might be a little too clingy, a little too revealing. She could sense his eyes on her curves, following the slope of her hips and swell of her breasts. She sat up a little straighter.

Her brain kept trying to temper her body's responses. *Runaway Groom. He's the Runaway Groom. He's absolutely, definitely* not *for you.*

Was she ready for all this? Not a chance.

Will wasn't quite sure what was happening. He'd virtually face-planted himself into his last four relationships and engagements. He'd been swept along with the early joy and the passion.

But this was something else entirely.

All he wanted to do was reach across the table and grab her and kiss her. It didn't help that the world was plotting against him and the sun had started to dip slightly in the sky, silhouetting her figure and perfect blonde hair on her shoulders. Or, more importantly, highlighting her silky skin and waiting-to-be-kissed lips.

It was automatic. The thought made him lick his lips and he could swear he could still taste her from earlier. He pulled his hands back from hers and lifted the wine glass to his lips. Empty. Darn it. It seemed as if both of them had inexplicably dry mouths.

He made an attempt to focus on the list. *Out of bounds.* He had to keep saying it over and over in his head.

His eyes scanned down the list of wedding items. There. That would stop him. Nothing like a list of wedding to-dos to temper his libido.

'What about catering? Do you have anyone in mind?'

Rose visibly jerked in her chair. It was as if her brain had been circling in the same clouds as his. At least that was what he was hoping.

She groaned. 'Oh, no. That will be a nightmare. Mum and Dad are so fussy about food.'

'You can't pull any special favours?'

She shook her head. 'I've already pulled special favours for the tour. And that was only to cater for five members of the band. We don't even know how many people they're inviting yet but I can guarantee you—it won't be five.'

Will frowned. 'It's such short notice. I hate to say it but you might need to take what you can get.'

'Oh, don't say that.' Rose put her head on the table, her blonde hair flicking up dramatically behind her. He smiled. She might appear calm on the surface but when the moment occurred it appeared that Rose could do drama.

He frowned. 'There's a conference on Monday at the Newbridge Auditorium. It's for businesses but there are always lots of caterers in attendance, trying to tout for business at events.'

She lifted her head just a little from the table. He could only see one eye beneath the long locks. 'Catering for a business event isn't even in the same league as catering for a wedding.'

He arched his eyebrow at her. 'You'd be surprised. Some of these events have cordon bleu chefs. Again—numbers might be an issue. And you'll need to have some idea of a menu. Do you know what they like?'

'That's easy. Mum likes chicken and Dad will want steak with all the trimmings. But it has to taste just right.'

'Like mother, like daughter?'

She straightened in her chair. 'Yeah, I guess so. Though in most things I'm most like my dad.' She picked up a pencil. 'Dessert will need to be something chocolate for Mum—usually with orange—and anything with strawberries or raspberries for Dad.'

She screwed up her nose as she studied the list. 'Balloons, seat covers, wedding gifts, evening favours, wedding cake, hors d'oeuvres, and a bar.' Her head thumped back on the table. 'I can't do all this!'

Will reached over and grabbed her hand, this time propelling her from her chair and pulling her towards him. She barely had time to think about it before he plunked her down on his knee and wrapped his arm around her waist. 'I'm helping you. That's what the deal is. By Monday night we will have a caterer. By Tuesday we'll have sorted the chair covers, balloons and favours. If you pay enough you can pretty much get what you want.'

He stood up and turned her around in his arms, reaching up to touch her cheek, trying not to drink in the feel of her. 'Rose, stop worrying. I've already told you—the biggest things are sorted.' Her hands had moved automatically to his waist, her fingers gently pressing through his shirt. He wanted them to move. He wanted to feel them stroke across the expanse of his back and shoulders. He wanted to feel them running up the planes of his chest and wrap around his neck. If they could just move a little closer...

She was staring up at him with those big blue eyes. It made his breath catch in his throat. She'd never looked so beautiful. And for a second he was sure she was looking at him exactly the way that he was looking at her.

But then she blinked. And it was as if something had just flicked on in her brain. 'Yes, because you know all about this stuff, don't you?' Her hands fell from his sides and she took a step back.

What had just happened?

He gave himself an internal shake. 'Okay. Sit down. I'll go and get some of Judy's pavlova for us and some coffee. Then you can tell me all about your PR ideas for my homeless charity. Fair's fair.'

He picked up the plates and gave her a smile as he headed back inside. It only took a few minutes to be out of her sight and he stopped and pressed his head against the cool corridor wall. What was he thinking?

He was going to have to put a No Touching sign on her head.

Because if he didn't—he'd get himself into a whole load of trouble.

The pavlova looked magnificent, with lots of layers of gooey meringue, lashings of fresh cream and oodles of strawberries, raspberries and kiwi fruit. A girl might think she was in heaven. That, followed by the smell of rich coffee, was making her already full stomach think it might have to squeeze a little more inside.

She was ready. She was prepared. She'd taken the few moments of Will's absence to gather herself. A quick dash to the bathroom and a splash of water on her face and wrists had cooled her down. Technically speaking. It hadn't stopped that crazy irregular pattern inside her chest that she was trying to ignore.

Now, she was in control. And Will was back to his amiable, joking self. No more hot looks of what might be. No lingering glances or widening pupils.

'So what's the plan for PR?'

His voice sounded so calm, so laid-back. Now was the time to find out if he really was.

She savoured the last mouthful of pavlova and set down her fork. Her words were simple and she said them as if they were the most obvious thing in the world. 'The plan, Will—is you.'

He wrinkled his nose. 'What?'

She waved her hand. 'I didn't know you were associated with that homeless charity until you told me. And then I asked myself why. Because you've had more than enough media coverage in your time.'

He gave a shake of his head. 'But that was all the wedding stuff. It was all personal. It doesn't really count.'

She shook her head and leaned towards him. He really didn't get it. 'But that's just it, Will. *You're* the story. *You're* the person people want to read about. People love you. Your reputation as the Runaway Groom precedes you and it's time to use it to your advantage.'

The frown seemed to be spreading across his face. 'No. I don't agree. I hate all that stuff. How on earth can being known as the Runaway Groom help a homeless charity?'

She took a deep breath. It was obvious he was going to take some persuading. 'You've seen all the TV shows with phone-in voting?'

He nodded warily. 'Yes, all the wannabe pop-star stuff?'

'Exactly. They often have the same things in newspapers. Vote for your favourite TV soap star. Vote for your favourite model.'

He was nodding slowly. 'I still don't get it. What does that have to do with me?'

She gave him her best PR smile. 'We're going to do something similar with you.'

He was shaking his head again. 'Why on earth would anyone vote for me?'

Rose sucked in a deep breath and talked quickly. 'People love the fact you were the Runaway Groom. Imagine we had a number of trials or dares for you to do. All hideous. All things that people would cringe at. We can ask the public to vote on which of them you should do for the homeless charity—earning money and raising awareness along the way.'

'But why on earth would people be interested in that?'

This was it. This was when she finally revealed her master stroke.

'Because there'll be four separate possibilities. All set by each of your jilted brides.'

'What?'

Rose jumped in quickly before he had too much time to think about it. 'Just think about it. I bet some of them still want revenge on you. They'll probably take great pleasure in making a hideous suggestion for a dare. And I can spin it. From what you've told me, each one of your brides-to-be were interested in being in the media. If I pitch it to them as an opportunity to take a bit of revenge on you—plus the fact the money will be going to charity *and* you'll have to do whatever the winning dare is—I'm sure they'll take part. What's more the press will eat it up.'

Will's head had been shaking from the second she started speaking. His face wasn't pale as if he were shocked—it was starting to go red as if she'd made him angry. 'You have got to be joking. *This? This* is your plan?'

She shifted in her chair. 'If you'll just take a minute to consider it…'

He stood up sharply and his chair flew backwards. 'Take a minute? Take a minute to consider humiliating myself in front of millions? Have people talk about me instead of the charity? I'd be a laughing stock.'

Rose stayed as cool as she could. She lifted her coffee cup and took a sip as if guys shouting at her happened every day. In New York it wasn't that unusual and she was made of sterner stuff.

'Yes, you would,' she said simply. 'But people would be interested to know why you were doing it. Why the world's most eligible bachelor would put himself through it. That would lead them to the homeless charity.'

His fists were clenched and pressing down on the table.

She could see the flicker of an angry tic in his jaw. But after a few moments his breathing seemed to ease and the flush in his face died down. Rose sat quietly, sipping her coffee and looking out over the view.

This was the perfect solution to his PR problems. It had come to her earlier on and she'd known he wouldn't like it. But if he was as committed to the charity as he claimed to be, he'd realise just how much this could work.

He glanced behind him and grimaced as he picked up the chair. After a few seconds he sat back down and put his head in his hands.

Patience. Men had to be left to think things through. In a few days Will Carter would probably be claiming the idea was his own. Or maybe not.

He lifted his head slightly, his deep blue eyes locking on hers. 'You really think this could work?'

She nodded slowly. 'I think it's a darn sight better idea than dealing with El Creepo footballer. You know he's a recipe for disaster.'

Will groaned and leaned back in the chair. 'I know he is. But people like him. Even if he is a prat.'

She smiled at him. 'No, Will. People like *you*.' She let the words hang in the air for a second or two.

He was still looking sceptical. 'Do you honestly think you could persuade my exes to take part?'

She bit her lip. 'If I pitch it right they will be jumping all over this. There's nothing like a woman scorned.'

He grimaced. 'But I never wanted to hurt any of them. And this will just bring all those bad feelings to the surface again.'

'And some of those bad feelings are exactly what we need. Those bad feelings will probably give us some spectacular dares that the public will be willing to pick up the phone and vote for.'

She hated that it sounded so mercenary. It wasn't really Rose's nature but the reality was, if Will really wanted publicity for his charity in a short space of time this was exactly the way to do it.

He started pacing. She could almost see his brain ticking over all the pros and cons.

'I'm still worried. Two of my exes will probably be fine. They've moved on. They've got married. Both of them have told me they were glad things didn't work out between us.' He waved his hand and gave a rueful smile. 'They know we just weren't right for each other. And they've got their happy ever after with someone else.' He frowned. 'Another has got into the media spotlight. The extra publicity will probably suit her. Looking back, I'm sure that's why she dated me in the first place. But the fourth? I just don't know...'

'Is this the one you actually left at the altar?'

He nodded and shook his head. 'Melissa was fiancée number two. I still feel terrible. She didn't take things well and she still hates me.'

'Might this be a little redemption for her? A way to draw a line under things?'

'I just don't know.' He pulled out his phone.

'What are you doing?'

'I'm going to talk to Violet.'

For the weirdest reason her heart plummeted. 'You are?' How ridiculous. Violet was his best friend. Of course he wanted to talk to her. It was only natural.

But it made her stomach curl up in the strangest way.

A way she'd never felt before.

She'd never once been jealous of her sister. They were close. They always supported each other. They'd never had a serious falling-out. Only the usual sisterly spats. But all of a sudden she was feeling strangely jealous of the relationship between Violet and Will. He trusted her. He valued her opinion. And it was almost as if he were second-guessing her advice.

The call lasted only a minute and there was nothing secret about it. She could hear Violet's shrieks of laughter at the other end of the phone. 'It's perfect. The press will love it. I told you my sister was a genius!'

Guilt flooded through her, heat rushing to her cheeks. Violet always had her back, always—even in the worst of circumstances.

Will glanced at her, uncertainty still lacing his eyes. She held her tongue. There was nothing she could say at this point to persuade him. He had to think it through for himself. There was only one natural conclusion he could come to.

She stood up and held out her hand. 'Thank you for a lovely evening, Will. I'm feeling tired. I think I'll go to bed. I take it you've got no ill effects from your headache and I'll be free to go home tomorrow?'

He stared at her outstretched hand for a few seconds. Maybe it was the strange formality between two people who'd kissed a little earlier? But he took a few steps and walked over and shook her hand.

Darn it. There it was again. The little shot straight up her arm, tingling all the way. No matter how many times she tried to ignore it, it wasn't a figment of her imagination. His hand was warm and firm.

It was the first time she'd been around Will and he looked anything less than confident and sure of himself. Her suggestions for publicity had obviously unsettled him.

'Thank you, Rose,' he said distractedly.

She turned away to head back in the house. It was odd. The strangest feeling. She'd much preferred it when the atmosphere between them had been light and flirty. This horrible unsettled feeling was uncomfortable. As much as she didn't want to admit it, being around Will Carter was a lot more interesting than she'd first expected.

Her head told her one thing, and every female hormone in her body told her a whole other. It was exhausting.

But she was curious to see where it would take her.

'Rose?' She turned at the sound of his voice, her heart giving a little leap in her chest.

'Remember Monday—the business conference. We'll find you a caterer.'

'Sure.' She nodded, hoping to not let the disappointment show. 'Thanks.'

She turned back and lengthened her strides back into the house.

Monday had never felt so far away.

CHAPTER FIVE

VIOLET AND ROSE waited impatiently on the chaise longue. Their mother was doing her usual—making them wait. 'Do you have your phone to text Daisy?' Violet asked.

'No pictures,' yelled their mother from the other room. 'I don't want there to be any possibility of a leak to the press.'

The girls rolled their eyes at each other. Sherry had already tried on eleven dresses from various designer friends ranging from barely there to tulle princess. None of them had really suited. 'Has she given you any instructions on the flowers yet?' Rose whispered.

Violet nodded. 'And I'm sworn to secrecy. I've not to say a word.'

'But you can tell me.'

Violet shook her head. 'Not even you.'

Rose felt the indignation rise in her chest. 'You've got to be joking. After everything that's been dumped on me— you're not allowed to tell me about the flowers?'

Violet shrugged. She was entirely used to their mother's little quibbles and obviously didn't think it was worth getting tied in a knot about.

She shot Rose a look. That kind of look. 'So how's things with you and my best friend?'

Rose could feel the hackles rise at the back of her neck. She was instantly on the defensive. 'What do you mean?'

'Have you kissed him yet?'

'What? Why on earth did you ask me that?'

Violet counted off on her fingers. 'Because he's Will Carter. He's charming. He's lovable. And everyone loves him.' She lifted her eyebrows. 'And you two haven't met before. And don't think I didn't notice the little buzz of chemistry yesterday. What's going on?'

Rose was annoyed. 'Chemistry? There was no chemistry. The guy climbed into my bed and I cracked him over the head with a vase. How is that chemistry?'

'But you spent all day yesterday with him *and* you spent the night at his place.'

If only she knew that Rose had spent the whole night tossing and turning in the bed at Gideon Hall wondering— even for a second—if Will might appear. Useless thoughts. Ridiculous thoughts. And thoughts that had made her even angrier and made her feel even more foolish as the dark hours of night had turned into the early hours of morning.

'Nothing happened. Absolutely nothing. You know exactly why I had to stay there—because *you* wouldn't help me.'

Violet gave a few tuts. 'Wow. I think the girl protests too much,' she joked. 'Watch out. He'll sucker you in.'

Rose sucked in a deep breath, ready to erupt at her sister but she didn't get that far.

'What about this one?' Their mother's voice cracked a little as they turned to face her.

Sherry Huntingdon had never lost her model figure or her mane of golden locks. She easily looked fifteen years younger than she actually was.

Rose gasped and lifted her hand to her mouth. 'Oh, Mum, that's it. That's the one. It's perfect.'

Violet was on her feet, walking over to touch the ruched fabric scattered with tiny jewels. The dress was a showstopper. It hugged every curve of her frame, fitting like a glove in satin covered in tiny sparkling jewels with a huge fishtail.

'You think?' Yes, her voice was definitely breaking. It was all getting too much for her. It was the perfect dress for the perfect wedding.

'I love it, Mum,' said Rose with pride. Her mother had never looked quite so stunning as she did today.

'Veil or no veil?'

'No veil.' Both girls spoke in unison, then turned to each other and laughed.

Their mum hesitated a second. 'I've picked a dress for all three of you. You just need to pick a colour each.' She held up a bright blue dress on a hanger. It had sheer shoulders, a fitted bodice with a jewel clasp gathered just under the breasts and a loose full-length skirt. 'Do you think it will suit Daisy? I didn't want to pick something that made her pregnancy so obvious.'

Rose nodded. 'I think it looks great.' She held the layers of material in the skirt and swished it from side to side. 'What colour do you want, Violet?'

'Either red or dark purple. What about you?'

'I like this bright blue. Will we wear jewel colours? Do you think Daisy would wear emerald green?'

'I don't see why not.' She nodded. 'Bright colours would be nice.' Violet exchanged a glance with her mother. It was obvious thoughts were spinning through her brain. Rose was curious. What were they thinking about?

'We'll talk colours later,' Sherry said quickly before spinning around. 'Now, will someone unzip me so we can talk headpieces?'

Rose was exhausted. Her mother's dress was picked. Their dresses were more or less agreed on, and they'd tried on an endless amount of jewellery and headpieces yesterday. And that was only the dresses.

She'd emailed a number of caterers and not had one single response. Marquee companies were being equally silent and it was all starting to make her panic. Hopefully things would be better with Will today.

He'd assured her that as long as they were willing to pay a premium price they'd be able to find someone suitable.

She shifted nervously on her feet and fiddled with an earring while she waited for him to arrive. Two minutes later she could hear the purr of a car coming down the driveway. Will pulled up in a car identical to her father's vintage Rolls-Royce only this time in silver. She raised her eyebrows in surprise as he climbed out and walked around to open her door for her.

'What?' He grinned. 'Did you think only your dad had one of these?'

She climbed in. 'I thought you would have wanted something more modern—more environmentally friendly.' It was a nice touch—a man opening a door for her.

He slid into the seat next to her. 'Quality and class. I spent a number of years waiting to buy this car. Now I've got it, I fully intend to drive it.'

She squinted at the row of stitches on his head. The swelling had definitely gone down now and she could see the edges pulled tightly together. 'How's your head? Does it hurt?'

'Is that concern after what—two days?' He was mocking her, trying to get a rise out of her. He leaned a little closer conspiratorially. 'It's itchy. I thought I was going to have to put a set of gloves on last night to stop me scratching it in my sleep.'

'Ouch. Isn't there a cream or something you can put on it to stop it itching?'

He shook his head as the car sped along the winding country roads and headed towards the motorway. 'I'm not to touch it at all. So scratching is definitely not allowed!'

There it was again. That annoying little flutter in her stomach that let her know this was her fault.

'Do you really think we'll find a caterer today? I'm getting worried. I've contacted a few and heard nothing.'

He nodded as they turned towards the motorway. 'I think we'll find someone. I hope you're hungry.'

'Why?'

'Because they'll all have workstations and they'll be cooking so all the businesses can sample their food. Catering an event is a really big deal. It pays big bucks. They go all out at these events.'

'Really? We'll get to eat the food?'

He smiled. 'Really. I guarantee you. You won't be able to eat for a week after this.'

She sighed and leaned back into the comfortable leather seat as they started to hit the traffic. 'It's just a pity we can't clone Judy and get her to make all the food. That chicken the other night was great.'

He smiled in appreciation. 'She's great. And no. You can't have her. She's my secret weapon.'

She shuffled in the seat. 'Have you given any more thought to the publicity?' Great. She could see his knuckles tighten on the steering wheel and start to blanch.

'Let's talk about it later.' He leaned over and turned on the radio. The conversation was obviously over. Rose turned and looked out of the window. She was still ticking off things in her head. She'd have to talk to Will about marquees; they were proving a real problem. If she could get the caterer sorted out today that would be at least one more thing off her list. Then it would be into the murky world of wedding favours and table decorations.

Will signalled and pulled off the motorway towards the conference centre. The car park was already jam-packed but he moved straight to the valet parking at the front and jumped out. Rose didn't even want to consider how much this was costing.

The conference centre was full of people in designer-cut suits and Italian leather shoes. She looked down at her simple fitted beige trousers and white loose shirt with a variety of beads. 'You should have warned me I'm under-dressed,' she hissed. 'I could have changed.'

His brow wrinkled as he walked forward. 'You look perfect. What are you worrying about?' He glanced at the map in his hands. 'Here, Hall C is where all the caterers are. Let's head there.'

He nodded and said hello to a few folk as they wove their way through the crowds. There really wasn't much need for the map. The smells emanating from Hall C would have led them in the right direction.

It was definitely the busiest part. Will didn't hesitate. He made his way straight over to the first booth and picked up a disposable plate and fork. 'Come on,' he whispered. 'Have a quick taste. If you don't like it we'll move on.'

The aroma of spicy chicken and beef was wafting around her, making her ravenous. She took a spoonful and grabbed a taste just as Will did. Her eyes watered and she turned to face him, trying not to laugh.

Within a few seconds he had a similar expression on his face. He gestured towards a nearby table stocked with iced water and glasses. 'Water?' The word squeaked out and she had to put a hand in front of her mouth. She nodded and followed quickly to the table, grabbing the glass of iced water that he poured. She swallowed swiftly and allowed the cool water to ease her scorching throat.

'Wow. I think they overdid the chillies.' She could almost feel a tear in her eye.

Will gulped down a second glass of water. 'Well, that was a wake-up call.' He grabbed her hand. 'Here, let's go somewhere things will be more soothing.'

He pulled her over towards an Italian stand where lasagne, spaghetti bolognaise and chicken *arrabiata* were all waiting to be sampled. They both played safe, taking a small sample of lasagne and spaghetti. It was good. Meaty, creamy with just the right amount of herbs. 'It's lovely,' Rose sighed. 'But it wouldn't do for Mum and Dad's wedding.'

Will nodded. 'Let's try some more.' Half an hour later they'd tried some Chinese food, some sushi, some Indian food and lots of traditional English dishes. Rose was no closer to finding something she really liked. She was pushing some food around her plate. 'Oh, no. This chicken looks a bit pink. I'm not eating that.'

Will whipped the plate out of her hand and dumped it in the rubbish bin. 'Wait. There's someone I know. His food is good. Let's try him.'

He walked with confidence, his hand encircling hers just as it had all day. It sent nice little impulses up her arm and gave her a strange sense of belonging. England had always been her home. She'd lived at Huntingdon Hall since she'd been a little girl. But spending most of her time in New York these last three years had given her a bit of space and distance.

Being around Will was making her think hard about her choices. Her father had already mentioned she would need to be back here for the band's European tour. But as much as she loved New York and her friends, it was beginning to lose its shine. Seeing her younger sister Daisy get married had made her feel a little flutter of homesickness.

Knowing that Daisy would have a baby soon and wanting to be around her new niece or nephew definitely made her want to stay close to home.

Will steered her over towards a new stand. 'Hi, Frank. This is my friend Rose Huntingdon-Cross. We're hoping to get an event catered soon.'

Frank put his hand out and shook Rose's hand warmly. 'Pleasure to meet you. Tell me what you want to taste. Any friend of Will's is a friend of mine.'

Rose smiled. The first stall that seemed promising. 'My parents' tastes are simple. My mother likes chicken. My father steak. They just like them to taste exquisite. What you do with them is up to you.'

'Chicken and steak. My two favourite English dishes. Give me a second.'

He knelt behind the counter and put up a range of plates. 'Okay, steak. Here's a plain sirloin. I can give you gravy, pepper sauce or whisky and mushroom sauce. Here's my version of steak stroganoff, and another steak traditional stew. For chicken I have chicken with cider, apples, mushroom and cream, a chicken stew with tomatoes and pepper and a traditional Balmoral chicken with haggis and pepper sauce.'

The plates appeared one after another with a variety of cutlery. Will smiled broadly. This guy could be perfect. As Rose worked her way along the row each dish tasted every bit as good as the one before. She sighed as she reached the end.

Frank was standing with his arms crossed. 'What's your dessert wish list?'

She turned to face Will, who was finishing off the sirloin steak with some mushroom sauce. 'Really? You knew this guy and didn't phone him straight away?'

Will smiled. 'He's my secret weapon. Everyone's tastes are different. Frank's always my number one choice.'

She looked up at Frank. 'Dessert would be something chocolate and orange for my mother and something strawberry or raspberry for my father.'

'No problem.' He disappeared again and started thumping plates up onto the deck. 'Chocolate and orange torte, raspberry pavlova, strawberry cheesecake, chocolate and cherry gateau and chocolate and raspberry roulade.'

Rose felt her eyes widen. 'I've just died and gone to heaven.' She lifted a fork and worked her way along the dishes, reaching the end as her taste buds exploded. 'All of them. I want all of them.'

Frank's smile reached from one ear to the other. He pulled out a diary. 'When's your event? Next year? Two years away?'

Rose gulped and glanced at Will for help. 'Eh, just under four weeks.'

'What?' Frank's voice echoed around the surrounding area.

Will moved swiftly behind the counter, putting his arm around Frank's shoulders. 'This is a very big event, Frank. And if I tell you money is no object, would it help?' He pointed towards Rose. 'Her mum and dad are renewing their wedding vows. They have a massive kitchen that you will be able to have full run of. You might have heard of them: rock star Rick Cross and ex-model Sherry Huntingdon. It's pretty much going to be the celebrity wedding renewal of the year. Everyone will be talking about who catered it.'

Frank's face had initially paled but as Will kept talking she could see the pieces falling into place in his brain. 'I have reservations for the next two years. Taking something on like this would be no mean feat. I'd have to hire other staff and make alternative arrangements for my other booking without scrimping on quality.'

Rose's stomach was currently tied up in knots. His food was perfect. His food was *better* than perfect and would suit her mum and dad and their exacting needs far more than anything else she'd seen today.

'Please, Frank. Can you have a look at your diary and see if you can make this work? Your food is fantastic. Mum and Dad would love your menu.'

He hesitated as he flicked through an appointment book in front of him. 'That date is for a corporate event—not another wedding. I'd be able to let my second-in-command take charge. But I'd need extra staff.' He stared off into the distance as if his brain was mulling things over. 'I'd also need to see the kitchen before I make a final decision.'

Rose found herself nodding automatically. She was sure the kitchen would meet his standards and if there was anything else he needed—she'd find it. 'Any time, Frank. Any time you want to see the kitchens would be fine with me. Just say the word.'

He glanced between Will and Rose once again. 'This will be expensive. You realise that, don't you?'

Rose answered quickly as she pulled out one of her business cards and handed it to him. 'I've tasted your food. You're worth it. Don't worry about the costs. Do you need a deposit?' She pulled out the corporate credit card she usually used for all the band expenses. It had the biggest credit limit.

He waggled his finger. 'I haven't seen the kitchen yet.' Then he laughed and turned to Will. 'Where did you find this one? She's your best yet—by an absolute mile.'

Rose felt her cheeks flush with colour. 'No, I mean… we're not… There's nothing going on between us.'

Frank winked. 'That's what they all say.'

Will tried to break the awkwardness, but his immediate reaction was to slide his arm around her shoulders and pull her closer. 'Rose and I are just good friends. I'm helping her out with the wedding stuff for her parents and she's helping me out with some publicity for the homeless charity.'

Frank looked at her again. This time she could see a flicker of respect behind his glance. He held out his fist towards Will's and they bumped them together. 'See you Wednesday night at the soup kitchen?' He waved the card. 'I'll call you later today and arrange to come and see the kitchens, okay?'

'Absolutely. That's great. Thanks very much.'

Will steered her away and over towards an ice-cream stand. The warmth from his arm was seeping through her shoulders. She should object to him holding her so closely—particularly when there was no reason. But something felt right about this. It was almost as if she were a good fit.

She gave him a nudge. 'I forgot to tell you. There's a wedding fair on Saturday in one of the nearby hotels. Will you come with me to try and sort out some of the other arrangements?'

He groaned. 'I can't think of anything worse. I hate wedding fairs with a passion. I've been at more than I could count.'

She grinned. 'Good. Then it won't be a problem. I'll come for you at ten o'clock.'

He raised his eyebrows. 'You'll come for me?'

She nodded. 'I'll try and drive something inconspicuous. The sooner we get in, the sooner we get out.'

'Okay, I can live with that.'

'You never told me you volunteered at the shelter, too.'

He looked down at her. 'Didn't I? I just thought you

would know. Violet's come along a few times to help when numbers have been short. I go there once a week. It helps me try and connect with the people I'm trying to help. Some of their stories would break your heart.' He stopped walking and turned her to face him, placing his hands on her shoulders. 'I'm completely serious about this.'

'I know that. I get that.' She could see the worry and concern on his face.

'That's why I'm so hesitant to do what you suggested. I get that it's a good idea. But I don't want this to be about me. I want it to be about *them*.'

She lifted her hand up to his arm and gave it a squeeze. 'I understand. I really do. But our world doesn't always work the way we want it to, Will. If it did—none of those people would be homeless in the first place. I can't give you a long-term fix here. What I can give you is a way to get people talking about the charity—because that will happen. But first, we need an angle.'

He sighed. 'And the angle is me.'

The guy standing in front of her now wasn't the Runaway Groom. He wasn't a guy that had made a host of headlines in all the tabloids. He was sincere. He was committed to his charity. And he wanted to do the best he could for it. There was a whole other side to Will Carter that no one else knew about. If she'd thought he was charming before, she hadn't counted on how much a little glimpse into the real Will could actually impact on her heart.

She nodded. 'Are you worried about the trials your exes might suggest?'

He shook his head and gave a rueful smile. 'I probably should be, but that's actually the last thing I'm worried about.' He reached over and tucked a wayward lock of blonde hair behind her ear. It was the simplest movement.

But the feel of his finger against her cheek sent her back

to the church on the island. Back to the feel of his lips on hers. Back to the surge of hormones that had swept her body and done crazy things to her brain.

If she stood on her tiptoes right now their noses would brush together and their lips could touch again.

She needed a reality check soon.

And there was only one way to get it.

She gave his arm another squeeze. 'Then let's get this done. You need to give me details on who they are—and how to contact them. Leave it to me. I can deal with them.'

There. Nothing like a bucket of cold water over the two of them to break the mood.

His arms dropped from her shoulders. 'Sure. Let's see what I can do.'

He walked away in front of her, heading towards the exit. She waited a second. Letting her heart rate come back to normal and trying not to fixate on his backside.

Her stomach gave a little flutter. Nothing like hearing about all Will's bad points from his multitude of fiancées to give her a little perspective.

CHAPTER SIX

WILL WOKE UP with his head thumping. A wedding fair was the last thing he needed. Helium balloons and tiny bottles of whisky were not filling him with joy.

He threw on his running gear and went for a run in the grounds, circling the house and gardens a few times, then pounding around the lake. Running was always therapeutic for Will. It helped him clear away the cobwebs and get some clarity on things.

But the cobwebs this morning were Rose shaped. And they didn't plan on moving no matter what he did.

The last thing he wanted to do was let her down. So, no matter how much he hated it, he would spend the day talking about wedding favours, chair covers and balloons.

Everything about this should be making him run for the hills. But the promise of being around Rose again was just far too enticing. He pounded harder on the driveway. No matter how hard he tried, Rose Huntingdon-Cross was finding a way under his skin. It didn't matter the messages that his brain was sending. The messages from his body were a whole other matter. And they were definitely leading the charge.

He rounded back to the main front door just as his phone beeped. A text. From Violet.

What you doing today?

His stomach dropped with a surge of guilt. He texted quickly before he changed his mind.

Helping Rose with wedding arrangements.

He waited. Expecting Violet to send something back. But she didn't. And it made him feel even worse. It had only been a few days but he was neglecting her. Any day she'd call him on it and ask him what was going on.

Then he'd be in trouble.

He strode through the hallway and up the stairs, hitting the shower in his room. He automatically pulled a suit from his cupboard, then stared at it, and put it back. This wasn't a suit kind of day. Hell, the last thing he wanted was to be mistaken for a groom.

He pulled on a short-sleeved shirt and a pair of army trousers before driving to the local surgery and getting the nurse to remove his stitches. The scar was still angry and red but she assured him it would fade over time and he arrived back just as Rose was pulling up outside the house. She gave him a hard stare as he climbed into the tiny Mini.

'You got your stitches out?'

He nodded. 'It's official. I'm now Harry Potter and I'll get all the girls.' He looked around. 'What's up?' She had her black planner sitting on her lap.

Rose was perfect as always. She was wearing a pink and white fifties-style dress. It was demure and gave nothing away. But he'd already seen and touched what lay beneath those clothes. His fingers started to tingle.

'Is this the casual look?' she asked stiffly.

'What—you wanted me to wear a suit and pretend to

be a groom? You think I haven't had enough practice at that?'

She frowned. 'Well, it could have been part of our disguise. I'm not sure I want to tell people today that I'm organising a wedding renewal for my parents. The news isn't exactly out yet.'

'Haven't you contacted their friends with the date?'

He didn't want to appear critical. But he could only imagine that most of Rick and Sherry's guest list would already have bulging diaries.

Rose was concentrating on the road. She was cute when she was driving, glasses perched at the end of her nose.

'I have. But there's always a few I can't get hold of.' She rolled her eyes without diverting them from the road. 'And you know, they're the ones that have a monster-size tantrum if they hear the news from anyone else.'

'Tell them to get over it.'

'What?' She seemed shocked by his abrupt tone.

'These people are adults. If they want information they should check their emails or answering machines. I hate the way some of these celebrities want to be spoon-fed. They act like a bunch of toddlers.'

He heard her suck in a breath as if she were thinking what to say. Had he just offended her? Violet was so normal he just assumed that Sherry and Rick didn't behave like other celebrities. Rose was biting her lip.

He couldn't help himself. He couldn't wait. 'Are you mad?'

She shook her head. 'No. I'm not mad. And I guess you're right. It's just I get used to dealing with these kinds of people.' She wrinkled her nose. 'And it starts to all seem normal to me instead of outrageous.'

She turned the car towards a country estate. The road

was already backed up with cars and Will sank lower in his seat. 'I've got a bad feeling about this.'

She laughed and gave him a slap. 'Oh, come on. How bad can it be?'

'You've never met a bunch of Bridezillas, have you?'

She pulled over. The car park was jammed and the traffic was virtually at a standstill.

'You're parking here? On the driveway?'

She nodded and smiled. 'Why not? In the next five minutes everyone else will, too. Let's go.'

She climbed out into the morning sun and waited for Will to join her. Everywhere they looked there were people. The doorway was crowded, so they walked around the large mansion house and went in another entrance at the back. Will pulled out some cash to pay their entrance fee and picked up a leaflet with a floor plan.

Rose had an amused smile on her face. 'These things have a floor plan?'

He laughed and put an arm around her shoulders. 'Let me introduce you to the world of crazy brides. If we hang out here all day I guarantee at some point we'll see two brides scrapping over a date somewhere.'

'No way.'

He nodded solemnly. 'Way.' He glanced at the plan. 'What first?'

She screwed up her nose and leaned against him, her scent reaching up around him. It was light and floral, like a summer day. Just exactly the way a girl called Rose should smell. 'We don't need to wait for the fashion show of the bridal dresses. That's all sorted. Let's hit the favours. I'm still not really sure what we should get.'

Will guided her through the large mansion rooms. 'Lots of people just go for the traditional—miniature bottles of whisky for guys and some kind of trinket or chocolates for the women. Lottery tickets are popular, too.'

Rose shook her head. 'I don't think my mother would be happy if I gave her wedding guests a lottery ticket. It has to be something more personal than that.'

'More personal for around two hundred people?'

He could see her bite the inside of her cheek. 'More like three hundred.'

The room was already crowded and they walked around. Some things were cute. Some things were practical. And some things were just quirky.

Rose held up flip-flops in different colours. 'What are these for?'

The girl behind the counter smiled. 'It's our most popular item right now. Flip-flops for the women who've been wearing their stiletto heels all day and want to spend the night dancing.'

Rose nodded. 'Good idea.' She moved on to the next stall, which had personalised notebooks with pictures of the bride and the groom on the front. Little heart-shaped glass pendants. Handkerchiefs with the bride and groom's name and date of wedding stitched on them.

He could see her visibly wince at some of the more cringeworthy items. She turned and sighed. 'I don't see anything I love.'

Will breathed in deeply and caught the whiff of something sweet. In the far corner there was a glass counter from one of the most well-known stores in London. 'How about chocolates?'

She walked over next to him. 'Isn't that a little boring? A few chocolates in an individual box for the guests?'

'How about you try and personalise it? Strawberry, orange, blackcurrant, limes—you could find out people's favourites. In fact,' he bent forward and whispered in her ear, 'if you speak very nicely to that man behind the counter and showed him your guest list I bet you he already knows some of the favourites of the people on it.'

Will bent over and picked up a triangular bag of popcorn. 'Some of the guys might prefer this. They've got shortbread, too. They even do mini-doughnuts.' He shrugged. 'Everybody eats. Everybody likes food. If you personalise it as much as you can it could be a hit.'

She was beginning to look a little more relaxed. The room was starting to get crowded. She shot him a smile. 'Give me five minutes to see what I can do.'

She disappeared across the room in a flash and within two minutes was behind the counter charming the white-gloved chocolatier. She pulled out a list and the two conferred over it for a few minutes before the chocolatier carefully folded it and put it in his pocket. Rose pulled out her chequebook and quickly scribbled a cheque, leaving her card.

She came rushing back over with a small basket of chocolate creams in her hand.

'Success?'

She was beaming. 'Better than success. He's even going to come to the wedding and set up the counter for the day.'

'As well as do all the favours?'

She picked up a chocolate and popped it in her mouth. 'Mmm…strawberry, delicious.' She held out the basket. 'Do you want one?'

'I'm not sure—is it safe? If I didn't know any better I'd say you were guarding them with your life.' He was laughing. Even though she'd offered a chocolate she'd automatically pulled the basket back to her chest as if she were daring anyone to try and take one.

She looked down at the basket and reluctantly pushed it forward again. He waved his hand. 'Forget it. I know when there's a line in the sand.' He leaned forward. 'Are you going to tell me how much all this is going to cost?'

Rose smiled and popped another chocolate in her mouth. 'Absolutely not. Now, let's look over here. The chocolatier just gave me the best idea in the world.'

They walked towards a smaller stand at the back of the hall. It was covered in jewellery and different mementos, a lot of them encrusted in crystals. She picked up the nearest one and shot the guy behind the table her biggest smile.

'I think you're about to hate me, but Paul, the choco-latier, sent me over.'

The guy smiled and rolled his eyes as Rose let out a gasp and picked up a little jewelled guitar. 'Oh, this is it. This is so perfect.' She spun to face Will. 'How perfect is it? A jewelled guitar for Rick and Sherry's wedding re-newal?' She could feel the excitement building in her chest. Trouble was, the workmanship of the guitar set with jew-elled stones was beautiful. How long did it take to make?

She took a deep breath. 'What would you say if I asked for three hundred of these in three weeks' time?'

The guy's jaw bounced off the floor. 'I'd say, "Do you know how much that would cost?"'

She nodded. 'I think I have a pretty good idea.'

He held out his hand towards her and walked around the table. 'John Taylor.' He wrinkled his nose. 'Rick and Sherry? Are you talking about Rick Cross?'

She nodded. 'He's my father. My parents are renewing their vows. I'd really love it if we could have some of the mini-jewelled guitars as favours.'

She could see him bite his lip. 'I'm a huge fan.' He sighed. 'The guitars are ready. The stones just need to be glued in place. They're semi-precious crystals. It takes a bit of time. But…' he paused '…for Rick Cross? I think I could pull out all the stops.'

'You could?' Rose let out a squeal and flung her arms around the guy. Will's face creased into a frown but she was too busy pulling out her credit card and setting up the order to pay too much attention.

After a few minutes she glanced around, placing her hand on Will's arm. 'Now help me find, accost and probably blackmail some company into hiring me a marquee for the day.'

He rolled his eyes. 'You'll need an even bigger chequebook for that.'

But Rose was getting lost in the atmosphere of the place. 'I think I want ones that have those fairy lights at night—you know, so it looks all magical?'

Her hair tickled his nose as he bent forward. 'Watch out, you're in danger of turning into one of the Bridezillas. I think you've been bitten by the bug.'

She stopped walking abruptly and turned around. 'Oh, no. Don't be fooled. Not for a second. This is my mother's dream wedding. Not mine.'

'And it was pretty much Daisy's, too.'

She nodded. 'I know. But I don't want any of this.'

He wasn't convinced—not for a second. 'Doesn't every girl want a dream wedding and to feel like a princess on the day they marry?'

But Rose's face was deadly serious. 'Absolutely not. Seeing all the chaos with Daisy getting married just made me even more convinced. The only part of that wedding that mattered was the two people standing at the front and looking at each other as if they couldn't wait to say they'd love each other for ever.' A Bridezilla pushed her from behind as she hurried past, and Rose almost faceplanted into his chest.

He pulled her close and put a protective arm around her waist. She sighed. 'I definitely don't want all this. I want me and my Mr For Ever alone—just the two of us—saying our vows without any of the kerfuffle.'

He smiled at her choice of word. 'Kerfuffle? I don't think I've heard that in years.'

She raised her hands to the bedlam around them and lifted her head towards his. 'Well, isn't that the most accurate description? Who needs it? Not me.'

Something soothing and warm was washing over him. Four fiancées. And not one of them had ever wanted this. He'd known all along how different Rose was. He'd known she was sneaking under his defences in every which way. He just hadn't realised how much. And it was the way she'd said those words. *Me and my Mr For Ever alone*. The words *Mr For Ever* should have terrified him. But for the first time in his life they didn't.

'Really? You really don't want all this?' He knew she'd loved the church on the island and remarked how perfect it was. But he hadn't been entirely sure that wasn't just saying she didn't want a big wedding. But the one thing Rose couldn't hide was the sincerity in her eyes. His head was crammed full of thoughts of the palavers over wedding plans with the four previous fiancées. Not one of them would have agreed to walk away from the dream and just have the husband.

Today was totally different. Today he didn't want to run from the room in the start of a mild panic. That could be easily explained. This wasn't his wedding and Rose wasn't his fiancée. But everything about this felt different. And it felt different because of Rose.

Her face was just inches from his. Her pale blue eyes unblinking. 'I really don't want any of this,' she whispered.

The buzz around him was fading away. All he could concentrate on was the face in front of him. All similarities to her sister had vanished in the mist. This was Rose.

This was only Rose. The woman who was having more of an effect on him than he could even begin to comprehend.

Any minute now a white charger would appear in the room and he'd just pick her up and sweep her off somewhere.

But being Rose, she would probably object.

She lifted a hand up and placed it on his chest. The warmth from her palm flooded through his fine shirt and their gazes locked and held for a second.

Was she really having the same kind of thoughts that he was?

Then it happened. A wayward thought he could never have dreamed of. He could actually imagine doing all this kind of stuff with Rose.

Was it because her vision of a wedding was close to his? Because the funny thing was, even if she changed her mind, he could see himself doing all this planning with Rose. Rose felt right. Rose felt like a part of him.

For Will it was like a revelation. Fireworks were going off in his head. His brain was spinning and his mouth resembled the Sahara desert. Was this it? Was this what it felt like for other people? Was this what it felt like for Rick and Sherry?

Her eyes twinkled and a grin appeared on her face. 'Come on, wedding guy. There were three things on the list today. Favours—done. But you promised me marquees and balloons—you better deliver.'

The spark in her eyes broke the increasing tension between them and brought him back to reality. He had to be sure. He had to be *more* than sure. The last thing he wanted to do was hurt Rose.

He nodded and grabbed her hand. 'Let's see how quickly we can do this. There's a bridal show about to start. Everyone will disappear to watch that.' All he really wanted to do was get out of here and get Rose all to himself.

It didn't take long. It just took an exceptional amount of money. But they finally found someone who could supply a marquee—complete with twinkling fairy lights—on the date they needed. Once they heard the magic words *Rick Cross and Sherry Huntingdon* the deal was done.

The balloons were another matter. One side of the hall had a whole range of displays and colours, from table decorations with a few helium balloons to archways covering the whole top table.

'Do you know what colour scheme your mum will want?'

'Yep, jewel colours. Bright and bold. Red, green and blue.' She wandered between all the stands touching all the metallic bobbing balloons, some held down by balloon weights and some tied to walls and chair backs.

'What's the story?' he asked. 'Were you the kid that never got bought a balloon?'

She smiled and tipped her head to the side. 'I just like them, that's all. Don't get me wrong—if you ever tried to get me in a big balloon—up in the sky—I'd run in the opposite direction. But these…' she jiggled her hand amongst an array of bobbing balloons '…I just love.' She pointed ahead. 'See those ones, all heart-shaped and just the colours I need? I'd love a really big display like that in all four corners of the marquees.'

Will stared at the bobbing balloons. They made him nauseous. He couldn't understand the attraction. The heat in the mansion house was starting to rise. The number of people surrounding them seemed to be growing and growing. He couldn't wait to get out of there. He had a one-track mind—get Rose away from all these people and just to himself.

The double doors in the large room they were in opened out onto the wide gardens. But the air was hardly circulating around them.

Rose took a few moments to place her order and pay by cheque. She walked over smiling. 'I love those. I think they'll be perfect.'

'Good. Can we get out of here now?'

She pivoted on her heels, her dress bouncing out around her. He could see several eyes in the room on her. She really didn't have any idea just how pretty she was, or what a statement her older-style dress made. It was like having Doris Day in the room with them. He couldn't help the smile that spread from one ear to the other.

It was official. This was the Rose effect.

'What about cakes? We haven't looked at cakes yet...' Her voice drifted off as her hand trailed against silver and pink heart balloons in a wide arch next to her.

The bridal show must have just finished as people started to surge through the entrance towards them. Rose stumbled on her square-heeled shoes and fell into the display balloons, dislodging them and making them drift free from their anchor and rise up all around her.

For an instant the whole room held its breath as two hundred balloons escaped their tethers and started floating and bobbing free. Will could see the horror on her face and grabbed her hand as he stifled a laugh and pulled her towards one of the open garden doors.

It was infectious. Rose started laughing too as they burst from the doors, out into the grounds as several balloons escaped around them.

Behind them there were squeals and bedlam. But Will couldn't have cared less. The fresh air of freedom was just too much as they ran across the grass together to where the cars were parked.

The last thing he saw was a pink and silver balloon floating in front of them as they dashed to the car.

CHAPTER SEVEN

ROSE WAITED NERVOUSLY as the phone rang. She was regretting her suggestion big time right now. 'Hello?'

The voice was sharp at the end of the phone.

'Hi, there. This is Rose Huntingdon-Cross. I'm looking for Melissa Kirkwood.'

'Violet's sister? What on earth do you want?'

She cringed at the instant recognition. Melissa was the bride who had been jilted at the altar. She was always going to be the most difficult.

'I'm phoning you because I'm doing some charity work for Will Carter and his homeless charity.'

There was a hiss at the end of the phone. 'Don't even say his name to me!'

It came out with such venom that she was actually taken aback. Although her brain was telling her to stay calm, her tongue just went into overdrive. 'I'm sorry to upset you. It's just—I thought you might be interested in this. We're contacting all of Will Carter's ex-fiancées to see if they would be willing to participate in a charity event. All you'd be required to do is put forward some kind of trial or dare that you'd like Will to do, and it will go to a public vote with all proceeds going to the charity.' Her mouth was gaining momentum like a steam train. 'You can be as horrible as you like with the dare or trial. Pick something you know he would hate to do.'

Oh, no. Had she actually just said that out loud? It was too late. Her PR head had gone into salvage mode. She couldn't take it back now.

There was silence at the end of the phone and a deep intake of breath. Rose's heart thudded in her chest. Part of her wanted Melissa to refuse, the other needed her to say yes. 'We've already negotiated a deal and coverage with the national press—and there will be television interviews, too. So you'll be able to show the world how you've moved on.'

Please let her have moved on, prayed Rose. Will had described some of his exes as a little fame hungry and eager to be in the spotlight. Hopefully the temptation would be too much.

'Just how hideous can I make his dare?' The voice had developed a calculating edge.

'As hideous as you like. At the end of the week's voting he will have to carry out the one with the most public votes.'

She could almost hear Melissa's brain ticking at the end of the phone. 'I need a day to think of something suitable.'

'Absolutely no problem at all. How about I call you back on Tuesday and set up an interview with the press for you then, too?'

Best to kill two birds with one stone. She really didn't want to have prolonged conversations with any of Will's exes. No matter how curious she was about the collection of women. Once she'd made the initial phone calls she was backing out of the limelight and letting the momentum carry the whole thing forward. The newspaper editor had loved it, and one of her favourite morning TV presenters had already agreed to interview all the women on TV.

The tone in Melissa's voice had changed. It was almost as if her brain was currently contemplating exactly what she could plot. 'Tuesday will be fine.' The phone went down with a click and Rose gulped.

She made a mark on the list in front of her. One down. Three to go.

'Rose? Rose, are you there?'

Will's voice echoed down the corridor and his head appeared around the corner of her bedroom door. He was clutching something in his hand and looking a little wary.

By the time she'd finished the phone calls she was exhausted and had adopted the starfish position on her bed. She hadn't moved for the last twenty minutes and didn't have any intention of moving any time soon.

She turned her head. 'If you ever get engaged to a crazy woman again you and I are never talking.'

He winced. 'You've done it? You've called them all?'

He didn't wait to be invited in. He just crossed her room in long strides and sat down at the edge of her bed.

Her head flopped back. 'I've called them all and you owe me—*big time.*' She turned on her side and rested her head on her hand. 'Where on earth did you find them?'

He frowned. 'Don't be like that. All of them have good points. I'm just not their favourite person.'

Rose laughed. 'Oh, you can say that again. Just wait till we find out what the trials are on Tuesday. I have the feeling that some of these ladies will spend the next two days plotting.'

He rolled his eyes. 'Not some. Just one of them.' His fingers drifted over and touched the edge of her trousers. 'I didn't mean to hurt any of them. Things just got out of hand.'

Rose pushed herself up the bed. 'Once or twice I might

let you off with. But four times. Do you never learn your lesson?'

'Looks like I'm about to.' There was something about the way he said the words. He was pretending to be flippant. But the atmosphere had changed quickly around them. She might be relaxed around Will, but it didn't deplete the buzz of electricity she felt whenever he walked in the same room as her.

She sighed. 'What's that?' She pointed to the curled-up newspaper in his hand and flopped back onto the bed.

'Yeah, about that.' Will flopped back onto the bed next to her.

The corners of her lips turned upwards. 'We've been in this position before.'

He smiled, too. 'I know. I remember. I even have the scar to prove it. I'm just hoping I'm not about to earn another one.'

She wrinkled her brow. 'Why would you do that?' It was disconcerting having those dark blue eyes just inches from hers. This was exactly what waking up next to Will Carter would feel like. All six feet four of him just inches away. That rogue thought was doing strange things to her stomach.

He moved a little bit closer. She could see the tiny freckles on his nose, feel his warm breath on her cheek and certainly smell his fresh aftershave. Her senses were scrambled. Was he about to kiss her?

'I think your PR campaign has just taken off in an unexpected way,' he whispered as he unfurled the newspaper.

She was muddled for a sec. The kiss wasn't coming. Her eyes tried to fixate on the coloured picture on the front of the red-top newspaper.

The effect was instantaneous. She sat bolt upright just as the text sounded on her phone.

The photo looked staged. It was just too perfect. Rose with her Doris Day–style dress and blonde hair streaming behind her and Will in his casual shirt and trousers. But it was the expressions on their faces that gave everything away—they were laughing and the elements of pure joy shone from their faces, in perfect unison with the pink and silver heart-shaped balloons escaping into the sky behind them.

If Rose worked in PR for the movies, she would have paid a fortune for a shot like this.

But it was the headline that took her breath away. *Has the Runaway Groom finally found his bride?*

'What?' She snatched the paper from his hands. 'What on earth is this?'

Will opened his mouth to speak but nothing sensible came out. 'I'm not sure… It's just a picture… It will blow over in a couple of days.'

The paper was crumpling beneath her fingers. Rose worked in PR. She knew exactly how big this was. She also hated the fact it was her face staring back at her from the front of the newspapers. It brought back horrible memories of a few years ago when she'd made every front page. She'd hated every second of that and never wanted to repeat it again. 'How many, Will? How many calls have you had this morning?'

He flinched. 'About a dozen.'

'A dozen!' She was shrieking and she couldn't help it. If it was any other girl—any other girl in the world right now photographed with Will—she'd be doing a happy dance. This would be a great kick-start for the publicity for the homeless charity.

But it wasn't any other girl. It was her. And she hated the fact this could blow out of proportion. Hated the fact it was her in the headlines. How ironic. She hated the media but had learned how to use them to her advantage. Maybe this was a wake-up call for her? Maybe she'd started to get a little complacent?

Something twisted inside her. 'Violet,' she breathed.

Will's cool hand touched her arm. 'I called her. She laughed. And warned me off again.'

'She laughed?' Rose could feel the waves of panic washing over her. She hadn't even hinted to Violet the thoughts that were clamouring through her head about Will. How on earth could she? She couldn't make sense of them herself. The last thing she wanted to do was tell her sister she was falling for the Runaway Groom.

'All those calls I made this morning. Just wait until your exes see this. They'll think I'm next on your hit list. They'll think I'm just doing this because you've sucked me in.'

'Sucked me in how?' His voice was low and tinged with anger. He reached over and grabbed the newspaper from her hands. 'You know what they say about this—today's news, tomorrow's chip paper. It's a photo snapped by someone at the wedding exhibition yesterday. There's nothing we can do about it.' He shrugged his shoulders. 'If you go to a public place there's always a danger you'll get papped. You must be used to it.'

He had no idea. No idea what had happened a few years ago and how it had changed everything for her. Changed how she felt about herself. Changed how she thought her parents felt about her.

She took a deep breath and tried to think logically.

He was making sense but she couldn't even acknowledge it. 'But this is a disaster. What happens when I phone those women back? What if they refuse to participate because of this?' She pointed at the paper again. She hadn't even read the whole article. 'I mean, it's all rubbish.'

'No. It isn't.'

She turned quickly to his voice. Will was still lying on the bed. He reached up his hand and pulled her back down next to him.

'What are you talking about?' She couldn't help the tremble in her voice. They were back in their original position. Lying on the bed next to each other with only a few inches between their faces.

'Rose, stop pretending that nothing is happening between us. We both know that it is.' He lifted his finger and touched the side of her cheek, oh, so gently. She shivered. She couldn't believe he'd actually just said it. Acknowledged it out loud.

She wasn't going crazy. She wasn't imagining things. He felt it, too.

But he'd felt it four times before. History proved that. She didn't want to be number five.

This was the one and only time she'd felt like this.

Part of it was horrible. Last time she'd felt this vulnerable was after her friend's death when she'd been splashed all over the media.

Rose had learned quickly it was better to be the person to try and control the PR, than the person *in* the PR.

And the more her feelings grew for this guy, the more she questioned herself and her ability to trust her instincts. What had happened three years ago had affected her more than she'd ever realised. She would always regret leaving her friend. She would always regret the fact she hadn't hung around when there was even a possibility that Autumn could have put herself in harm's way. She'd spent the last three years playing the *if only* game.

And she couldn't afford to do that any more. She had to live in the real world.

And only her parents really knew that she'd been aware

of Autumn's drug-taking. What would Will think of her if he knew the truth? If she revealed all her flaws to him?

'Why couldn't you just be an ordinary guy?' she whispered.

Will smiled. He was so much more laid-back about this. He didn't seem to have a single problem trusting his instincts—and that was probably part of the problem. What was more he didn't have a shadow of doubt in his eyes. Not like the clenched hand she currently felt protecting her heart.

'Why couldn't you just be an ordinary girl?'

He leaned forward and brushed his lips against hers. She was scared to move at first. Acknowledging it was one thing. Seeing where it might take them was entirely another.

But everything he did was completely natural. From edging closer so their bodies were touching, to his hands wandering through her hair and around her face and neck. Each kiss was designed to lead on to the next. To make her want more. And she did. *So* much more.

All the sensations in her body were on fire. As if Will had more than one set of hands and they were currently skimming her erogenous zones as if he were reaching out and kissing and caressing each one in turn.

Rose pulled back sharply.

'What's wrong?' Little creases appeared around his eyes.

'I don't know. I'm just nervous. I'm not sure about any of this.'

'What part are you not sure about?'

Her hand was resting on his bicep. She could feel the heat of his skin through her palm. Every sense in her wanted to run her hand up under the short sleeve of his shirt and feel more.

'I'm not a spotlight kind of girl, Will. I agreed to help you with the PR but I don't want PR for myself.'

She felt him suck in a deep breath. 'I'm afraid with me it might be part of the package. We could release a statement about your parents' renewal. That would explain why we were there. They may well leave you alone after that.'

Forget about it. Forget about everything. Act on impulse, Rose, and just kiss him the way you really want to.

But she couldn't. For Rose this was all about control. Since her friend's death she'd become a control freak. It was why she did the job so well for the band. Nothing left to chance.

Now people were taking pictures of her she didn't know about. Pictures of her that told the whole world exactly how she felt about Will.

And the whole world exactly how he felt about her.

It was like a jolt—and probably just as well she was already lying down.

Her silence had obviously worried him. 'Am I overstepping the mark, Rose? Do you want me to leave you alone?'

'No.' It was the first concrete thought in her head.

She was so confused right now. She didn't want to be the next girl to be swept along in the flurry of love that surrounded Will Carter.

She wanted a chance to be normal. To be just Rose and just Will. Two people that were attracted to each other. The electricity sparking between them was everywhere. But while this was all new to her, every precautionary bone in her body kept reminding her it wasn't for Will.

And no matter which way she looked at it—it hurt.

'I can't be number five.' Her words came out solidly. Definitely.

Will looked sad as he shook his head. 'You're not num-

ber anything. You're Rose.' His hand touched her cheek
again. 'Can't we see where this relationship takes us?'

'But that's just it, Will. You don't have relationships.
You have engagements, wedding plans and then nothing.
You're a commitment-phobe—even though you can't see
it for yourself. I can't set myself up for that. I don't want
to start a relationship that won't ever go anywhere.'

'That won't happen, Rose.' She'd expected him to say
something different. She'd expected him to crack a joke
about her being way too keen and these things being years
away. He couldn't possibly know the surge of terrifying
emotions in her chest.

She could see him trying to find the words and the
thought he was trying to placate her made her wish the
ground would open up and swallow her. Even saying those
few words had been too much. She should have known
better. She shouldn't even have acknowledged anything
between them.

'This is different.' His words were unexpected. But she
just couldn't let herself believe them—no matter how much
she wanted to.

'I bet you've said that before.'

The wave of hurt on his face was obvious. And even
though she should probably want to take the words back,
she just didn't. It had to be said. Will's reputation had gone
before him. It didn't matter that her own experience of him
felt entirely different. For all she knew, all the other girls
had thought that, too.

Will sat up on the bed as her phone beeped again. 'I
don't know how to show you this is different, Rose. I don't
know how to explain.'

She sat up and pulled out her phone. It was from her
father.

Can you come and see me? There's something special I want you to do for me.

'It's my dad. I'd better go.'

Will nodded reluctantly. 'Rose?'

She'd already started towards the door. She hated the way she spun around, desperate to hang onto his words.

'Let's just see. Let's just see where this takes us.'

She couldn't speak. She couldn't even explain to herself why she felt so hurt. She just gave a reluctant nod before she disappeared out of the door and the hot tears started to snake down her cheeks.

Her dad was waiting for her in the kitchen, sketching with deep concentration on a bit of paper.

'Hi, Dad, what's up?'

His eyes narrowed for a second when he lifted his head. He'd always been able to read her like a book. She could see him think about asking her what was wrong, but the paper in front of him was a definite distraction.

He hesitated, then pushed it towards her. 'What do you think?'

It was a pencil drawing of a bangle with little scribbles next to each part. Three strands of gold in different colours pleated together with a little flower intersecting the pleat at each third of the bangle—a rose, a daisy and a violet.

'It's beautiful, Dad. What's this for?'

His well-worn face sagged in relief. 'It's for your mother. It's her gift for her wedding day. I wanted to give her something special. You will make it for me, won't you? And you'll be able to get the yellow, white and rose gold?'

Something surged inside her. Even though alarm bells were sounding all around her head about the amount of time the bangle would take to make, and the intricate details, there was just no way she could ever say no to her father.

The thing that struck her most was the absolute love she could recognise on his face. The fact that he'd spent a lot of time and effort on this design was obvious. But what was even more evident was just how much he loved her mum. After all these years he still wanted to do something to make her heart sing.

That was what she wanted. That was the kind of relationship she wanted. That was the kind of love she wanted. One that would last for ever.

She felt a tear spring to her eye again as her dad put his arm around her shoulder. 'Don't worry, Dad, I've got the three kinds of gold. It will be perfect. Mum will love it.'

But now that he'd sorted out his wedding gift her father's attentions had shifted immediately. Rick Cross was no fool. Particularly when it came to Rose.

'So what's wrong? What's going on with you and that Will Carter? Violet's moping around like a lost cause.'

'She is?'

'Of course she is. You've stolen her favourite pet.'

A tear slid down her cheek as everything just threatened to spill out. 'But I haven't. I was helping him—and he was helping me with the wedding arrangements. It's just that we've been spending so much time together. I didn't mean to leave Violet out. I'll phone her—no, I'll go and see her.' She was babbling and she just couldn't help it. Wasn't it Will that normally did this?

Her father shook his head. 'Rose? What's wrong? I was only joking. Violet can take care of herself. I just wondered if there was something I should know. My daughters seem to be getting married in short order these days.'

Rose felt her breath catch in her throat and her father noticed immediately. She'd just had that awkward conversation with Will. A conversation nobody should be having after such a ridiculously short amount of time. It was almost as if her father could read her mind—and heaven knew what he could find in there!

But Rick Cross was cooler than your average dad. 'I like that fella. Always knew nothing would happen between Violet and him. But you?' He gave a little shrug of his shoulders. 'I guess that depends how you feel.'

He left the words hanging in the air. It was awful. She wasn't ready to have that kind of conversation with her dad. He was still her *dad*. Then again, she wasn't ready to have that conversation with anyone.

She focused back on the drawing. 'Leave this with me. This will be fine.' Where she would find the hours from she had no idea. But if this was what her father wanted—this was what he would get.

If he noticed the abrupt subject change he didn't say anything. She picked up her bag. 'Oh, I forgot to tell you—the guy you wanted to write your biography, Tom Buckley from New York? He emailed today to agree the terms and conditions. He'll have full access to the band tour backstage. I'm just arranging flights for him now.'

A huge smile broke across her dad's face. This was something that was really important to him and he'd been quite insistent about who he wanted to do the job. Just as well Rose had worked with Tom in the past and could use her maximum persuasion skills—along with a hefty salary—to persuade him to write the biography in the timeframe her dad needed. One more ticked box and another thing off her plate. She felt a little surge of pride. Her dad was happy with her.

Her dad gave her a hug and a kiss. 'That's great, honey.

Thanks for doing that. Now, if there's anything you need to talk about, come and see me. Or pick up the phone and I'm there.'

Her heart gave a little squeeze. He wouldn't pry. He wouldn't interrogate her. Just as well, as she didn't know what to say. But it was her dad's way of letting her know that he'd noticed. He'd noticed something was wrong. Dads didn't come much better than Rick Cross. When the whole press thing had blown up when Autumn had overdosed he'd been her biggest ally—her best spokesperson. And he'd done exactly the same for Violet when her sex-tape scandal had hit the press. Rick Cross didn't take kindly to people trying to hurt his family.

He'd taken Rose in the car to see her friend's parents. He'd spent hours talking to them and comforting them— but in no way letting them blame Rose for their daughter's actions. And when the press had started to get nasty a few days later he'd made lightning-fast arrangements and got her out of there. She was lucky that her family were so supportive.

It gave her a little strength. A little fortitude. Maybe it was time to look at herself again. Maybe it was time to start trusting her instincts?

Her father had just told her he liked Will Carter. Will had been Violet's best friend for the last three years. And the man she knew in person didn't measure up to what she'd read in the press.

She reached over and gave her dad a quick hug. 'This bangle will be perfect. I'll make sure of it. Don't worry, Dad. You can trust me.'

He brushed a kiss against her cheek and gave her a curious look. 'Always, Rose.' Before he walked across the kitchen he paused in the doorway. 'Rose?' She looked up

again and he gave her a rueful smile. 'When you know—
you just know,' and then he turned and walked away, leaving her with the drawing clutched in her hands.

CHAPTER EIGHT

FOUR HUNDRED AND sixty emails. That was how many he had to read. Will groaned and put his head in his hands. This was getting out of control.

He couldn't concentrate. He couldn't focus. Because his head was so full of Rose.

The sensation he'd felt the other day at the wedding fair with Rose had swamped him. The words Rick Cross had said at their first meeting were echoing around his brain. *When you know, you just know.* But it was more than that. It was the way Rick had looked at Sherry, too. The zing between them. He'd never had that before. But he had it with Rose.

Trouble was, he didn't know what to do next. How on earth could he convince Rose that everything about this just felt different—just felt right?

He didn't blame her. He really didn't. How would he feel if Rose had been engaged before? He was lucky she would even stay in the same room as him.

But he just couldn't help how he felt about her. It was taking over every waking minute of his life. He looked at the calendar, then walked over to the window. The island was right in front of him and from this view he could see the roof of the church. Something curled inside him.

A tiny seed of an idea. A wild idea. A crazy idea.

If he told Violet she'd probably dunk him in a bath of ice. If he told Rose she would run screaming for the hills...

For the first time ever Will felt as if he could see himself grow old with someone. It should be terrifying. But instead a warm feeling spread across his chest.

And something about this idea was taking shape in his head. He only had to do one thing. One thing that he hoped no one would find out about.

And it could make all the difference to his life.

Rose put the phone down and laid her head on the desk.

'Was it that bad?' Violet was standing laughing at the door with her arms folded.

Rose didn't even lift her head. 'Worse,' she sighed.

Violet walked over and lifted up the piece of paper on Rose's desk. First it was a gasp of shock, then it was a snort, then it was just a peal of laughter. By the time Rose lifted her head Violet was wiping a tear from her eye.

'I came up to tell you Will's just pulled into the car park. I bet you can't wait to tell him what all his dares are.' She shook her head as she kept looking at the list. 'I can't wait to see his face.'

'Really?' She half hoped Violet wasn't joking. 'Then you can tell him.'

She raised her eyebrows. 'Oh, no, girl. That's your job.' She gave Rose a nod of her head and walked back to the door with her shoulders shaking.

Rose heard the murmur of words down the corridor as she obviously met Will. A few minutes later he appeared at the door, face pale. 'Oh, no. What have they suggested?'

Rose gestured towards the seat opposite her. 'You better sit down.'

For once Will did exactly as he was told.

She started carefully. 'The good thing is that these will definitely generate media interest.'

'And the bad news?'

She gulped as she passed over the piece of paper. 'You might not like some of them.' She bit her lip. 'The thing is, the newspaper already knows about all the dares. So we can't get anyone to change them.'

His brow wrinkled. 'Why would they need to be changed? Are any of them going to kill me?'

She shook her head swiftly. 'No. No. That was one of the conditions they were given—nothing fatal.'

'Please tell me that you're joking.'

She shook her head again and gave him a half-smile. 'Eh, no.'

'Dangling from Tower Bridge and getting dunked in the Thames?'

Rose tried not to smile. There was no doubt the press would have a field day with these. To say nothing of all the TV and media interviews she'd arranged for the ex-fiancées. This could end up being one of the most successful PR campaigns she'd ever been involved in.

Will had been right. Three out of four of his exes had been fine. And even Melissa had started to come round. She was gearing herself up for TV interviews and appeared to be quite happy at the prospect.

'Dress for a day as a gladiator/warrior and parade around Piccadilly Circus? Wear a thong and work in a women's underwear department for the day?' His voice was getting more incredulous as he continued to read.

Rose couldn't help but start laughing. 'Those last two came from Angie and Marta. They were definitely going more for the laughs than the cold, hard revenge.'

Two of Will's ex-fiancées were now married with children. They were happy to help the charity auction and had obviously had fun thinking up what he should do. Both of them had seemed very nice and very happy with their lives.

The third, Esther, had looked on it as good publicity for her new TV-presenting career. She'd been quite mercenary about it. She wasn't that interested in the charity but she was certainly interested in raising her profile.

Will slumped further down the chair as he finished reading. 'A full body wax on live TV?' The paper was now crumpled in his hand. 'Which do you think will win?' he said resignedly.

Rose tried to be rational. 'I think it's a toss-up between a dunking in the Thames and the man thong.' She held a scrap of luminous green material with her pen. 'Look. Marta tried to be really helpful. She even sent the thong.'

Will's eyes nearly popped out of his head as he reached forward and snatched the tiny item. 'You have got to be joking. There's absolutely no way on this earth I'm ever putting that on. Or dressing like a blooming gladiator.'

But Rose was on her feet in an instant. 'Oh, no, you don't. You agreed to this. This isn't about you. This is about the charity. Think how much money will be raised by people phoning in to vote on this stuff. I bet you'll be able to employ some new workers. Don't start being a wuss on me now.'

He groaned and sagged down again, staring at the thong in his hand. 'But people won't be talking about the charity. People will be talking about me and my utter humiliation.'

'So what?' She was feeling annoyed now. This had taken time, effort and persuasive skills she hadn't even known she had. 'It will also raise the profile of your charity—which, if you remember, was exactly the brief you gave me.'

His eyes fixed on hers. For a second it seemed he was

assessing her. If he found her wanting she would find the nearest vase and whack him over the head again.

He stood up. His imposing figure in front of hers. His broad chest filling her vision. His voice had a determined edge to it. 'It has to be about more than this. It has to be something else.'

'What? What else do you want from me, Will?' she shouted, all patience finally lost. 'What else can I do?'

'I want a night.'

'What?' She was losing the plot. None of this made sense to her any more. She had too much going on. Too much to think about. Sisters, fathers, mothers, weddings, band tours, bangles, promotion, interviews, Will, Will and more Will.

Any minute now she would spontaneously combust.

But Will was on a roll. 'I want a night. I want to show people what this is really about. I want to spend a night on the streets the way my friend had to when he was homeless —when he didn't know where to turn. I want people to understand how terrifying and dangerous it can be. I want to give them a real feel for the vulnerability—and the stories—of the people I want to help.'

Her brain started spinning. It was genius. It was perfect. It would complement the other publicity perfectly. People might have fun voting, but if they watched something like that it would really bring the message home. But when he'd said the words 'I want a night' it wasn't quite what she'd hoped to hear. And now she was annoyed with herself for even imagining he might have meant something else.

Will was still mumbling. 'And I want you to do it with me.'

The words clicked into place in her brain. 'Me?'

'Yes. You.'

She was baffled. 'But why?' Could her head really get any more confused?

'Because you're the perfect person to do it with. People know who you are. A famous couple's daughter? They'll love it. They'll think it's something that a girl like you, and—' he pointed to himself '—a guy like me would never do. Let's show them how hard it is. Let's show them just how difficult it is. Let's tell them some of the stories of the people out there.'

Boy, when he wanted it, his charm just came out in spades. And it was rational, businesslike sense. It put another edge to the publicity. She kind of wished she'd thought of it herself. But she kind of wished he wanted to do it with someone else. Could she really put herself in the spotlight again?

His hands rested gently on her shoulders. She could smell him. His scent was invading her senses. It was like a magic potion winding its way around her. She could almost see its tendrils wrapping around her body and throwing all rational thoughts out of the window.

'I need you, Rose. I need to do this. And I need to do it with you. Do you understand that?'

There it was again. That way he made her stomach twist and turn. He knew just how to speak to her. Just how to reach in and touch the little parts of her that couldn't say no to him. Part of this terrified her.

She wasn't in a situation where she couldn't say no. She just didn't want to. And even though this was completely different from years ago, a tiny little bit of her still remembered feeling so distracted by a man she'd forgotten about everything else. The guilt still consumed her. She didn't ever want to be that way again.

It didn't matter this was Will. It didn't matter there was no element of danger. This wasn't about him. This was about *her*. And her ability to trust. She still hadn't completely learned to trust her instincts. And a guy with Will's history? He didn't really have trust stamped all over him.

Still, she couldn't ignore what was happening between them. She couldn't ignore the way her body reacted every time he was near. She'd never felt this way about a guy before. Was this what love felt like? Or was this just infatuation?

'Rose, are you okay? Do you need some time to think this over? Please tell me you'll think about it. I really want to do this with you.'

She took a deep breath. Was she prepared to do this for a charity? No matter how uncomfortable and scary it was? Of course she was. She was lucky. She'd had a privileged life. Her parents had always drummed into her and her sisters how lucky they were. They made a point of supporting their favourite charities and the work her mother did was never-ending. Of course she could spend one night on the streets.

She took a deep breath. This seemed like so much more. It seemed like a partnership. It seemed like a way of cementing things between them—to see if their paths could truly connect or not.

'I'll do it.' There. She said the words before she had too much time to think any more. To mull things over.

And Will did the thing she'd longed for. He sealed it with a kiss.

The interviews were set. The voting lines would be announced tomorrow. With so much publicity for the homeless charity and the papers filled with all his ex-fiancées everyone seemed to have forgotten about the picture of him and Rose in the press. Everyone but him.

For the first time in his life he'd cut a picture from the

press. He'd even saved it and printed it from one of the press Internet sites.

He loved it. He loved the way they were captured in it. Daisy was the photographer in Rose's family and he'd heard her talk with passion about her pictures and what she wanted to capture in them. But he'd never really got *it* before.

Not before now.

Not before he could see the look on both his and Rose's faces. Captured for an eternity. And he loved it. He was actually going to frame it.

But it made him nervous. Now, everything else paled in comparison to how he felt about Rose. He could see it now. He could see the infatuation. But he'd never felt the love. Not like this.

How would she be when he told her what he'd done? If she felt the same way he did, everything should work out fine. If she didn't?

He'd need to learn to live with having a runaway bride.

CHAPTER NINE

PAUL SCHOLAND WAS her favourite ever TV presenter. With his bright, sparkling blue eyes and prematurely grey hair the female audience just loved him. He had all the exes eating out of the palm of his hand and had got the mixture of personal and publicity just right. Rose's tightly tied-up stomach was finally starting to relax. Particularly when she got a text about the sudden upsurge in voting. Things were going better than she could ever have imagined.

Will had spent most of the morning pacing around the room; Violet had come in every now and then to howl with laughter at some of the comments and then left again. Will's segment had been pre-recorded and when his face filled the screen Rose took in a deep breath.

The camera loved him. She'd always known it, but she'd never really appreciated it before. His eyes were even more remarkable than Paul's, his dark hair framing his face, with tiny lived-in lines around his eyes enhancing his good looks. But better than everything was his easy, laid-back attitude. The whole world was falling in love with him right now—her included—and Rose was feeling sparks of jealousy.

This was her Will. Hers. She didn't want to share him.

'Is it over yet?' He was watching from beneath his fingers. She nodded. 'Just about.' She turned her phone towards him. 'Look how things have gone.'

His eyes widened and he dropped his hands. 'How much?'

She smiled. 'Yeah, that much. And it's only the first day. You were on the front page of one of the red tops today, too. People are talking about this—talking about your charity.'

He looked a little doubtful. 'I'm being made a laughing stock on national TV.'

Rose stood up and walked towards him. 'Paul handled those interviews really well. In the meantime, money is being raised for your charity. You've got another interview on the main news channel tomorrow. That will give you an opportunity to speak about your friend and why you're doing this. You'll be able to talk about the night on the street, too. It will all balance out, Will. This is a good thing that you're doing.'

He stood up next to her. 'I know. I just wonder what I'm going to end up doing.' He shook his head. 'It could be a disaster.'

'It will be fine. No matter what it is at the end of the day, it'll be worth it.'

He nodded slowly. 'You're right. Of course you're right.' He lifted his hand and twisted his finger through a lock of her hair. 'So where are we with your list?'

For a second her thoughts were jumbled, then her woolly brain came into focus. 'The wedding list, yes.' She turned and walked over to the table and picked up her black planner. 'Okay, venue, marquees, food, band all sorted.'

'Is your dad playing at his own wedding?'

She sighed. 'Of course he is. But not till later. Their support band is playing for most of the main event. But there's no show without punch. At some point my dad and the guys will want to get up there and rock out.'

She ran her finger down the rest of the list. 'Violet's doing the flowers—apparently my mother's already given her instructions. Mum's got her dress and we've all picked ours. Daisy is doing some of the wedding pics and her assistant is doing some others.'

'What about everything else?'

'Well, the wedding favours and chocolates are sorted, as are the chair covers and balloons. I've just got to sort out a wedding cake and to choose wine and a drinks list for the bar.'

'When do you need to do that?'

She wrinkled her nose. 'In around an hour. I was kind of hoping you would come with me and help me choose the last few things.'

Will shrugged. 'I can choose wedding cake and the wine is already sorted. Sounds like every guy's dream date.'

She opened her mouth to stop him, to tell him it wasn't a date, and then stopped. She was almost glad he was thinking like that. It felt kind of nice.

She took a few minutes to finish up with emails and phone calls, finalising the flight arrangements for the reporter flying in from New York to write her father's book. She'd worked with Tom Buckley on numerous occasions and he was great. The only hiccup this time was the scheduling. Tom was on another job and the soonest he could get here was the same day as her mother and father's wedding renewal. She'd have to leave at night to pick him up from the airport. It couldn't be helped.

Will finished on his phone around the same time she did. 'Ready?'

She nodded and they walked outside to his car. 'Do you have an address?'

She bit the inside of her cheek and turned her phone

around to show him. He blinked. Twice. 'Really? What on earth…?'

'Yeah, I know. When I phoned Angie to ask her to take part in setting a dare she asked me how things were. Before I knew it, I'd told her about my parents' wedding renewal and how difficult it was to find everyone at short notice. She said her sister would be delighted to make the wedding cake.'

'Does she know I'm coming along?'

Rose looked at him nervously. 'It might be a little awkward but I'm sure it will be fine.'

'I sure hope so. Otherwise we're both in trouble. You won't get any cake and I'll probably end up wearing some.'

She laughed. 'I'm sure it won't end up like that. Angie was great on the phone. She couldn't have been nicer. She seems really happy now she's married with a baby of her own.'

He looked thoughtful as they continued along the road. 'Angie is nice. She's great, in fact.'

The words did strange things to her insides. She liked Angie. She really did. She just didn't want to think about the history between her and Will. She couldn't even bear to think about it.

'She just wasn't right for me—like I wasn't right for her.'

It was like a wave of relief washing over her. And it was almost as if Will realised her apprehension because one of his hands left the wheel and squeezed her leg through her dress as he glanced sideways at her.

'You're right. I'm sure it will be fine.' He put his hand back on the steering wheel and they continued along the road until they eventually reached the address.

Angie's sister Deb was the ultimate professional. Small and petite with a bright red bob, she had a whole portfolio of cake photos to show Rose along with lots of samples of her baking.

They were all laid out before her. 'Here are the sponges—try a bit of each. If there's a special request I can make it. I have traditional fruit cake, carrot cake, chocolate cake, strawberry and white chocolate, dark chocolate and orange, coconut and vanilla sponge, lemon sponge and coffee sponge.' Each one was more delicious than the last.

'Do you like them?'

'I love them all.' Rose kept flicking through the cake book. It was difficult to know which style and what kind of decorations to choose. She turned the book towards Will. 'What do you think? A traditional tiered cake or something more novelty?'

'What do your parents like best?'

'That's just it. I don't know. For birthdays we quite often have novelty cakes. But I'm not sure if they'd want that for their wedding.'

'How many tiers do you want? Do you know how many guests are coming?' Angie's sister had her order book poised.

Rose groaned. 'It could be three hundred.'

Deb blinked twice. 'Do you want some advice?'

Rose nodded. 'Gladly. I know nothing about this kind of stuff. I just don't have a clue.'

Deb flicked through her portfolio. 'Keep it simple— or as simple as you can with that amount of guests. How about an eight-tier cake with one of every kind of sponge? That way your guests will be able to find something they like. I can cover it in royal icing with some pale ribbons and you could get your florist to do a display for the top that matches your mum's flowers.'

Rose nodded quickly. She was happy to take any suggestion right now that made things a little easier. Deb pointed to the cakes in front of her. 'I'll go and make you some tea. Just pick which sponge for each layer.' She handed over a diagram. 'Remember sponge one will be the biggest and sponge eight the smallest so all you need to do is decide the order. I'll give you some space because this can take a little bit of time.'

She left Rose and Will together in the room. Will had barely said a word since they got there. 'Are you okay?'

He gave the tiniest nod. 'It's just weird, that's all. She hasn't even mentioned the dares or the press stuff.'

'She probably doesn't want to.' Rose pointed to all the sponges. 'This is her business and doing Mum and Dad's cake will be good publicity for her portfolio. I'm expecting her to charge a lot more because of the short notice but I'm just so relieved to have someone.'

Will frowned. 'This wedding is costing a lot of money.'

Rose nodded.

'But doesn't that kind of go against your mum and dad's principles?'

She wrinkled her nose. 'I know what you mean. To be honest they probably give away the same amount of money that they spend.' She shrugged. 'From a strictly PR perspective the wedding will look ostentatious. It will feed the public image that they're successful and doing well. But it also means that they can continue to give to all the charitable causes they want to—with or without publicity.'

Will nodded. He looked thoughtful and picked up a piece of one of the sponges. 'Which is your favourite?'

'I can't decide. They're all delicious.'

'What would you pick for your wedding cake?' It was a simple enough question. 'If it was up to me I'd have the whole thing chocolate.'

'Oh, no.' She waved her hand. 'I wouldn't want a wedding cake anyway.'

'You wouldn't?' He was surprised. He knew she'd said she didn't want a big wedding. But just how small did she actually mean?

Rose shook her head and waved her hand. 'I don't want any of it. Any of it at all.'

A horrible feeling crept over him. 'Do you mean the wedding?'

She tilted her head to the side. 'No, but that's all I want. The wedding. A dress and a bunch of flowers for my hands.'

He raised his eyebrows. 'And presumably a groom?'

She threw back her head and laughed. 'Well, hopefully that's part of the package and not an optional extra.'

Relief started to flood through him. It was odd. He hadn't actually realised that when Rose said small, she actually meant minimal. It wasn't quite what he'd imagined. But the more he got to know her, the more he understood.

Rose lifted a little piece of carrot cake and nibbled. 'This one is delicious.' She sighed and lifted up the strawberry and white chocolate. 'But I like this one, too.' It crumbled as she bit into it and Will reached over and put his hand under her chin. She spluttered as he caught the crumbs. 'Never thought of you as a messy eater.' His eyes twinkled as he lifted some of the chocolate cake. 'Here, try my favourite.'

She hesitated. There was something so intimate about being fed by someone else. Even if it was in the middle of the day in someone else's house. Her eyes darted to the door. Deb was nowhere in sight.

She opened her mouth as he positioned the light, moist sponge at her mouth. The chocolate frosting was perfect, sending little explosions around her mouth, to say nothing of the ones as his fingers contacted her lips.

His thumb smudged across the edges. 'You've got a little bit stuck,' he whispered.

'Where?' She looked around for a napkin.

'I'll get it,' he offered as he bent forward to kiss her. His lips touched hers, lightly at first, delicately, before he eased her lips apart and joined their mouths together. His hand slid around the nape of her neck and through her hair, making her want to beg for more. This was it. This was what he did to her. Gave her a little taste that left her begging for more.

The voices started in her head. She was getting in too deep. Every kiss took her a step closer to never wanting to go back. *Angie's sister's house* floated around her head. There was a thought to chill her heated blood. She pulled back and made a grab for a napkin. It was perfect timing as Deb appeared with the tea, her bright smile still firmly in place.

Rose picked up the diagram and quickly numbered each tier of the cake with the sponge she wanted. 'Thank you so much, Deb, for doing this. Let me know how much I owe you.'

Deb hesitated but shook her head. 'It's fine, but I'd be really grateful if you could get a photo with your mum and dad and the cake for my portfolio.'

'Of course. Of course. No problem at all.'

Deb gave a hopeful smile. 'Thanks.'

It only took them a few minutes to get in the car and leave. Rose was feeling happy. All the things on her wedding list were finally ticked off. For once, she could relax. All she needed to focus on now was making the bangle for her mum.

Then there was the horrible sinking realisation that she really had no reason to spend time with Will any more. All of a sudden his proposition about being on the streets one night didn't seem quite so scary.

Will seemed laid-back. 'So, are you ready for your night on the tiles with me?'

'When a guy invites a girl for a night on the tiles he doesn't usually mean it literally.'

Will glanced over at her. 'I like to do things a little differently. Anyway it will take my mind off those hideous dares. Have you heard any more about them?'

She nodded and smiled. 'It's a definite split vote between the gladiator, the thong and the total body waxing.' She shrugged. 'Personally I thought people might be more inclined to go for the more venomous one—the dunking in the Thames. But no, it seems it's humiliation all the way.'

'Does the total-body hair wax include the hair on my head?'

'Absolutely.'

He shuddered. 'It just doesn't seem that appropriate for a homeless charity.'

'But dressing in a thong and working in a lingerie department does?'

His eyes were fixed on the road but his lips turned upwards. 'No, that's definitely pure humiliation all the way.'

He was taking it really well. The whole dare thing didn't seem to bother him or annoy him. He was prepared to take it on the chin.

It was just another reason to like him all the more. Somehow she knew spending a night out on the streets with Will wasn't going to be the best idea in the world. He was already ticking so many boxes for her. Was she really prepared to let him tick the last few?

'What will I need?'

'Warm clothes, especially a jacket and shoes. It can be really cold at night.'

'Do you think we'll get any sleep at all?'

'I have no idea. I guess we'll find out. Is one of the reporters from the paper coming along?'

She screwed up her face. 'He'll do a cover story. It took quite a bit of persuading. But I don't think he'll stay all night.'

Will's phone sounded and he lifted his hip slightly. 'Can you pull that out for me?'

She stretched over and slid her hand into his pocket. The skin next to the thin cotton lining of the pocket was warm. She tried not to focus on that as she made a grab for the phone. She pulled it out and glanced at the screen.

'It's Violet. She wants you to phone her.' Her stomach did a little flip. This was her sister. Will was Vi's best friend. She had no reason to feel jealous.

Will gave a slight nod of his head but said nothing. It just made her feel worse.

'Just drop me back at home,' she said abruptly. 'I need to spend some time on my mother's bangle.'

'Okay.' They drove in silence until he reached her parents' house and she jumped out of the car as quickly as she could. 'Thanks. I'll text you about Saturday night.' She slammed the door quickly as she strode inside, passing Violet in the corridor. 'Is Will outside? I need to talk to him.'

Violet wandered past her and outside as Rose made her way to her workshop. She needed to get a hold of herself. She needed to get things into perspective. Her mind was playing tricks on her these days. Making her think irrational thoughts. Was this what it felt like to be in love? Because if it was—it wasn't good. All of a sudden she felt sick to her stomach.

There was no getting away from it. Saturday night on the streets was going to be make or break for her and Will. He knew it. And she knew it.

CHAPTER TEN

IT WAS THE final dress fitting. Daisy was back now with her ever expanding tiny bump. The green dress covered it to perfection and standing side by side the three sisters in their green, blue and purple dresses made a striking picture.

Sherry clapped her hands. 'Oh, my beautiful girls. You all look perfect.'

Rose tugged at her hair. 'Do we need a tiara or a fascinator or something?'

Sherry exchanged a look with Violet. 'We've got that all under control. You'll have a fresh flower for your hair.'

Daisy was distracted. She sat down and eyed her jewelled sandals suspiciously. 'Can I wear Converse instead?'

'No,' Sherry said swiftly. She held up an alternative pair of flat jewelled sandals. 'I've got you flatties for the night. You only need to wear the heels for the renewal vows.'

Sherry turned to Rose. 'Everything is ready? Everything is done?'

Rose nodded and started to reel everything off. 'Marquees will be set up the day before. Violet's taking care of the flowers, Daisy the photographs. Dad's backup band is organised. The chairs and tables come the day before. The favours and cake are organised—along with the menu. Everything will be perfect, Mum, you don't need to worry about a thing.'

Sherry enveloped her in a hug. 'That's why we trust you with everything, honey. You're just so good at organising. I don't know what we'd do without you.'

Rose beamed; she didn't even know about the bangle yet. Her mother would be delighted. But Violet didn't look delighted. Violet looked mad. As if her mother's words had just irked her.

Rose had no idea what was going on. But she'd too much to think about right now.

And most of her thoughts were around a runaway groom...

He could hardly even see her face. The hood of her parka came right down over her nose. He stuck his face inside. 'Is anyone alive in here?'

'You said it would be cold. I'm just trying to make sure I'll be warm.'

He slid his arm around her shoulders. 'It will be cold. But I'll do my best to keep you warm.'

She glanced around. There were a number of people in the homeless shelter drinking tea and soup. 'What time does this place close?'

'Eleven.'

'And where does everyone go then?' She was looking around at the array of figures in the room. Most weren't dressed very well; all of them were in layers. He saw her look down and knew exactly what she'd see. Lots of the people who slept on the streets had shoes that were mismatched and falling apart. Once they found a pair of shoes that fitted they wore them until they literally fell off their feet.

'That's just the point. I guess we'll find out.'

Rose inched a little closer to him. Will was used to coming here. He often came and helped out in the food kitchen. He wasn't fazed by the sometimes unkempt people that used it. This place was a safe haven. Somewhere they could be fed and get a few hours' warmth. It was staffed completely by volunteers and Will would like nothing more than for it to be open for longer.

As the staff in the kitchen started to clean and tidy up Will moved forward to help. Rose was right by his side, washing dishes and cleaning worktops. It was all hands on deck here.

By the time they locked the front doors darkness had fallen. Rose was glancing around at the people gathered in small clumps around the door. Few words were exchanged. Most were trying to decide where to stay safe for the night.

'I had no idea so many people stayed on the streets,' she whispered. 'Can't they get emergency accommodation from the council?'

Will shook his head. 'Some of these people have been through the system—some haven't. A few have addiction problems and weren't able to manage a tenancy even though the council had found one for them. Managing money is a skill that some people find really difficult. There's just not enough support out there.'

A thin, wiry teenage boy walked past, head down and hands in his pockets. Rose sucked in a breath. 'Will,' she whispered, 'he doesn't even look sixteen.'

Will's heart squeezed. 'That's Alfie. And he's seventeen. He's been on the streets for the last two years and he won't let me help him. I've tried.'

Rose looked horrified. 'Why on earth would a kid that age end up on the streets?'

Will shook his head. 'That's just it. He won't say. And he's one of about twenty kids I know that really shouldn't be here.' He nudged her with his elbow and pointed across the road. 'That's Danny, one of the voluntary workers.

He'll spend most of the night keeping watch over the young ones to try and keep them safe. He's a real godsend.'

Rose's brow was wrinkled and she turned to face him. 'I don't get it. Why don't these kids want to be under a roof and sleeping in a bed?'

'Because not all homes are like yours and mine. Not all homes are safe. I suspect some of these kids have come through the care system and slipped through the net. Others are escaping abuse. Some have mental health disorders that make it difficult for them to cope.' He looked around and pointed towards a group of middle-aged men. 'And it's not just the young ones. Last year they estimated around three thousand people slept rough in London, people who just don't have family or friends to help them. Lots of them ended up homeless because of redundancy or domestic abuse. There's a whole host of different reasons people end up like this.'

Rose slipped her hand into his. 'Your friend. How is he?'

Will felt himself bristle. It was the whole reason he was here but it was still a sore point. He still felt as if he'd let his friend down. 'He's getting there. It took a long time before he'd let anyone help him. That's just it. I could stand here in the street and announce I'd give everyone somewhere safe to sleep for the night but most of them wouldn't believe me—wouldn't trust me. They wouldn't come.' His voice was tinged with sadness as Rose's fingers curled around his own. He couldn't imagine being here with anyone else. He couldn't ever have imagined any of his previous girlfriends agreeing to do this with him—he wouldn't have wanted them to.

But this was different. This was important to him. And if the decision he'd made about Rose was right, this was the kind of thing he needed to share with her—he needed her to understand.

He pointed to the dark streets. 'Are you sure you're okay with this?' She looked nervous, even though she was obviously trying her best not to.

'I'm fine,' she said quietly before adding, 'I'm with you.'

He nodded and took a few steps down the street. 'Then let's go. Let's see how you survive on the streets at night.'

This London was completely different from the London that Rose knew. She wasn't naïve. She knew people slept rough and there were homeless hostels all over London but, while she'd taken part in a lot of charity work with her parents, she'd never worked in any of these places.

London at night for Rose and her sisters had involved trendy streets and clubs. Coming out late at night, clamouring into a cab and grabbing some food from an eatery on the way home. The streets they were walking down now were unfamiliar to Rose. Dark, damp, creepy.

Will took her down alleyways, stopping by rubbish bins to speak to people hidden in the shadows. Handing out biscuits and cards with addresses for assistance. As the cold crept around them and the night became even darker they kept going. Tramping unfamiliar streets without fear. Occasionally they met other workers, voluntary organisations and a few cops on the beat. Will seemed to recognise most of them, stopping to compare notes and talk about trouble spots. A few made jokes about his press coverage, though all thanked him for trying to raise the issue.

Fatigue started to settle in. Her muscles were tiring. The cold was creeping down to her very bones. Will steered her towards one of the bridges spanning the Thames. 'This is a hotspot,' he murmured. 'Lots of people sleep under this bridge at night. Stay close. Fights sometimes break out.'

The rain had started to fall. Thick, heavy drops that soaked straight through her jacket. They hurried under the bridge. There was no lighting under here. It was almost completely black with only a flicker from the occasional match somewhere.

At the other side there was a fight starting over some cardboard boxes. Rose drew close to Will, wrapping her arms around his waist and shielding her face away. The fight ended as quickly as it had started, with the victor claiming his spoils and arranging his cardboard box on the ground.

'They were fighting over a cardboard box?' Rose whispered.

Will nodded. 'You've no idea what has value on the street. Especially on a night like this. Here.' He pulled her over to the wall under the bridge and pulled her down next to him. The cold concrete quickly wound its way through her clothes and she shifted on the ground. Will still had his arm around her shoulders and she snuggled closer to get some body heat. 'Are we going to stay here?'

It all seemed so alien to her. So cold. So uncomfortable. So unsafe.

He nodded. 'This is it. This is where a lot of the people on the streets spend the night. How long do you think you could actually sleep for?'

'I don't think I can sleep at all,' she whispered, not wanting to offend any of the huddled figures around her.

'I know. But we have to try. We have to understand what it is these people go through every night. That's the message I want to get out there.'

Something struck her. 'What happened to the reporter?'

Will sighed. 'He got waylaid with something else. He interviewed me earlier and I've got a little camera attached to the pocket of my jacket. He should pick up some things from that.'

Rose put her hand on the freezing ground. 'But he won't

pick up this. He won't pick up how cold it is out here. He won't get how the wind whistles under the bridge and the raindrops still reach you even though you're in the middle.'

Will smiled. 'But you do.'

Something fleeted across her face. 'Yeah, but I don't like it, Will. I'd be terrified if I was here myself. I can't stand the thought of living every night like this.'

He looked out over the darkness of the still water of the Thames. 'This is where Arral used to sleep at night.'

'Your friend?'

He nodded. 'I still can't fathom how it happened. How a guy who did so well at university, got his first job and flat just ended up on a downward spiral that ended up with him stabbed and in hospital.' He shook his head as he looked at the bodies huddled around them. 'Arral was married. But when he lost his job and his home, his wife just upped and left. She didn't take her vows seriously. The whole for better or worse part just seemed to pass her by. I've thought about it for the last few years. How marriage was about good and bad.' He squeezed his eyes shut for a second. 'It always made me second-guess things. It always made me scrutinise my relationships. Would this person still want to grow old with me if I didn't have the fancy house, jobs and cars? It made me question my abilities to choose wisely.'

She frowned. 'But I've met all four of them. Marta and Angie seemed nice. Both of them weren't bitter. They knew they weren't destined to be with you. Esther is focused on her media career. And Melissa?' She shrugged. 'She seems to have her own demons. I doubt very much you can do anything about them.'

She squeezed his hand. 'This place gives you a whole new perspective on life, doesn't it?' She was looking around. Looking at the array of faces, some hidden beneath hoods or cardboard boxes. There was a real mixture of people here. Mainly young and middle-aged. There were around forty people under this bridge, but only two she would have termed elderly.

'Are you okay?'

She shivered and huddled a little closer. 'Yes. I'm just remembering, I guess.'

'Remembering what?'

'My friend, Autumn,' she said sadly. 'She died from a drug overdose at a party one night. We were both there, but I made bad choices that night. We both did.' Her voice started to shake. 'No one knows, Will. But I knew that Autumn had dabbled with drugs before. I knew and I still left her alone that night to go off with some guy. I wasn't a silly teenager. I was a twenty-four-year-old woman and I left my friend behind. I let her down. I let myself down. And I let my parents down. They had to deal with the fallout of my actions. They had to deal with my bad choices.' She was ashamed to say those words out loud. What would Will think of her now he knew all about her flaws? 'I wonder how many of these people didn't even get to make a choice to end up here?' she murmured. 'It seems so unfair.'

Will nodded. She couldn't really tell him how horrible she found this.

'I had family. I had a really strong family. My dad took over. He came with me to speak to Autumn's parents. He was there for hours.' She glanced up at Will. 'People just don't realise what my dad is made of. "Rock star" doesn't equate with supportive parent.' Will gave her shoulder a squeeze. 'But after the funeral was over I just couldn't take it. I couldn't take the bad press. I'm not a good person, Will. I'm the most flawed person you could meet.' She was shaking her head in disbelief.

'I went to New York to escape. To start again.' She held up her hand as the tears formed in her eyes. 'But now I feel a thoroughly pathetic human being. I didn't feel strong enough to cope—so I left. But what if you don't have the means to leave?' Her voice was starting to waver. 'Or what if the means to leave makes you end up on the street?' Being out here was scary. Having this as your reality must be terrifying for some of these people. 'I wasn't strong enough. I couldn't take what the press said about me. I hated having my picture in the paper. I couldn't take the lies. I didn't trust my judgement any more and I hated the fact that I felt as if I'd let my parents down. But I still had my family. I still had them around me. Is this what happens when you don't have family to support you?'

He tilted her chin up to face him. 'Rose, you and Violet are two of the strongest people I've ever met. The press has had a field day with you both. You, with your friend's death and Violet, with her leaked sex tape. But it hasn't dragged either of you down. If anything, it's made you both stronger. You didn't run away. You regrouped. You've spent the last few years working hard for your dad. You haven't hid away. And you've found something else. You've found something that you love—your jewellery making. And you've worked hard at that, too. How does that make you weak? How does that make you a failure? We've all got to take what life throws at us and deal with it the best we can.'

He stroked a finger down her face. 'Is this it, Rose? Is this what you're so afraid of? The press putting things you can't control about you in the papers? Letting your parents down? Trusting your judgement?'

He gave a gentle laugh. 'Have faith, Rose. Have faith in yourself. Because I have faith in you, and so does every member of your family. You've organised your parents' renewal vows in record time. *They* trusted *you* to do that.' He emphasised the words by pressing his palm against her chest. 'They trusted your judgement—even if you don't.' He leaned closer. 'And I trust your judgement, Rose, more than you can ever know.'

His face nuzzled against hers, his cold nose sending little delicious waves down her chilled bones. 'Do you think I would have brought anyone else here? Do you think any of my previous girlfriends would even have made an attempt to understand this?' She could hear the conviction in his voice. He really believed in what he was saying. 'It could only ever have been you, Rose. Just you. You're the only person I could share this with.'

He straightened a little. 'I told you about Arral and his wife leaving. I told you that in the lead-up to my weddings I started to have doubts. Doubts about whether I could see myself growing old with that person.' He touched her cheek. 'I don't have any doubts about you, Rose. I can see myself growing old with you. You've got to give us a chance. You've got to know that this is real between us.'

There they were. The words she'd thought she wanted to hear. Every ounce of him believed what he was saying. How could she tell him that even though he was sure, she was the one with doubts?

Realisation was seeping through her with the cold concrete beneath her. This wasn't really about him. This was about her.

Will might well be the Runaway Groom. It was a label that was never going to disappear. Every instinct told her to trust him. Every instinct told her to believe what he was saying.

But she hadn't learned to trust her instincts again yet. It was the one thing that was holding her back. The wary part of her brain said he was in the first flush of romance again. That in a few months none of this would be real. How well could you possibly know someone after a few weeks?

But then there was Daisy. She'd had one night with Seb and returned weeks later to give him baby news. They'd married in the space of a few weeks, and, while there might have been a few initial doubts, on their wedding day their faces hadn't lied. It was two people, totally in love with each other, who'd said those vows. If it worked for Daisy—why not for her?

It was so easy to get sucked in. Will was gorgeous. Will was charming. And even on a wet, rainy, cold night he made her feel like the most special person in the universe.

'Once we get through this, let's go someplace else. Let's go someplace it's just the two of us. I didn't want to share this with anyone else, Rose. And I don't want to share you either.' His lips were hovering just above her own. His warm breath heating her skin.

All she could see in this dim light was the dark blue rim around his eyes. The thing that she'd first noticed about him. The thing that had drawn her in and made her heart do that first little flip-flop.

There were no alarm bells ringing. No 'do this and you'll regret it' voices screaming in her head. Maybe, for the first time ever, she was really ready to take a chance on love?

His lips made contact with hers. It was the briefest of kisses. The warmest of kisses. Telling her everything she wanted to know and sending signals that her body was screaming for.

She couldn't walk away from Will right now if she tried.

So she stayed there, with Will's broad arms wrapped around her, sending a little heat into her numb bum and chilled bones. It felt right. It felt secure. It felt as if this was the place she was supposed to be.

Part of her brain kept ticking. She'd need to come clean with Violet. And Daisy. She'd need to tell her sisters how she really felt. All of this wasn't true until she'd done that. Her family were so important to her. But she would wait. She would wait until after the whole PR announcement tomorrow and the wedding renewal.

It would give her a little time—a little space to have confidence to trust her instincts once again.

Nothing would happen before that—surely?

CHAPTER ELEVEN

HER EYES FLICKERED OPEN. She could hear Will's breathing next to her, feel the rise and fall of his chest against her back. His arm was curled around her. Waking up next to Will this time was an entirely different sensation.

Her eyes wandered to the clock and widened in shock. It was nearly midday. Will had booked them into a boutique hotel in the West End of London. When they'd finished their night on the street she'd been utterly exhausted. The journalist had been waiting for Will and he'd done a short interview without letting go of her hand. Then he'd brought her to this hotel and done a whole lot more before they'd finally fallen asleep.

Her heart started thudding against her chest. There was a host of further interviews later today, then the TV show tonight with the reveal of the winning dare. She'd promised she'd be there. But right now she had to get home and do some work on her mother's bangle. Time was running out. She didn't just have commitments to Will to fulfil— she'd commitments to her family.

Especially now. Especially after what had just happened between them. She needed to talk to Violet sooner rather than later.

In a familiar motion she slipped out from under the covers. Her clothes were lying across the floor and she picked them up and slipped them back on. She should wake him. She really should. But he'd been every bit as exhausted as she'd been. She could let him sleep and order him breakfast in an hour or so. That way she'd have time to get across London and put in a few hours' work on the bangle before she had to get back for the TV show. If she woke him now he might try and distract her. And it was likely that she wouldn't say no.

She grabbed her phone. Out of charge and she'd forgotten to bring her charger—typical. She bent over the bed and laid a gentle kiss on his forehead. He didn't even flicker. Just kept breathing deeply. So she smiled and slipped out of the door, remembering exactly what had happened earlier that morning on her trip back across London.

Something wasn't right. The space in the bed next to him wasn't filled with a warm, comfortable body. There was just a little divot in the bed where that warm body should be.

Will's eyes flickered open, first to the space beside him, then to the bathroom door. Every part of his body was coiled up right now, hoping that any second there would be a flush, a sound of running water and Rose would walk out of the door. But everything was silent.

The knock at the door nearly gave him heart failure and sent him bolt upright in bed. The door opened with a member of the staff carrying a tray that he set next to the bed. 'Breakfast for you, Mr Carter.'

'I didn't order breakfast.' His stomach grumbled loudly as if it were part of the bad joke.

The staff member gave a nervous smile. 'The young lady ordered it for you.'

Will flung the cover back and went to stand up—right until he realised he wasn't wearing anything. The poor guy was already walking backwards to the door. He covered himself quickly. 'The young lady? Where is she?'

The guy couldn't get out of the room quickly enough. 'I think she left, sir,' he said as he pulled the door closed behind him. The smell of bacon, eggs and coffee filled the room as Will sagged back on the bed.

She'd left? Why on earth would she leave after the morning they'd had together? Will's stomach curled. Had he misread the signals? Had he misread Rose completely?

He grabbed his phone and dialled her number. Straight to voicemail. He sent a text. Delivered. He held the phone in his hand for a few minutes, willing her to reply. Nothing.

This couldn't be happening. Why on earth would Rose send him up breakfast but leave without saying goodbye—or, worse, without leaving a message? He looked around for pen and paper. But there was nothing obvious.

He pushed the breakfast tray away. He couldn't stomach anything right now. Not while everything he'd wished for was hanging in the air. His phone beeped and he jumped. But it wasn't a message. It was a reminder that the TV studio car would be picking him up in an hour. He wasn't on until six that night but they wanted to rehearse and since the whole show was about him and his charity he could hardly let them down.

Clothes. He needed new clothes. His fingers were still clenched around his phone, rapidly turning white. Rose would have to wait until later.

She was out of breath and cursing herself like mad.

'What's the name?' The guy at the front desk looked distinctly uninterested.

'Rose Huntingdon-Cross.'

He gave a cursory glance at the list and shook his head. 'Not on it.'

'What do you mean I'm not on it? I'm the one that arranged the interview.'

The guy almost sneered. 'You're not on the list.'

She could feel the pressure building in her chest and resisted the urge to grab the guy by the nape of the neck and drag him across the desk. She'd never use the 'Do you know who I am?' card but she hated ineptitude.

She folded her arms across her chest. 'I'm here for Paul Scholand's interview with Will Carter—you know, the Runaway Groom? I can give you the name of each and every one of his fiancées that must have checked in with you by now.'

The guy didn't even blink. 'Not on the list,' he said again. It was almost like a challenge.

She took a deep breath. 'Why don't you check under Cross? People often list my surname wrongly.'

His eyes went reluctantly to the page again and he blinked. 'Hmm. Cross by name, cross by nature?' he said in a sing-song voice. She really could pull him across the desk and thump him.

'You bet,' was her reply.

He gestured with his hand, waving her in, and she strode past without a second glance.

Once she was through she found the studio no problem. Paul Scholand had been interviewing out of the same studio for the last five years and Rose had been there on a number of occasions with the band—in fact, she was due back in another month.

But today was a bit different. The studio was normally always slick and smooth but with four extra women, who for reasons unknown to Rose seemed to be being kept apart, along with Will—who seemed to be being kept apart from *everyone*—the studio runners and assistants seemed harassed to death.

This thing had just taken root and sprouted into a complete forest. One she wasn't even sure she wanted to enter. She gulped. If this was how she was feeling—how on earth must Will be feeling?

She reached into her pocket. Nothing. Then remembered she hadn't even charged her phone from this morning. Darn it. Things had got a bit fraught when she was in her workshop. There had been problems with one of the kinds of gold. She was going to have to get more and it would take more than a day to arrive. All cutting into her time to work and make the bangle on time. It was her own fault. She'd been distracted when she'd started work and not totally focused on the job. Under normal circumstances she would have noticed a problem with the gold straight away. But no. She was too busy dreaming of the feel of Will's hands on her skin and his lips coming into contact with that sensitive area at the bottom of her neck.

Her hand automatically lifted to the area. Whenever she thought of him her skin tingled.

She looked around, trying to see him through the crowded studio. Her eyes locked on another set that was watching her carefully. Angie—one of Will's ex-fiancées.

Her feet hesitated for a second before she put a smile on her face and walked over, holding her hand out. 'Angie, it's so nice to meet you. Thank you for doing this. The phone lines are doing brilliantly. We're raising lots of money for the charity.'

Angie gave a controlled nod of her head. She was in the middle of getting her hair and make-up done. 'That's really good to know. I'm glad it's going well.'

Rose felt something creep up her spine. Angie was being very reserved. Had she done something to offend her?

'And thank you so much for putting me in touch with

Deb. Her cakes are to die for. It was a real weight off my mind.'

As if on cue Angie pushed forward a plastic tub towards Rose. 'Deb sent something else for you to try. This is chocolate and hazelnut sponge. She wondered if you wanted some extra cupcakes for later?'

Rose picked up the tub straight away. She couldn't wait to try it. 'Oh, thank you, this is great. I'll give her a call later.'

Angie glanced sideways, as if to check to make sure no one else was listening. 'Be careful,' she said in a low voice. 'You've got that glow about you, Rose. Believe me, it can fade quickly. You're a nice girl.'

Rose opened her mouth to deny everything but the studio hairdresser had appeared again and was fussing around Angie. She walked away with her mouth hanging open. *Angie could tell just by looking at her?* How was that even possible? Nothing had happened until this morning. Up until then it had only been a few kisses. Nothing of any significance. And if she kept saying that she might actually believe it.

Will was at the other side of the studio with Paul Scholand. She lifted her hand to give him a wave and he wrinkled his brow, as if he was trying to work out who it was. She was forgetting. The studio lights were directly in his eyes.

She wandered closer. Round the back of the cameras and right round to the other side of the studio.

'You,' came the voice behind her. She spun on her heels and pulled the plastic tub a little closer, as if it were some kind of shield. Melissa Kirkwood had that kind of effect on people. This was a woman that certainly hadn't got over the Runaway Groom. She was the one who'd suggested dunking Will in the Thames.

'What can I do for you, Melissa?' Rose tried her sweetest voice. She'd no intention of doing anything for Melissa; she already couldn't wait to get away from her.

Melissa folded her arms across her ample chest. She was wearing a bright pink dress with a slash right down the front. One of the studio hairdressers was behind her, teasing her hair into waves. Melissa had obviously decided there was no need to be as discreet as Angie.

'So are you floating on a cloud right now? Thinking that Will could never look at another woman the way he looks at you? Has he told you that he loves you yet?' she sneered. 'Because we've all been there, honey. Don't think you're special.'

It was like having someone tip a whole bucket of ice over your head.

What was it with these women? Did she have a neon sign above her head?

'I have no idea what you're talking about,' she said quickly.

'Sure, honey, that's what they all say before the engagement ring appears, then your groom races down the aisle like he's being chased by killer zombies. It's written all over your face. You're just the next sucker in line.'

She could feel the colour rush up into her cheeks. Two ex-fiancées in almost the same number of minutes accusing her of the same thing. Was there a camera in the hotel room this morning? Last thing she wanted was to end up part of a sex-tape scandal like her sister.

She turned and walked away from Melissa. She'd already heard enough.

Will was standing at the edge of the set now while one of the make-up girls dusted some powder on his face. She was batting her eyelids and talking incessantly, but his gaze came into direct contact with Rose's.

It only took two strides to cross the space. 'Where did you go? I called you. Why didn't you call me back?'

Rose hesitated; her cheeks were still flushed from the comments from Angie and Melissa. She hated that people seemed to be able to read her so easily—particularly when she hadn't even had a chance to speak to her sisters. Was she really ready for this?

Her hesitation caused something to sweep over Will's face. He looked hurt. Even a little angry.

Paul Scholand was on his feet. 'Are you ready, Will? It's time for the countdown.'

Will nodded. 'Wait here,' he said quickly to her, shooting her a glance that made her insides curl up.

Everything about her felt in flux. She wanted to tell him the truth. She was confused. She needed time to think. She needed time to talk to her family. Last night and this morning had been great. She'd almost been convinced that he meant everything that he'd said.

But being here, in amongst the women he'd 'loved' before, was overwhelming. Words that he'd never said to her. She felt crowded—swamped. She felt as if there weren't enough room in the building for her own feelings while there was a huge rush of female hormones everywhere else. How on earth could she know how Will really felt about her here and now? This had disaster written all over it.

Will could feel the claustrophobia in the room. None of this was good. Paul kept looking at him reassuringly and patting him on the knee. He must sense that Will really just wanted to bolt from the studio.

The cameraman gave the signal and the theme tune started reverberating around the studio. On the other side of the studio, his four exes were being lined up on a curved sofa. He winced. Some of them had exchanged words in the past. He just hoped the studio had prepared for this adequately.

No matter how much he squinted at the spotlights he couldn't see Rose. All he'd felt from her was an overwhelming sense of panic. She'd left this morning as if she'd had second thoughts. She hadn't responded to any of his messages. And for the first time ever Will felt as if the shoe was on the other foot. He wanted Rose to feel the same as he did. He *needed* Rose to feel the same way he did.

Otherwise all his plans would be for nothing and he was about to make an even bigger fool of himself than normal.

Paul was talking now, playing the audience a clip showing each of his ex-fiancées talking about choosing their dare for him.

He looked at the four women. At one point he'd loved every one of them. At least he'd thought he had. He recognised it now as infatuation.

Nothing like what he felt for Rose. She was his first thought in the morning and his last thought at night. He'd seen her vulnerability last night. He'd wanted to do everything he could to protect the woman that he loved.

He wasn't running scared from Rose. Just the opposite. He was running towards her so quickly he was afraid he'd scare her off.

What if he'd misjudged the situation completely and she really didn't want to take things that far? All he knew was it was so important to him to show her that she was different. That she was *The One*. To show her he wasn't the Runaway Groom any more.

Paul touched his arm. 'Are you ready for the final figure?'

Will blinked. He hadn't been paying the slightest bit of attention.

Paul was still smiling his perfect TV smile. 'Would you

like to give the audience a little insight into why this charity is so important to you?'

Focus. Will nodded. This was the important bit. 'The charity is so important to me because I've had a friend affected by homelessness. There are a lot of misconceptions about people who live on the streets. Not all are drug addicts or alcoholics. Not all have been in trouble with the police. My friend hadn't done anything wrong, but because of the economic downturn his company went out of business. As a result he lost his home. He couldn't apply for jobs because he didn't have a permanent address. He didn't have family to turn to. He was embarrassed to tell his friends. I only found out after he was stabbed on the streets one night and the police contacted me because they found my card amongst his things. I want people to understand that there are a whole host of reasons people end up on the streets and there are lots of things we can do to help prevent it. Find out where your nearest shelter is. See what you can do to help. It doesn't have to be a lot. It can be donating clothes, donating food. It can be helping out in the kitchen. It can be helping people learn new skills.'

Paul nodded solemnly and turned to the camera. 'The votes have now closed. We're just about to find out how much money has been raised for charity. Ladies, are you ready?'

The camera panned along the four women with smiles on their faces. This was so not Will's idea of a good time. But if it got the message across he really didn't care.

'Is there any particular dare you'd like to avoid, Will?'

He shook his head. 'Paul, I'm willing to do whatever the public voted on no matter how humiliating it is. I just want to thank each and every person who picked up the phone and voted, contributing to the fund.' He put his hand on his chest. 'Thank you all from the bottom of my heart.'

Paul waited for the drum roll. It seemed to last for ever. Dramatic TV seemed to be his forte.

'Voting on the dares has finished. Will Carter, the total amount of money raised for your homeless charity is...one point one million pounds!'

Will's legs took on a life of their own and he shot upright with the wildest yell, punching the air. 'Yes!' His brain was jammed full of all the things the charity could do with the money. All the things that would make a difference for the people on the street. Staff. Housing. Employment. Rose was a genius. He could kiss her. He would kiss her.

Paul was still talking as Will pushed his way through the buzzing studio. He'd stopped listening to Paul. He'd stopped worrying about the cameras. All he wanted to do was find Rose.

Rose. There was a stunned smile on her face as he elbowed people out of the way to get to her. He picked her up in his arms and spun her around. 'Way to go, Rose! Have you any idea what this means?'

He didn't wait for an answer, just lowered her down and planted a kiss square on her lips, reaching his hands up to either side of her face. She tasted of strawberries. Sweet, juicy strawberries.

But she wasn't kissing back. Not as she usually did.

The buzz in the studio seemed to have died down a little. Will felt a tap on the shoulder. Paul, with a camera and light at his side. 'Will, who is this? Is this someone that we all should meet? Could this be your newest fiancée?'

He felt her bristle under his touch, every muscle in her body tensing. She pulled her lips away from his.

Panic. That was all he could see in her eyes. He'd misjudged this so badly. The one thing he didn't want to do. He'd just been swept away by the momentum of the event, and the memories of this morning. He hadn't even asked Rose if she was ready to go public and now, he'd just kissed her on national television in front of all his ex-fiancées. Could he get this any more wrong?

'Rose. Don't panic. This will be fine. Let me handle this,' he whispered.

But she looked horrified. Her hands fell from his sides. 'I'm not ready for this, Will.' Her words were cold. Definite.

Will stepped back as if stung. She looked hurt. She looked confused. *He'd* done this to her.

Will was used to women falling in love with him. He wasn't used to them stepping away. But Rose was different. And he'd known it from the start. It was why he loved her.

He turned to Paul. Right now, he could cheerfully punch him. Paul knew exactly who Rose was—he'd worked with her often enough.

'Rose is just a friend,' he said quickly before turning and beaming at the camera. 'I don't think I'm quite ready for another fiancée, do you?' He gestured towards the four sitting women. 'Let's find out what dare I will be doing.'

Paul led him back over towards the TV sofas as his head spun round and round. How was he going to get this back? How was he going to sort this?

He glanced behind him. But the spot that Rose had been standing in was empty. She was gone.

Rose had never walked so quickly. Hot tears were spilling down her cheeks. *I don't think I'm quite ready for another fiancée, do you?*

How much more of a wake-up call did she need? Fiancées. He collected them like some kids collected dolls, or rubbers, or cars. Will Carter made promises he couldn't keep. He never saw things through to the main event.

That wasn't for her. It never would be. Rose was a traditionalist. She wanted what her mum and dad had. Love to last a lifetime. Nothing less would do. She wouldn't, *couldn't* settle for anything else.

She waited until she burst from the studio doors and the cool fresh air hit her before she finally released all the pent-up sobs. Home. She needed to go home. She needed to see her sisters.

Because at a time like this—only sisters would do.

CHAPTER TWELVE

WILL'S PHONE SOUNDED and he bolted across the room,
knocking over a chair and leaping over his bed to reach it.

'Rose?' he answered breathlessly.

'Violet,' came the snarky reply. 'And I'm going to kill
you with my bare hands, Will Carter.'

He sagged onto the bed. 'I thought it was Rose. I've
left her a dozen messages and sent about a hundred texts.'

'I know. I've read them all. I'm in charge of Rose's
phone now.'

He winced. The messages were private. They weren't
really for family viewing.

'Please, just let me talk to her.'

'You did my sister, Will.' The blunt words cut through
him. 'Of all the women in the world, you had to break my
sister's heart.'

'No,' he cut in quickly. 'That's the last thing I want to do.'

'Well, it's too late.' He'd never heard Violet like this.
They'd been good friends for years with never a cross
word.

'Violet, how long have you known me?'

There was a pause. 'Three years.'

'Have I ever lied to you?'

The pause stretched on and on. 'Well...no.'

'Violet, I love Rose with all my heart. I've even done

something really crazy to prove it to her. But it's a bit hard to tell her about it if she won't even talk to me. I need your help.'

He could almost hear Violet's brain ticking over at the end of the phone. 'Violet, please. This is it for me. *Rose* is it for me. There won't ever be anyone else. Help me prove it to her.'

There was a loud sigh at the end of the phone. 'This better be good, Will.'

The relief was immense. 'It's better than good, Vi. I promise you. Here's what I need you to do…'

She hadn't had a minute. The last week had been frantic. Finalising every detail of her parents' wedding renewal. Trying to make sure that Daisy wasn't doing too much in her current condition and avoiding the messages from Will.

She'd had flowers every single day. Followed by balloons and cupcakes and the chocolates she'd loved at the wedding fair. It was nice. It was charming. But it was a token from a guy who was good at giving tokens, just not good at giving his whole heart.

Violet initially had been mad. Daisy had been sympathetic. But for the last few days both sisters had been surprisingly quiet. Maybe they were as caught up in the arrangements as she was.

But at last everything was ready—or at least it should be.

The marquees were finally in place and their corners filled with metallic heart-shaped balloons. The flower arches and covered chairs for the outside ceremony were complete. The weather had even decided to let the sun shine for the day.

People had been arriving at Huntingdon Hall since this

morning. One celebrity friend after another with their little lists of demands. Rose had ignored every one of them. They were big enough to sort themselves out. She had her mother to deal with.

Daisy was lying across the chaise longue in her green gown, her hair in curls around her shoulders. 'Do you think I'm getting kankles?' she moaned.

'What on earth are kankles?' asked Violet. Her purple gown fitted perfectly and the beautiful exotic flowers that their mother had picked were the perfect explosion of colour against the rich jewel-toned gowns.

'Puffy ankles. Pregnant woman ankles. Do you think I'm getting them?'

Violet gave a cursory glance at Daisy's perfectly normal ankles in her flat jewelled sandals. 'Oh, belt up, Daisy.'

Rose winced. That was sharp—even for Violet, but she seemed a little on edge today.

'Well, girls, what do you think? Am I ready to face the world?'

Sherry Huntingdon looked magnificent. Her cream lace fishtail gown hugged every inch of her perfect body. All three girls were around her in an instant. Group hug. It was something they'd done since early childhood.

'You look spectacular, Mum,' said Rose quickly, trying to bat back the tears from her eyes. 'Dad won't be able to take his eyes off you.'

Daisy gave a little nod. 'Let's go to the staircase and get some pictures of that gown on the stairs. It will be gorgeous.' She was already thinking like the professional.

But Rose couldn't relax and be happy for the family portraits—even though she wanted to. Her stomach was wound like a tightly coiled spring. She should be able to relax. Everything was coming together. All the hours she'd spent working on the plans were finally coming to fruition.

The endless nights she'd spent in her workshop working on the gold bangle for her mother would be worth it. She was sure of it. So why didn't she feel good?

Everything was perfect. Everything was hitch free. Three hundred people attended the wedding renewal ceremony. Amongst them, somewhere, would be Will—but she hadn't seen him yet.

After the renewal ceremony there were more photos, cake cutting, hors d'oeuvres and lots of wine. Then it was time for the sit-down meal.

Her father stood up to make a speech and she felt her breath hitch in her throat. He raised his glass. 'I want to thank you all for coming today, to see the wedding that my beautiful wife always deserved.' He gave a little laugh. 'Even if I am twenty-eight years too late. Most of you know that Sherry and I got married on a whim in Vegas. We hardly knew each other at all. But—' he raised his glass and looked at his wife '—when you know—you just know.' There was no hiding the love and devotion in his eyes. 'I want you all to know that every day that has been filled with Sherry has been perfect. We've fought. We've argued. There has been the odd occasion that we haven't spoken. But there hasn't been a single day I haven't wanted to be part of this partnership—part of this family with our three wonderful, if challenging, daughters.'

He picked up a box from the table. 'Lots of people buy new wedding rings for a renewal ceremony. But Sherry and I didn't want to do that. We've had these rings for twenty-eight years and they've seen us through the good, the bad and the beautiful. They're sort of our lucky charms. So...' he gave a little nod to Rose '...with the help of one of our fabulously talented daughters, I got her something else.'

He handed over the box to Sherry, who opened it with

shaking hands. She took out the bangle, the three twisted strands of gold intersected with a rose, a violet and a daisy. The recognition was instant and she leapt to her feet and wrapped her hands around Rick's neck. 'It couldn't be more perfect,' she declared.

The waiters were standing behind everyone, ready to put down the perfectly made first courses. But Rose's stomach was done. She couldn't even try a mouthful.

She'd always known it. It had played along in the background all along. This was what she wanted. This. The perfect part of knowing that every day, no matter what, there was one person you wanted by your side.

'Excuse me,' she said quickly to the person sitting next to her. 'I have to powder my nose.'

Her footsteps covered the gardens quickly, taking her back to the sanctity of the house. The quiet of the house, the coolness of the house.

She took a deep breath, closed her eyes and leaned against the cool wall. Hold it together. Stop being so pathetic. This is your parents' wedding renewal. All you need to do is get through the day. This isn't about you. This isn't about Will. This is about them.

The voices circulated in her head, but they did nothing to stop the tears pooling behind her eyelids. There was a small thud beside her, the sound of another pair of shoulders hitting the wall right next to her. Violet. Then a hand slid into hers. A broad, thick hand, its fingers interlocking with her own. Not Violet.

Her eyes flew open. 'Will.' She didn't want him to see her like this. She wanted him to see her when she was sure of herself, when she knew exactly how to react around him.

He let go of her hand and stepped in front of her, placing one hand above each shoulder, fencing her against the wall.

'Rose,' he said matter-of-factly. 'No phones, no messages.' He gave a wry smile. 'No flowers, no balloons, no cupcakes. Just you. And me.'

Her breath was caught somewhere in her throat. Halfway up and halfway down and not being of any use at all.

'I… I…' She couldn't find any suitable words.

He shook his head. 'Not I. Not you. Not me. Us. We need to talk about us, Rose.'

'There is no us.' The words rushed out.

'But there should be.' His reply was equally quick.

Her brain was working on overdrive. She had so many things she wanted to say. 'I'm sorry. I couldn't handle that day at the studio. When I saw all your exes lined up and looking at me I just felt as if I were the next lamb to the slaughter.'

He blinked. It wasn't her best choice of words. But her brain wasn't treading carefully right now.

'It was too much, Will. It was too soon. After what we'd just done and then Angie said something, then Melissa… and then you kissed me and Paul cracked that joke.'

He lifted a finger to her lips. 'Stop, Rose. Just stop.'

She stopped babbling and tried to think straight. He lifted his finger gently from her lips and placed it over his heart.

'Angie, Melissa, Paul.' He shook his head. 'You are the person that matters to me, Rose. All those women were my past. None of them matter. You're what matters, Rose. You are my future.'

She opened her mouth again and he shook his head to silence her. 'I should have known how you would feel in the studio. I didn't want to be there—why on earth would you? It was claustrophobic. They hadn't spent the night we just had. They hadn't seen what we'd just seen, or shared what we'd just shared. When Paul told me how much money we'd raised the first person I wanted to see, the first person I wanted to share that with, was you, Rose. Nobody else. You were the person I wanted to celebrate with.'

He raised his eyebrows and his mouth quirked. 'And I want to thank you for not coming to that department store and helping me sell women's lingerie all day dressed in nothing but a thong.'

She couldn't help but smile. The pictures of Will's butt had probably sold a million newspapers. The store had never had such good sales and had pledged part of them to the homeless charity.

She sighed. 'I just couldn't, Will. I needed some time. I needed some space.'

He reached up and wound his finger through one of her blonde curls. 'I get that. I do. But I've missed you. I've missed you every single day, Rose. I don't want to spend a single day without you.'

The lump in her throat was growing by the second. He was good. He was really good. And he was being sincere. But she still had the horrible doubts that she wasn't the only woman to hear those words and it was breaking her heart.

He touched her cheek. 'I love you, Rose. I don't want to be without you. I don't want to be without you ever.'

A tear slid down her cheek. She should be singing with joy and while part of her wanted to, she couldn't face the heartache that being left at the altar might bring. Not when she loved him with her whole heart.

It was just the two of them in the corridor. She had a clear, unblinking view of the dark rim around his eyes. Something she could spend the rest of her life looking at.

'And I can prove it.' He reached inside his jacket and her heart lurched.

No. Not this. Anything but this.

'I don't want to be your next fiancée,' she cried. The words just blurted out.

'And I don't want you to be my next fiancée,' he replied coolly. His hand came out slowly from his jacket pocket. It wasn't a ring box. It wasn't anything remotely like jewellery he was holding. It was a piece of paper. No matter what she'd said before, her heart gave a little sag.

He handed it to her silently and took his other hand down from the wall next to her head.

Her hands were trembling as she unfolded the paper. She stared at it for a few seconds. Blinking at the words. She couldn't make sense of it at all because she'd never seen anything like this before.

'What is it?' Her voice was shaking.

'It's our wedding banns. For tonight, for a wedding in the church on the island. I don't want you to be my fiancée, Rose. I want you to be my wife. I didn't know how else to prove it to you.'

'But…but…how did you do this?' Her hands were still trembling as she looked at the date. Sixteen days before. Now she really couldn't breathe. Her legs felt like jelly beneath her. 'You knew then?'

He nodded. 'I knew then, Rose. I didn't doubt it. The only person I had to convince was you.'

'You want us to get married today?'

He smiled and knelt down. 'This is how I'm supposed to do it, isn't it? I guess I just was scared you wouldn't let me get this far.'

He reached up and took both her hands. 'Rose Huntingdon-Cross. I love you with my whole heart and I want you to be the person I wake up next to every morning. And I don't care what continent we do that on. If you want to go back to New York and work, I'll come with you. If you want to keep designing wedding jewellery—I'll build you a whole workshop. Whatever you want, Rose, I'll do it.'

He bent forward and kissed the tips of her fingers, one after the other. 'I've listened to every single thing you've told me. You don't want a big wedding. Check. You loved the church on the island. Check. You don't want a runaway groom. Check. You want things to be simple. Check. All you want is a dress, flowers and I've taken a gamble on a string of fairy lights. Check. You want someone who loves you with their whole heart. Check. You want the kind of love that your parents have—' he winked at her '—Violet let me in on that secret. Check. So, will you do me the honour of becoming my wife tonight? I love you, Rose. I'll never love anyone like you, and I'm hoping you feel the same way. Because I want that kind of love too, Rose. The kind that your parents have—the kind that lasts for ever.'

She couldn't believe it. She couldn't believe her ears. 'You really want to do this now—tonight? You planned this two weeks ago?'

'I planned this two weeks ago.'

'But how could you possibly have known?' She couldn't wipe the smile from her face.

He tilted his head. 'Because when you know, Rose, you just know. Remind you of anyone we know?'

The words flooded over her. He'd used her father's expression and it had never seemed so apt. It was time. It was time to let go and trust her instincts. She'd grown more than she could ever have predicted in the last three years. It was time to throw off the seeds of doubt. Will was standing in front of her declaring his love. He'd done all this for *her*. He'd done all this because he loved *her*. And she loved him with her whole heart.

She smiled. In her head she could see them already. Sitting on a little wooden bench with grey hair growing old together—of that, she had no doubt.

He stood up and put his hands on her hips. 'Ready to visit our island?'

She grinned. 'Our island. I like the sound of that…'

CHAPTER THIRTEEN

WHEN HER STOMACH flipped over now it was with pure excitement. They pulled up straight next to where the boat was moored. Even from here she could see multicoloured fairy lights strung across the thick trees on the island.

'What about witnesses?' It was the first time she'd given it any thought. The drive here had just been a blur.

Will touched her face. 'I spoke to Violet. If we'd tried to sneak your sisters away from the renewal it might have attracted some attention. They'll be waiting for us when we get back. Our witnesses—as long as you're happy—will be Judy and my friend, Arral. I invited him along specially.' She smiled and nodded as tears pooled in her eyes. He'd thought of everything.

She fingered the fine material of her blue dress. It wasn't quite what she'd imagined herself getting married in, but then again, this was how she'd always wanted to do it—just as her parents had—no fuss, just two people who loved each other saying their vows.

The journey to the island was smooth as silk. He helped her out of the boat at the other side and pointed her towards the cottage. 'There's a surprise for you in there. I'll give you a few minutes.'

She nodded as she walked into the cottage. It was just as beautiful as she remembered. But the ambience had changed. Last time it had been full of pent-up emotion and surging hormones. This time it was balanced. This time it was full of hope, promise and love.

She caught her breath. A full-length dress was hanging part way from the ceiling, just within her reach. It was a real-life wedding dress. Cream embroidery at the top with an embroidered tulle straight skirt, it was exactly what she would have picked for herself.

It only took a few minutes to slip out of the blue dress and into the cream one. On a table at the side were a few lemon roses tied with lemon and cream ribbons. All the while she'd thought Will was helping her plan her parents' renewal he'd actually been planning their own wedding.

There was a knock at the door. 'Rose? Is everything okay? Are you ready?' He sounded a little nervous.

She walked over and opened the door. He'd changed into a grey suit with a matching lemon rose buttonhole. Her husband-to-be couldn't have looked more perfect.

She slid her hand into his. 'I can't wait.'

They walked hand in hand to the church. Will smiled as he opened the door and a wave of heart-shaped foil balloons burst from the doors and floated into the sky above. Then he led her down the aisle where their witnesses and celebrant stood waiting.

It was perfect. It was magical. The room was lit with fairy lights and candles. The evening light behind the stained-glass windows sent beautiful shards of rainbow reflections over the white walls.

She walked over and gave both Judy and Arral a kiss on the cheek. 'Thank you for coming,' she whispered. 'Thank you for sharing this with me and Will.'

The celebrant nodded. 'Can we begin?'

Rose took a deep breath and nodded, looking into the

eyes of the man she loved. No Runaway Groom. No waiting. Will was about to become her husband.

They repeated their names and made their declarations. For a second Rose expected the church to be invaded by a wave of angry objecting ex-fiancées, but everything was silent.

Will turned to face his bride, holding up a plain yellow band. 'This was the one thing I couldn't plan. I could hardly ask my wife to make her own wedding band without letting her in on the secret. So, I decided we'd make do for now because she'll have the rest of her life to change them if she wishes.'

Rose nodded. 'These will be perfect.'

Will held the ring poised at her finger. 'Rose Huntingdon-Cross. I love you more than I ever thought possible. I've shared things with you that I could never share with another living soul. You complete me. You are my world. I want to spend the rest of my life getting to know you more and promise to love you more each day until the end of my life.' He smiled at her. 'Because when you know—you just know.'

She let out a nervous laugh and picked up his wedding ring, her fingers trembling as she slid it onto his finger. 'Will Carter, you burst into my life in the most unpredictable way and will probably bear the scar for the rest of our lives. I love you, Will Carter, even though I was afraid to. You've taught me that after three years it's okay to trust my instincts again. You've taught me that people aren't always what we presume they are. You've taught me that there's a whole world out there that I knew nothing about. I want to spend the rest of my life working side by side with my husband and helping those who want to be helped. I want to grow with you, Will. I want to love you more each day.

And you'll never be my runaway groom, you'll always be my husband, the man who has captured my heart.'

She leaned forward and they kissed. His hands sliding down her back and cupping her backside, pressing her against him. She wound her hands around his neck. She couldn't have planned anything more perfect. This was all she'd ever wanted from a wedding. Her and her husband saying their vows at a beautiful setting. Two people who loved each other for ever.

'Do we get to have our honeymoon in the cottage?' she whispered.

He shook his head. 'Oh, no. The honeymoon is a complete surprise. We'll be gone for three weeks.'

She pulled back. 'Three weeks? But what about the tour and the charity concert?' She put her hand to her mouth. 'Oh, no. I'm supposed to pick up that reporter from the airport in a few hours.'

Will laughed and shook his head. 'Oh, no, you don't. That's all under control. For the next three weeks Violet is in charge. I've given her your black planner and she's picking up Tom Buckley at the airport. She's even packed your case. All we need to do is go back and tell your parents and Daisy that we're married.'

'Really?' He'd thought of everything.

He held out his hand towards her and she slid her fingers into her husband's. 'Really.'

By the time they arrived back her father had just finished rocking out on the stage with his band. His hair was damp with sweat and his jacket and tie had been flung aside.

Daisy and Violet were pacing. It was obvious Violet hadn't been able to keep things to herself.

She rushed over straight away. There was no mistaking the look on her face; she was genuinely delighted. She grabbed hold of Rose's left hand. 'Have you done it? Are you genuinely Mrs Carter?'

Rose gave the tiniest nod; she couldn't hide the grin that spread from one ear to the other as she looked at her brand-new husband. 'Mrs Carter, wow.' She hadn't actually said the words out loud and they seemed unreal.

But that didn't stop Violet. 'Wheeeee!' She let out a yell and jumped on Will, sending him flat out onto the grass. 'Finally!'

Will couldn't stop laughing. 'I take it you approve.'

Violet bent forward and kissed him on the forehead. 'Finally, I stop having to pretend to like all your fiancées.' She winked at Rose. 'This one, I love!'

'Rose!' Her mother's voice cut through the crowd of people.

Will stood up from the grass, dusted himself off and slid his hand into hers.

Sherry was gorgeous as ever. Her eyes widened slightly as she noticed the change in Rose's dress. She wrapped her arms around her daughter's shoulder. 'You look beautiful, darling.'

She reached her hand over to touch Will's cheek. 'I take it you have something to tell me, Mr Carter?'

Rick appeared at Sherry's side, sliding his arm around her waist. Rose was holding her breath, well aware that both her sisters were doing the same thing. But Rick Cross grinned and held out his hand towards Will. 'I take it she said yes?'

Will shook his hand. 'You've no idea the relief I felt.'

Sherry's eyebrows rose. 'You knew?'

Rick laughed. 'Of course I knew. Will's a traditionalist. He asked me a few weeks ago.'

Sherry shook her head. 'And you kept it a secret from me?'

Rick rolled his eyes. 'You and secrets, Sherry? Oh, no. I wasn't getting myself in that much trouble.'

'I've got something to tell you, too, Dad.' Rose's heart was thudding in her chest. She'd never been so sure of anything.

'What is it, honey?'

She intertwined her fingers with Will's. 'When I come back from my honeymoon I'll help with the final plans for the tour and then I'll be resigning.' She shot Will a smile. 'I'm going to be working on my jewellery collection full-time.'

Her father gave a little nod of his head. It was almost as if he'd been expecting it.

He leaned over and kissed Rose's cheek. 'I take it you got the wedding you always wanted, beautiful?'

She breathed in deeply. Her parents were happy for her. Her sisters were happy for her.

And she had a husband she loved and trusted with her whole heart.

She leaned up and whispered in his ear. 'Can the honeymoon start now?'

Will slid his hands around her waist as his blue eyes twinkled. 'Absolutely.'

* * * * *

FALLING FOR THE BRIDESMAID

SOPHIE PEMBROKE

For George and Karen, for making this book possible through coffee, childcare and cheerleading!

Thank you both, so much.

CHAPTER ONE

THE SWEET SMELL of rose petals filled the evening air, giving the falling dusk a sultry warmth. Music sang out from the band on the patio, romantic with just an undertone of sexy. Fairy lights twinkled in the branches of the trees and inside the marquees, and around them leaves rustled in the still warm breeze.

The whole set-up was so perfectly loved-up Violet thought she might be physically ill if she had to suffer through it a moment longer.

Glaring down at her lavender bridesmaid's dress, she slunk to the edge of the celebrations where she could watch the live band play in peace. She needed to make more of an effort to enjoy the evening, and maybe the music would help. Her parents' vow renewal ceremony had been beautiful, and the party that followed a huge success. Later, she had no doubt, her dad and the boys from The Screaming Lemons would take to the stage and wow the remaining guests all over again, even though they'd finished their official set an hour ago. Knowing Dad, it would probably be a lower key, acoustic set the second time around.

Keeping Dad off the stage was always more trouble than getting him on there, and he always wanted one more encore. But for now the support act seemed to be doing well enough. The courtyard in front of the stage was filled with people dancing, or just holding each other, or kissing. Falling in love.

Violet scowled and looked away.

Of course, the situation wasn't helped by her family. There, leaning against her new husband—Lord Sebastian Beresford, Earl of Holgate, if you please—was her youngest sister, Daisy. No, the Lady Holgate now. Hard to believe that Daisy-Waisy was an honest-to-God countess, but somehow not quite as impossible to process as the slight swell of her baby bump under her carefully chosen emerald-green bridesmaid's dress.

Just a few more months and Violet would officially be the maiden aunt of the family. Hell, she was already doing the church flowers most weekends, and taking tea with her mother's 'ladies who lunch' crowd. Maybe she should just skip straight ahead to adopting a three-legged cat and taking up crochet.

Actually, she'd quite like to learn to crochet, but that wasn't the point.

Seb rested his hand against his wife's stomach, and Daisy's soft smile grew into a fully fledged grin as she tilted her face for a kiss. Violet turned away, suddenly embarrassed to be staring.

But unfortunately her gaze just landed on Rose and Will, looking equally wrapped up in each other. Her twin sister and her best friend. Violet had to admit she really hadn't seen that one coming either. An attraction, perhaps, or maybe even a fling. Not that Will would give up his runaway groom status for good and marry into her family. But there Rose stood in her own wedding dress, after sneaking away for their own secret marriage ceremony once their parents' vow renewal service was over.

Maybe she just had no sort of love radar at all. Or maybe it was broken. That would explain a hell of a lot, really.

Will glanced up at just the wrong moment and, this time, Violet couldn't look away quick enough. Even staring pointedly at the band, she couldn't miss the whispered conversation between Rose and *her* new husband. Probably trying to decide whose responsibility Violet's hurt feelings were now.

Violet sighed. It wasn't that she wasn't happy for her sisters—she really, truly was. And she knew that their happiness shouldn't make her own sorry situation feel so much worse. But it did.

Swallowing, she looked down at her feet, and the high heels pinching her toes. It would pass, she knew. Any day now she'd be able to look at all the happy and loved-up people around her and just smile, without the bitter tinge that threatened to colour her whole world.

That day just wasn't yet, that was all.

'She thinks you're cross with her, you know. Or me, possibly,' Will said, standing beside her with his hands in his pockets. Such a familiar sight at these events. Usually Will's presence was a comfort, a reliable soul to help her through the amused looks, the only half-whispered comments, and the occasional drunken suggestion from guys she barely knew but who clearly thought they knew all about her—and her sexual proclivities.

Today, though, he was just a reminder that things wouldn't ever be the same again.

'Cross with Rose?' Violet asked, mustering up a smile. 'Why on earth would I be cross with her? For stealing you away from me? Good riddance, I say.'

The startled look on Will's face told her she'd misjudged something very badly.

'Uh, no. She thinks you're mad because you got landed with picking up that reporter guy from the airport tonight, so you're missing out on the good champagne. That or the whole Benefit Concert thing.'

Ah, that. Yeah, that would make more sense. Especially since she hadn't been completely silent about her unhappiness that the reporter was coming at all.

'I hadn't really…you think she stole me away from you?'

Violet gave him a withering stare. 'Yes, Will. I've been lusting after you, pining away for you through every one of your ridiculous engagements and runaway groom stunts. And now you've finally married my sister, I don't think I will ever recover.'

Her deadpan delivery apparently sold it because Will laughed with obvious relief. 'Good. That's…okay, then. And you're not mad about the reporter either?'

'I'm mad about the champagne. Otherwise, I'll cope.'

'You're sure? I know you're a little…'

Violet tried to guess the word he was avoiding saying. Nervous? Worried? Paranoid?

Probably paranoid.

'Apprehensive about him coming,' Will finished.

Violet sighed. Apprehensive wasn't the half of it. But her dad had made up his mind that he wanted to tell his story, have that official biography on the shelves, and he'd picked this guy to do it. Rose had looked at her with worried eyes when he'd announced it, but even she admitted it made sense to do it now, ahead of the new tour and album. The reporter guy would have exclusive access, in-depth interviews and enough connections to get a real buzz going in the media.

'Rose says he's nice,' Will tried. 'They met in New York before she came home.'

'I'm sure he's a doll,' Violet replied. It didn't matter who he was. He was press, and only interested in them as a story, as something he could sell.

Violet had learned that lesson the hard way.

Will frowned. 'Maybe if you talk to your dad...'

Shaking her head, Violet gave him a gentle smile. 'It's fine. I promise.' Dad had made up his mind and that was it. As always. Nothing Will, Daisy, Rose or Violet could do to change it. And so there was no point dwelling on it. She'd just stay out of his way as much as possible and hope for the best.

What else could she do?

'And about the Benefit Concert—' he started, but Violet cut him off.

'Go on, Will.' She pushed against his arm. 'Go whisk Rose away on your honeymoon. I'll take care of things here, I promise. Since you've apparently already texted the reporter guy my phone number, he's my responsibility now, and I think I can manage one airport pick-up. You two go relax for a bit. Get used to being married for once, instead of just temporarily engaged.'

'Okay. See you soon, kid.' With a quick hug and a peck on the cheek, he headed back towards Rose, and Violet was alone again.

As usual.

She hadn't exactly *lied* to Will, she decided. She had never thought of Will as husband material—or even one-night stand material. He was worth far more to her as a friend, and she'd never felt that spark, that flash of something more that hinted that they could be anything else.

It was just kind of weird that he obviously felt that flash with *Rose* of all people. Her so-identical-it-was-actually-spooky twin sister.

Although, really, she should be used to people seeing something in Rose that they never saw in her. After all, hadn't their parents made Rose stay home instead of going back to the States after Daisy's wedding, just so she could organise their vow renewal ceremony and party? Even though Violet had been right there, with time on her hands, happy to help?

Not that she was bitter. She knew why they hadn't asked—because they'd been sure she wouldn't want to do it. Wouldn't want to have to deal with so many people, so many knowing eyes.

And they were probably right.

Will hadn't thought about that as he'd told her where to find Rose's black planner, though, and asked her to make sure everything kept ticking over for the annual Huntingdon Hall Benefit Concert while they were away on their honeymoon. Maybe he'd just been too caught up in the flush of true love to think about it. Or maybe he expected her to hand it over to some agency person, hired to cover Rose's job.

Maybe she should. After all, she knew absolutely nothing about how to organise a concert for thousands of people. Will had insisted that Rose had already done all the hard work, that there'd be practically nothing left for Violet to do.

Because obviously otherwise they'd have found someone more competent to put in charge.

Violet shook her head. She was being ridiculous. She hadn't wanted to organise the vow renewal anyway. Or the Benefit Concert, come to that. She had other obligations. But now that Rose had told their dad she'd be stepping down from her job managing the PR and events for The Screaming Lemons once she got back from her honeymoon…well, someone would have to do it. And Violet couldn't ignore the very small part of her brain that thought that person could be her.

No. She had no experience, and no desire to deal with people who laughed at her behind her back all day long.

She'd just stick to things she knew she was good at. Like arranging flowers, thank you very much.

The flower displays she'd designed for the vow renewal were, she decided, by far her best displays yet. Lots of exotic blooms in deep jewel colours. Striking and memorable, just like her parents. Her flowers rocked, everyone said so.

There you had it. Twenty-seven years on the planet, and that was all she could say about herself.

Violet Huntingdon-Cross—kick-ass flower arranger, wannabe crocheter. Potential cat lady in waiting.

No, that wasn't all. That was just all that other people saw—and she was happy to keep it that way. She made a difference in the lives of young people and teenagers every day, even if no one ever knew it was her. After all, if word got around that Violet Huntingdon-Cross was manning the phones at the troubled teen helpline, their calls would skyrocket with people wanting to ask her about her own past, or just talk to a minor celebrity—and the kids she really wanted to help wouldn't be able to get through at all. So she helped where she could. Even if she wished she could do more.

Her parents did the same, helping out charities anonymously when they could. The only difference was, they also did enough charity work—as well as music and the occasional modelling gig respectively—in public that everyone assumed they already knew everything there was to know about Rick and Sherry Cross.

But with Violet…well, Violet could only imagine what they were *still* saying about her. Probably the nicest was that she'd become a recluse.

Still, that was a hell of a lot better than what they'd been saying about her eight years ago.

Pulling her phone from her tiny clutch bag, she checked the time and then double-checked the email Will had sent her from Rose's account with the reporter guy's flight details. Thomas Buckley...that was his name. She must make an effort not to just call him reporter guy all the time. Although it never hurt to have a reminder that the press were press and always on the record, whatever they said. Not something she ever wanted to forget again.

Time to go. She'd get changed out of her bridesmaid's dress, grab the ridiculous name card Rose had left for her and be at Heathrow in plenty of time to grab a coffee before his flight landed. And, best of all, she wouldn't be stuck in romance central another minute.

Moving towards the side door to Huntingdon Hall, Violet paused as she caught sight of her parents, dancing in the light of the just risen moon. So wrapped up in each other that the couple of hundred people watching, who'd come all this way to celebrate with them, might not even be there at all. Sherry Huntingdon and Rick Cross were famously crazy about each other, but it wasn't until Violet caught them in moments like this that she really believed the media hype.

And that, she finally admitted to herself, was the real reason all this love stuff was getting to her. Deep down, she'd always believed that she'd just fall into a perfect relationship like her parents had, like both her sisters had now found too.

Instead, she'd got something else entirely. Like anti-love. The sort of relationship that tore up your insides and made you someone else. After that, if she was honest, Violet wasn't sure she'd ever have the courage to try again.

Her phone rang in her hand and Violet answered it automatically, glad for the distraction. 'Hello?'

'I was under the impression that you, whoever you are, were supposed to be meeting me at the airport about twenty minutes ago.' The American drawl made Violet's eyes widen. The reporter guy. Except Rose's email had him landing in an hour and a half. Dammit!

'I'm so sorry, Mr...' Oh, God, what was his name?

'Buckley.' He bit the surname out. 'And I could care less about apologies. Just get here, will you? I'll be in the bar.'

And, with that, the line went dead.

Picking up her skirt, Violet dashed for the garage and prayed no one had blocked her car in. She'd have to borrow one of her dad's if they had. No time to change now, or even pick up that specially made name card of Rose's. If she ever wanted to be relied on for more than flowers, she needed to not screw this up. And since the bad impression she—and by extension her family—had made on the reporter guy was already done, she needed to find a way to fix it. Starting with getting to Heathrow as fast as humanly possible, *before* he started drafting his story. She knew journalists. The truth seldom got in the way of a good story, and once they thought they knew all about a person it was almost impossible to convince them otherwise.

And Violet had already earned the Huntingdon-Cross family enough bad press to last a lifetime.

CHAPTER TWO

TOM PUSHED HIS way to the counter, dragging his suitcase behind him like a weapon. A coffee shop. What the hell kind of use to him was that, especially at this time of night? He needed a drink—a proper one. But that was arrivals for you—never as good as the departures lounge. After so many years travelling the world, you'd think he'd remember that. Except he was usually being collected straight off a plane these days, and got whisked through arrivals to some hotel or another without even clocking his surroundings.

He'd just have to hope that whoever the ditsy woman Rose had assigned to pick him up was would check her phone and see his text telling her to meet him here instead.

Staring at the menu above the counter with bleary eyes, Tom tried to figure out his best option. He'd already consumed so much caffeine in the last two weeks that his muscles appeared to be permanently twitching. Add that to the distinct lack of sleep, and he wasn't sure another shot of the black stuff was quite what he needed. Of course, what he *needed* was a big bed with cool sheets, a blackout blind and about twenty-four hours' solid rest.

None of which was a remote possibility until his ride pitched up.

Ordering a decaf something-or-other, Tom tossed his

jacket and laptop into the nearest bucket chair and hovered impatiently between it and the counter while he waited for his drink. If he'd flown first class, or even business, he could have had as many free drinks as he liked on the plane. But old habits died hard and, since this job was entirely on spec and therefore on his own dime, he'd been paying for his own flight. Something inside him still baulked at shelling out that much cash just for a better seat, even though money wasn't really an object any more. Certainly not the way it had been growing up.

His music journalism career had taken off enough in the past few years that he could rely on his contacts for a good life and a better income. He'd come a long way from his first big, explosive story, almost ten years ago.

So yeah, he could have afforded the upgrade, easily, and without tapping those savings. And if he'd remembered about the free booze aspect of things, he probably would have done. As it was…

Snatching his coffee from the girl behind the counter, he settled at his table and prepared to hang around a while. God only knew how long it would take his ride to get there from wherever she was, but he might as well get some work done while he waited. Even if he felt as if his eyes might jump right out of his head if he didn't close them soon.

At least the work was worth travelling all the way from New York for. A story like this, a break this big…it could make him, permanently. He'd be the go-to person for anything to do with The Screaming Lemons, and that was serious currency in the industry. It would give him access, and opportunities with the newer bands coming through. He'd have the pick of jobs.

He'd already made a pretty good name for himself with the bigger music magazines, websites and even the colour supplements. But this trip, these interviews, this was something more—it was a book in the making. That was what Rick Cross had promised him. And Tom was going to make sure the old man made good on his word.

He was annoyed to have missed all the upheaval in the Huntingdon-Cross family over the past two months, but it couldn't be helped. He'd already been committed to another project at home in the States and, anyway, who could have predicted that one of Rick and Sherry's famously blonde and beautiful daughters would get married and knocked up all within the space of eight weeks? And who knew what was going on with Rose now? She'd been in the press recently herself, he remembered, pictured with the famous Runaway Groom—who he'd *thought* was famously her sister *Violet's* best friend. Maybe something had happened there—and he'd missed it, again. All *he'd* had was a text message when he turned his phone back on after the flight, with a contact number and the information that, due to unforeseen but brilliant circumstances, someone else would be collecting him.

Or not, as the case might be.

Tom sighed. He'd just have to make sure he got good interviews with them all when he could. And, wherever Rose might be, at least one daughter was still living at home—probably the most famous one, if you counted notorious Internet celebrity, which Tom did.

Opening his laptop, he pulled up his notes on the family. He was staying at the family home, Huntingdon Hall, so he needed to be prepared from the get-go. He'd spent weeks compiling old interviews, articles and photos of the whole family, and felt he had it pretty much down. And after speaking with Rose in New York and on the phone while planning the trip, he'd thought he had at least one ally there—until she'd decided to swan off and abandon him with no notice.

Presumably she'd got an offer too good to refuse, no matter how much it inconvenienced anyone else. Celebrity kids—always the centre of their own world, however nice and normal Rose had seemed when they met. He needed to remember that.

He'd only had one conversation with the man he was really there to see, though—Rick Cross himself. Rock star, family man, reformed wide boy. The interviews Tom had on file dated back almost thirty years, back to when The Screaming Lemons were the next big thing on the rock scene. Nowadays, they were the old standards—and they had to try harder to shock or surprise.

With his plans for a tell-all book about the band and his family's history, it looked as if Rick had plans to do both.

Tom had asked him, 'Why now?' It couldn't be money—the band still sold enough greatest hits records and got more than enough airplay that it didn't matter if their latest album tanked. But all Rick would say was that it was time.

Scrolling through his family crib sheet, Tom reminded himself of all the most pertinent facts.

Most people in Britain and the States could pick Rick Cross out of a line-up and tell you his story. Same for his wife, the beautiful and rich mostly ex-model and now English society stalwart, Sherry Huntingdon. With his fame and her family, they made quite the impact.

Then there were the girls. The youngest, Daisy, was the newest Lady Holgate, which seemed pretty much par for the course for celebrity kids, Tom decided. After all, if you already had money and fame, surely a title was the only thing left to go for? Especially in the UK.

The twins were a few years older at twenty-seven. Rose, he knew from personal meetings with her, had been living in New York for the last few years, although she had planned to be in England until the annual benefit concert at least.

And then there was Violet. Tom had enjoyed the hell out of researching her. The thought made him smile even as he rubbed at his gritty eyes.

A commotion at the counter made him look up, and he blinked at the sight of a tall blonde in a ridiculous dress and heels crashing past a table full of customers. Was that Rose? Or a sleep deprivation induced hallucination?

'Sorry!' the blonde yelped, and he decided that she was probably real. Hallucinations didn't usually yelp, in his experience.

Shaking his head to try and wake up, Tom packed up his laptop. It looked as if his ride had made it after all. Any time now he could fall into that nice, peaceful, quiet bed and sleep for a week. Or at least until Rick Cross summoned him for his first interview.

From all the reports he'd read, Tom was pretty sure Rick wasn't an early riser. That lie-in was practically in the bag.

'Rose,' he said, hoisting his bag onto his shoulder and reaching for the handle of his suitcase. 'I thought you were going away? You didn't have to come all the way out here just because the idiot you asked to pick me up forgot. I could have just caught a cab, you know.'

Rose looked up, eyes wide, her hands still gripping her skirt. 'Oh, um, no, it's fine. Thomas. It's fine, Thomas.'

Why did she keep repeating his name? And why was she calling him *Thomas* instead of Tom all of a sudden? They'd spoken plenty of times before, and even had lunch once. It wasn't as if she might have forgotten it all of a sudden.

Unless…

The smirk formed unbidden on his lips. 'I'm sorry, *Violet*. I thought you were your sister for a moment. And it's Tom.'

'That's okay. You're not the only one to get confused.' She pulled a frustrated face, and Thomas couldn't help but laugh. It was just so *familiar*. And not from Rose.

'What?' Violet asked, obviously startled by his outburst. Maybe he should have had caffeinated coffee. Obviously the sleep deprivation was starting to affect him.

'I'm sorry,' he managed, trying to keep his smirk in check. 'But for a moment you looked just like you did in the—' Self-preservation kicked in as her face turned stony and he cut himself off.

'No, really. Do continue.' Her cut glass accent was sharp enough to wound, and any humour Tom had found in the situation ebbed away. 'I believe you were about to finish that sentence with the words "leaked sex tape", right?'

'I'm sorry,' Tom started, realising he'd apologised to this woman more in the first three minutes of meeting her than he'd normally need to in even a month of *dating* someone. But Violet interrupted before he could get to the part about sleep deprivation and inadequate impulse control.

'That's right,' she said, a little louder than Tom thought was strictly necessary. 'I'm the famous Huntingdon-Cross Sex Tape Twin. Not one of the two sisters who found true love and settled down. The one who men only want so they can film us together and put it on the Internet. Get your autographs here.'

The café was almost empty, but a couple of guys sitting at the table nearest the front definitely had their camera phones out. What kind of audacity did it take to stand up in public and admit to being the star of a ridiculously ex-plicit sex tape watched by half the world? The sort only the rich and famous had.

'And apparently, according to the frustrated and an-noyed look on my face, it can't even have been good sex. Personally, I don't remember, but Mr Buckley here has obviously watched it often enough to be considered an expert. Do feel free to ask him questions, if you like. I'm not in a hurry. I mean, I'm only missing my parents' marriage renewal ceremony to be here. Carry on.'

Waving an imperious hand towards him, Violet perched on the edge of a stool by the counter and waited. Feeling the heat of embarrassment in his cheeks, Tom grabbed the last of his things from the table and headed for the exit. Violet Huntingdon-Cross might be used to this sort of exposure, but he certainly wasn't.

'No questions? Oh, what a shame. I suppose we'd better be on our way, then.' Violet hopped down and followed him out into the arrivals hall.

'I suppose I deserved that,' he muttered as she held the door of the terminal open for him. He had laughed first. But she'd been over an hour and a half late to collect him. So the sleep deprivation was at least partly her fault, right?

'I suppose you did,' she replied. 'And I'm very sorry for being late to collect you. Rose gave me the wrong flight times.'

Damn. There went that argument.

'This is where you apologise to me for humiliating me in front of a crowd of people,' Violet prompted, and Tom raised his eyebrows.

'Me? Trust me, sweetheart, you did the humiliating all by yourself.' As if a performance of that sort was second nature to her. Which, judging by the sex tape, it might well be. He'd heard that Violet had calmed down in more recent years, but maybe the family had just got better at hiding her exploits from the media.

Her whole face flushed bright red at his words, and she pushed past him as they left the terminal. 'I'm parked in the short stay car park,' she called back over his shoulder.

He was pretty sure he wasn't supposed to hear her muttered words as she strode off towards the car, but he did. 'Hopefully not as short as your stay with us, though.'

Tom allowed himself a smile. Violet Huntingdon-Cross was definitely a worthy interview subject. And if he could get some new or hidden scandals on the eldest family wild child to help sell his book proposal, well, he'd be an idiot not to. Right?

CHAPTER THREE

VIOLET'S HANDS WERE still shaking as she tried to get the key into the ignition. At the back of the car, Tom was struggling to open the boot for his cases, but she had no intention of helping. Not least because the way her body was trembling meant she'd probably be even worse at it than him.

What on earth had possessed her? Eight years of best behaviour, of keeping her head down, of politely ignoring all the comments and jokes—all gone in one moment of frustration and humiliation in an airport coffee shop.

It had been his laugh, she decided, as the key finally slid home. It had made it so abundantly clear that she wasn't a real person to him, just a hilarious anecdote. One she had probably now ensured he would be dining out on for all time.

She was used to being seen as a public figure more than herself. She was always Rick and Sherry's daughter first, and often Rose or Daisy's sister before she was ever a person in her own right. Except when she was the Sex Tape Twin. And, quite honestly, she'd rather be nobody than *that*.

Except that was all she ever seemed to be to anyone outside her own family. And God, was she sick of it.

The car boot slammed shut; Tom must have managed to stow his cases away. Any moment now he'd slide into the passenger seat beside her and they'd have to make polite conversation all the way home. That, or sit in frosty silence. Violet wasn't sure which would be worse.

She sighed. Yes, she was. Silence would be worse. Because only her dad had any idea how long Thomas Buckley would be staying at their house, and she couldn't simply send him to Coventry indefinitely. This wasn't boarding school; it was real life. And somehow that had turned out to be even more confining and stifling than the strict Catholic school they'd all been sent to.

She was a grown-up now. The mistakes of her youth were *supposed* to be in the past. She was more than the stories people told about her. Which meant sucking it up and making nice with the offensive American music journalist who would be writing some sort of tell-all about her family and their life any time now. And hoping he'd forget what a disaster this whole night had been.

It was like her dad had said, back when That Tape had first hit the internet and suddenly her sex face was splashed all over magazines and newspapers everywhere. He'd left the rest of the band in some hotel somewhere, mid-tour, and come home to check on her. While she'd lain sobbing on her bed, he'd rubbed her back and told her, 'At least you know now, honey. Not everyone out there wants what's best for you. And only you can decide who to trust.'

Well. There was an easy answer to that one, Violet had found. Don't trust anyone—except family.

Will had been an exception to the rule, and a hard-won one at that. But it helped that he'd only ever been friend material. She wouldn't trust even her best friend with her whole heart. Not like Rose had done.

The passenger door opened and Violet sucked in a breath before plastering on a smile. 'All okay?'

Tom gave her a slightly wary look, as if uncertain

whether she might just drive off with him half in and half out of the car. She couldn't really blame him; she hadn't been exactly consistent since they'd met.

Time to start mending fences before he started writing articles.

'Fine.' Tom slid into the seat beside her. 'And, uh, you?'

She forced her smile to brighten further. 'Just dandy.'

'Right. And are you always prone to such extreme mood swings?'

Oh, God, he was probably thinking that she was on drugs, or bipolar, or something else that would make a good story. This was *not* going well.

Violet sighed. Time to try honesty. 'Okay, look. We got off to a rotten start here, I know. But Dad wants you staying with us, working with him, and Dad doesn't change his mind once it's made up. So I just have to suck it up and get on with things, right? And since I don't particularly want to spend the next however many weeks avoiding you or trading insults on sight, I figure the easiest thing is to pretend the last half an hour didn't happen. Okay?' Partial honesty, anyway. She didn't need to mention—

'Plus you don't want me to tell the story of this evening in any future articles or books?'

Damn. 'Well, do you blame me?'

Tom was quiet so long that she had to glance over to check that he hadn't fallen asleep. When she looked, he was holding out his hand.

Eyebrows raised, she took it, biting her lip at the slight tingle she felt at his skin against hers. For heaven's sake, it was a handshake! Had it really been so long since someone she wasn't related to by blood or marriage had touched her that her body had forgotten what it felt like?

'I'm Tom Buckley,' he said with a half smile. 'Nice to meet you. Thanks for coming to pick me up.'

'Violet Huntingdon-Cross. Sorry I was an hour and a half late.'

He chuckled. 'Let's just blame Rose for everything, yeah?'

'That's what I've been trying to do for the last twenty-seven years,' Violet said, and sighed. 'Sadly, it never seems to stick.'

At Tom's laugh, she slipped the car into gear and pulled out of the parking space. 'Come on. Let's get you home. I bet you're tired after your long journey.'

'Exhausted,' Tom admitted, and when she looked she could see the dark circles under his eyes, even in the poor lighting of the airport car park. 'That's kind of my excuse, actually. For, well, everything. Sleep deprivation. It's been a hell of a week.'

'I'm sure. Rose said you were working out in Miami?'

He nodded. 'For the last week. Then a flying visit home to New York to repack my bags, then straight here. I feel like I haven't slept in a month. I'm looking forward to some peace and quiet, actually. Your dad told me that Huntingdon Hall is out in the middle of nowhere, right?'

'Ye—es,' Violet said, biting her lip as she remembered the party she'd left just a couple of hours before. It was long gone midnight. Surely everyone would have gone home by the time they arrived, right? Oh, who was she kidding? Rick and Sherry's parties were legendary. They'd be lucky if they didn't find anyone passed out on the tennis court in the morning, this time.

'That sounds ominous,' Tom said. 'Do they have guests? Wait…' Glancing over, she saw him frown, the moment it clicked into place for him. 'Oh, hell. It's their vow renewal today, right? You said you were missing it… That's why you were so annoyed about having to come and fetch me?'

'And why I'm wearing this fetching yet inappropriate

dress,' Violet confirmed. No need for him to know that, actually, she'd been happy to get out of there. 'I'm afraid there's a very real chance the party might still be ongoing.' She glanced at the dashboard clock. 'In fact, I think Dad and the boys will probably be taking the stage for their encore session right about now.'

Tom groaned and let his head fall back against the headrest. 'So, no sleep tonight is what you're telling me.'

'Basically. Sorry! Maybe you can get some sleep in the car?' She should feel worse about this. The guy was obviously exhausted to the point of losing all social niceties. She should feel bad that her parents and their friends were going to keep him up for *another* night.

She really, really didn't, though.

It seemed to Tom that no sooner had he closed his eyes than a car door was slamming, then another opening, and cool night air flooded over his face. Followed swiftly by his ears being assaulted by one of The Screaming Lemons' classic hits being played as an acoustic number.

Normally, he'd be up at the front of the stage, soaking in the moment, tucking the memories away for future articles, trying to find the right words to describe the perfection of that three and a half minutes.

Tonight—or rather this morning—he just wanted it all to go away. Including Violet Huntingdon-Cross.

'Wake up, Sleeping Beauty,' she said, in a voice far too jolly for someone who had recently glared at him with such loathing. 'You're missing the party.'

He cracked open one eyelid and waited for the yellow blur of her hair, the pale fuzz of her face and the purple blotch that was her dress to come into focus. Then he blinked; she was closer than he'd thought, and suddenly the only things in focus at all were her bright blue eyes, peering down at him.

'Oh, good,' she said, straightening up. 'I thought for a moment I was going to have to leave you here for the night. That or get someone to come carry you to bed. That sort of thing never makes a terribly good first impression, you know.'

Unlike, for instance, pointing out a woman's sex tape history within five minutes of meeting her. God, when he woke up properly he was going to have to work at getting Violet back onside. As the only daughter living at home, he had a feeling she could make life difficult for him if she wanted.

And he rather suspected she might more than want to. It might actually be her burning life ambition at this point.

'I'm awake,' he half lied, forcing himself to straighten up. Another couple of moments and he might even make it out of the car.

Violet grabbed his hand and, even through his sleep fog, he couldn't help but be aware of the feel of her smooth, cool skin, or the way something indefinable crept up his arm at her touch. Something that seemed to crackle with possibilities.

Something that woke him up completely.

Blinking again, he twisted round to get his feet firmly on the ground and stood up, belatedly aware that he was still gripping onto Violet's hand, probably rather tighter than she'd like.

He dropped it fast, but her blue, blue eyes were still fixed on his and the puzzled crease between her eyebrows told him that whatever he'd felt, she'd felt it too.

At least he had the excuse of sleep deprivation. What justification was she using?

Violet shook her head and stepped back, nicely out of

his personal space. 'I know you're exhausted. But given that sleep is likely to be impossible for the next couple of hours at least, and since you *are* here to observe and interview and write about the band... Why don't you come and meet Dad?'

Dad. Even after an hour in the company of one of the most famous celebrity kids in the world, it still felt strange to hear her refer to the infamous Rick Cross as 'Dad'. How different a world must Violet live in to the real one he inhabited, to so casually be able to think of Huntingdon Hall as home, and one of the most recognisable couples ever as Mum and Dad?

Different, certainly, to the kid from New York who never even knew who his father was, only that he wouldn't have done him any good in life if he'd stuck around anyway. The kid whose mother had so disapproved of the method he'd used to get out of the gutter, she hadn't spoken to him for three years before her death.

Yeah, there were worlds between him and Violet. And however long he stayed at Huntingdon Hall, he had to remember that.

'Isn't he still playing?' Tom said, hoping it wasn't painfully obvious he was stalling. Rick had seemed sharp on the phone, the sort to see through people's masks. He wanted to be on top form when he sat down with Rick for the first time.

Violet tilted her head to the left, listening to the music, he presumed. 'This is usually his last number. He'll be off stage soon and still on that performance high. It's a good time to meet him if you want him to like you.'

'And do *you* want him to like me?' Tom asked. It seemed strange that she would, given everything.

A look of annoyance flashed across Violet's face, as if

she weren't used to being asked this many questions about her motives and feelings. Maybe she wasn't. 'Yes.'

Tom couldn't resist. 'Why?'

'Does it matter?' Violet tossed her hair back over her shoulder as the last chord rang out from the stage. 'We're going to miss him.'

'You haven't answered my question.' Tom folded his arms, leant back against the car and waited.

With an impatient huff, Violet grabbed his hand and started dragging him towards the stage. Tom didn't budge until she started talking.

'Because Dad makes up his mind about people and things in an instant, and that's it. You're here; you're going to be writing about him and us. If he likes you, he'll show you his best side, the stuff *I* want you to be writing about. If he takes a dislike to you…'

'Things could get messy?' Tom guessed.

Violet sighed as they reached the edge of the stage area. Even though the party was obviously filled with friends and family, the cheering as the band came off stage was still as loud as Tom had heard in any stadium.

'Let's just say this whole experience will be a lot less fun. For all of us.'

Suddenly, the familiar craggy face of Rick Cross appeared at the top of the stage steps, mouth open and laughing at something his band mate was saying behind him.

'Showtime,' Tom whispered, and Violet flashed him a quick grin—the first honest smile he'd seen from her.

Tom took a breath. Time to meet the parents.

CHAPTER FOUR

VIOLET HID A grin at the slightly shell-shocked look on
Tom's face as Dad and the boys traipsed down the temporary stairs at the side of the stage set, all laughing, chatting and still clearly caught up in their own world—a world
that consisted of music, noise and melodies.

She knew the kind of impact they could have, just off
stage. When she was younger, just old enough to be allowed to stay up to watch the occasional gig from the
wings, she and Rose had found it hard to understand this
part—when Dad wasn't Dad, just for a moment. He was
all Rick Cross, rock star, right now. And that was a sight
to behold.

The adrenaline would wear off soon enough, Violet
knew. He'd come down, hug his wife, ask for a drink, and
before too long he'd be heading to bed to sleep it off. Well,
maybe after a little more time with his closest friends—
drinking and talking and probably singing.

Right now, in this moment, he was exactly who Tom
Buckley had come here to interview. She hadn't lied when
she said that this was the best time for Tom to make a good
impression with her father. But it was also the best time
to remind Tom that this wasn't just *anybody* he'd come
here to write about.

The press could publish all the stories they liked about

her and her sisters—and heaven knew they would. But they couldn't touch her parents. Rick and Sherry were rock royalty, beyond reproach. There were no affairs, no addictions, no mistakes made—nothing to latch on to and use to make their lives hell. It might have been different back in the day, but not any more.

Now they were national treasures, and Violet was unbearably proud of them for it.

'Mr Cross.' Stepping forward, Tom stuck out his hand, smiling warmly. Violet had to give him credit—if he hadn't been slumped over in her passenger seat for the last forty-five minutes, she'd never have known he was utterly exhausted. He looked professional, ready to do a great job.

She just hoped that Dad's idea of a good job and Tom's meshed.

'Mr Buckley, I presume!' Rick's famous smile spread across his face. 'Great to have you here.' He shook Tom's hand with what looked like painful enthusiasm. 'Boys, this is the guy I've invited over to write our musical life story.'

'And your family's,' Tom put in. Violet rolled her eyes. As if any of them would forget that he was here to expose all their private lives as well as their public personas.

'Oh, he's here for the dirt, Rick.' Jez—Uncle Jez to the girls—the band's lead guitarist and Rick's best man, elbowed his friend in the ribs. 'Time to hide those skeletons in better closets!'

Rick laughed, his head tipped back in pure amusement and joy. Violet bit the inside of her cheek and just prayed there wasn't anything hidden there that she didn't know about. She couldn't imagine how there could be, given how closely she'd been involved in her parents' lives and work since she'd moved back home eight years ago.

But you could never be too careful when it came to the

press. And if Dad had any secrets, Uncle Jez would be the one to know them.

'Trust me, I'm just here to write the best, most honest story I can for your legion of fans. They're only interested in the truth.' Unlike Tom, presumably.

'And that's just what you'll get.' Rick clapped a hand on Tom's back, and Violet knew the reporter had passed some test that no one but her father would ever understand. 'The complete unvarnished truth, ready to be written down for posterity.'

Relief warred with apprehension inside her, and Violet clenched her fists so tightly her nails bit into the palms of her hands. On the one hand, the fact that her dad liked Tom would make the interviews go more smoothly, reducing the chances of a story about a recalcitrant, difficult star. On the other, it opened up the opportunity that Rick would get *too* close to Tom. As much as he talked about the unvarnished truth, surely her father realised there were some parts of their family lives, and history, that none of them wanted shared with the world. For the umpteenth time in some cases.

Well, there was nothing for it now but to see how things went. And try and keep tabs on both Tom and Rick, so she could try and head off any prospective trouble *before* it turned up in the papers this time.

'Darlings, you were brilliant as always.' Sherry floated up to them, kissing each of the band members on the cheek before planting a rather more thorough kiss on her husband. Tom, Violet noticed, was politely staring at the floor. Everyone else was too used to it to even bother.

'Mum, this is Tom Buckley,' Violet said once the public display of affection was over. Might as well get all the introductions over in one go. 'He's the writer Dad—'

'The writer who's going to tell our little story! Of

course.' Sherry held out a hand, although whether she intended it to be kissed or shaken Violet wasn't sure.

Tom went for the handshake. Not fully charmed yet, then. Mum might have her work cut out with this one. Obviously he wasn't taken in by her disingenuous description of his subject matter. Nobody in the world would describe the history of The Screaming Lemons and the Huntingdon-Cross family a 'little story'. Least of all anyone who had lived it.

'It's a pleasure to meet you, Mrs Huntingdon-Cross,' Tom said, releasing her hand.

'Oh, call me Sherry, please.' Mum flashed that legendary wide smile, the one that had been seen in magazines and on billboards for decades now. 'Anyone who stays here at Huntingdon Hall rather automatically becomes part of the family, I'm afraid. You might as well get used to it!'

Tom Buckley, part of the family? Not on Violet's watch.

But that was the problem with her parents. It wasn't that they were overly trusting or naïve, particularly. They knew the dangers of fame as well as anyone, and took care to live their lives circumspectly. But once they'd taken someone in and claimed them as a friend…it took a lot to shake their faith in them. And that could be dangerous.

'Where's Daisy?' Violet asked. She needed backup here and, with Rose and Will already gone on their honeymoon, Daisy-Waisy was going to have to be it.

'Oh, she and Seb have already turned in, I think,' Sherry said with a dismissive wave of her hand. 'Daisy was exhausted, poor thing—pregnancy is extraordinarily tiring, you know,' she added as an aside to Tom, who nodded, despite the puzzled crease between his eyebrows. 'And I think Seb wants to get off back to Hawkesley first thing.'

Curses. With Tom about to collapse from sleep deprivation, the chances weren't good that he'd be up in time to meet Daisy before she left. Which meant Violet was on her own trying to keep this whole project from blowing up in their faces. Lovely.

'And Rose has already left?' Tom asked politely. 'I met her in New York last month, and I know she'd planned to be here right through until the concert…' He left the sentence open. Not actually a question, so not really prying, but enough that politeness insisted that someone fill the gap. Tricky.

'Oh, yes,' Sherry said, beaming. 'She and Will left on their honeymoon a couple of hours ago.'

Tom's eyebrows inched up towards his hairline, and Violet winced. 'Honeymoon?' he asked. 'I didn't realise that she was planning a wedding.'

Or that she was even dating anyone, just like the rest of them. In fact, Violet was willing to bet that what Tom really meant was: *Two daughters married in a suspiciously short space of time, and one of them pregnant…there has to be a story here.* Especially if he'd seen the photos of Will and Rose in the papers.

Time to put a stop to that.

'Oh, yes,' she said, smiling cheerily. 'Will has practically been a part of the family for years now. We're delighted that they've made it official.' All true—Will *was* part of the family—certainly more than Tom Buckley ever would be. And why did he need to know that up until the last month or so, Will had only been there as Violet's best friend? And if he never realised that Will and Rose hadn't met until Daisy's wedding…well, that would be great. She just hoped that Tom Buckley didn't keep up with the UK celebrity gossip too closely.

Rick slung an arm around Tom's shoulders as the rest of the band wandered off in search of a drink or a bed. He had to reach up quite a bit to do it, Violet realised.

'That's the only downside of having daughters, you know,' Rick said, grinning at Violet. 'Having to give them away to unworthy men.'

'Oh, hush,' Sherry said. 'You know you adore Will. And Seb is going to be a wonderful son-in-law.'

'True. I have lucked out.' Rick turned his wicked grin onto Violet, and she felt her stomach clench at what he might come out with next. The inability to keep his inappropriate comments to himself was definitely a downside to the post-performance adrenaline. 'Makes me worry who Violet might decide to bring home. I can't possibly get that lucky three times in a row.'

Heat flooded Violet's cheeks. She'd spent more time blushing in front of Tom Buckley than actually talking to him at this point, she was sure.

'*Not* something you need to be worrying about, Dad.' Or be talking about in front of reporters.

Rick's face turned a little sad. 'No, I suppose not.'

'Anyway, Rose will be back soon enough, and you'll be able to catch up with her then,' Violet said with forced jollity. Tom gave her a look that left her in no doubt he knew exactly what she was doing—steering the conversation away from anything interesting. Violet made a mental note to warn Rose that it might look better if her whirlwind romance with Will hadn't been quite so…whirlwind-like. Rose would understand. Once she got home, everything would be so much easier.

'Actually, darling,' Sherry said, her smile just a little too wide, 'I spoke to Will as they were leaving. I understand they're going to be away for four weeks.'

Four weeks. Suddenly, with Tom Buckley standing there, it seemed longer than ever. Just when she really needed her twin at home with her. What had Will been thinking? Not about his best friend, stuck at home with the man who wanted to ferret out all her secrets. No, he'd been thinking about getting her twin sister naked for longer.

Damn men and their inability to think about more than one thing at once.

'That's right,' she said, forcing a smile. 'Although I couldn't get him to say where they were going.'

'Me neither,' Rick said. 'Will said he couldn't risk it. You know your mum would have texted Rose on the way to the airport and ruined the surprise.'

'Anyway. They won't be back until two days before the Benefit Concert, but Will said he'd left Rose's notes with you.' Mum had her 'tiptoeing' voice on. As if she was taking the long way round getting to the point.

'Yeah, it's all in Rose's study, apparently. Her black planner and all the files and contracts and stuff.'

'And…Will mentioned that you'd agreed to, well, keep an eye on things while they were away.' Ah, that was what Mum was working up to. Of course. Concern that Violet had agreed to something that, when it came down to it, she wouldn't be able to, or want to do.

Well, maybe it was time for her to prove her parents—and Tom Buckley—wrong. If Rose could organise a benefit concert, so could she.

'That's right.' And she'd do it too. But she really didn't want to get into this with Tom standing right there. Then again, there wasn't a chance of her getting any sleep tonight if they didn't agree a plan for the concert. The last thing they needed was the annual benefit being an utter disaster zone because Rose wasn't there, the one year they had a reporter on site recording all the behind the scenes activity for posterity.

Damn it! How could Will and Rose do this? Clearly, love had driven them crazy. It was the only explanation.

'You're looking worried, honey.' Her dad wrapped an

arm around her waist and hauled her close for a hug. 'But there's nothing to fret about. Rose has been running this thing like clockwork for years. The set-up's all done; everything's been booked for months.'

Violet turned her head to raise her eyebrows at her father. If everything was already sorted, then why was Rose always running around like a mad thing in the last few weeks before the concert every other year?

'Maybe your dad is being a little optimistic,' Sherry said. 'But really, darling, everything is in hand. All that's left is the fiddly last-minute stuff. And I'm sure we can find someone to handle that, if you don't want to. Rose and Will would understand. I'll call up an agency or something.'

Agency staff. Another stranger in their home all the time, taking responsibility for the biggest concert in The Screaming Lemons' calendar. Someone who had absolutely no reason to care if things went perfectly or just well enough to get paid.

Violet risked a glance at Tom. She could almost read the story writing itself behind his tired eyes. Thoughtless wild child celebrity daughter disappears on eve of major charity event after whirlwind romance, leaving benefit concert in chaos. Sex Tape Twin decides she'd rather pick flowers than take on the job.

Almost as bad a start as her scene in the coffee shop.

'No. I can do it. We don't need to call the agency. I'll take care of the concert. I've seen Rose do it, and I'm sure she's left really good notes. I can do it. I'd like to.'

A complete lie. The last thing she wanted to do, when she should be keeping an eye on Tom, was take on a high profile project that would put her in the public eye and require speaking to all the people she'd been happily avoiding for eight years. But sometimes proving a point—especially to someone like Tom Buckley—required sacrifice.

'Are you sure, darling?' Her mother's perfect face crinkled up into a frown. 'It doesn't really seem like…well, like your sort of thing.'

Of course it didn't. As much as she might have moaned about her parents calling Rose in to organise their wedding, she knew exactly why they'd done it. To spare Violet the misery of having to brave the public and the publicity again. It was bad enough doing so as a guest at endless charity functions, or just appearing at the benefit concert. Anywhere there were cameras, her nerves started to tremble. And this…this would mean liaising with pop stars, working with celebrities.

There were going to be a *lot* of cameras. Her fingers felt shaky just thinking about it.

'I'm sure,' she said as firmly as she could. 'The Benefit Concert is important. I want to make sure everything goes just as well as it would if Rose was here.'

Maybe she could just pretend to be Rose. Maybe no one would notice that she was actually the *other* twin. You know the one.

'Well, honey, if you're sure.' Rick's forehead had matching creases. Then he broke into a smile and clapped Tom on the back. 'Hey, maybe Tom here can give you a hand!'

CHAPTER FIVE

TOM COULDN'T BE sure if it was the sleep deprivation or if he really was missing something in the conversation going on around him. It felt as if there were actually two discussions taking place—one with words and one entirely conducted through concerned eyebrow gestures.

Still, he was pretty sure he didn't stand a chance of understanding the eyebrow conversation until he got some actual sleep. In fact, he was just plotting the best way to get shown to his room when Rick volunteered him.

'Me?' Tom wished that had come out slightly less squeakily. 'Help with the Benefit Concert?'

Sherry clapped her hands together. 'What a brilliant idea! I knew I married you for a reason.' She planted another kiss on her husband.

Violet, Tom noticed, hadn't responded at all. In fact, she looked as though she'd been sent into a state of severe shock and might need therapy to even deal with the idea.

God, he just had the best way with women, didn't he?

'Unless…Violet, darling, are you sure you really want to do this?' Sherry's eyebrows were doing the very concerned thing again, mirrored by Rick's. Yeah, Tom was definitely missing something here.

But Violet shook off the shock, smiled widely and said, 'Of course I do! And I'd appreciate any help that Tom is able to give me, in between the work he's *actually* here to do.' She even managed a sincere smile for him as she spoke, which Tom thought might be a first.

'Well, that's settled then.' Rick clapped his hands together, but his eyebrows suggested that nothing was settled at all. Tom suspected there'd be some private family conversations going on once he'd finally found a bed to fall into.

Well, so be it. Despite Sherry's enthusiastic welcome, he wasn't actually family. He didn't need to know all their tiny moments and their every word. He just wanted the stories. And, he'd admit it, the secrets. *They* were what would set his book apart from everything else ever written about Rick Cross and co.

And he was pretty sure he'd get them. Starting tomorrow.

'Guys, if I'm going to be ready to start interviews, write a book *and* organise the best concert in the history of benefit concerts, I'd better get some sleep.' Tom gave them all his friendliest all-in-this-together smile.

'Oh, of course!' Sherry immediately went into hostess mode, something Tom imagined she had honed and perfected over years of events, guests and parties. 'Violet, why don't you show Tom to his room, darling?'

Violet's smile was starting to look a little fixed, but no one except Tom seemed to notice. 'Of course. I might turn in myself.' She kissed her parents on their cheeks. 'It was a brilliant day. Here's to many more happy years of marriage.'

Tom followed Violet away from the stage, across the gardens. The party had obviously started to wind down after the Lemons had left the stage. The fairy lights in the trees shone down on abandoned glasses and plates and grass-stained marquee floors. A few stragglers still loitered by the temporary bar, where the last remaining barmaid yawned expansively, but most people had already headed home to bed.

Tom applauded their sensible natures. Of course, it was gone 4:00 a.m., so maybe they weren't that sensible.

Glancing over his shoulder, Tom saw Rick and Sherry making their way across to where the rest of the band sat with their partners or friends under the moonlight. Jez was strumming an acoustic guitar and laughter and conversation floated among the notes in the night air.

'I don't know how they're still going,' Violet said, following his gaze. 'I'm knackered. But they're always the last ones standing at a party. I think it's a point of pride these days. And they always finish the night together, just the gang of them who've been there from the start.'

He should be over there, soaking up the moment. Taking in the atmosphere that would make his book authentic. Except…it was a private moment and he was new on the scene. He couldn't force his way into that close-knit group. He had to earn his place, and that would take time and trust.

Violet was giving him an odd considering look. 'You still want to go to bed?' A slight flush of colour hit her cheeks in the pale lights, and he knew somehow that she was waiting for him to make a joke about whether that was an offer to join him. So he didn't.

'Alone, I mean. Not with me,' Violet babbled, as if he had. She must get that a lot, although he'd expected her to just brush it off or turn it back on the joker to embarrass *them*. After her display in the airport café, he knew she had the confidence and the fire.

Except…here, now, this seemed like a different Violet. One who'd known humiliation and pain. One he hadn't expected to meet when he'd sat in Miami and New York reading up about the wild child Sex Tape Twin without shame.

She'd never even put out a statement, he remembered. No apology for being a bad role model, for letting down her fans or those young girls who looked up to her. No regret for the shame and embarrassment she'd brought on her family.

Why was that? Suddenly, he desperately wanted to know. But those questions too required patience and trust to be earned. Maybe in a few weeks. After all, they were going to be working on the concert together. He had all the time he needed to learn everything there was to know about Violet Huntingdon-Cross, and her family.

'Honestly, Violet, I think I'd pass out on you tonight even if it was an offer.' He gave her a friendly smile to show it was a joke, that he didn't mean any offence. But, as her gaze met his, even his exhausted body had a moment where it wished that wasn't the case. That maybe, just maybe, this beautiful, confusing woman might actually make that offer to him.

Which was clearly ridiculous. They had nothing in common. She'd never understand him or his life, and he'd long since grown out of sleeping with any beautiful woman who offered. He liked his sexual encounters to mean something these days. Maybe not true love and forever, but a meaningful connection at least.

He couldn't really imagine any connection between him and the self-absorbed daughter of a celebrity. Still, he felt a little relief as the colour in her cheeks faded and she gave a quick nod.

'Come on then. Your bedroom's this way.' Violet started off towards the main staircase.

Tom bit his tongue to stop himself asking where hers was as he followed.

Violet woke up exhausted. Maybe it was all the excitement and chaos of the day and weeks before, but even once the big vow renewal was over and Rose was safely off on honeymoon she couldn't relax enough to sleep—despite the fact it had been gone four by the time she'd made it to bed. Eventually, after an hour of fitful tossing and turning, she'd given up and turned on her bedside light to read for a while.

She'd woken up four hours later, with the light still on and her face smooshed against her book. Not the perfect start to the day.

Scrubbing a hand across her face to try and persuade her eyes to stay open, she glanced at the clock. Nine thirty a.m. Chances were, the rest of the household would be sleeping in until well after lunch, but there was a nervous energy running through Violet's veins that she knew from experience wouldn't let her go back to sleep.

A shower, her most comfortable jeans and a T-shirt in her favourite shade of lavender-blue made her feel a little more human. She scraped her hair back into a clip to dry naturally, slathered on what claimed to be a rejuvenating moisturiser and headed downstairs in search of coffee.

'Coffee will make all things better,' she murmured as she switched on the espresso machine. The lie was a soothing one, at least. How could one poor drink be expected to deal with all the worries that had piled on in the last twenty-four hours?

'Think it can even help your poor old dad?' Rick leant against the door frame from the hall, his weathered face looking a little grey under his summer tan. 'I think I'm getting too old for the partying lark, honey.'

'Never.' Violet grabbed another espresso cup from the shelf. 'You'll still be rocking with a walking stick when the rest of us have grown old and boring.'

Except she didn't even need to age to grow old and boring; she was already there, wasn't she? Her entire existence already fitted within the grounds of Huntingdon Hall. Or it had. Maybe the Benefit Concert would be her chance to spread her wings.

'Only if I have my girls there to help hold me up,' Rick said, settling himself into one of the chairs at the kitchen table. 'Wouldn't be any fun without you all.'

'Mum sleeping in?' Violet handed her dad his coffee, then sat down to blow across the surface of her own cup.

'She says she needs her beauty sleep.' Rick laughed. 'Course, we all know she's plenty beautiful without it.'

'I didn't expect anyone else to be up for hours,' Violet said.

'I've got a shift down at the centre this morning,' Rick said. 'No one else could cover, so...' He shrugged.

Violet gave him a sympathetic smile. While everyone knew that Rick and Sherry supported all sorts of charities publicly, very few people were aware of all the private time they put in. Her dad did a lot of work for Alzheimer's charities, as well as helping out at a local drug rehabilitation centre, while her mum put in time on a children's helpline, amongst other things. Would they share that side of themselves with Tom? Violet had no idea.

'I'll be back to give Tom his first interview this afternoon, though,' Rick said, suggesting that he might. Violet was glad; more people should know about all the good they did. 'And what are you up to today?'

Violet sipped her coffee. 'I was planning on raiding Rose's files to get an idea of what I've let myself in for with this Benefit Concert.'

Rick's face turned serious. 'Now, honey, you know you don't have to take that on. It's not too late to change your mind.'

'Don't think I can do it, huh?' Violet said, eyebrows raised.

'Violet, I truly believe you could do anything in the world you dreamt of, if you decided to. It just comes down to if you really *want* to.'

Violet bit her lip. Dad thought she could do it. He had faith in her. And maybe, just maybe, he knew something she didn't. At the very least, she wanted the *chance* to prove him right.

'I want to do it,' she said, ignoring the way her whole body felt as if it might start trembling any second. This was her chance—her golden opportunity to do that *something more* she'd been wishing for. 'It's important to me, and I think it's time.' Time to stop hiding behind the walls of Huntingdon Hall at last. Time to start living in the real world again, even if it was still filled with monsters.

The smile that split Rick's craggy face was reward enough for her decision. 'I think you might be right, honey,' he said, and pressed a kiss to her hand across the table. 'I think it's time the whole world got used to seeing the *real* Violet Huntingdon-Cross for once.'

Violet smiled back through her nerves. *Wouldn't that be something?*

CHAPTER SIX

HUNTINGDON HALL WAS ridiculously large, Tom decided, after getting lost on the way to the kitchen for the third time. Tastefully redecorated, with none of the attempts to recreate the Regency or whatever that he'd half expected from the almost aristocracy. But then, this family were unusual in almost every other way, why not this one too?

There were so many contradictions for him to uncover, but that was half the fun.

Contradiction one. Sherry had inherited this hall from her blue blood family—but had obviously renovated it entirely using her husband's money—or her own, Tom supposed. She had enjoyed a very lucrative modelling career, after all. Anyway, the point was, while the outside of Huntingdon Hall still looked like something from a period novel, the inside was entirely modern.

As Tom made his way down a corridor that looked almost exactly like the one he'd just explored, Violet's directions from the night before seemed even more ridiculous. *Just follow the walls,* she'd said. *Eventually all of them lead back to the main staircase.* Follow the walls? What kind of advice was that? Especially since it appeared he'd been following the walls in the wrong direction for the last five minutes. Why wasn't there a helpful servant around here somewhere?

Of course that led him to contradiction two. In a house this size, with a family this rich, he'd have expected dozens of flunkies running around doing things for them. But he'd seen nobody. Oh, he was sure there was a housekeeper somewhere, and he highly doubted that Sherry did her own cleaning, but apart from that? Everything seemed to be kept in the family. Rose took care of the band's PR and everything else that needed organising, it seemed.

At least until she ran away on her honeymoon and Violet stepped in, rather than hire someone else.

Violet was, without a doubt, most definitely contradiction number three.

Tom turned another corner, dutifully following the wall and, finally, stumbled across the staircase. At last, his path towards coffee and maybe even breakfast was clear.

He hopped down the stairs in double time, smiling as he heard voices coming from what he hoped would prove to be the kitchen. Part of him was surprised not to be the first up—it had been a ridiculously late night, but even with his exhaustion level he'd found it impossible to sleep past ten. Too many years of risking missing the tour bus or a flight somewhere had left him a very light sleeper.

'Good morning.' Both Rick and Violet looked up at his words, and Tom got the unerring feeling that he'd interrupted something.

'Ah! Our guest awakes.' Rick moved towards the coffee pot. 'Strong and black? Or do you drink what can only be described as "warm milk with a coffee scent" like my daughter?'

'Strong and black, please,' Tom replied. Actually, he normally preferred it somewhere in between, but he wasn't taking the chance of failing the Rick Cross coffee test. Or any other tests he threw his way before Rick actually opened up to him and gave him the material he needed.

Rick nodded as he poured. 'Good choice. Now, about today.' He handed Tom a tiny steaming espresso cup with an apologetic smile that made Tom's heart sink. There were going to be no interviews today, he just knew it.

This was always the risk in coming here. Staying at Huntingdon Hall gave Tom unprecedented access, yes. But it also gave the subject the illusion of limitless time—and plenty of excuses to dodge sitting down and talking to him.

Tom did not have limitless time, and he needed this story.

'I was hoping we could make a start on some questions about what the Lemons are doing now,' Tom said, hoping the allure of potential publicity for the new album would draw him in. 'I've got a couple of possible slots in magazines and supplements coming up, and it would be good to let people know what's next for the band.'

'Rose would kick me if she heard me turning down the publicity, but I'm afraid I have some commitments today that I need to take care of before I can sit down with you.' Rick reached for his own coffee mug—which, Tom noticed, had milk in it, damn him. 'Sorry, Tom. I'll be back this afternoon, though. And I'll get Sherry to book some time with you too, as well as the boys from the band. I want us to get the bulk of the first few interviews down over the next week or two, so we've all got more time to focus on the Benefit Concert when it comes around. That sound okay to you?'

'That's…great, actually.' So much for the old man trying to avoid the interviews. Maybe Rick Cross was as serious about this book as Tom hoped after all. 'And I can probably find something to entertain me around here this morning.'

He hadn't meant to look at Violet, but somehow his gaze just sort of slid over in her direction. Her blonde hair looked darker—was it wet?—and strands were curling around her face. In jeans and a bright blue T-shirt, without make-up, she looked a lot younger than she had the night before. And, from the redness around her eyes, more vulnerable.

What had she been discussing with her father before he walked in? Suddenly, Tom wished he'd stopped outside to eavesdrop.

'You can help Violet go through all Rose's files!' Rick sounded immensely pleased with himself at the idea. 'Get up to speed on all the plans for the Benefit Concert. I just know my Violet is going to knock this one out of the park.'

He reached across and squeezed his daughter's shoulder, and she gave him a rather weak smile in return.

'Still, everyone needs a little help sometimes, right, honey?' Rick went on.

'Yeah, I guess.' With a deep breath, Violet straightened her shoulders visibly and looked him in the eye. 'So, Mr Buckley, how about it? You up for a challenge?'

'Absolutely.' Tom drained his espresso and smiled, unsure if the challenge was the concert or understanding the woman sitting in front of him.

'Okay. So…Will said that Rose left everything she had to do with the Benefit Concert in here.' Violet approached the door to the seldom used study on the first floor with more than a little trepidation. She hadn't been in this room since it was their homework room, years ago. Since she'd handed in her dissertation, she hadn't so much as opened the door.

It was Rose's room, not hers. As close as the twins were, Violet had to admit that they'd lived very separate lives over the last few years. With Rose in New York, that distance had only grown.

Oh, they still talked about pretty much everything. Violet still knew her sister's mind and heart, and she knew that if she needed anything Rose would be there in a heartbeat. But their lives were different. Rose jetted around the world, building her career working for The Screaming Lemons' PR, but also cultivating her passion making jewellery. The wedding rings she'd crafted for Seb and Daisy, and the bracelet she'd designed and made for their mother, were amongst the most beautiful things Violet had ever seen. Rose had real talent, and Violet knew that Will would encourage that—especially now Rose had made the decision to give up the PR side of things and follow her dreams.

Maybe it was time for Violet to do that too, she thought as she pushed open the door. Starting with the Benefit Concert.

'Huh.' Behind her, Tom stared over her shoulder. 'Did Will say where, exactly?'

It was a valid question. Violet's heart sank as she took in the piles of paperwork, the overflowing files and the stack of wedding magazines on the desk. Poor Rose had been swamped for the last month or more, with preparations for the band's latest tour, album promotion and not to mention planning their parents' vow renewal service and party. No wonder she hadn't had time to tidy up.

Well, that just made step one in the 'get-back-out-there-and-show-the-world-what-Violet-Huntingdon-Cross-is-really-made-of' plan all the more obvious.

'We need to start with a clean sweep,' she said, picking up Rose's battered, precious black planner from the middle of the piles covering the desk. 'We'll sort through everything in here, clear up and find all the relevant stuff, then set up my office in here. Will sent me the link to the Dropbox folder Rose was using for all the electronic stuff, and she's given me access to the email account she uses for the Benefit Concert each year. So I should have everything I need to get started…'

'Once you can find the desk,' Tom finished for her.

'Yeah.' She turned to look at him. 'Sorry. This probably isn't what you were hoping to do this morning.'

Tom shrugged. 'Not entirely. But this afternoon should make up for it. And it doesn't have to be a total waste. I can ask you some basic interview questions while we're working.' He pulled out his smartphone and scrolled through to an app with a microphone logo. 'You don't mind being taped, right?'

Violet's body froze, her back so stiff she thought it might snap. At least he was asking, she supposed. She hadn't been given that courtesy last time.

'I think maybe today we should just focus on getting this office sorted.' She knew her voice was stilted, but she couldn't seem to do anything about it. 'If I'm going to be on the record, I want to be sure I'm giving your questions my full attention.' That way, it would be harder for him to sneak in trick questions, or twist her words around later. She'd spent some time, after everything, researching the best way to deal with the media. Of course, when every question was about a sex tape, there was only so much you could do. But she knew more now than she had at nineteen and that knowledge gave her a little confidence, at least.

She could deal with Tom Buckley. As long as she kept her wits sharp.

'Okay. Fair enough.' Tom slipped the phone back into his pocket and Violet's shoulders dropped back to their usual level. If he had any idea why his request had her so rattled—and surely he must—Tom didn't show it. He was a professional, she supposed. 'So, where do we start?'

Violet surveyed the room. 'The desk? I mean, that's probably going to have her most recent stuff on it. And once we've cleared that, at least we have somewhere to work.'

'Sounds like a plan.' Shifting a pile of papers and a red polka dot cardigan from the leather chair on the visitor's side of the desk, Tom grabbed the first stack of files from the edge of the desk and took a seat.

Selecting her own pile, Violet settled into the desk chair and started to read.

'So, is your sister always this messy when she works?' Tom asked, and Violet's hackles instantly rose.

'She's been incredibly busy recently,' Violet said. 'I'm sure that, if she were here, she'd know exactly where everything was, though. She's very efficient.'

'I'm sure she is.' Tom dropped his first file onto the floor. 'That's my "wedding vow renewal" pile, by the way. I guess that must have taken up a lot of her time. You all helped, though?'

'Where we could,' Violet replied. Of course, with Daisy suffering from first trimester woes, and herself relegated to flower arranging, it had mostly been Rose. As usual. 'Mum was pretty burnt out from organising Daisy and Seb's wedding, so she left a lot of it to Rose. I took care of the flowers, though.'

Tom's gaze flicked up to meet hers, faint disbelief marring his expression. 'You arrange flowers?'

'I do.' Violet looked back down at the file in her hands. This, at least, had to be a safe topic. No one expected the Sex Tape Twin to spend her weekends fiddling with oasis and floristry wire in the church hall, right? 'I took over the local church flower committee a few years ago now.'

That, of course, had been a local scandal in its own way—she was too young, too inexperienced, or just had too much of a reputation. But, whatever anyone said, that scandal hadn't made the national press, at least.

'Huh. I always imagined church flower ladies were…' Tom trailed off and Violet raised her eyebrows at him as she waited for him to finish the sentence. 'Married?' he said finally, as if asking her to tell him what to say to get out of the conversation.

Violet huffed a laugh and reached for the next file. 'Married. That's the best you could do?'

'Well, okay, fine. I thought they were older, more boring, greyer and considerably less beautiful than you.'

Despite the warmth filling her cheeks, Violet resisted the urge to say, *You think I'm beautiful?*

He'd just think she was fishing for compliments, anyway.

'As it happens, I'll have you know that floristry is more popular than ever.' She had no idea if that were actually true, but it sounded good. 'Young women across the country are taking courses in flower arranging.' Probably.

'Did you?' Tom asked. 'Take a course, I mean?'

'Not…exactly.' Damn. There went the legitimacy of her words.

'So how on earth did you get to be head of the church flower committee? I've watched enough rural British murder mysteries to know that kind of job is usually enough to kill over.'

'We live in Buckinghamshire, not Midsomer,' Violet pointed out. 'We haven't had a murder in the village in almost seventy years.'

'Still, I bet there was a queue of blue-haired ladies waiting to take over. Weren't they a tad annoyed when you swanned in and stole it from right under their noses?'

Well, yes, of course they had been. But Tom made it sound as if she'd just rocked up and demanded she be given the job because of who her parents were, just like some people she'd known back in the day had demanded access to exclusive nightclubs. And usually been let in, too.

'I'd been trained up by the last head of the committee for five years,' Violet said, trying not to notice the lump that still formed in her throat when she thought about Kathleen. 'When she got sick, she insisted that I take over. She dictated arrangements to me over the phone, made me bring her photos to show her I was doing it right. When she died...I was voted in the day after the funeral.' Kathleen had actually tried to leave her the position in her will, but of course it hadn't been hers to give. So there had to be a ballot of the whole committee—which she'd won by just one vote.

Still, Violet hoped she'd won over the doubters over the last few years. God knew, she'd achieved very little else. Until now. It might be a bit of a jump from flower arranging to concert arranging but, come hell or high water, she'd prove herself here just like she had on the committee.

'But you obviously wanted it.' Tom tilted his head to one side as he studied her. It made Violet want to flinch, so she worked really hard at keeping her muscles still instead. He *wanted* her to flinch, she was sure of it. And she wasn't giving Tom Buckley *anything* he wanted.

'It meant a lot to Kathleen that I take it on,' she said evenly. 'And I get a lot of pleasure from working with flowers.'

He nodded absently, as if taking everything she said as accepted truth. But then he fixed her with his clear green eyes and said, 'So, tell me. How did the daughter of rock royalty go from starring in her very own porno to arranging the Easter flowers?'

CHAPTER SEVEN

VIOLET WENT VERY still for a moment, the fingers clutching her file almost white from tension. Tom sat back and waited. He knew this part. In any usual interview, this was the bit where the subject tried to recall all the advice from the PR guru on how to spin their misdeeds in the best possible light.

And Miss Violet Huntingdon-Cross had clearly had some ambitious PR advice, probably from her twin sister, actually. Keep your head down, take on some charity work, or work in the community. Rehabilitate your character until everyone forgets the part about how they saw you naked on the internet, mid pretty boring sex.

Was this why Rick had pushed for him to help her out with the Benefit Concert? Tom had no doubt that Rick's first concern was publicity for the band, but maybe the relaunch of his eldest daughter as an upstanding member of society was a nice side benefit. Hell, maybe that was why he was doing all this now. With two daughters married, he could happily portray them as settled down and mature—and Violet could ride in on their coat-tails.

Except Tom had seen her lose it in the middle of an airport café. He'd glimpsed the real passionate, wild Violet—and he really wasn't buying the Sunday school teacher act.

'I thought we agreed that this wasn't the time for an interview,' Violet said, her voice stiff and prim.

Tom shrugged. 'It's not. I'm not recording anything. Just asking an idle question.'

'Sure.' Violet's mouth twisted up into a bitter smile. 'I bet we're off the record and everything, right? No, thanks. I know how that works.'

'If I say something is off the record, I mean it.' Tom sat up straighter, bristling a little at the implication. 'Your dad brought me here because he knows my reputation as a fair, honest, accurate reporter. I'm not trying to trick you into anything here, Violet.'

He'd worked too hard at building up that reputation—after the story that made his name—to risk it now, over one blonde wild child. If his mother were still alive, even she'd have to admit that he'd turned it around. He was respectable now, dammit.

Violet met his gaze, her blue eyes wide and vulnerable. She'd probably practised that look in the mirror, too. 'Okay, then,' she said finally, giving him a small nod.

But she didn't answer his question. Instead, she turned back to the file in her hand, giving it her full attention as a little crease started to form between her eyebrows. Tom wanted to ask her what she was reading—until he realised there was a much more pressing question to be answered.

'What did you mean, when you said you "know how that works"?'

Violet shrugged, not looking up. 'You know. Off the record is only valid until someone says something worth breaking the rules for.'

'That's not true.' The defence of his profession was automatic—even as he admitted to himself that for some reporters it was entirely true. The sort of reporter who would hack voicemails or intercept emails didn't care very much about a verbal agreement about 'the record'. Hell, it was barely more than a social convention anyway, a nicety to make interview subjects feel more comfortable.

But he'd stuck by that convention for his entire career, bar one story. And he didn't intend to ever break it again.

'Really?' Violet raised her pale brows at him in disbelief. 'You really believe that all reporters honour the privacy of things said off the record?' She shook her head without waiting for an answer. 'The only way to be safe is to assume that you're on the record at all times. Whatever anyone says.' The way she said it, the conviction she gave the words…this wasn't just some advice from a media expert. This was the mantra Violet lived her life by—or at least it was now.

'When talking to reporters?' Tom asked, wanting her to admit to what he suspected. 'Or when talking to anybody?'

Her gaze slipped away from his. 'Depends on who you're talking to. And whether you trust them not to sell your story to the papers.'

'And who do you trust that much?' Tom had an inkling it would be a very short list.

'Who do you?' Violet threw his own question back at him, and he blinked in surprise.

'Trust me, no one is interested in any story about me.' Just the idea of it made him laugh. He was a reporter, always behind the scenes, shedding light on other people's lives. No one ever needed to examine his—and he really didn't want them to.

'Just suppose they were. Hypothetically.' Violet leant forward and, even with the desk between them, her piercing stare made her feel uncomfortably close. 'Imagine that something happened in your life—you won the lottery, or wrote the next Harry Potter, or married a celebrity, whatever. Suddenly everyone in the world wants to know your secrets. Who would you still tell the truth to?'

No one. The thought felt empty and hollow even as it echoed through his brain. There was no one he trusted with that much of him. No one he'd tell about his hopes and dreams—and no one he'd trust with his failures or regrets.

Oh, he had friends, plenty of them. Enough in every country that he always had someone he could meet for dinner, or go out for drinks with. And he'd had girlfriends, too—also plenty. The fact he didn't have one right now made absolutely no difference to the trusted person question. He hadn't told any of the previous ones any more than he thought they needed to know. His mother had probably been the last person he'd trusted that way, and she was a long time gone. Not to mention the fact that even telling *her* the truth hadn't ended so well.

He wasn't the story. He never was. That was kind of the point of being a reporter.

'Never happen,' he said as breezily as he could. 'My utter unremarkableness is one of the main reasons I've managed to build up a successful career as a music journalist. So, go on, your turn. Who do you trust that much? Rose, I imagine. And Daisy and your parents. Who else?'

'I think that's plenty, don't you?' Violet sat back and picked up her file again. 'After all, it's obviously still four more people than you have,' she added, not looking up.

Tom didn't have an answer to that one, either.

It was going to take them forever to wade through all of Rose's files. Violet bit back a sigh—Tom would only have a sigh-related question waiting for her. Maybe ask her if she was frustrated by her sister's departure or, worse, in love with her new brother-in-law. She had a feeling it was only a matter of time before someone noticed that Rose had married the man who'd been squiring her twin around for the last few years and jumped to the obvious—but erroneous—conclusion that there was a really juicy story there. She'd place money on it being Tom, and before the week was out.

Sneaking a glance at him across the desk, Violet considered the way he'd evaded his own question about who to trust in this world. On the one hand, she'd been surprised to find someone whose list was shorter than her own. But then, given his profession, perhaps that wasn't so surprising. He had to know that everyone had their price, when the story—or tape—was good enough.

Still, she'd have expected him to have *someone*. A trusty sidekick best friend, perhaps. Or a loyal, long-suffering girlfriend. Not everyone was lucky enough to have a built-in best friend from the day they were born, like she and Rose had been, but she'd have thought he'd have found at least one person to trust over the last few decades.

Strangest of all was the feeling she'd got, watching him dodge the question. The odd sensation that in that moment they'd both looked past a mask neither of them usually lifted, and seen something they never intended the other to see. Had he really seen her fear, her mistrust in a way that even her family couldn't quite grasp? Or had she imagined that strangely searching look?

And what about him? Had she truly recognised another person who understood that the truth was a private thing, that who a person was deep down didn't always need to be shared? At the least she knew he didn't trust people any more than she did.

Was he lonely? Or did he like being alone? Did it make it easier for him to do his job, not worrying about friends or family who might be disappointed in him, or disapprove of the stories he chose to tell?

Or had he had someone once and betrayed them for a story, like Nick had done to her?

Shaking her head, Violet looked back down at the file in her hand. She was projecting now. Whatever Tom's history was, and whomever he chose not to share it with, she was pretty sure it had nothing in common with hers.

Violet added the file in her hand to the 'album promo' pile and was just reaching for the next one when her phone buzzed in her back pocket. Standing to fish it out, she checked the name on the screen.

'It's Rose,' she said, her finger hovering over 'answer'. 'I'll go take it in the other room.'

'See if you can find out where she's hidden all the bands' contracts while you're at it,' Tom said. 'And the notes on the riders. They'd be really useful around now.'

Violet nodded and escaped into the sitting room next door to talk to her sister. She really didn't want an unreliable audience when she was talking to one of her four people.

'Hey, where are you?' Violet shut the door carefully behind her, just in case Tom got it into his head to eavesdrop. 'Is it glorious and sunny and beautiful?'

'All of the above,' Rose said with a laugh. 'I have to admit, Will has outdone himself. But you'll have to wait and see the photos when we get back. I want to see who guesses where we've been first.'

'Meanie.' Violet pouted but, since her sister couldn't see her, the effect was rather wasted. 'Are you happy, though?'

'Very,' Rose promised, her tone suddenly serious. 'Really, Vi...I'm so much happier than I thought I could be. Ever.'

Violet's heart ached at the truth in her sister's words. 'I'm so, so happy for you,' she said as sincerely as she could. But even as she spoke, she rubbed the space between her breasts, just over her heart, and wished that she could find such happiness.

'What about you?' Rose asked. 'How are things there?'

That, Violet knew, was her cue to tell her sister light-hearted stories about everything that had happened in the less than twenty-four hours since she'd left. Only problem was, she was struggling to think of any.

'Um, fine. Nothing much to report, really. Mum and Dad stayed up super-late with the guys, and Dad headed off for his shift at the centre today looking half dead, even after a couple of coffees. Mum still hadn't surfaced last time I checked.'

'So, the usual,' Rose summarised.

'Pretty much, yeah.'

'How about Tom? Did you find him okay at the airport?'

'Yeah, eventually.' Violet bit the inside of her cheek. She really, really wanted to point out that Rose had given her the wrong flight times. But if she did she'd have to explain what happened next. She was just trying to think of a way to fudge the subject when Rose spoke again.

'Hel—lo. What happened? Tell me immediately.'

'I don't know what you're talking about,' Violet lied.

'Yes, you do. That was your "I'm mad at you but don't know how to tell you" voice. Twin here, remember?'

'Okay, fine. You gave me the wrong flight times! He ended up calling and demanding to know where I was, so I rushed all the way over to Heathrow in my bridesmaid's dress and heels then humiliated myself in front of everyone in the coffee shop.' Violet finally took a breath and relaxed once the words were out. Not telling Rose stuff took far more energy than just telling her everything.

'Will just forwarded you his email with the flights on,' Rose said mildly. 'If they were wrong, it was his own stupid fault. Now, humiliated yourself how, exactly?'

Maybe it would have been worth holding back that part, though.

'His fault? Fantastic. So it was all over nothing in the end, anyway.' Violet sighed. 'I was so determined to make a good impression—to make him like us so he'd write nice things about us. But after his call and the traffic, I was kind of flustered. And it had been a really, really long day.' A long, loved-up, excruciating sort of day for the one single girl in a family of people madly in love with their spouses.

'Oh, God, what did you do?' Rose asked with the sort of dismayed expectation that came from having been witness to every single one of Violet's screw-ups for the past twenty-seven years.

'He thought I was you!' Violet said. Rose knew how much she hated that. And after the day she'd had...well, some sort of blow-up was inevitable.

'Tell me you didn't berate that poor man in public for not being able to tell apart identical twins he's barely met.'

'Of course not! In fact, I played along for a moment or two, but he figured it out pretty quickly.' Violet swallowed at the memory. She hated this bit, but Rose was going to hate it even more. 'He said he recognised my facial expression. From the video.' No need to say which one.

Silence on the other end. But only while Rose caught her breath, Violet imagined.

'I will fly home right now and beat him up if you want.' Rose swore, quite impressively. Violet recognised a few words they hadn't learnt at boarding school. 'I can't believe I thought he seemed like a good guy! I thought we could trust him with this interview, with Dad. But now... I'll call Dad. Get him to send him back to whichever rock he crawled out from under.'

Warmth filled Violet's chest at her sister's unqualified

support. But part of her couldn't help but feel a little responsible too.

'In fairness, he was severely sleep deprived and over-caffeinated at the time,' she said. 'And he didn't really say it in an offensive manner. Well, as far as you can remind someone of the biggest mistake of their life without meaning to offend them.'

'It wasn't your fault,' Rose said automatically, just as she had every time it had been mentioned for the last eight years. 'You trusted him. And you had no idea he was filming you—let alone that he'd put it out on the internet. Do not blame yourself for the actions of Nefarious Nick.'

'*Anyway,* I don't think Tom meant to cause offence. And I might have overreacted a little bit.'

'Overreacted?' Violet was pretty sure she could *hear* Rose wincing. 'What did you do?'

'Announced to the whole coffee shop that yes, I was the Huntingdon-Cross Sex Tape Twin and if they had any questions they should ask Tom, since he'd clearly watched it plenty of times.'

Rose let out a burst of laughter. '*Really?* Oh, that's brilliant. And the first time I've ever heard you joke about the whole thing.'

'I wasn't joking,' Violet muttered.

'So, did he make it to Huntingdon Hall alive? How are things going? I mean, after that kind of a start I'm assuming he's probably part of the family already.' Apparently, Rose's romantic happiness hadn't dulled her ability for sarcasm.

'Actually, we agreed to start over. He's helping me with the Benefit Concert.'

'You took it on?' Rose asked. 'I kind of hoped you might when Will said you'd agreed to take care of things. But I wasn't sure if you'd…well, feel comfortable doing it. You know, you can always get someone in from the agency we use if you're not happy.'

'It's fine. I said I'd do it and I will.' And hearing how everyone else expected her to pull out every five minutes was only making her more determined that it would be a raging success. 'Although we're having some fun trying to sort through all your papers.'

'Yeah, sorry about the mess. But there's a system, I promise.'

'Care to explain it to me?' Violet asked, settling back on the sofa to take detailed notes as Rose explained the meanings of different file colours, and how the left side of the desk was only ever used for pending stuff. She just hoped she and Tom hadn't already messed up whatever weird system Rose had developed…

CHAPTER EIGHT

TOM STARED AT the blank laptop screen in front of him, then rubbed his eyes. He'd been at Huntingdon Hall for almost a week, sat down for detailed, open interviews with both Rick and Sherry, plus most of the band members. He had hours of audiotape, plus a whole notebook full of scrawled notes. He'd even managed to put together a preliminary article for one of his favourite editors, talking about the exciting opportunity he had, staying at Huntingdon Hall. When it went to print in one of the supplements this weekend, it should build excitement for the Benefit Concert, help with the album promo and even start some buzz for the eventual band biography. It had been a productive, worthwhile week.

So why the hell was he still thinking about Violet Huntingdon-Cross, drowning in paperwork in her sister's study?

She was the only one he wasn't certain he could get to open up, that was all. He had appointments to talk with Daisy, and even her new husband, in a couple of weeks when they came for the benefit, and he felt sure he could collar Rose and the new Mr when they got back from their honeymoon. But Violet…she was right there in the house with him, and yet he couldn't get close. Even when they were in the same room, she made it very clear there was an exclusion zone around her—one he would never enter.

Maybe he'd got too close with their conversation about trust—even if he had come out the worst for it. But that only meant he needed to push a little further.

Tom closed his laptop. He could take a break from writing if it meant getting Violet to open up. After all, her parents were off doing the first of many promos for the Benefit Concert—radio today—her sisters were both busy being married and happy…it was just the two of them there now. They might as well get used to each other's company.

Another thing he had managed over the last week was learning his way around Huntingdon Hall. At least he no longer got lost looking for the kitchen.

Tom knocked on the study door, waiting for Violet to call for him to come in, but she didn't answer.

After a moment, Tom pushed the door open, just enough to peer through the crack.

'Yes, I understand that, Mr Collins. But—' Violet sat at the desk, phone clamped to her ear. Strands of hair were escaping from the clip she'd used to keep it back, and she rubbed her forehead with her free hand. 'And, as I've already told you—' A sigh, as she was presumably cut off again.

Slipping through the open door, Tom took the seat opposite the desk and she glanced up at the movement.

'Who is it?' he whispered.

'Olivia's manager,' she mouthed back. Damn it. Olivia was the hot new American act Rose had booked for the benefit. Tom had interviewed her once or twice before, and each time the star's list of demands had grown. Word in the industry was that no one could wait until her star burned out and she had to start begging *them* for the press. But while the kids were still downloading her music…

Reaching over, Tom stabbed the speakerphone button with his finger, and Mr Collins's diatribe became audible.

'All I'm saying is that I think I need to talk with someone with a little more authority over there. Olivia isn't just some local act, taking part for the exposure. She's the biggest thing in pop music right now, and I don't think that some girl who's only famous for who her parents are and for getting naked on the internet can really appreciate—'

'Mr Collins—' Tom struggled to keep his tone professional as inside him indignation and anger burned brighter '—this is Tom Buckley. We've spoken before, when I've been commissioned to write pieces about Olivia.'

'Tom. Right.' A little unease threaded through Mr Collins's words now he knew he was talking to the press. Tom didn't imagine for a moment that he had *much* power in the world, but the ability to make famous people look ungrateful, stupid or plain mean was always worth something. 'You're covering this concert?'

'I'm helping Miss Huntingdon-Cross organise it this year.' Maybe his words were a little sharp, but Mr Collins deserved a hell of a lot worse. 'All for charity, you know. I've got Olivia's rider right here.' He held out a hand and Violet passed it over. Tom scanned through the pop star's list of demands for her performance and backstage requirements, eyebrows raised. 'She does realise that all the profits from the day go to very worthwhile charities, yes?'

'Well, of course she does,' Mr Collins blustered. 'She's always keen to help those less fortunate than herself.'

'In which case, I'd imagine that she wouldn't want the sixty-seven requests she's made to result in us not being able to meet our giving targets for the year, right? I mean, I'm sure that nobody would ever say that Olivia places more importance on having the appropriately named Diva vodka available backstage than she does on starving children getting a hot meal, but...well, you have to admit, it doesn't look all that good.'

There was a pause on the other end of the line. Tom waited it out. The next move had to be the manager's.

'I'm sure Olivia would be satisfied with a more...easily available vodka,' Mr Collins said eventually.

Tom drew a gleeful line through the words reading 'Three bottles of Diva vodka' on the piece of paper in front of him. 'I'm sure she would too. In fact, why don't you go back to her and see which other items she might be willing to forgo? For the sake of the children.' And her publicity, of course. Tom was under no illusions about that.

'I'll see what I can do.' Mr Collins hung up.

Beaming, Tom handed the rider back to Violet. 'And that is how you deal with ungrateful, self-important, egotistical teenage stars.'

'By threatening to expose them in the press as terrible people?' Violet, for some reason, didn't look quite as pleased with his victory as Tom thought she should.

'By making them aware of the truth of their situation,' he replied. 'They're public figures, and their attitudes and behaviour are noted. Don't you think the world should know that she wanted a bottle of three-thousand-dollar vodka more than she wanted to help the charity she was supposed to be appearing for?'

'No. Yes.' Frustration crossed Violet's face. 'Look, the point is, I didn't need you to save me. I could have dealt with it myself.'

'I'm sure you could.' Something told him this might be the time to tread gently. 'But sometimes these guys react better to the press than to...' Hell, now he was stuck. How to describe her in a way that wouldn't make her fly off the handle?

'Some girl who's only famous for who her parents are and for getting naked on the internet?' Bitterness filled Violet's voice as she quoted Mr Collins.

'Okay, I definitely wasn't going to say *that*.'

'But it's what you were thinking, right?' Violet gave him a sad smile. 'I know how people see me.'

The disappointment on her face made her look more fragile than he'd imagined she could, especially after their explosive first meeting in the airport. This wasn't a woman who revelled in her notoriety, who defended her mistakes and delighted in the press coverage. This wasn't the woman he'd watched—very briefly, before embarrassment got the better of him—in that sex tape.

'Does that happen a lot?' he asked, suddenly furious at the idea that it wasn't just one stupid man belittling Violet, but a whole host of them.

'Mr Collins?' She shrugged. 'Sometimes. I don't… Mostly, I'm not around people like that, so it's fine. If we're at a charity event or something, usually people won't say it to my face. But I hear the snickers and see the smiles, you know? I guess it's the only thing I'm famous for, so it's all anyone wants to talk about.'

'But it's not all that you are.' It surprised him how strongly he believed that—and how ashamed he felt that, when he'd arrived, he'd probably thought the same. What had changed?

'Was this why you didn't want to be in charge of the Benefit Concert?' he asked.

'I do want to do it,' she snapped. 'But…it's why my parents were worried about me doing it, yeah.' Her hands were busy playing with some stress toy she'd found in Rose's drawer when they were sorting the study—a globe that she could stretch and squeeze. After less than a week, it already looked considerably more worn than when they'd discovered it. 'They know I don't enjoy dealing with people so much these days. That was always left to Rose, really.'

These days. Since the sex tape? Tom frowned. Since

then, she'd stopped trusting anyone outside her immediate family, and avoided other people as much as possible.

Huh. Perhaps the stories he'd read when researching Violet Huntingdon-Cross weren't all there was to know. And he was a reporter—he always wanted to get to the truth, the real story.

Standing up, Tom reached across the desk and rescued the poor battered globe from between her fingers. 'Come on.' He took her hand and pulled her to her feet.

'What? Where are we going?' That puzzled frown line between her eyebrows was actually kind of cute, Tom decided.

'Lunch,' he told her. 'Completely off the record. I promise.'

It quickly emerged that Tom had no idea where they could actually go for lunch. 'Hey, you live here,' he said. 'Where's good?'

Rolling her eyes, Violet grabbed her handbag and car keys. 'Come on.'

As she started the engine, and tried to ignore Tom fiddling with the radio, she weighed up her options. There was the Peacock in the village, but that was just across the road from the church and the vicar's favourite afternoon haunt. She could almost guarantee that having lunch there with Tom would mean that the whole flower committee would be talking about her again by Sunday. There was the Three Tuns in the next village over, but Mum and her ladies sometimes took lunch there mid-week, and Violet couldn't remember if it was one of those days. Even if Mum wasn't there, the ladies might be.

So that left the Fox and Hounds, three villages over and with hand-cut chips to die for. Violet felt she could live with that.

'Is there any reason we're crossing county lines to grab a sandwich?' Tom asked as they drove past the turning for the village.

'Hand-cut chips,' Violet replied. It was only a partial lie, at least.

'Fair enough.' Tom settled back into his seat, the radio playing something obscure and jazzy, and folded his hands behind his head.

'So, these questions you want to ask...' It made Violet a little nervous, how relaxed he was. As if he already knew the answers to the things he was going to ask.

'When we get to the pub.' Were his eyes closed? Violet snapped her gaze away from the road ahead just long enough to check. Yep, he was half asleep in her car. Again.

'Okay, but you know I don't believe in off the record, right? I distinctly remember having that conversation.' That too revealing, too intimate conversation. Since then, she'd taken care to keep their interactions to a minimum. When he'd stopped by to see if he could help with the Benefit Concert a few days ago, she'd handed him a call sheet and left him to it. And when he'd been helping her sort the study, it had been easy to just boss him around.

Until today. Violet was under no illusions who was in charge today, even if she was the one holding the steering wheel. And she really didn't like it.

Beside her, Tom sighed, brought his hands down to rest in his lap and opened his eyes. 'Okay, look. This is how this is going to work. We are going to have lunch. Over lunch, we will make friendly conversation. We will probably talk about our families, our friends, our lives. Because that's what people do when they go out for lunch.'

'Not always,' Violet interjected. 'When we have flower committee lunches we mostly talk about other people. In fact, most lunches I've ever been to have been filled with people talking about other people.' Seemed people were always more comfortable gossiping about people they barely knew than about themselves. In fact, they especially seemed to like talking about her, she'd found.

'Fair point,' Tom conceded. 'Okay, then, imagine we're at some sort of internet dating meet-up thing.'

Violet couldn't help but laugh. 'No way.'

'Why not?'

'Because no logical computer programme in the world would ever put us together!' The journalist and the woman who got screwed over—quite literally and in front of millions—by one. Not a natural match.

'You don't know that!' Tom twisted in his seat to grin at her. 'We're both relatively young, relatively attractive…'

Violet tossed her hair over her shoulder, the way her mum did when she was dealing with idiots who didn't know they were idiots. 'Relatively?'

'In your case, relative to the pop stars and supermodels of this world. In mine…relative to everyone else.' Tom shrugged, as if to admit he knew the argument was kind of weak.

Violet raised her eyebrows as she pulled into the car park of the Fox and Hounds.

'Regardless of our relative attractiveness levels, I can assure you that our personality profiles would be very, very different.' Violet switched off the engine.

'Oh, I think we could have stuff in common.'

'How would you know? You don't know the first thing about me, apart from what you've read on the internet.' And watched, of course, although she didn't feel the need to remind him of that.

'Exactly.' Tom flashed her a grin and opened the door. 'And you don't know anything about me.'

'Except that you're a reporter.'

'That's my job, not who I am.' He got out of the car.

'So who are you then?' Violet called after him.

'Come to lunch and find out.' Tom leant down, rested him arms on the door frame and peered in at her. 'I'll do you a deal. For every question you answer of mine, I'll answer one of yours. Off the record.'

'I told you, I don't believe in that.'

'You might by the end of lunch. Now come on. I'm starving.'

CHAPTER NINE

VIOLET HAD BEEN RIGHT—the hand-cut chips were definitely worth the trip. The conversation, not so much. So far, over a pint of bitter for him and an orange juice for her, they'd discussed the menu, the merits of starters over puddings and the general preference for both, whether a table by the window might be nicer than one by the bar, and if the couple arguing in the car park were ever coming in.

But now, as the waitress retreated after leaving them their meals, he had his chance.

'So, do you want to go first, or shall I?' Tom popped another chip in his mouth while Violet considered her answer. Then, since it seemed to be taking her a while, he ate another. 'That wasn't meant to be such a brainteaser, you know.'

'It's a big decision!' Violet said. 'Like that bit in *The Princess Bride* with the iocane powder. You know… *Are you the sort of person who'd put poison in your glass or my glass? That bit.'* She looked down and selected her own chip, biting it in half.

'How, exactly, is lunch with me like deciding whether to drink poison or not?'

'Not lunch. The question thing,' Violet said. 'I mean, if you ask first, then I'll know the sort of level of questions we're asking, which makes it easier for me to come up with mine. But if I go first, then I can see how good your answers are before deciding how good *my* answers should be. See?'

'Sure.' Or, you know, not at all. 'So, you like movies?' Tom asked, oddly charmed by her uncertainty.

Violet's gaze flew up to meet his. 'Is that your first question? Because I hadn't decided…'

'Okay. Not an official question. Just an idle wondering.' Anything that got her talking was good with him.

'Then, yes. I like movies.' She took a breath. 'So, my turn.'

'You've decided, then?'

Violet nodded. 'I think so.'

'So was that me going first, or did that one not count and this next question is you going first?' He grinned at the frustration that crossed her face.

'Does it matter?'

'Not really, I suppose.' Tom settled back in his chair. 'Go on, then. Ask away.'

'Why did you agree to come and stay at Huntingdon Hall, and work on this book for Dad?'

Was that an easy one, to lull him into a false sense of security? Or did she just have no idea what to ask? Either way, he wasn't going to be so gentle.

'Because it's the chance of a lifetime,' he said with a shrug. Faint disappointment coloured Violet's face, and he realised suddenly that maybe this wasn't an easy question. Maybe she was asking more than he'd first thought. He paused, and considered the real answer. 'The Screaming Lemons were my mum's favourite band; they were the soundtrack to my childhood. So even if this wasn't a great opportunity to really make my name—and hopefully some money—I'd still have wanted to take the job. Your dad, his friends, your family—you're part of modern history. You matter to the collective memory of music lovers everywhere. I don't want that to be lost when we're all dead and gone.'

'The music would live on,' Violet said, her head tipped slightly to one side as she studied him. 'Isn't that enough?'

'In lots of ways, yes. But the Lemons were more than just the music. They're people too—people who mean a lot to their fans, like my mother. And I don't want the truth of who they are to be lost to the stories and anecdotes of people who barely knew them.' Had he even realised why this mattered to him until she'd asked? He didn't think so. Until this moment, he'd thought he was just there to do a job—a fun, fulfilling and hopefully lucrative job, but a job nonetheless. Now it felt more like a vocation.

'So is your mum pleased you're doing it?' Violet asked.

'That's a separate question,' Tom pointed out with a frown. Why had he even mentioned his mother? She was the last thing he wanted to talk about, and he had put the idea in her head. He was normally sharper than this. 'My turn first.'

Violet took a deep breath, as if steeling herself for something deeply unpleasant. 'Go on, then.'

What to ask? Or, rather, what to ask first? He had a lengthy list in his head of things he wanted to know, but where to start? If he went in with something too heavy, she might shy away. But if he started out gentle and they ran out of time, or she called a halt earlier than he'd like, he might never get to the important questions. Tricky.

In the end, he went for something in the middle.

'How do you feel about your twin sister marrying your best friend?'

Violet rolled her eyes and picked up her sandwich with both hands. 'I wondered how long it would take you to get to that.' She took a bite of her sandwich—a stalling tactic,

Tom decided. Something to make her look busy while she considered her answer.

'You promised me the truth,' he reminded her.

Violet swallowed her mouthful. 'I know, I know. Okay, it's a little bit weird, but I'm honestly really happy for them. I thought I was going to have to spend the rest of my life pretending to like Will's fiancées, then celebrating when he inevitably ran off and left them at the altar. This time, I was praying for him to go through with it. They're a good match.'

'So why is it weird?' Tom asked, hoping she wouldn't notice him slipping in the extra question.

Violet tilted her head to the side, considering. 'I guess just because it was never like that with us. Rose is practically my double, but there's a chemistry and a connection between them that just never existed between me and Will. And now it's my turn again.'

She smiled, her gaze catching his, and Tom found himself mesmerised by those bright blue eyes once more. He knew what she meant about the chemistry. He'd met Rose, had a very pleasant lunch and conversation with her. But he'd never found himself wanting to uncover all her secrets, or wanting to reach across and tuck a rogue strand of hair behind her ear. If Rose had told him that no dating agency in the world would set them up, he'd have laughed with her—not stubbornly set out to prove her wrong.

Which was ridiculous. Violet was right—they had nothing in common, no shared history or world. So why was he trying so hard to find a connection between them? Even he wasn't oblivious enough to pretend it was just for a story.

'Go on, then,' he said, breaking away from the look first. 'Ask.'

'I already have. Is your mum pleased you're doing this story?' Violet asked, and Tom's gaze flew away from hers.

'Sorry, only…you mentioned her before—that she was a big fan of Dad's. I just wondered if you were close, I guess.'

'She's dead,' Tom said, wincing at how blunt it came out. 'I mean, she died, about seven years ago now. So, uh, she doesn't know I'm here, but if she did…yeah, I think she'd be pleased. I think she'd have wanted to come too!'

'I'm sorry.' Violet's eyes were wide and sad. 'The way you talked about her, I just assumed… It must have been awful.'

Tom shrugged. 'It was. Still is, in lots of ways. I miss her, of course. And I think about her a lot. But…' Did he want to tell her this? One confidence in the hope of winning a lot more from her in return. 'When she died…we weren't on the best of terms. That's what I regret most. Not having the time to make things right with her before she died.'

He'd expected the sympathy in Violet's eyes, but not the sadness. 'I really am sorry, Tom. But I think she must have known how much you loved her—I can tell just from five minutes speaking with you, and she knew you your whole life.'

'I hope so.' Tom reached for his pint as a distraction. 'My turn. So…' This was it. This was his chance to ask the question he really wanted to know the answer to, while she was still feeling sorry for him. So why didn't he want to ask it, all of a sudden?

He pushed himself to, though. 'The sex tape. Why did you never issue a statement about it? An apology or an explanation?'

'Because it was nobody's damn business,' Violet snapped. 'If they want to watch it, fine, I can't stop them. But I don't have to acknowledge it.'

'Yeah, but a leaked sex tape… There's always talk that the subject might have put it out themselves. For the publicity or whatever. You didn't even deny that.' And *everybody* denied that. That was what made the whole Sex Tape Twin scandal so strange.

Violet looked him straight in the eye, her mouth hard and her jaw tight. 'Since I didn't even know I was being filmed at the time, it seems unlikely that I'd have been able to leak it to the media, doesn't it?'

'You didn't…you honestly didn't know you were being filmed?' Because that made it a whole different story. That…well, that explained a lot about why Violet was so touchy on the subject of trust.

'Of course I didn't! Do you really think I'd let someone film me doing…that?' She shook her head. 'Of course you do. Because you don't know me at all, just like I said. All you know about me is what you've read on the internet, the same as everyone else. Despite the fact you've spent the last week in my home—and apparently learnt nothing at all.'

'I didn't… I just assumed…' His arguments sounded stupid now. Of course Violet wouldn't—this was the woman who trusted no one outside her family. Why would she trust someone to film her being that vulnerable? Except, of course, something had to have happened to make her that wary. And it would make sense for this to be it. 'You looked straight into the camera, Violet. You had to know it was there.'

She blinked at him, shock in those blue eyes. 'I…I did? God, how many times did you watch it, Tom?'

'Not even once all the way through,' he promised. 'But there are stills…'

'Oh, I know. Someone sent a whole pack of them to my parents, along with a note that read "Your daughter is a whore" in bright red lipstick.'

'That's…wow. That's awful.'

'Yeah.' Reaching over, Violet stole his pint and took a sip. Then she sighed. 'Okay, look. I will tell you the story of the sex tape saga. But then that's it for today, yeah? And if you use *any* of it in this damn book of yours—'

'I should. You should want me to,' Tom interrupted. 'The world thinks that you filmed that tape on purpose. Half of them probably think you leaked it yourself. That's all the world knows of you. Don't you want them to know the truth?'

'I just want them all to forget,' Violet whispered, and something in Tom's chest clenched tight at the misery in her voice.

'Tell me what happened,' he said, reaching across the table to take her hand.

Violet looked up, her eyes wide and sad, and said, 'Okay.'

Oh, God, she didn't want to talk about this. Didn't want to admit all over again how stupid she'd been. Stupid, naïve and blind. Or, as Rose put it, nineteen.

'So, after I left boarding school, I took a gap year. I did some work experience at a newspaper because I thought I wanted to study journalism.'

'*You* wanted to become a reporter? You?'

Violet rolled her eyes at the mocking disbelief on Tom's face.

'Yes. I was eighteen then, and a totally different person. And this will go a lot quicker if you don't question everything.' If he interrupted her too much, Violet wasn't sure she could get through to the end of the story at all.

'Sorry. Carry on.' Tom took a big bite of his burger to show he wasn't going to talk any more.

'Okay, so I was working on this paper where no one cared who my parents were—or if they did, it was mostly only to complain about it. I wasn't getting paid, and mostly I fetched coffee, made photocopies and—eventually, once they realised I wasn't an idiot—checked copy and wrote filler pieces from press releases that got emailed in.'

'Sounds familiar,' Tom said through a mouthful of lunch.

'While I was there, I met a guy.'

'Less familiar.'

Violet tried to smile, to acknowledge his attempt to lighten the mood. But just thinking back to those days made her chest hurt. She'd been so young, so carefree. She'd really believed she could do anything she wanted, could be anyone if she just worked at it hard enough.

Finding out she was wrong had almost broken her.

'He was called Nick. He was one of the paper's senior reporters and he kind of took me under his wing. At first I thought it might be because of who my parents were— even then, I was used to people trying to get close to me just so they could get closer to *them*. But Nick didn't seem interested in them. Only me.' He'd made her feel so special—as if her family were the least interesting thing about her. No one had ever managed that before.

Of course, it was all a lie, which might have made it easier.

'What happened?' Tom's expression was already grim, knowing how the story ended. Violet didn't blame him. It wasn't pretty.

'We dated for a bit. He took me places I'd never even thought of going before. I thought…' So, so naïve. 'I thought it was something real. That he loved me as much as I believed I loved him.'

'But he didn't?' There was no pity in Tom's eyes, which she appreciated. The pity was almost worse than the laughter.

'He filmed us in bed together without my knowledge, then put it out on the internet. I believe he also sold some of the photos to the highest bidder first.'

'Bastard.' Violet had never heard quite so much vehemence put into two syllables before.

'The worst thing was…it took me a while to realise what he'd done. I thought it was a fake, or that someone had filmed us without our knowledge…' She swallowed, not wanting to relive the next part. But she'd promised him the truth. 'I went to see him, talking about lawyers and what we could do to get it taken down…and he laughed at me. As did the woman who was in his bed at the time.'

Tom winced at that. 'Jesus. That's…what a piece of work. No wonder you've been hiding out at Huntingdon Hall for the last eight years.'

Violet shrugged. 'It's safe there. I don't have to deal with the press, or the public, or what everyone thinks they know about me, most of the time.'

'So…that's when you stopped trusting people?'

'Do you blame me?' Violet asked.

Tom shook his head. 'No. But one thing I don't understand. Why didn't you let people know the truth? Put out a statement, or sue the scumbag?'

Rose had wanted her to, Violet remembered. Had wanted her to fight back, to fight as dirty as Nick had. She'd wanted to use every connection their parents had to ruin Nick's life the way he'd wrecked hers.

But Violet had said no.

'I didn't want to be that person,' she said, wondering if Tom would understand. Rose had, eventually, but it had taken years. 'I didn't want to drag things out in the papers and on the news. I didn't want to make things all about me. I just wanted it to go away. For people to forget.'

'Except they never did,' Tom said.

Violet stared down at her plate. 'No. They didn't. And it's too late now to change anyone's ideas about me.'

'Maybe not.' Tom leant back in his chair, studying her so intently that it made Violet's skin itch.

'What do you mean?'

Tom shrugged. 'I just wondered if maybe your dad's determination to have me write this book, now, might have something to do with telling the truth about your story, too. Letting the world know what really happened at last.'

Violet shook her head. It wasn't enough. 'Why would they believe it? It's too late now, anyway. It's much harder to change entrenched beliefs than just telling the truth.'

Tom's smile was slow and full of promise. 'Then you clearly haven't read much of my writing. Just wait and see what I can do.'

CHAPTER TEN

'So, where do you want to start today?' Rick Cross lounged back in his chair in the little sitting room off his studio, looking utterly relaxed. A complete contrast to how his daughter had looked when Tom had asked *her* a few innocent questions over lunch at the start of the week.

Focus, Tom. He had *the* Rick Cross here ready to interview, and he did not have time to be distracted by thoughts of Violet.

'Well, we've covered the basic history of the band—although there are lots of areas I want to dig deeper into later, when we have more time. But since I know you need to head out again in an hour…maybe we should use the time to talk about where The Screaming Lemons are today, and where they're headed next?'

'And the family. Don't forget that,' Rick said. 'I want the story of my family to be told, as much as the band. And it's exciting times around here at the moment.'

'Of course.' Including, presumably, Violet's story. How did she feel about that? he wondered. On the one hand, it would mean everyone knowing the truth—and hadn't he promised her he'd change the minds of the Great British—and American—public with his words? But even if the new press attention was more positive than it had ever been before, it would still put her front and centre again. And leave people talking about her sex life more than ever.

From what he'd learned of Violet, that wasn't going to go down well.

'But let's start with the band,' Tom said. He wanted to talk to Violet some more himself before he started discussing her with her father.

Rick gave him a knowing look. 'Okay. What do you want to know?'

Tom already had every detail of the upcoming tour and album launch, what singles they were planning to release when, who'd written most of which song, and who'd done the cover art—and nothing that he couldn't have got from an informative press release.

He needed to go deeper.

'What issues did you run into writing and recording this album that you maybe haven't had to worry about before?' he asked.

Rick smirked. 'You mean broken hips and playing the guitar with a walking frame now we're all so old?'

'Not necessarily.' Tom gave him an apologetic smile. 'But your last album was five years ago now, and life has to have changed for you all. Two of your daughters have got married, your first grandchild is on the way... Jez got divorced a couple of years ago, right?' Rick nodded. 'And the world—the music scene particularly—has changed too. How did that affect things?'

Leaning back in his chair, Rick brought one ankle up to rest on his opposite knee, obviously belying the need for hip replacements. He was only sixty, if that, Tom thought. There was a lot more music to come from the Lemons yet.

'I think...the music scene changes by the minute. You can't write songs to that. I let the marketing people worry about it, and we just get on with writing the best tunes we can. As for the family stuff… Every year we become more settled, happier in the place we're in. We're fortunate. We're all healthy, living the lives we want to live.' An uncomfortable look crossed his face and Tom knew he couldn't *not* ask any more.

'Except Violet,' he said softly.

'Except my Violet,' Rick confirmed.

Tom put down his notepad on the low table between them, dropping his pen on top of it. His phone was still recording, of course, but he knew he wouldn't use whatever Rick said next. Not officially, anyway.

'Is that one of the reasons you asked me here?'

Rick raised an eyebrow. 'You think you can make Violet happy? Get her to follow her dreams at last?'

'Not that.' Tom shook his head, hoping he wasn't actually blushing in front of a rock legend. As if he'd be so presumptuous as to think he could fix Violet's life. 'I meant…the world never got to hear the true story. Their image of Violet, their beliefs about her—that's a large part of what keeps her hiding away here. It did cross my mind that you might want this book to change that. To let people see the real Violet.'

Rick studied him for a long moment before answering, and Tom fought his impulse to look away. He had a feeling that this moment in time, this answer, would set the tone for every interview that followed. That Rick was judging him and his abilities right now, making a decision about how much to tell him—for this question and every one that came after.

And Tom really, really wanted to be found worthy.

'I think, in the end, that Violet will be the one to show the world what she's really made of. She'll be the one to stand up and say, *You were wrong about me.*' Rick flashed a quick smile. 'But anything you can do to help that along would be appreciated.'

Violet glared at the piece of paper in front of her as the phone in her hand clicked over to voicemail again.

'You've reached Jake Collins, music agent. You know what to do at the beep.'

She hung up. If Olivia's manager hadn't responded to any of the other messages she'd left him in the days since their last phone call, not to mention the emails, then why would this message be any different?

Maybe she should threaten him, like Tom had. Except she was very afraid that Mr Collins would just laugh at her and go right back to ignoring her. Not ideal.

Placing her phone back on the desk, she read through Olivia's contract to appear in the concert again. That, at least, was signed. But since she'd somehow got a clause included that meant it was only valid with the accompanying agreed and signed rider, it wasn't worth the paper it was printed on. The rider was not only unsigned, but nowhere near agreed.

Violet had emailed over a revised version after their last conversation, deleting the request for ridiculously overpriced vodka amongst other things, and leaving in the more reasonable stuff. Since then, she'd heard nothing from Olivia's camp.

A knock on the door roused her from her thoughts and she looked up to see Tom loitering in the doorway. She scowled at him by reflex.

'What did I do to put such a look on your face today?' he asked good-naturedly, dropping to sit in what Violet had somehow come to think of as his chair. 'Since you haven't actually seen me since breakfast, when I think I was mostly inoffensive.'

'Jake Collins isn't answering my calls. Or my emails.'

'Olivia's manager?' Tom shook his head. 'He likes his games, that one.'

'I'd rather figured that out for myself, actually,' Violet snapped. 'And this particular game is down to you, I think.'

'You think he's ignoring you because of what I said to him the other day?' Tom shrugged. 'He still deserved it.'

Which was true, but not particularly helpful. 'I think he's stringing me along, making me fret until the very last moment when he'll show up with both the signed rider and my big name act for the concert.'

'Then why are you worrying?' Tom asked. 'Just ignore his little mind games and get on with everything else.'

He made it sound so easy. 'Because there's always the possibility that he's playing a different game. Olivia's contract is pretty much meaningless without the signed rider and if they pull out at the last minute, once all the concert publicity is done and the programmes printed…'

Tom winced at the implication. 'So what are you going to do?'

And wasn't that the three thousand dollar bottle of vodka question? What did she do? Keep phoning and emailing like a desperate person? The ballsy thing to do would be to cancel Olivia altogether, unless the rider was signed by the end of the day—Violet was sure that was what Rose would do. But Violet didn't have Rose's connections to help her find a suitably starry replacement at the last moment.

Which only left door number three.

'I'm going to go and find Jake Collins and his teenage pop idol and get a signature on this bloody rider, that's what I'm going to do.' Violet wished she felt as confident as she sounded. Turning her laptop so Tom could see, she elaborated. 'Olivia's in the middle of a UK arena tour at the moment. Today's Friday, so she's in…' she ran a finger down the list of tour dates on the screen '…Brighton. So that's where I'm going.'

Tom blinked at her, then a slow smile spread across his face. 'Road trip. Cool. When do we leave?'

'We?' That wasn't the plan at all. 'No we. Just me. I need to do this myself.'

'Hey, I'm not planning on interfering,' Tom said, holding his hands up in a surrender pose. 'I just want to see you take Jake Collins down yourself this time. Off the record, of course.'

'Of course,' Violet echoed with disbelief. As much as, oddly, she found she wouldn't mind Tom's company on the trip, she wasn't sure this was an episode she wanted finding its way into his book.

'Besides, I know the PR staff at the venue. I can probably get us press credentials to get us into the gig in the first place.'

Okay, now that would be useful. She hadn't even thought beyond getting to Brighton to how she'd actually get past security to see the star and her manager.

Decision made, Violet closed the lid of her laptop. 'Better grab your stuff then. If I want to get there before the gig, I need to leave in…' she checked her watch '…twenty minutes.'

Tom grinned and jumped to his feet. 'I'll be ready in fifteen.'

Which was all very well for him. Violet wasn't sure she'd ever be ready for a road trip with Tom Buckley.

CHAPTER ELEVEN

TOM WAS ALREADY leaning against the car when Violet emerged from Huntingdon Hall eighteen minutes later, overnight bag in hand. He hadn't wanted to risk her disappearing without him.

Inviting himself along on her little road trip had been a spur of the moment decision, but he'd decided while packing that it was a good one. From a purely professional standpoint, watching Violet take on Jake Collins could be pure gold for the book—not to mention the fact that a couple of hours trapped in a car together would give him plenty of time to interview her on the way to Brighton. For once, she wouldn't be able to escape his questions.

He was less comfortable with his other reasons for wanting to accompany her. Because he had to admit the truth—to himself, if not to Violet—that when he'd made the decision to join her he hadn't been thinking professionally at all. He'd been thinking about the look on her face when Jake Collins had spoken to her as if she were nothing. He'd been thinking about her plucking up the courage to face him and demand a signature.

He'd been thinking that he didn't want her to have to do it alone. And he wasn't sure he wanted to know why it mattered so much to him that he would be there to protect her.

Shaking his head to clear his rebellious thoughts, Tom grinned at Violet as she drew close. 'Ready?'

'As I'll ever be.' She gave him a less certain smile. 'You know, you really don't have to come. I'll be fine.'

Tom shrugged. 'I know. But I've been in the country for over a week now, and still haven't seen anything but the airport and Huntingdon Hall. I'm ready for a road trip.'

Violet opened the trunk and they both stashed their bags. 'You've been to Britain before, though, right?' she asked as she slid into the driver's seat.

'Loads of times,' Tom admitted. 'But I've never seen any of it with you.'

She opened her mouth as if about to answer, then closed it again, frowning at the steering wheel. 'We should get going, then.'

Tom settled back into the passenger seat as Violet started the engine, turned on the radio and pulled out onto the long driveway. At least he wasn't the only one a little unsettled by their connection.

They travelled mostly in silence, content to listen to the radio, until they reached the motorway—and stationary traffic. Tom's only attempts at conversation—gentle precursors to the questions he actually wanted to ask—had been rebuffed by a sharp, 'I'm trying to concentrate on the road right now,' from Violet. Not that he believed her. He knew a stalling tactic when he heard one.

But as the motionless cars spread out ahead of them as they crested the slip road, he straightened up in his seat and prepared to try again.

'Looks like we might have to catch Olivia after her performance,' he said, as casually as he could.

Violet swore in response, and he hid a grin. Where had a nice girl like her learnt words like that?

'That was off the record, by the way,' she added.

'Of course,' Tom said, as seriously as he could manage.

'Dammit.' Violet thumped a hand against the steering wheel. 'Can you check the traffic reports? See how bad this is likely to be?'

Tom nodded and reached for his phone but, before he could find it, a shrill ringing filled the car.

'That's mine.' Violet nodded towards where her phone sat in a little space below the dashboard. Cars up ahead jerked forward, just enough for her to try and edge the car onto the main motorway. 'Is it Mr Collins?'

Tom fished out the phone and looked. 'It's your mother.'

'Of course.' Violet sighed. 'I'll call her back when we get there.'

'Or I could just...' Tom swiped the screen to answer, and gave Violet an innocent smile in response to her glare. 'Hello, Sherry. Violet's just driving at the moment. Can I help?'

'Tom, great—yes, please. Can you tell her that I just had Frances Littlewood on the phone, asking who Violet is bringing as her plus one for Henry's wedding next weekend? She says one of Henry's ushers is single if she's stuck...'

Sherry sounded harried, which was very unlike her. But then, Henry Littlewood's wedding was the theatre dynasty event of the summer. In fact, he had a feeling that Rick and Sherry were godparents to Henry himself. The Littlewoods had the same sort of money, prestige and power in the acting world as Rick and Sherry had in the music one. It was bound to be quite the event. Quite the *public* event. Just the sort of thing Violet usually avoided, as far as Tom could tell.

He covered the phone with his hand. 'She wants to know who you're taking to Henry Littlewood's wedding next weekend. Otherwise, Frances Littlewood is setting you up with an usher.'

Violet swore again and Tom grinned, glad Sherry couldn't hear.

'Not looking forward to it?' he asked, already pretty sure of the answer.

'Henry's a family friend, and his mother made his fiancée make me one of her bridesmaids too, which she probably hates me for.' Violet sighed. 'I want to go for him, and Mum and Dad will be there, probably Daisy and Seb too… It's just…'

'You don't want to face all the people. And the cameras.'

'Yeah.'

Tom considered. There was a chance Violet might never forgive him for what he was about to do. On the other hand, if he could convince her of the truth—that it was the act of a friend, that he honestly had no ulterior motive for this… maybe it could bring them closer.

Maybe, one day, Violet would learn to trust him.

He lifted the phone to his ear again.

'Sherry, if it's okay with you and Rick, I'm going to accompany Violet. As her date, not a reporter on this occasion!'

'Well,' Sherry said, sounding taken aback, 'that sounds lovely. I'm sure we'll all have a delightful day.'

'Me too.' Although, judging by the shocked glare on Violet's face, only if he lived that long. 'See you later, Sherry.'

Silence reined in the motionless car for a long, long moment.

Then Violet said, 'You are never answering my phone again.'

What was he thinking? Well, actually, Violet was pretty sure she knew exactly what he was thinking—what a perfect way to further his career by sneaking into a society wedding under the guise of being her date. It wasn't as if she hadn't got used to being used for her name and family over the years, but this one really did take the biscuit.

'I meant what I said,' Tom told her, his expression deceptively earnest. 'I'm not going to the wedding as a journalist.'

'No, you said you were going as my date. Aren't you supposed to *ask* a girl before declaring something a date?' Because if he'd asked she could have said no. And she almost certainly would have. Probably.

'Well, it was kind of a spur of the moment decision. Much like this road trip.' He shot her a sideways glance she pretended not to see. 'Is it such a bad idea?'

'Yes!'

'Why?'

'Because…oh, so many reasons. Because you're not my boyfriend; you're the guy who's here to research and write about me and my family. Because you're always, always a reporter, no matter how much you pretend you're taking a day off. Journalists don't do off-duty.'

'Okay, answer me this one question honestly.' Violet stared out of the windscreen at the road as he talked. Because she needed to concentrate on driving, not because she was ignoring him. Really. Even if the car wasn't moving. 'Will the wedding be more or less fun with me there to keep you company?'

Damn him. Violet bit the inside of her cheek to keep from answering. Even with Daisy and her parents there, it would be better with Tom. Because Daisy and Seb would be all loved-up again, and so would Mum and Dad probably, and everyone would start telling stories about their own weddings or engagements or romantic moments… and, for once, she wouldn't have to sit there as sorry single Violet whose heart had been betrayed and broken by the only man she'd ever loved.

'Violet? More or less fun?' Tom pressed.

'More.' The word came out begrudgingly.

'Great! Then it's all settled.' Tom beamed at her and Violet almost missed her chance to move forward two metres.

Settled wasn't the word she'd use at all. In fact, things felt more unsettled than ever to Violet.

'So, how many times will you have been a bridesmaid this year, after this one?' Tom asked.

Violet tried to pretend her cheeks weren't getting warm. 'Three, including Mum and Dad's renewal. And you know what they say…'

'No idea, actually,' Tom said cheerfully.

'Three times the bridesmaid, never the bride,' Violet quoted. 'Of course, this is actually the sixteenth time I've been a bridesmaid, so I think we're long past worrying about that.' Not that that would stop everyone there thinking it, or whispering it behind her back, she was sure.

Tom let out a low whistle. 'Sixteen. That's, wow. A lot.'

'Yeah. Most of them were as kids—you know, family friends or people who just wanted cute, famous twin girls to walk down the aisle with them or to make sure Rick and Sherry were photographed at their wedding. You know how it goes.'

'Yeah, I guess.'

'I've only done it five or six times since I left university. Mostly for friends.' Why was she still talking about this? He couldn't possibly care.

'Still, it's a good job you look so great in bridesmaid dresses,' Tom said with a grin.

No pretending she wasn't blushing this time. But thinking about bridesmaid dresses just made her remember the one she was wearing when she'd met him, and what had followed next.

Still not her finest moment.

'Did you check that traffic report?' she asked, eager for a change of subject.

Tom pulled out his own phone and jabbed at the screen for a while. 'Okay, it looks like this carries on for the next couple of junctions. Then we should be clear.'

Violet sighed. 'So, after the gig it is. There's no way we'll make it before at this rate.' They'd been cutting it close as it was. And by the time the gig was over she was going to be exhausted, even if things went well.

'Want me to see if I can find us rooms at a hotel somewhere near the arena?' Tom asked, as if he'd read her mind. It was kind of disconcerting.

She bit her lip. Did she? It would mean a whole night away with Tom Buckley, plus the drive home tomorrow. He was bound to use to his advantage, even if she was slightly reassured by his use of the plural 'rooms'. But was that more dangerous than driving home exhausted? No. Of course it wasn't.

She sighed. 'Yeah, I guess so.'

They inched forward another few metres as Tom frowned at his phone screen. Eventually he gave a little cheer of triumph, and tucked his phone away again.

'Got something?'

'Nothing near the arena,' Tom said, 'but I got us two rooms right on the front, in some hotel with an old-fashioned name. I'm not sure I've ever seen the ocean in Britain.'

'It's the sea here,' Violet corrected him. 'And the British seaside is an institution, I suppose. You should see it.'

A broad smile split Tom's face. 'Great! Only thing I

can't figure out is why one of the rooms was half the price of the other.'

Violet could guess. Not all of those old seaside hotels were in the best of repair these days. 'Well, tell you what, you can take that room and find out. Okay?'

Tom's smile didn't even fade an iota. 'Whatever you say, boss.'

Violet turned her attention back to the traffic ahead of her. She had a feeling it was going to be a very long night.

CHAPTER TWELVE

THE CONCERT HAD to be well underway by the time Violet swung her little car into the car park nearest to the arena. Tom had exercised discretion as the better part of valour and avoided asking too many questions for the latter part of the journey, as Violet's expression grew stony and set as the traffic worsened.

He almost pitied Jake Collins, the mood she was in. But only almost.

'You can definitely get us in there, yes?' Violet asked, switching off the engine and lights. At high summer, the sun was still going down but it still felt late.

'It's done.' Tom stretched his legs out of the door, feeling his back pop as he arched it. 'There should be passes waiting for us at the door.' He didn't mention exactly how much favour currency he'd exchanged for that privilege.

Violet stalked off in what he presumed was the direction of the arena and he hurried to catch her up, pausing only briefly to admire the look of her determined walk and her behind in tight blue jeans.

As he'd promised, they were waved through backstage without any noticeable delays. From the amused look one of the security guards gave Violet, Tom had a feeling that she could probably have talked her way in there without him anyway. She had a very famous face, after all. Not to mention the rest of her.

Violet paused for a moment in the empty corridor backstage as they approached the star dressing room. The sound of Olivia's latest hit echoed around the hallways. Tom stood beside her as she leant against the cool painted wall.

'You ready for this?' he asked, his voice low, relying on his close proximity to ensure he was heard.

'No.' She gave him a wobbly smile. 'But I'm going to do it anyway.'

God, you had to admire that kind of spirit. That kind of grit. The woman he'd thought she was when they met wouldn't have been afraid, and the one he'd come to know in his first days at Huntingdon Hall wouldn't have dared. But this Violet—the woman he was beginning to think of as his Violet, without any justification—she was braver than either of those other women he'd thought he knew.

She was magnificent.

'I'll be right here,' Tom promised. 'But you won't need me.'

Her smile firmed up a little at that, and something in his chest grew warmer. Was it his heart? It had been so long he could hardly tell.

Slowly, Tom leant forward to press a kiss against her forehead, but she tilted her head up to look at him and then…well, it was only natural for him to place that kiss on her lips, right?

'Yeah? Well, you tell them not to call me again until we're talking about top billing, okay? My girl headlines or nothing at all.'

The terse voice cut through what Tom thought was pretty much a perfect moment. Violet jerked back, putting unwelcome inches between them, and Tom bit back a growl of frustration.

'Mr Collins,' Violet said, in what Tom recognised as a dangerously sweet voice. Shaking off the kiss fog that had filled his brain, he tried to focus on what was happening in front of him. How much had the agent seen?

Jake Collins blinked, then jabbed at the screen of his smartphone and slipped it into his pocket. 'Miss Huntingdon-Cross. What a...surprise. And Mr Buckley, correct? Now, what can I do for you two lovebirds?'

Damn. That answered the question of whether Jake had noticed them kissing. Violet's cheeks grew a little pink and Tom cursed his lack of impulse control. Couldn't he have waited to kiss the girl *after* she'd taken care of business?

'I won't take more than a moment of your time, Mr Collins,' Violet continued smoothly, ignoring Jake's amused look and raised eyebrows. Tom stayed a few steps away to the side, close enough to see everything, but not so close that Jake Collins would be able to turn things round and try to deal with him instead. This was Violet's rodeo.

'We're actually in the middle of a pretty big gig here right now, in case you haven't noticed.' Jake's gaze flicked over to Tom. 'I realise you may have had other distractions to deal with.'

Again, Violet ignored the innuendo, so Tom resisted the urge to land a punch on the manager's face. Just.

'Trust me, Mr Collins, I'm here on business,' Violet said crisply. 'Olivia hasn't signed the revised rider yet. You may not be aware but the contract for her to appear at the Benefit Concert is void without the signed rider.' Jake's mouth twitched up at that. Of course he was aware. But Violet kept talking. 'Since I couldn't get hold of you by phone or email, I thought the simplest thing would be to come down here in person with the rider.' She pulled a folder out of her bag and handed it over.

Jake didn't even open it. 'Obviously you realise that

Olivia needs to sign this? And she's a little busy right now.'
As if to punctuate his statement, Olivia hit the high note
of her latest single and the walls around them vibrated
with the sound.

'We can wait.' Violet smiled patiently and Tom brought
his hand to his mouth to hide his own grin.

With a sigh, Jake flipped open the cover of the folder
and glared at the paper inside. 'This isn't what I agreed
with your sister.'

'That is the standard rider that every other act appearing in the concert has signed, plus a couple of the more
reasonable requests from Olivia's original list,' Violet said.
'If it isn't acceptable to you, or to Olivia, I need you to tell
me now. We have just over a week until the concert and if
I need to find a replacement I need to do it immediately.
I'm sure you understand.'

Tom glanced down at Violet's hands, resting at her
sides, and noticed they were trembling, just slightly. Jake
wouldn't have noticed, he was sure. No one who wasn't
looking, or who didn't know Violet, would. She sounded
completely in control of the moment, of the man even.

Only Tom knew she was terrified.

Had she been scared that night at the airport? He hadn't
known to look for the signs, then. Had just assumed that
she was the cocky, self-assured celebrity kid he was expecting.

Now he knew her better. And cared for her all the more
for it.

'You really think you could find an act of the same calibre as Olivia in a week?' Jake shook his head and laughed.

'It's not the calibre I'd be worried about,' Violet shot
back. 'The same level of fame may be a problem, but I
could call a dozen better acts and have them on the stage
in moments.' Tom winced at the sting in her words.

'Of course, the real problem would be the fans,' Jake threw back. 'Because, whatever you think of her talent, Olivia is the one they want to see. I'd like to see you fill that concert without her.'

Violet nodded, her face solemn. 'And I'm sure Olivia would hate to let down her fans. Which is why, if she's not planning to appear, it would be best to know now. So I can put out an official statement apologising to her fans on Olivia's behalf. I'm sure they'll understand when I explain that we were unable to divert enough money from the charity account to satisfy her. Especially when that information comes in a paragraph after a detailed description of all the good causes that money is used to support.' She looked thoughtful for a moment. 'Maybe I'll get Dad to put out the statement. After all, it's his concert, and his charities. We could include a list of all the acts who waived their fee for the concert altogether for comparison. What do you think?'

It was more or less the same threat Jake had made himself, but with more teeth. If Olivia pulled out now, Violet would eviscerate her reputation. Jake didn't want a diva on his books—even if that was what he had. He needed Olivia to appear wholesome and loving and giving, so the kids' mums would let their pre-teens buy her music.

Jake Collins glared at Violet for a long moment before flicking his gaze over to Tom. With a 'What can you do?' smile, Tom shrugged.

'Fine.' Jake snapped the word out as he flicked the folder closed again. 'I'll get her to sign it tonight and courier it to you tomorrow.'

'Perfect.' Violet's smile was sharp, with a hint of teeth. 'And if it's not with me by Monday, I'll issue that press release.' She held out a hand, which Jake took, obviously reluctantly. 'I'm so glad we were able to clear this up. I hope the rest of the tour goes well.'

Jake Collins turned on his heel and stalked away down the corridor without so much as a goodbye. Tom watched him go, aware Violet was doing the same. Then, once he'd disappeared around the corner, Tom let out a long breath.

'You did it,' he said.

'I really, really did.' Violet's eyes were wide, her expression stunned. 'I did it, all by myself.'

Tom grinned. 'So what now?'

The shock faded from Violet's face, replaced by elation. 'Now we celebrate!'

CHAPTER THIRTEEN

THE HOTEL BAR was mostly deserted, but Violet managed to scare up a barman to fetch them some drinks, while Tom carried their bags in from the car and got them checked in. She was glad of the few minutes alone; it gave her a chance to process everything that had happened since they'd arrived in Brighton. And somehow the confrontation with Jake Collins was fading in her memory, compared to the brief, soft, mesmerising kiss she'd shared with Tom beforehand.

But all too soon Tom was back and Violet found herself trying very hard not to stare at his mouth. Why had he kissed her? And was he planning on doing it again?

And if he wasn't, would she?

'Here's to beating that scumbag at his own game.' Tom raised his pint to Violet's glass of wine, and she dutifully chinked them together.

'You don't think I went too far?' Violet asked. After all, it was one thing to stop Jake Collins from trying to ruin her concert, another to behave just as badly to get her own way.

Tom shook his head. 'Trust me, I've seen too far. That was just far enough. Your sister would be proud.'

'Except we're not going to tell her about this, right?' Violet said. 'And it's definitely not going in your book.'

'But it's such a great story!' Tom protested.

'About me,' Violet replied. 'A story about me. And the book is supposed to be about the band, in case you've forgotten.'

'And your family. Your dad has been very specific about that.'

Violet rolled her eyes. 'I have no idea why. Him and Mum, yeah, I get. People want to read about their epic romance. And okay, maybe a tiny section on Daisy marrying into the aristocracy, or looking at all the work Rose has done with the band. But what is there to write about me except a sex scandal I'd much rather no one ever mentioned again?'

'I don't know,' Tom said. 'That's what I've been trying to find out.'

'By asking a thousand questions.'

'That you don't answer.' Tom raised his eyebrows. 'Why is that?'

God, he was unstoppable. 'I answered every question you asked me at lunch the other day. I told you everything you could possibly want to know.'

'About one bad experience with a guy eight years ago, yeah,' Tom said. 'But what about who you are now? What's happened in your life since? Your entire existence can't revolve around one bad sex tape, Violet.'

Except it did, however much it hurt to admit. 'Why does it matter so much to you that you know everything about my life?'

'Because I want to understand you!' Violet glanced around her to make sure no one else had come into the bar and started listening, but Tom obviously didn't care if they had. He was on a roll. 'Violet, you are a mystery to me. And uncovering mysteries is kind of my job.'

'But why do you care?' Violet whispered, knowing she

was really asking *Why did you kiss me?* and wishing she didn't need to know the answer so much. How had he got so cleanly under her skin? She'd only known the man a couple of weeks, but suddenly all she wanted in the world was to hear him say that she mattered to him.

'Because…because you're more than your past. You're…God, Violet, you could be anything you wanted, and you're hiding away at Huntingdon Hall. I want to understand you, to know the truth of you. I want…I want you to trust me.'

Didn't it always come down to that? Violet took a breath. 'I came here today, didn't I?'

'You did,' Tom admitted. 'And why was that? I mean, why did you take on the concert at all if you're not desperate to get back to doing *something* with your life?'

Why had she? It seemed so long ago already that she'd agreed to it. 'I think it was partly to prove a point to you,' she admitted. 'After we met at the airport… It felt like you thought I was nothing more than my parents' name and my own infamous internet appearance. I wanted to prove I was something more, I guess.'

'Good! Because you are. And I'm so damn glad you're starting to see it.' He took a long sip of his pint, then frowned. 'If that was only part of the reason, what was the rest?'

He was sitting too close to her to let her think straight. Violet wished she'd picked one of the other tables, one with two chairs on opposing sides, rather than this booth table with one long semi-circular seat. Here, he could keep sliding round until their legs were nearly touching and she couldn't concentrate on anything else…

A question. He'd asked her a question.

'I guess…I didn't want to let Rose down. Or my parents. And…'

'Yeah?' Another inch closer, and she could feel the length of his thigh against hers, warm and comforting. His arm was almost around her shoulders, resting on the back of the booth behind her, cocooning her, keeping her close and safe. Letting her know she could tell him her secrets.

'I wanted to do…more, I guess. I know you think I've just been hanging around at home, arranging the odd bouquet or something. And maybe that's what I wanted people to think, because then they wouldn't expect too much. I don't know.' She took a breath. This wasn't like her past, this was her life, and she wasn't ashamed of it—actually, she was pretty proud of it.

'I do a lot in our community, besides just the flowers, you know. I help out with pensioners' lunches at the church, I run a counselling group and…Mum and I, we set up a helpline. It's national, and it doesn't have our name on it anywhere. But we take calls from kids and teenagers who just need someone to talk to, or need help escaping from dangerous situations. I do a shift on the phones most days, and I take a lot of calls from teenage girls in their first relationships. Girls who've got in too far too fast and don't know how to get out again. I help them.'

She stopped, aware that Tom's hand was on her shoulder now and he was staring down at her, his eyes full of intensity and feeling she couldn't quite decipher.

'So, anyway. Not just sitting around arranging flowers,' she said. 'But I wanted to do more, and the concert… well, it wasn't about me, so it seemed like a safe way to try and do it.'

Tom shook his head. 'Every time I think I've got you sussed out, you go and surprise the hell out of me again and prove you're more than I could have even imagined.'

Violet stared up at him. 'Yeah?'

'Yeah.' Their gazes locked, and she knew before he dipped his head that he was going to kiss her again. And she wanted it so much…but something made her pull back.

'Wait,' she said, and hoped she wouldn't regret it for the rest of her life.

The woman was trying to kill him. That was all there was to it.

Swallowing hard, Tom backed up. Not too far—not far enough to let her forget that gorgeous chemistry that sizzled between them. Just enough for her to know that he wouldn't push anything until she was ready.

'What's the matter?' he asked, trying to find some rationality. But all he could think about was kissing her again, even when she'd made it very clear she didn't want that.

God, he was an idiot. What was he doing? Hell, what was he thinking? She was a subject. Not even that, the daughter of his subject. A secondary interest, worth about twenty pages in the book.

Not someone he should be falling for.

'I don't know.' Violet stared down at her hands, and Tom wished he could read her mind. 'I just…I'm not sure this is a good idea.'

Tom was. At least his body was damn certain it was the best idea he'd had in years.

'Why not?' he asked, disappointment clenching his chest even as he tried to fight it off. She was wary, he knew that. He just needed to win her over. Talk her round. It was all just words—and he was good at words. It was kind of his job, right?

'Because you're a reporter. Because I don't really do relationships. Because you're working for Dad. A million reasons.'

'None of which sound like you don't feel the same things I do when we're together.' She had to feel it too, right? No way that kind of connection only worked one way. It wasn't possible.

Violet sighed. 'Look, I'm not saying I'm not…that there isn't… Okay, fine. Yes, I'm attracted to you, even when I don't want to be. But that doesn't mean we need to…do anything about it. You're staying with my family, working with my parents… We can't risk screwing all that up.'

'It would be worth it.' He was damn sure of that. Even if she was only making the same arguments that had been buzzing round his head for days.

'Come on, Tom.' Violet's lips twisted up in a half smile. 'This is your big break. Don't tell me you'd be willing to risk that just for a quick tawdry fling with the Sex Tape Twin.'

'Don't say that,' Tom snapped. How could she still say that, after everything she'd just told him? 'That's not who you are. Not any more. And never to me.'

'I was, though. That was the first thing you knew about me. And the first thing I knew about you was that you'd watched that damn video.'

'It was work. I didn't…' God, there was no excuse here that would work, was there? 'You weren't…you to me then. You weren't Violet.'

Violet's smile was sad. 'But that's the point, isn't it? I'm not me to anyone. I'm just that stupid, naïve girl in a sexy video. I'm never just Violet.'

'You are to me now,' Tom promised.

'I hope so.' She looked up at him at last, blue eyes wide. 'But in lots of ways you're still just The Reporter to me. I don't…it's weird to think that I've opened up to you more than anyone since Will, but I still barely know anything about you.'

Well, that he could fix, surely? 'What do you want to know?'

'Everything,' Violet replied. 'But not tonight, I don't think. I need a little time to…process everything. I mean, I did something huge today, facing down Jake Collins. I couldn't have done that before, not even a month ago—I just froze up in front of people like that, knowing they were laughing at me inside. I'm changing, and I like it, and I think…I think a lot of it has to do with you being here. But it's all happening so fast, and I still have so much left to do for the concert, and…'

'You need time. I get that.' Disappointment warred with relief inside Tom. She wanted to know everything—and that meant she wasn't the only one who needed time. He needed to think about this too. To figure out how much he could tell her, how far he could let her in before she reached the stuff that would just make her kick him out completely. 'This wouldn't…this isn't a fling, Violet, not for me. And I don't think it is for you either. So we can take our time.' Even if the restraint it required was physically painful.

He managed a small smile for her, and shifted just a little further back. 'We'll talk soon, yeah? I need to go figure out all my cutest childhood tales and stories of selfless behaviour to win you over with.'

Violet paused with one hand on her handbag and threw him a serious look. 'Those aren't the ones I want to hear, Tom. I want the truth, same as you. It's the only way I can learn to trust you.' She leant over and pressed a kiss to the side of his mouth before grabbing her room key from the table and heading for the lobby.

The truth. Tom stared after her as she disappeared into the elevator, her golden hair flowing behind her.

The truth was the one thing he definitely *couldn't* tell her.

Draining the rest of his drink, Tom grabbed his own room key and prepared to head up. He had a lot of thinking —and writing—to do.

CHAPTER FOURTEEN

VIOLET HAD A horrible feeling that Tom was avoiding her.

They hadn't talked much on the way home from Brighton, mostly because Tom had been passed out in the passenger seat after muttering something about the mini bar, a spring sticking in his back, a broken window and a dripping shower keeping him awake. Violet hadn't slept much better, but since her room had been perfectly comfortable the only excuse she had was her own thoughts.

She did think, as she got back onto the motorway, that if he'd been that uncomfortable he could have always come and slept in her room…

Except she'd made it very clear that was off the cards, at least until she got to know him a little better. She'd been in a relationship before where the guy knew all her innermost thoughts and dreams and it turned out she didn't know him at all, and look how that ended. But while she knew that was a perfectly sensible decision in principle, that hadn't made it any easier to dismiss the thoughts of what might have happened if she'd just let him kiss her again.

In the days since then, he'd been nowhere to be seen. He hadn't even joined them for dinner last night. 'Working hard', her dad had said with a wink. And Violet might have believed it if it wasn't now *Friday* and she'd seen neither hide nor hair of him all week.

Oh, he'd been around, she knew that much. Locked away in the studio with her dad conducting more of the interviews he had, in fairness, travelled thousands of miles to do. She'd even overheard him talking with her mother once or twice—more interviews, she supposed—before she'd stopped listening at doors and got back to what she was supposed to be doing.

At least getting on with the planning for the Benefit Concert had mostly distracted her. With only a week left to go, she was reaching the hectic last few pages of Rose's carefully made lists. Jake Collins had even sent in the signed rider, so she didn't have to follow through on her publicity threats.

Things were good, and dealing with Jake had given her added confidence to get on with her job. She was on top of everything, had spoken with almost everyone involved, or at least their representatives, personally—without a single mention of the words 'sex' and 'tape' in the same sentence. She was making progress.

But, she had to admit, she missed Tom.

'Miss him how, exactly?' Daisy asked when she came over to try on potential wedding outfits the day before Henry Littlewood's wedding. 'I mean, he's right here.'

Violet sighed, and tried not to think that Rose would have understood. Even her twin would probably have struggled with this one, especially since Violet wasn't sure even *she* understood it.

'I guess I'd just got used to having him around.' She grabbed another dress from the pile of maternity evening-gwear Daisy had brought with her. 'How about this one?'

Daisy shook her head. 'Lily Taylor wore that one to a gala last month. It's already been photographed, and I don't want to be in any of those "which mum-to-be wore it best?" comparison pieces.'

So why did you bring it? Violet wanted to ask, but didn't. Pregnancy had made Daisy a little touchy.

'And he's still around.' Daisy shifted on the bed, her hand cupped around her growing baby bump. 'He's just a bit busy interviewing Dad and Mum, I suppose. And me.'

'He's interviewed you?' Violet stopped looking through outfits and stared at her sister.

Daisy blinked back blankly. 'Well, yes. He's interviewing all of us, isn't he?'

'Of course. Yeah.' She'd just imagined that he might start with her.

Daisy shifted again to tug on Violet's hand and make her sit on the bed. 'Okay, seriously. What's going on with the two of you? He's coming as your date tomorrow, Mum said the two of you disappeared to Brighton, of all places, last weekend, and now you tell me you haven't seen him all week. I know you'd probably rather tell Rose, but she's not here. So, fess up—what's going on?'

Violet bit her lip. In some ways, it was probably for the best that Rose wasn't there. She'd have sussed out there was something going on by the time Violet and Tom went for that first lunch. As much as she loved her twin, maybe it was better that she didn't have her über-protective identical sister around right now.

And Daisy…Daisy had always been a good listener, when they'd given her something to listen to.

'To be honest, I have no idea.' Violet fell back to lie on the bed, feeling lighter just for saying it. 'He indicated that he has…feelings, I guess. For me.' By kissing her and making her whole world spin.

'And you said?'

'That it was a bad idea.' Which, now, a week later, felt like a fairly epic mistake in its own right.

'Why?' Daisy asked, eyebrows raised in astonishment.

'He's gorgeous, seems nice, Dad adores him, which is always a good sign, and you're obviously a little bit besotted. So what's the problem? He's…oh. He's a reporter.'

Rose would have got there half an hour ago, but in some ways it was more useful to hear the reasons why Violet *should* say yes. Or maybe that was just wishful thinking.

'Actually, for a reporter, he's kind of…un-slimelike.' The admission didn't come easy.

'You really do like him, don't you?'

Violet sighed. Did she? She thought back over the last couple of weeks. Even after their awful first meeting, when really what she'd most wanted to do was strangle him, there'd still been a weird connection when she'd taken his hand. And he truly had been a help with the Benefit Concert. The way he'd spoken to Olivia's manager… He'd stood up for her, been offended on her behalf. And then he'd taken her out for lunch to cheer her up—and interrogate her, of course. Then he'd come all the way to Brighton and stood back and watched her deal with things herself, and knowing he thought she could had given her the confidence she needed to do it.

He understood about not trusting people. And she hoped he'd understood when she'd told him that she needed to know him better to trust *him*. Hoped he realised that just thinking she might eventually be able to trust him was a huge step for her.

Hoped he wasn't actually avoiding her.

'I do,' she admitted. 'I do like him. I just…he's asking all these questions about my life and my family. By the end of this book, he'll be an authority on all things Screaming Lemons and Huntingdon-Cross. I just want to know him as well. Does that make sense?'

'Of course it does!' Daisy stroked a hand down Violet's arm. 'Oh, Vi, I hope he opens up to you. And if he does…

if he gives you what you've asked for…you'll give him a chance, right? I know it's risky—relationships always are—but we all want to see you happy, and if Tom can make you that way…you have to let him try. Okay?'

Violet nodded. Eight years was too long to hide away, anyway. She'd dealt with pop stars, managers, suppliers and even the press covering the concert over the past week. She could deal with one date with a reporter who made her skin tingle. Right?

Saturday morning came almost too fast for Tom. He'd had a plan, a way to convince Violet that he was worth a chance. She wanted to know all about him? Fine. He'd tell her, up to a point. Nobody really needed to know everything about another person, right? She just needed to feel as if she understood where he came from, and that much he could give her.

Except, he realised quickly, he was always better with the written word than the spoken one. So he'd decided to find the time to write it all down, starting in a freezing, leaking hotel room in Brighton and continuing in between interviews and typing up his notes and a rush job on a short article for an editor who'd called and offered him a last minute slot.

Somehow, it wasn't until Saturday morning that he realised that what he'd written was his own obituary.

Tom stared at the words printed in front of him. Perhaps not the most auspicious start to a relationship, but it did give her all the pertinent information. At least all the information he felt able to share. And it was a start, right? A sign that he could give her what she wanted.

And besides, it was too late to change it now.

A quick shower and Tom dressed in his best suit, ran some gunky stuff through his hair to try and make it behave, and hoped he'd be good enough for the Littlewoods. And Violet.

Rick was already in the kitchen pouring the coffee when Tom made it downstairs, and Daisy's husband, Seb, sat at the counter sipping his own mug as he read the paper.

'Ah, our third compatriot,' Rick said, grabbing another mug and filling it to the brim with hot, strong black coffee. Tom took a sip the moment Violet's father handed it over. Somehow, in the last three weeks, he'd actually converted to *liking* his coffee black. 'This, gentlemen, is the part where we wait.'

Tom checked his watch. 'Aren't we supposed to be leaving soon?'

'Theoretically? Yes. But in reality?' Rick shook his head.

'We told them we needed to leave an hour before we actually do,' Seb explained. 'That way, we might actually get out of here on time.'

Taking a seat, Tom tried to imagine Violet taking hours to get ready. For someone who mostly lived in neat jeans and blouses, with her hair clipped back, it seemed unlikely. But, then again, once Sherry got involved…yeah, he could see things taking a while.

Violet, as a bridesmaid, should, by rights, have stayed at the hotel the night before with the rest of the wedding party. But, as she'd pointed out to everyone at dinner earlier in the week, she was only a bridesmaid on the bride's sufferance, so she wouldn't inflict her presence too early. 'There are, like, ten others anyway. No one is going to miss me.' So, instead. she'd arranged to have her hair and make-up done to match everyone else's at the house and would travel down early with the rest of them.

If she ever finished getting ready.

Two cups of coffee later, Violet appeared, dressed in a

pale blue bridesmaid's dress that left her shoulders bare. Her hair had been pinned back from her face and fell in curls at the back, and her wide dark-lashed eyes looked bluer than ever.

'They are coming, honest. Daisy's just changed her mind about which dress to wear. Again.' Violet swished across the room, her skirt floating around her legs, to fetch herself a coffee. Her shoes were silver, Tom realised. And sparkly.

And he was totally staring.

Blinking, he tore his gaze away, just in time to see Rick hide his smirk behind a coffee cup. Fantastic.

'I'll, uh, go see if the cars are here, shall I?' Tom said, heading out to the front of the house before anyone had time to reply. Maybe the fresh air would help clear his head.

Since they weren't expected for another thirty minutes, of course there were no cars. Stepping to one side of the front door, Tom leant against the brick wall.

'Hey.' He opened his eyes and found Violet standing beside him, cup of coffee in hand. 'You okay?'

'I'm fine,' Tom lied. 'No, actually, I'm not. I have something to give to you, and I'm not sure if I should, if it'll help or if it will scare you off for life…'

Violet raised her eyebrows. 'Well, now you have to give it to me. Because the things I'm imagining just *have* to be worse than whatever the reality is.'

Reaching inside his suit pocket, he pulled out the carefully folded sheet of paper.

'Okay, so you said you wanted to know about me. About my life. And so I thought I'd write it down—that's what I've been doing this week, when I wasn't interviewing your family. So…here it is.' He held out the piece of paper and waited for her to take it, half wishing that she wouldn't.

But she did, her wary eyes huge as they met his. Then she unfolded it, looked down and her eyebrows drew down as her brow furrowed.

'This is… Is this your obituary?'

'Kind of.' Tom hunted for a way to explain. 'When I used to work on a local newspaper, one of the things I was in charge of was keeping the obituaries up to date for local celebrities. So that if anything happened, we were ready to run. I have a few on hand for musicians I've written about or interviewed a lot, too, ready for when the time comes. So when I sat down to write about my life…it just kind of came out that way.'

Violet stared at him. 'You really are a journalist all the way to your core, aren't you?'

'Apparently so.' He just wished that wasn't the one thing she didn't want him to be.

'Is the car here yet, darling?' Sherry's voice floated down the stairs and out of the front door. 'We don't want to be late.'

Violet folded the paper again and slipped it into the tiny silver bag she carried. 'I'll read this later,' she promised. 'And then…maybe we can, uh, talk again?'

'I'd like that a lot,' Tom replied. Of course, first they had to get through the Littlewood wedding. Suddenly, he'd never been so unexcited at the prospect of spending a day with the rich and famous.

CHAPTER FIFTEEN

'So, what do we think?' Daisy asked as they finished up their puddings later that evening. 'Better or worse than my wedding?'

'Our wedding,' Seb put in, around a mouthful of chocolate and pistachio torte. Daisy waved a hand dismissively at him.

'Not a patch on yours, Daze,' Violet assured her sister. 'Was it, Tom? Wait, you weren't there, were you?' Maybe that third glass of champagne had been a bad idea. Bubbles always did go straight to her head.

But there'd been so many people, so many knowing glances. And even with Tom on her arm, she'd needed something else between her and all of them.

'I was not, unfortunately.' Tom smiled across the table at Daisy. 'But, delightful as today has been, I can't imagine it being a patch on a wedding organised by Sherry Huntingdon.'

'A safe bet,' Seb murmured.

Leaning back in her chair, Violet tried to spot the waiters coming round with coffee. Maybe that would help her focus on the special day going on around her.

Because all she'd been able to think about so far was the piece of paper folded up in her clutch bag.

She'd tried to concentrate on smiling as she and the

other bridesmaids walked in front of the beautiful bride down the aisle, and on Henry looking handsomely nervous at the front of the church. And she'd tried to listen to the vicar talking about the importance of love and forgiveness and understanding in a marriage. But really her mind had been buzzing with the knowledge that in her lap she held the history of Tom Buckley. His life and times. His secrets.

And she really, really wanted to know them.

But she wanted the time to savour them, too. To absorb and understand them. And she couldn't exactly sit there and read it at the dining table surrounded by her sister and brother-in-law, and three of Henry's cousins and their wives.

The cousins, fortunately, had wandered off towards the free bar before Daisy had started comparing weddings. But that didn't mean she could just get reading. Did it?

Violet glanced up. Daisy, Seb and Tom were deep in conversation and she didn't seem to be required. Mum and Dad were sitting three tables over, chatting with some old friends. It was entirely possible that no one would notice if she disappeared for ten minutes.

'I'm just going to…' She waved a hand vaguely in the direction of the bathrooms as she stood, but no one seemed bothered.

Pausing in the doorway to the main ballroom, where the wedding breakfast had been served, Violet checked to ensure no one was watching her, then headed in the opposite direction from the bathrooms—towards the gardens.

It was easy enough to find a secluded bench, hidden away behind the walls of the rose garden. If anyone stumbled across her, she could just say she needed a little air. After all, the weather was warm and the five hundred guests had made the ballroom a little stifling. No reason for anybody to suspect anything.

Especially not that she was hiding away to read the obituary of a man still very much alive.

She unfolded the piece of paper, wondering if the fact he'd written it told her more about him than even the words contained could. Only a journalist would think of doing such a thing, which was a permanent worry. But, on the other hand, he'd wanted her to have all the facts, the truth, laid out in a way they were only ever told after death.

This was who he was, how he thought he'd be remembered, everything he felt was important to say about his life. All in two pages—which Violet figured was probably a good page longer than hers would have been. Or a page and a half longer if you omitted the sex tape thing in the interests of good taste.

Yeah. No one was ever going to omit that.

With a deep breath, Violet focused on the words. Even with the dispassionate tone an obituary demanded, she could still hear Tom talking to her with every line.

She lived Tom's childhood in New York, his early career, his estrangement from his mother and his pain at her death, his tours with bands and his relationship history, all in his own words. And by the time she reached the end she almost, almost felt as if he was sitting there beside her.

'So, do you have questions?'

Violet jerked her head up at the sound of Tom's voice, blushing when she found him leaning against the garden wall watching her, one eyebrow raised.

'I probably will have, later.' After all, the plain facts weren't the same as actually *knowing* a person, were they? But after the last few weeks, it was really only the facts that she'd been missing. Swallowing hard, Violet got to her feet. 'But there's something else I want to do first.'

He didn't move as she stepped towards him, and she

understood that this was all on her now. This was her decision. And he would wait and let her make it.

She just hoped it wasn't a mistake.

She stopped, close enough that she could almost feel his breath on her face, but still not touching. Violet looked up into his eyes and saw the control there. He was holding back. So she wouldn't.

Bringing one hand up to rest against his chest, she felt the thump of his heart through his shirt and knew she wanted to be close to that beat for as long as he'd let her. Slowly, she rose up onto her tiptoes, enjoying the fact that he was tall enough that she needed to. And then, without breaking eye contact for a moment, Violet kissed him.

It only took a moment before he responded, and Violet let herself relax into the kiss as his arms came up to hold her close. The celebrity wedding melted away, and all she knew was the feel of his body against hers and the taste of him on her lips. This. This was what she needed. Why had she denied herself this for so long?

And how could it be that kissing Tom somehow tasted like trust?

Eventually, though, she had to pull away. Tom's arms kept her pressed against him, even as she dropped down to her normal height, looking up into his moss-green eyes.

'You liked my obituary, then?' he murmured.

Violet shook her head. 'Not one bit. I'd like it to never be written, please. But...I liked knowing you.'

'Is this where I give you some kind of line about getting to know me even better?' Tom asked, one eyebrow raised.

Violet's laugh bubbled up inside her, as if kissing Tom had released all the joy she'd kept buried deep down. 'I think it probably is, yes.'

'In that case, how long do you think we need to stay at this hootenanny?'

'There's five hundred people here,' Violet pointed out. 'What are the chances of them missing just two?'

'Good point.' And with a warm smile spreading across his face, Tom grabbed Violet's hand and they ran for the waiting car.

'Are you asleep?'

It was many hours later, and Violet's voice was barely more than a whisper. He felt it against his bare skin more than heard it.

'Not quite.' He shifted, pulling her closer against his side. Now he finally had her where he'd dreamt of her being, he wasn't willing to put up with even a centimetre between them. 'You okay?'

'Mmm, fine. More than fine. Kind of awesome, actually.' She smiled sleepily up at him, and he felt a puff of pride at the relaxation and satisfaction he saw in her face. She rubbed her cheek against his chest like a contented kitten.

'Told you this was a good idea,' he murmured into her hair.

Violet laughed, low and warm. 'You did. And you were right.'

Too damn right. This was more than a good idea. This was more than he'd dreamt it could be. He'd known from the first that he was attracted to Violet, but had never really expected to do anything about it. Never imagined he'd want to, not this badly.

But then he'd got to know her. Understand her. Even let her in a bit to understand him. And now look at them.

And she thought it was a good idea, at last.

'I'm glad you think so.'

'Plus, with the…last-minute nature of everything, I'm pretty sure you wouldn't have even had time to set up a video camera.'

It was a joke, he knew, but there was still something brittle behind the words. Something not quite healed. It made him want to wrap her up and keep her safe—not an emotion he was used to feeling about the women he dated. And in this case…he had a feeling that Violet had been kept safe for too long already. She'd had enough of being protected—and she was ready to take care of herself for a change.

Tom sank down a little lower in the bed, turning on his side until they were face to face. 'You know I wouldn't do that, don't you? You have to know that.' She might not need him to protect her, but she did need to trust him. To know he would never, never hurt her.

He wasn't that man any more.

'I do. I do.' Violet inched closer and placed another kiss on his lips. 'I'm just still…adjusting to the idea.'

'I can understand that.' Wrapping his arm around her waist, he pulled her against him. 'I just hope you can learn to trust me.'

'I think I already do.' The hope in Violet's eyes meant he just had to kiss her again.

But when they separated, the hope had faded away and left a question there. 'What is it?' he asked.

'I just wondered…in your obituary, you talked about your mum, how you fell out. And I know you said you hadn't made up when she died. But you never said what you argued about. I guess I just don't understand…what could have been that important that you didn't try to reconcile with her?'

Despite the warmth of the bed and Violet's body, a shiver ran through him and his muscles froze.

'Pride,' he whispered. 'What else? Stupid, pointless pride.'

Violet pressed a kiss against his collarbone. 'Tell me.'

Except he couldn't, could he? Because that one fact, that one omission from his obituary, was the one thing she'd never forgive. Still, he had to tell her something, and the trust in her eyes made him want it to be as close to the truth as he could manage.

'When I was just starting out as a reporter, I worked for a…less reputable paper. The sort that my mom felt was beneath me. It was run by a guy who believed that the ends—a good story—justified any means. And he expected his staff to do whatever they needed to, in order to get the copy.' And slowly, the longer he'd stayed there, the more desensitised he'd become to those methods.

'Mom said I was wasting my talents, that selling my soul for a job wasn't worth it.' He swallowed at the memory of his mother's face, full of righteous fury. 'She told me she'd brought me up better than that, that she didn't want to know a son who could sink to such depths.'

Tom risked a glance at Violet, where she lay silent, her cheek resting against his shoulder. Her eyes were damp and he fought back against the instinct to tell her how much he didn't deserve her pity or her tears.

'What happened next?' she murmured, her hand caressing his arm, a comforting, caring touch.

'I told her she didn't understand journalism, that she'd never get it. That this was what I had to do to build my career. She kicked me out of the house and told me to come back when I'd found my honour again.' He squeezed his eyes shut. 'It didn't take me too long to figure out she was right. But my pride made me stay away too long. I didn't know she was sick, and by the time I found out…it was too late.'

He'd quit the paper long before then, of course, the moment that terrible story broke and he realised what he'd done. But when he'd lost his mother's respect, he'd lost any respect he had for himself too. How could he go back until he'd regained that? And it turned out respect took far longer to earn than to lose.

Violet wrapped her arms tightly around his middle, shifting until she was almost lying on top of him, protecting him from the world. 'I'm so sorry.'

'It was a long time ago.' As if that made a difference to the pain.

'Still. I wish I could make it better.'

Tom curled his body around hers until they were touching skin at as many points as possible. 'Trust me, you are. Just being with you…watching you move past your own history, it helps.'

'Is that all that helps?' Violet raised her head slightly to look at him, and he felt himself warming at the heat in her blue eyes.

'I can think of one or two other things,' he said, and kissed her again.

CHAPTER SIXTEEN

VIOLET STRETCHED OUT against the sheets, listening to Tom's steady breathing beside her. The sun was almost fully up outside; it had to be around six. She'd heard her parents, Daisy and Seb returning hours ago, listened to their giggles and their good-nights. She'd texted Daisy from the car to say that she and Tom were heading home early—she figured she didn't really need to elaborate. Daisy might not be her twin, but she was still her sister. She knew her well enough for this.

What would they all think? Would they be pleased that she was moving on at last, or scared for her because of whom she'd chosen to move on with? Would they understand? And how would it affect the job that Tom was there to do?

'You're thinking too loudly,' Tom murmured, shifting beside her. 'Go back to sleep.'

'I will,' Violet lied. Running her hand down his arm, she listened until Tom's breathing evened out again. He probably wouldn't even remember his strange comment when he woke up.

But he'd remember the rest of the night, she was sure. That, at least, was impossible to forget. She might not be the most experienced of women, but the chemistry between them, the connection she felt when they were skin against skin…Violet had never felt anything like that before.

She stifled a laugh as she remembered Tom's first words to her—about how the frustrated look on her face reminded him of that hideous tape. Maybe Rose had been right when she'd recounted the incident to her. Maybe she really was finally able to laugh about the whole thing.

That had to mean she was moving on. And it was past time.

She glanced across at Tom, one arm thrown above his head as he slept, his dark hair rumpled and his bare chest so tempting. She could just curl back up beside him right now, rest her head on that chest and drift back to sleep until he woke up again for a repeat performance of last night.

The plan had many, many merits.

With one last look and a quiet sigh, Violet slipped out from between the sheets, slowly enough not to wake him. She needed to think, and that was practically impossible while in bed with Tom. The man was just too distracting—even asleep.

Grabbing a pair of leggings and a long T-shirt from a drawer, and, giving silent thanks that they'd made it back to her room, not Tom's, the night before, Violet dressed silently, then crept out of the room. She'd use the bathroom down the hall to freshen up, rather than her own en suite bathroom, then grab some coffee and head to Rose's study. No one was likely to interrupt her there, at least not for a while. After the late night at the wedding, everyone was likely to sleep in, and Tom…well, he was probably a little worn out too.

She couldn't help the smile that spread across her face as she thought about it. One thing she had no doubt about— last night had *definitely* been a good idea.

Now she just had to figure out what happened next.

The study was blissfully cool, quiet and private. Resting her cup of coffee on the corner of the desk, Violet curled up in her desk chair and stared out of the window. There was probably work for the Benefit that she should be doing, but she knew she'd be good for nothing if she didn't sort out last night in her head first.

He'd talked about his mother, and about the dark side of reporting—as if she didn't know it well enough already. But he'd got out, and the guilt he carried from his mother not knowing that before she'd died…Violet knew that was strong enough to keep him honest for ever. Tom would never be the sort of reporter Nick was. He'd told her the truth about everything.

This could have been history repeating itself all over again—but it wasn't. Because Tom wasn't Nick. And, for the first time in a long time, she honestly found herself hopeful and trusting in her future.

The phone on her desk rang, and Violet frowned at it. Who on earth would be calling so early on a Sunday?

'Violet Huntingdon-Cross,' she said, answering it.

'Miss Cross. It's Jake Collins here.' Ah, of course. Only the most offensive manager on her list of acts—who else? Probably looking for a way to get back at her for the rider thing. 'We're in Dublin airport right now, about to fly back across to your own fair green isle for the Benefit Concert.'

Well, that explained the early morning wake-up call. But not why he was actually calling. And wasn't Ireland the fair green isle, anyway? At least he was sounding civil. Almost friendly, in fact. It was enough to make her suspicious.

'Mr Collins,' she said as brightly as she could, 'how can I help you today?'

'It's rather more a case of how we can help you, I think. I appreciate that the news isn't official just yet, but you know how the industry is. There were enough people at that party last night that it really wasn't a surprise.'

What party? The Littlewood wedding? But the only thing that had happened there… Violet bit back a groan. She'd place money on some camera somewhere catching a shot of her and Tom in the garden. But did anyone really care about that? And what on earth did it have to do with Jake Collins, anyway?

'I'm sorry… I don't understand.' And she wasn't sure she wanted him to explain it, either.

'Of course, of course. I totally get that you need to await the official announcement. And, of course, there will need to be the appropriate period of mourning, especially for your family. But no one would want to see the Benefit Concert cancelled, I'm sure. So all I wanted to say was… if your father feels it inappropriate for the Lemons to perform, Olivia would, of course, be more than happy to help out by taking over the headline slot.'

Mourning? Why would they…and what would make them think of cancelling the concert?

'Mr Collins, really—'

'Oh, I know, too soon. Too soon. But it's out there now. I'll call again at a better time and we can talk. So sorry for your loss. Please, pass my condolences on to your parents.'

The line went dead, and Violet stared at it in her hand for a long moment before a truly dreadful thought hit.

Rose and Will.

Violet's heart beat treble time in her chest. She had no idea where they were, what the time was there and she didn't care. Grabbing her mobile with shaking hands, she pressed the speed dial and prayed for Rose to pick up.

'Vi?' Rose's sleepy voice came over the line and Violet's breath burst out of her in relief.

'Oh, thank God. I just had the strangest phone call and

I thought…never mind. You're okay. Everything's okay. Go back to sleep.'

''Kay. Call you later.'

Violet hung up. Whatever Jake Collins's deal was, he was obviously mistaken. Everything was fine. Violet's heart rate started to return to normal and she reached for her coffee cup.

She only managed one sip before the police banged on the door.

'What's going on?' Tom asked as he stumbled into the kitchen, wishing he'd taken the time to go back to his own room and find something other than yesterday's suit to wear. But when he'd woken alone in Violet's bed, heard voices downstairs then spotted the police cars on the drive-way…he hadn't really been thinking about his own sartorial elegance.

Violet looked across from the coffee maker, her expression tense. There were lines around her eyes he didn't remember from the night before and they looked puffy and red, as if she was trying really hard not to cry.

Sherry wasn't even trying. How she managed to still look beautiful with tears streaming down her face, Tom had no idea. Rick had one arm around her, his other hand covering his face. Seb held Daisy in the corner, her face hidden against his chest.

And next to the kitchen table stood two police officers and a man in a suit—utterly incongruous in the Hunting-don-Cross kitchen.

'I'm sorry, sir,' the suit said, not sounding at all apologetic. 'I'm Detective Inspector Trivet. And you are?'

'Tom Buckley. I'm here interviewing the family.' Except he'd never felt more like an outsider than at this moment.

'You're press.' The detective's mouth hardened. 'I'm

sorry, but the family has requested no reporters be allowed in at this time.'

Tom's heart sank, a dead weight in his chest. Of course not. Whatever was happening, this was for family only. 'Right. I'll just—'

'No!' Violet said, too loud in the subdued kitchen. 'Tom's a…family friend. Right, Dad?'

Rick looked up just long enough to nod. His craggy face looked ten years older, Tom realised.

'In that case, I'll tell you just what I've told the others,' Trivet said. 'I'm afraid that in the early hours of this morning one of Mr Cross's cars was discovered along the riverbank, halfway between here and London. The man behind the wheel was Jez Whittle.'

The Screaming Lemons' lead guitarist. But, more importantly this morning, Rick's best friend.

'Is he…?' Tom hardly dared ask. The answer was already written on the face of everyone else in the room.

'It appears that he died in the early hours of this morning.'

'From the car crash?' Tom asked, but Violet shook her head.

'Mr Whittle died from a fatal overdose of heroin.' Trivet's expression was solemn as he spoke. 'People at the party he'd attended in London confirmed that he had seemed unstable before he left and had talked about needing "something more" to take the edge off.'

'He'd been clean for years!' Rick's head shot up, his distress clear on his face. 'I mean, twenty years. You don't just fall off the wagon after two decades. Not without talking to someone first. Without talking to *me*.'

Oh, God, he shouldn't be here. This wasn't meant for Tom to witness. He shouldn't be watching Violet go to her parents and wrap her arms around them both, tears on her cheeks. Because if he was here…he had to write about this moment. Had to tell this story.

And how could he, now?

'What happens next?' Seb asked, his voice low and even. He was family now, even if he'd only married in. He could take charge and ask questions and take care of people. While Tom had to just fade into the background and pretend he wasn't intruding on this incredibly private grief.

Except he wanted to. He wanted to take Violet in his arms the way Seb had held Daisy, wanted to make this easier for her, any way he could.

'There'll be an official inquest, of course,' the detective said. 'And we'll need to ask Mr Cross a few questions about the car and such. But mostly, I imagine, you can expect an influx of paparazzi, and soon. I can leave a couple of uniforms here to watch the door, if you want. Might dissuade most of them from trying anything extreme.'

Like climbing in through windows, harassing the family every time they even looked outside. Oh, God, this was going to be hell for Violet.

Seb nodded. 'Thank you. And if that's all…' The Earl had the aristocracy's way with dismissal hints, Tom realised, and almost smiled.

'For now.' Detective Inspector Trivet motioned towards the door with his head and the policemen all filed out, leaving the family alone. With Tom.

'I should…' Leave, he wanted to say. But how could he when Violet's head jerked up, her blue eyes huge and wide in her pale face and her gaze pleading. 'Make more coffee,' he finished. 'Or food. If anyone wants something to… Or something else. Anything you need.'

'Thank you,' Violet whispered. But no one else was listening.

'I don't *understand* it.' Rick crashed his fist down onto

the table, rattling the coffee cups. 'Why didn't he talk to me? Of all the people…he knew! He knew I could help.'

'I set up a drug rehab and addiction counselling centre years ago.' Rick's words from one of many interviews floated through Tom's mind. *'I always felt it was important to pay back, for all the narrow escapes friends have had. I wanted to help.'*

And was this why? Had Rick been thinking about Jez when he'd started that project? That it would have made his friend's life easier—or even that it would be there, ready for him, if he ever needed it again?

Stories of Jez's addictions had appeared in the papers regularly, back in the day. But the band had always closed ranks around him, Tom remembered from his research. And in those days they hadn't had the internet or camera phones to contend with. By the time they'd been invented, Jez had sobered up and flown right.

Until last night.

'He was probably on his way here, Rick.' Sherry sounded exhausted, even though they'd all only been up for an hour or so, Tom guessed. 'He always, always came here when he was in trouble, you know that. He came to us and we fixed it.'

'Except this time he left it too late.' Rick's melancholy tone tore another sob from Daisy, and Violet looked paler than ever. Her hands were shaking, Tom realised. He wanted to go to her. Wanted to know what to say, how to help.

But then the phone rang and Tom realised there was, at least, one thing he could do.

'That'll be the papers,' Sherry said softly.

'Vultures.' Rick glanced up. 'No offence, Tom.'

'None taken,' Tom assured him.

'Do we answer it?' Daisy asked. 'Or just leave it.'

'They won't stop calling,' Seb said.

Tom took a breath. It wasn't his place. He wasn't part of the family.

But he would do this for Violet.

'I'll deal with them,' he said. 'All of them. You just… look after each other, and don't worry about the press, or the photographers, any of it. I'll take care of it all.'

He wasn't quite sure if Violet's expression was grateful or concerned, but it didn't matter. If she didn't trust him completely after this, she never would.

CHAPTER SEVENTEEN

NOTHING WAS EVER going to be the same again.

It wasn't the first time Violet had experienced that sort of revelation in her life, but this time it felt impossible to see how her family would ever find their way back to being whole again. The grief they were all experiencing permeated the house, a silence that crept through the hallways and clung to the curtains.

That silence had sent her running for Rose's study, the place she'd spent the most time over the last few weeks. The place she'd hoped would help her take control of her life again, to grow up and start living instead of just hiding.

But hiding was all she wanted to do now.

Uncle Jez. She'd known him since before she was born, had grown up with him always there for birthdays and parties and jam sessions and just when he was craving ice cream. He had free run of the house—especially the kitchen if he felt like making pancakes. He'd treated Dad's collection of cars as his own, had famously said he could never marry because Rick had stolen the only woman worth settling down for, then gone on and married—and divorced—four times. He was wild and free and enormous fun and she would miss him, always, in a corner of her heart that would never heal.

But most of her grief was for her parents. For their loss.

And for the horrible, unexpected proof that everything they'd told her, her whole life, was wrong.

Everything wouldn't be okay if they just stuck together. As long as they had each other, terrible things could still happen. There were some things in this world that family just couldn't fix.

And the worst thing was that she'd known that, really, of course she had. But she'd never actually believed it until this morning.

'Hey.' Tom stuck his head around the door at the same time as he rapped his knuckles lightly across the wood. 'Do you need anything?'

He hadn't asked if she was okay, which she appreciated. In fact, he'd been great at avoiding the stupid, unnecessary comments and questions and just getting on with what needed to be done. He'd gone out and faced the pack of press hyenas outside the house and asked that they respect the family's privacy and grief at this terrible time—not that any of them imagined that they would. Still, it had made it clear that no one intended to make a fool of themselves in front of them, or give them a new sound bite or photo to focus on.

Violet had watched him on the telly, too scared to even risk appearing at a window hiding behind a curtain to see it live. He'd looked in control, but also as if he cared.

As if he was part of the family.

Violet took a breath. 'To be honest, I could do with a hug.'

'That, I can do.' Tom smiled and shut the door behind him. Stepping forward, he opened up his arms and she practically jumped into them. How had it only been a matter of hours since she'd been curled up naked in his arms? And how could so much have changed since then?

'Rose is on her way back,' she murmured after a long

moment of just being held. 'At least she hopes so. She and Will were heading to the airport to see if they could get an earlier flight home when I spoke to them last. Although, since I still have no idea where they are, God only knows how long it will take them. I said I'd go pick them up if they let me know when their flight gets in.'

'I'll come with you,' Tom said. 'Just let me know when.'

'I'd like that.' Violet wondered if he could sense the relief in her voice. She could have sent a car, but it was important to her that Rose saw family when she arrived. But that didn't mean she wouldn't appreciate some backup when the inevitable comments and photos and looks started at the airport.

Strange to think that this time they'd be because of Uncle Jez rather than her own mistakes.

'How's your dad doing?' Tom asked and Violet pulled back from his arms with a sigh. Back to the real world.

'He's…devastated, basically. Mum's with him, though, so that will help. Daisy and Seb are going to stay on for the next week, too. Seb's popped home to get their stuff, and Daisy has gone for a lie down.'

'And you? How are you doing?' That question at last. She supposed even Tom couldn't hold off asking it for ever.

'I'm…angry. At Uncle Jez, at those vultures outside our door—no offence—at the world.' But Violet had learned that just being angry didn't get you anywhere. You had to do something with it or it was just wasted.

She'd spent the last eight years being pointlessly angry, and look where it had got her.

'I realised I'm angry because it's so meaningless,' she said, looking straight into Tom's eyes. 'So I decided to make it mean something.'

Tom blinked. 'Mean something. How, exactly?'

Taking a deep breath, Violet held up the new poster

mock-up she'd spent the morning working on. 'I know the concert's only five days away, and I know this would mean a ridiculous amount of work to pull it off—especially since we don't even know if Dad and the rest of the boys will even want to get on stage. But what do you think? Will you help me?' Violet glanced down at her newly appropriated poster, now proclaiming the Benefit Concert to be wholly in support of addiction support centres across the country. It would be a lot to do. But it would definitely mean something. It would be worth it.

A smile spread across Tom's face, and she knew she had him.

'Just tell me what you need me to do,' he said.

Violet had spent two days working like a woman possessed. Tom watched her in awe, taking every task she gave him and completing it as efficiently as possible, mostly because he wanted to get back to watching her work. If he'd ever thought of her as a spoilt celebrity kid who only wanted the spotlight without having to do anything beyond getting naked to earn it—and, okay, he had—she was proving him wrong by the second.

She amazed him. All day long she made the calls he knew would have terrified her a few weeks ago, speaking to not just people in the business but the media too. She fended off questions about her family and her dad's reaction to Jez's death like a pro, as though they didn't touch her at all. Tom knew they did—knew that when she clung to him in their bed at night she was thinking of all those people out there, desperate to know every detail of her life and use it against her.

He did his best to distract her at those moments.

And she amazed him there, too. When she wasn't being professional Violet, organising the Benefit almost from the ground up again, or family Violet, taking care of her distraught parents and pregnant sister, or even community Violet, fending off well-meaning locals who came with flowers or food. When she could just be his Violet, alone in the dark, letting him see the heart of her. As if Jez's death had torn down the last of her barriers and given him a clear path in to the real Violet.

They'd never really had The Talk—the one about their future and what they both expected out of this relationship, if it even was a relationship. But somehow, Tom felt, they didn't need to. They'd instinctively moved past that, to an understanding that this was what it was—and it was what they both needed right now. They mattered to each other, and the world was easier with each other in it. That was all Tom cared about.

'Okay, so what's left?' Violet asked, tapping her pen against her notepad as she frowned down at her list.

Tom refrained from pointing out that she was the one with the checklist in front of her. Instead, he moved behind her, rubbing her shoulders firmly as he looked down at the lines after lines of her handwriting, all with tiny check boxes beside them.

'Well, most of the stuff that needed printing—the new signs and programmes and stuff—that's all taken care of,' he said, assessing the ticks in the check boxes. 'And we've spoken to every act and sponsor and media partner between us, so they all know the score.'

'And they're all on board,' Violet added, a hint of amazement in her voice. As if she couldn't believe that *she'd* actually talked them all into it.

'With your incredible persuasive sell? Of course they are.' Tom dug his fingers into a particularly tight knot in her back. 'The riders for all the acts are sorted—even Olivia's. And all the technical stuff is more or less unchanged.

The new wristbands and such are en route, ready to hand out to the vendors when they arrive, to sell alongside everything else. What else is there?'

Violet's shoulders stiffened, beyond the power of his fingers to relax them. 'The headline act.'

'Apart from that.' Tom let out a long breath and moved his hands to just rest against Violet's skin, a reminder that he was there, that he wanted to help. 'Have you spoken to your dad yet?'

'Not about this,' Violet said. 'About the funeral arrangements, about the good old days, about the clinic, about what he'd have done to help if Jez had just come to him… But not a word on if The Screaming Lemons are planning to perform at the Benefit Concert.'

'He hasn't spoken to any of the rest of the band either,' Tom confirmed. 'Jonny actually asked *me* yesterday if I knew what was going on.'

'I need to ask him.' Violet put down her pen, obviously not willing to add this action to the list. 'If he wants to play…we need to get in another guitarist. They've worked with some great session musicians over the years…'

'Actually,' Tom said, the word out before he'd even completed the thought, let alone decided if it was a good idea, 'I might know someone. Someone I think your dad would approve of.'

Violet turned in her seat, twisting under his hands until she was almost in his arms. 'Really? Who?'

Tom shook his head. He didn't want to get her hopes up if it didn't work out. 'Look, you talk to your dad first. If he says he wants to go on…I'll make some calls.'

'Okay.' She gave him the sad half smile he'd grown too used to seeing over the past few days. 'Thank you, Tom. For everything you've done this week. I know this wasn't exactly what you came to Huntingdon Hall for.'

'Neither was this.' He dipped his head to press a kiss against her lips. 'And I wouldn't give us up for the world.'

A faint pink blush spread across her cheeks. Was that a step too far? Too close to the 'talking about things' line they weren't crossing? Because if there was one thing Tom had realised over the last couple of days, it was that he *wanted* to talk about things between them. He wanted to put a name on their relationship.

He wanted to tell her he had fallen in love with her.

But now wasn't the time. After the Benefit, once things had calmed down, and once Rose was back and her family was a little more stable again. They had time. He just had to pick the right one.

Love, it turned out, was worth waiting for.

'I mean it, Tom.' Violet's expression turned serious. 'You came here for a tell-all book, the exclusive stories that would make your name. And here you are, in the middle of the biggest story to hit the Lemons in thirty years, and you're spending all your time telling other reporters "no comment". I know it can't be easy for you—you're a born journalist; we both know that. But you haven't chased this story, haven't exposed Dad's grief. And I really, really appreciate that.'

Tom's smile felt fake and forced. A born journalist. Was that what he'd always be to her? And, worse, was it true? 'Of course I wouldn't. I'm here for you right now—and not as a reporter. When your dad is ready to resume our interviews, fine. But for now…let's just focus on the Benefit, yeah?'

Violet nodded. 'Are you still coming with me to the airport to fetch Rose and Will this afternoon?' The honeymooning pair had ended up having to take three separate flights over thirty-six hours to get home just one day earlier than planned, but Rose had insisted on doing it anyway.

'I'll be there,' Tom promised. 'I'll meet you at the front door at two, yeah?'

'Okay.' Violet leant up and pressed a kiss to his mouth. 'And, in the meantime, I need to go talk to Dad.'

'You do.' Neither of them were admitting it, but if the Lemons didn't play at the concert, the Benefit would lose a lot of impact. Yes, people might understand Rick's reluctance to get back on stage so soon after Jez's death, might even respect it. But without Rick Cross on stage, the Huntingdon Hall Benefit would just be another concert. And Violet, Tom knew, wanted this year's Benefit to be much, much more than that. She wanted to use it to change attitudes, to promote the availability of aid—for addicts and their friends and family.

She wanted to make a difference, and Tom honestly believed she might.

Plus, if there was anyone who could talk Rick Cross into anything, it had to be Violet.

'Wish me luck,' Violet said.

'You don't need it,' Tom told her, but he kissed her again for luck anyway. Just in case.

CHAPTER EIGHTEEN

VIOLET JANGLED THE car keys in her hand, barely resisting the urge to tap her foot. Where was he? It was quarter past two and still no sign of Tom. She really had to leave to fetch Rose and Will—unless she wanted them grumpy and fed up after a thirty-six hour flight with no one there to meet them.

'Any sign?' Sherry appeared through the kitchen door.

Violet shook her head. 'You haven't seen him either?'

'Afraid not. I checked the study again, and his room.'

'Did you ask Dad?' Violet asked, then regretted it when Sherry's face turned a little grey. Rick hadn't been in the best mood after Violet's conversation with him that afternoon.

'He's shut himself away in the studio,' Sherry said. 'I thought it best to leave him for now.'

'Yeah, I can understand that.' Guilt knotted in her gut. She shouldn't have pushed him, certainly not so soon. It was just that she was so desperate to make this year's Benefit Concert more of a success than ever. For Uncle Jez.

'Violet…' Her mother paused, and Violet felt the knot in her stomach twist tighter.

'I know what you're going to say, Mum. Don't worry. I'm not going to pester him again.'

But Sherry shook her head. 'It's not that. Sweetheart…

we're so proud of how you've stepped up these past few weeks. Taking over the Benefit, dealing with everything—even Tom being here.' She gave Violet a sly smile. 'Although I suspect that one wasn't quite the hardship you imagined, right?'

'Mum, I—'

'Darling, I think it's marvellous. He's a great guy, and it was past time for you to find something worth coming out of hiding for. No, all I wanted to say was…I'm so proud of what you're doing, turning this Benefit into a fitting memorial for your Uncle Jez, and a way to help others who might not know where to turn. It's important work, and I know how much it took for you to do it.'

Violet's eyes burned. 'Thanks, Mum.'

'So, so proud, darling.' Sherry wrapped her arms around her daughter and squeezed her lightly in a hug. 'And I do think the Lemons should play. I know your father isn't quite there yet, but I think he will be, once some of the fog clears. So…I'll talk to the boys, get them all on board. So we're ready when your dad bursts out of that studio ready to take to the stage, yes?'

'That would be great. Thanks, Mum.' Violet hugged her back, thinking, not for the first time, that the whole family would have been doomed years ago if Sherry hadn't been there to take them in hand.

'Now, you get off and fetch that twin of yours and her husband. We need all the family here right now.' She made a shooing motion with her hands. 'Go on. I'll tell Tom you couldn't wait for him when he shows up. He's probably on a call or something.'

Sherry was probably right, Violet decided as she pulled out of the garage and prepared to drive past the reporters still camped out on their doorstep. Tom wouldn't have left her to do this alone unless something important had come up. And since he'd taken on the job of distracting and dealing with the media and their many, many questions about Uncle Jez and the family, the chances were he was probably yelling 'no comment' down the phone at someone he'd previously considered a friend and colleague right now.

'Violet! Violet!' The calls started the moment her car pulled around to the front of the house and headed for the driveway out to the main road. She checked her windows were completely shut, but it didn't seem to do much for keeping the shouts out.

'How's your dad?' someone called.

'Any news on the car? How did Jez get hold of it?' yelled a less concerned reporter.

'Are Rose and Will coming home?'

'Is it true that Daisy went into premature labour and is now on bed rest?'

Violet had to smile at that one. Daisy was only five months pregnant and, if she was in bed, Violet was pretty sure she was 'seeking solace' in the arms of her rather attractive husband. Really, did they not think if something had happened to the baby they'd have seen the ambulances and medical experts lined up by the dozen? Sherry Huntingdon was taking absolutely no chances with her first grandchild.

The questions followed her as she sped down the driveway and faded away as she hit the open road. It was strange to think that the last time she'd driven this way had been when she'd headed to the airport to collect Tom. So much had changed since then, she barely recognised the frustrated, lonely woman who'd let loose on him in the coffee shop.

In the end, it turned out that Rose and Will's last leg flight had been delayed. Sighing as she checked the arrivals board for updates, Violet spotted a familiar-looking coffee shop and decided that was as good a place as any to try and avoid attention. Picking up a paper on her way, she grabbed a coffee, settled herself into a corner where she could still see the screens with flight information and prepared to wait.

She heard a few murmurs as people spotted her, probably exacerbated by the fact that the front page of the newspaper had a splashy sidebar about Jez's autopsy, but no one approached her directly, which Violet appreciated. In fact, it was possibly the most peace and quiet she'd had in days.

She should have known it wouldn't last.

Violet was halfway through reading an editorial piece about the price of fame, idly making her own comments in the margins with a pencil, when her phone rang. She didn't recognise the number, but that wasn't exactly unusual these days. She had all the main contacts for the Benefit Concert programmed in, but every time someone rang from a different office line or their home phone instead of their mobile, it threw her off.

'Violet Huntingdon-Cross,' she answered, trying to sound both welcoming—in case it was someone from the Benefit—and dismissive—in case it was another reporter who'd got hold of her number—at the same time.

'Hello, sweetpea.' The voice on the other end made her muscles freeze up, her whole body tense. For eight years she'd avoided that voice, and the man it belonged to. Eight years she'd spent trying to pretend he didn't exist—which was almost true. The man she'd thought she loved didn't exist at all. Only this man, who could betray her in a moment for a good story.

'Nick.' She should hang up, switch her phone off and pretend this never happened. Go back to hiding away from him and everything he represented.

Except she wasn't that Violet any more, was she?

'What do you want?' she asked, her tone clipped. She was so far past him now. One little conversation wouldn't kill her.

'The same thing everything wants from you right now,' Nick said. 'An official comment on the recent untimely death of your father's lead guitarist.'

Violet laughed, loud enough to draw attention from the people sitting at the next table. 'Why on earth would you imagine I'd give you that?' Or anything else he wanted, for that matter.

'Maybe for old times' sake?' Nick said. 'But I suppose I should have known better.'

'Too right you should.'

'I mean, you've got another journo on the line these days, haven't you? Stringing you along, just waiting for the story of a lifetime. I bet old Tom couldn't believe his luck.'

'You know Tom?' It wasn't really a question; Nick had always known everyone. Tom might be from the other side of the pond, but that wouldn't mean much. They ran in the same circles. But Nick was wrong if he thought Tom was anything like him.

'Doesn't everybody?' Nick said lightly. 'But I suppose the real question is how well *you* know Tom. I mean, have you ever read through his stories? Not the recent ones, but the early stories. The story that gave him his first big break, for example.'

'I don't know what you're talking about, and I don't want to.' Violet swallowed down the fear that rose up her throat as she remembered Tom talking about the first paper he'd worked for. The one that had caused such a rift between him and his mother. He'd never talked about the stories he wrote for that paper…a fact she'd wilfully ignored in the face of their romance. 'Tom's not like you. And what the hell does it matter to you anyway?'

'Maybe I just couldn't bear to see you taken in so completely all over again.' There was a pause, then Nick laughed. 'Okay, take this call as your reminder. When you figure out what he's really like and you realise that we're all the same, us journos, perhaps you might think *better the devil you know*, yeah? You've got to talk some time. Might as well talk to me as the next man.'

'It will never be you,' Violet bit out. How could he even think that? And what did he think he knew about Tom that would make *Nick* seem like the better option? She couldn't even think about it. 'Goodbye, Nick.'

She ended the call, her heart still racing. He was probably just winding her up. Taking a chance on having an in on the story of the century, or whatever. His editor had probably put him up to it. He couldn't have ever imagined she'd actually talk to him, right?

Which meant he was probably making it up about Tom, too. What the hell did Nick know, anyway? All Tom's stories were music based—even his early ones for that cursed paper were probably album reviews. What could possibly be contentious in that? Maybe he gave the Lemons two stars once or something, but that wasn't enough to drive a wedge between them. The past was the past; it didn't matter now.

Except…Nick had said they were all the same. And Violet knew some of the stories Nick had written. Had starred in a few.

Tom wouldn't write anything like that. Would he?

Violet glanced up at the arrivals screen. Still no word. So she had time to kill. It didn't mean anything.

At least that was what she told herself as she pulled her tablet out of her bag and began a search on Tom's name.

It took less time than she'd imagined. She wasn't exactly an internet geek, but even she could find basic information on a person—and the articles they'd written. And it wasn't exactly hard to figure out which one Nick had been referring to.

There, in amongst all the album reviews, band interviews and concert coverage, dated ten years earlier, was the story that had started Tom Buckley's career. And it made Violet's stomach turn just to read it.

Teenage starlet in nude photo scandal.

The photos had clearly been taken up close and in person, rather than by telephoto lens. Whoever had taken them had got close. Very close. And had been invited there.

Violet remembered the story breaking, remembered how these very photos had been splashed across the news, the papers and the internet within a matter of hours. And the text, the background info…he'd gone out looking for this, Violet could tell. Maybe he'd had a tip-off, maybe he'd played a hunch—whatever. Tom had deliberately and wilfully pursued and exposed this story. And maybe even seduced the actress to do it.

Kristy Callahan had been barely eighteen at the time, Violet remembered. She'd been famous for starring in a wholesome family sitcom. And Tom's story had destroyed her career.

Violet didn't want to know this. But now that she did… she couldn't pretend the story didn't exist. That she didn't know what Tom had done. He hadn't fallen out with his mother over the paper he worked for—it was because of this story. It had to be. He'd been lying to her after all, just at the moment she'd thought she had the truth. That she could trust him.

She glanced up at the screen; Rose and Will's plane had landed at last. She needed to find her sister and her best friend.

And then she needed to go home and find Tom.

CHAPTER NINETEEN

GOD, WHAT A DAY. Tom had been surprised when Rick had called him into his studio, and stunned when he'd insisted on doing an interview right now.

But the material he'd got was golden.

'I think, whenever you lose someone close to you, you always wonder if there was something more you could have done. Some small thing that would have kept them with you.' Rick shook his head, staring down at his hands. 'With Jez…knowing that I really *could* have done more—that I could have saved him if he'd let me, if he'd just called. That's going to be hard to live with. As is the guilt. Wondering if I should have seen the signs sooner, should have taken more precautions.'

Tom swallowed before asking his next question, reminding himself that today Rick was a subject, not a friend, not the father of the woman he was in love with. That he was here to do a job—one Rick had hired him for. That meant not shying away from the hard questions.

'Do you think…were there signs? Ones that you missed?'

Rick sighed. 'Probably. But, then again, maybe not. When an addiction takes hold…sometimes it can be a slow build towards cracking again, but more often it can just be one moment, one instant that flips you from recovering to addict again. There's such a thin line…and sometimes Jez liked to walk it. To put himself in the way of temptation.' He shook his head again. 'I don't know. If he wanted to hide it from me, he knew how. And with everything that's been going on here the last few months…maybe I wasn't paying the attention that I should have been.'

Guilt was etched in Rick's craggy face, whatever his words. Tom knew that guilt. That was the sort that never went away, the type you could never make up for once that moment had passed, the opportunity had been missed.

Rick Cross would blame himself for his best friend's death for the rest of his life, whether there was anything he could have done to prevent it or not. Facts didn't matter here, only love.

'Dad?' The door to the studio creaked open and Violet appeared through it. 'Rose and Will are here. And…have you seen…?' She trailed off as she caught sight of him. Tom gave her an apologetic smile, hoping she wasn't too mad about him missing the airport run. He'd planned to talk to her about it, but Rick had been very insistent that the interview was happening now or not at all.

'They're here?' Rick wiped his cheeks with the back of his hands and jumped to his feet. 'Sorry, Tom. We'll do this later, yeah?'

But Violet wasn't looking at her dad. She was still staring at Tom. And he had a horrible feeling that this might just have been his last interview with Rick Cross.

'I'm sorry I couldn't come to the airport with you,' Tom said as Rick shut the door behind him. 'Was it okay?'

'What were you talking to Dad about just then?' Violet's tone was clipped and her gaze sharp. 'Never mind; I'd rather hear it anyway.' She held out a hand for his phone and, with a sense of foreboding, Tom handed it over.

'He asked me to come in here,' he said as she fiddled

with the settings. 'He wanted to talk about some things with me now, while they were still fresh. He said you'd asked him about going on stage for the concert and he wasn't sure. He still needed to work some things out. He thought doing the interview might help.'

He sounded as if he was making excuses, Tom knew, when he had nothing to excuse. He'd been doing his job—and trying to help Rick at the same time. And Violet, for that matter, if it helped him get back on stage for the Benefit.

She had absolutely no reason to be mad at him, and yet he was pretty damn sure she was.

Violet pressed play and Rick's voice filled the room, cracked and broken and distraught.

I think, whenever you lose someone close to you, you always wonder if there was something more you could have done. Some small thing that would have kept them with you. With Jez...knowing that I really could have done more—that I could have saved him, if he'd let me, if he'd just called. That's going to be hard to live with. As is the guilt. Wondering if I should have seen the signs sooner, should have taken more precautions.'

Violet jabbed a finger at the phone and the voice stopped.

'This is why you came, isn't it?' she said, her voice too even, too calm. 'I think I forgot that, with...everything that happened between us. But you were only ever here to do a job, weren't you? To find out all the dirty little secrets in the closets of my family and friends and put them on display for the world to see. Uncle Jez said—' She broke off, and Tom could see her hands trembling as she held his phone. He wanted to go to her so much it burned. 'He told my dad to find a better closet to hide those skeletons in. But in the end, he was the biggest story you could have hoped for, wasn't he? You must have been so frustrated to miss all the drama of Daisy's wedding, and then Rose's too. But at least there was still one sister here for you to get close to and seduce. And then Uncle Jez overdosed in Dad's car and you realised you had the story of the century right here. An interview with a grief-stricken Rick Cross. All you had to do was make sure none of the other journalists got to him first.' She gulped back a sob, and the sound broke his heart. 'And to think I thought you were doing *us* a favour, turning them all away.'

'Violet, no. You're wrong.' She had to be wrong. None of this had been planned—least of all the part where he fell for her. 'I told you. I'm not that kind of journalist.' He just had to reason with her. She was upset, and that was understandable, but she'd come round once she calmed down and saw the truth. That was all. He just had to be patient and not lose his temper and everything would be fine. 'Your dad asked me to come here; you know that. And he asked for the interview today.' He stepped closer, reaching out for her, but she flinched away. 'And I know you've had bad experiences before so I understand why you might be a bit sensitive—'

'A bit *sensitive?*'

Tom winced. 'Bad choice of words. I mean, I can see why you might worry about these things. But you don't need to. I'm not like your ex. I'm one of the good guys.'

'Yeah?' Violet's expression tightened. 'And is that what you told Kristy Callahan?'

The bottom dropped out of Tom's lungs, leaving him fighting to suck in the air he needed to respond. Just the sound of her name sent the guilt crashing in waves over his shoulders and, in that moment, he knew just how Rick felt. Worse, because Rick hadn't actually done anything wrong. Whereas he had known exactly what he was doing and had done it anyway.

God, Violet was right. He was every bit as bad as her ex; he just hid it better.

'How did you…? Never mind.' It didn't matter now, anyway. She knew, and that was enough. 'I can explain. Will you listen to me?'

Violet barked a laugh, harsh and uncompromising. 'Listen to you? I don't even need to, Tom. I know exactly what you're going to say. That she knew what she was doing. She was a celebrity; she knew the score, and the risks. That it was different then—that she meant nothing to you. That *I'm* different…we're different. If you're really desperate, you'll probably trot out the love line. How being with me has changed you, that now you love me you could never do something like that again.'

The vitriol and bitterness in her words was sharp enough to cut, and the worst part was that she was right. He'd tell her anything to win her back right now. And she'd never believe it was because he truly did love her.

She'd never believe anything he ever said again.

But he still had to try.

'It was a mistake. I was just starting out and the paper I worked for… I didn't take those photos; you have to believe that much. I wouldn't do that.'

'No, you'd just syndicate them in papers and news outlets around the world.' Her mouth tightened again. 'This was the real reason you fell out with your mother, isn't it? This was what she couldn't forgive.'

'Yes. It was. But…it wasn't like you think.' He had to find some way to make her understand. She might never trust him again, and his chances of getting her to fall in love with him were non-existent now. He'd thought he had time, and now he was scrambling just to make her believe he wasn't the biggest scumbag on the planet.

Which, given some of his past actions, was a lot harder than he'd like.

'Really, Tom? You're going to try and tell me what it was like?' She gave him a mocking half smile. 'Trust me, I know. I lived it, after all.'

No. He wouldn't let her think that he was just like her ex. He'd made a mistake, sure, but he hadn't planned it. Hadn't deliberately set out to destroy that girl. And she had to know that.

'It's not the same. Violet, you have to listen to me—'

'No! I don't! Not any more. I listened to you, right from that first night. And I should have known better. I *knew* what you were, and I *knew* how this would end. I should never have let you in, never let you close.' She shook her head sadly. 'You said it the night we met. I was never anything more than the Sex Tape Twin to you. Someone you could use to get what you wanted because I didn't matter at all. I'm just a punchline, right? Just a grainy video on the internet for late night comedians to use to get a cheap laugh, even all these years later.'

How could she think that? After everything they'd shared, after the way they'd been together?

'You know the worst part?' Violet asked. 'I actually trusted you. All that talk about never trusting anyone outside my family and I just let you in. Because you were nice to me.' She laughed, low and bitter. 'How desperate must I have been? God, you must have thought you had it made.'

Anger rolled through his body, working its way up through his chest and finding its way out of his mouth before he could even think to censor his words.

'You talk about trust? If you trusted me one iota you'd listen to me. You'd let me explain. You'd trust me enough not to jump to the worst conclusion at the first sign of trouble.' Violet stepped back at the force of his words, and he wanted to feel bad about that but he couldn't find it in himself. 'How did you even find out about that story? Did you go hunting for a reason to put between us? Or did someone tip you off?' The faint splash of pink that coloured her cheeks told him that he'd hit the mark. 'Who was it? Rose? Or another reporter?' The obvious truth slammed into him and he almost laughed at the ridiculousness of it. 'It was him, wasn't it? After everything he did to you, you still trust his word over mine.'

'I trust facts!' Violet shot back. 'How I found out doesn't matter—except that it wasn't from you. If you want my trust, you have to give me the truth.'

'How could I tell you this?' Tom asked. 'Violet, you've been hiding away here so long, so scared of what people might think or say, you don't even know what trust looks like any more. You wouldn't even talk to me about whether we were in a relationship! I was falling madly in love with you and I couldn't even say the words in case I spooked you. In case you jumped to exactly the conclusions you ran to today.'

'The *right* conclusions,' Violet countered, conveniently ignoring all his other points.

'No.' The anger faded, as fast as it had come, and all Tom was left with was that cold, hard certainty. 'You're wrong about me. I made a mistake ten years ago. But since I've come here the only mistake I've made was believing that you could move past *your* mistakes, your history, and find a future with me.'

Violet stared at him, her eyes wide, and for just a moment he thought she might actually listen to his side of the story. Then she held out his phone and her thumb grazed the play button again.

'Do you think...were there signs? Ones that you missed?'

His own voice, pressing Rick for more answers, a deeper admission of guilt.

Violet's face turned stony at the sound.

Rick's heavy sigh echoed around the studio.

'Probably. But then again, maybe not. When an addiction takes hold...sometimes it can be a slow build towards cracking again, but more often it can just be one moment, one instant that flips you from recovery to addict again. There's such a thin line...and sometimes Jez liked to walk it. To put himself in the way of temptation.'

She pressed 'stop' again and dropped the phone to the table as if it were poisoned.

'I'm not ignoring the signs,' she said, each word like a bullet. 'And I'm not staying anywhere near temptation. I want you to leave. Today.'

'Your father—' He couldn't go. Never mind the story of a lifetime; if he left her now Tom knew Violet would never let him back in, no matter how fast he talked.

'Will understand when I explain exactly what you've done.' Her eyes were cold, her arms folded across her chest like a shield. 'You're just a reporter. I'm family. Trust me on this. I know which one he's going to choose.'

So did Tom. And he knew when he was beaten.

He gave a slight nod and reached for his phone. 'I'll pack now and be gone within the hour.'

He'd gambled everything on this being more than a story. Time to admit he'd lost.

'Goodbye, Violet.'

CHAPTER TWENTY

VIOLET STOOD SHAKING in the middle of the studio for long minutes after Tom left. She needed to move, needed to talk to Rose, needed to explain to her father what she'd done. But how could she when she felt as if her heart, along with some other essential internal organs, had been ripped out?

She'd known, from the moment she saw that story with his name on it, exactly how the day would go. Had known she'd be standing here alone again at the end of it. Seeing Tom abuse her father's trust and exploit his grief for a story had only made it easier.

She'd made the right decision. She'd got out before Tom could tear her life apart again.

So why did she feel so broken all the same?

'Violet, honey?' When had her dad come in? How had she missed that? 'Where's Tom? Your mum said she just saw him walking out the front with a suitcase.'

'I told him to leave.' The words came out as barely more than a whisper. Would Dad be mad? He'd invited Tom here, after all. He was his guest—his employee, really. It hadn't been her place to send him away.

But what else could she do?

His expression cautious, Rick put his arm around her and led her over to the sofa, away from the chairs he and Tom had been sitting in when she'd entered the room. How long ago was that now, anyway? Time seemed strange. Confused.

'What happened, honey?' he asked, sitting beside her. 'Tell your old dad.'

Violet frowned, trying to find the right words to explain. In the end, what came out was, 'Did you really ask him to interview you about Jez today?'

'Why, yeah. I did.' Rick's eyebrows lifted with surprise. 'Is that what all this is about? Vi, honey, it was my choice. When you asked me earlier about going on stage this weekend…I wasn't sure what I wanted to do. I figured talking it out some might help. And Tom, well, he's a good guy, right? And since all this will probably end up in the book eventually anyway, I wanted to get it down—how raw it feels right now. In case it helps anyone else going through the same thing.'

In case it helped someone else. Sometimes Violet wondered if her parents thought too much about that and not enough about themselves. But that was who they were and she loved them for it, all the same.

'Are you sure it was a good idea?' she asked. 'I mean, everyone wants that interview, and you don't know what Tom is going to do with it now he's—' She broke off with a sob before she could reach the word *gone*.

Rick tugged her closer and she buried her face in his shoulder. 'Do you want me to get your mum? Or your sisters?'

Violet shook her head against his top. 'No. I just…I just need a few minutes.' A few minutes to let the misery out. To let go of all the hope she'd clung to over the last week or so. The chance that her future might be different to her past.

Uncle Jez had probably had that hope too, and look where it had got him.

That thought set off another wave of tears, and Violet didn't try to fight them. She might be all grown up these days, but sometimes a girl still needed her daddy's shoulder to cry on.

Eventually, though, the sobs faded and her tears dried and she knew her dad was going to want some answers.

'You sent him away,' Rick said. Not a question, not even a judgement. Just an opening, to show he was listening if she wanted to explain.

'I found something out about him,' Violet replied, unsure how much she really wanted him to know. Except this was her dad. He'd been there through everything. He'd understand, right? He'd want his little girl safe and happy. 'I know you thought he was a trustworthy journalist, I know that's why you picked him to write your book. But Dad, he wrote a story once. A story that destroyed a girl's life—just like Nick destroyed mine.'

Rick stilled, his arms securely tucked around her. 'You're sure?'

'Very. He admitted it.' Well, sort of. 'He claimed it wasn't the same but then he would, wouldn't he?'

Rick sighed, deep and heartfelt. 'Then I understand why you did what you did. But Violet, I need you to remember something very important, okay?' He pulled back to stare into her eyes, and Violet gave a small nod. 'Your life wasn't destroyed. Remember that.'

Shame filled Violet's chest. Here she was complaining when Uncle Jez's life was gone for ever. And she'd give anything for him to be caught up in a sex scandal right now, even if it meant the papers dragging up her own sordid story all over again.

'I know. Compared to Uncle Jez—'

'That's not what I mean,' Rick said with a sharp shake of the head. 'Think about it, Violet. You still have your home, your family. They took your confidence, and I'll never forgive them for that. But you're still you. You're still my daughter. And you are still loved.'

Warmth filled her, from the heart outwards. 'I know. And I'm so lucky to have you all. But it felt like…they made me someone I wasn't. So they took away who I really am.'

'But they can't.' Rick tapped her on the forehead with one finger. 'She's still in there. And it looked to me like Tom was helping you remember who she is.'

'I thought so too.' Until she'd found out the truth.

There was a pause, and when Violet looked up she saw her dad had on his thoughtful face. The one that always made her mother nervous.

'How did you find out about it? The story he wrote, I mean?'

Violet grimaced. 'Nick called. Told me I should look into his earlier stories.'

'Nick?' Rick's eyebrows launched upwards. '*The* Nick? And you *listened* to him?'

'I hung up on him,' Violet said. 'But…I was curious.'

'As ever.' Rick sighed. 'Did you talk to Tom about it before you threw him out?'

'A bit. I think he wanted to say more,' she admitted.

'Maybe you should listen.' Rick threw up his hands in pre-emptive defence. 'I'm not standing up for the guy—you get to make your own choices about him, and if you tell me he's not someone we should trust then I'll can the whole book idea altogether. He can publish what he has in interviews, but there's not even enough for a novella there. But Vi, if he matters to you—and I think he does—then you have to hear him out. Don't let someone else's version of who he is make your mind up for you.'

Violet nodded, and Rick bent over to kiss her on the

top of the head before moving towards the door. 'Listen to your old dad, yeah? He's been around awhile and some-times, just sometimes, he knows what he's talking about.'

'I will,' Violet promised. But she couldn't help but be afraid this might not be one of those times.

'Hey, did you see this?'

Violet looked up from the file in front of her to see Rose in the doorway to the study, holding up a newspaper.

'It's less than twenty-four hours until the Benefit, Rose,' Violet said. 'I don't have time to read the paper.'

'You need to read this one.' Rose slipped into the room, revealing Daisy behind her. Daisy took the visitor's chair, rubbing her baby bump, while Rose perched on the edge of the desk, holding out the paper.

Violet sighed. Apparently she wasn't getting out of this without reading something. 'What is it?' she asked, reluctantly reaching out for the paper.

'Tom's first article from his interviews with Dad,' Daisy said, and Violet froze, her fingers brushing the edge of the newsprint.

'You really do need to read it,' Rose added.

God, but she didn't want to. One way or another, this would settle it. If he'd written the sort of story she expected him to, then there'd be no point listening to his side of the story about anything. It really would be over.

And if he hadn't…if by any chance he'd written the sort of story she'd want to read…what would she do then? Risk giving him a second chance?

She wasn't sure she could.

Swallowing, Violet took the newspaper from her sis-ter's hand and skimmed over the section she'd folded it over to. Then, letting out a breath, she read it over again, slower this time.

'It's good, isn't it,' Daisy said after a moment. 'I mean, the guy can really write.'

'Sensitive, too,' Rose added. 'He really got Dad. I've never read an interview with him that made me feel like I was actually there talking with him before.'

'Vi, are you sure…?' Daisy trailed off as Violet shot a glare at her.

She really didn't want to talk about this. On the one hand, she should have known better than to get involved with a reporter in the first place. And if he really, truly did turn out to be a different breed, the lesser spotted good guy journalist…what did it matter now anyway? He was gone. She'd sent him away, and for good reason.

'Did you hear who he got to stand in for Uncle Jez tonight, by the way?' Rose asked. 'God only knows how. I tried to get the band to play second billing to the Lemons when we first put together the programme, but their schedule was crammed. Tom must have really pulled some strings.'

'I'm organising the concert, Rose. Of course I heard,' Violet snapped, then sighed. 'Sorry. I know. He's been great. Right from the start.'

'And yet…' Daisy prompted.

Violet dropped the paper to the desk. If there was anyone she could talk to, anyone who could tell her what she should do next, surely it would be her sisters. Especially since *they* at least seemed to have love all sussed out.

'Have Will or Seb ever done anything, like, in their past? Something you're not sure you could ever understand? Or forgive?'

Rose laughed. 'Vi, honey, Will left four women at the altar, remember? You're his best friend; you know he's not perfect. And was I damn afraid he might do the same thing to me? Of course I was.'

'But you married him anyway,' Violet said.

Rose shrugged. 'It's like Mum and Dad always say. When you know, you know. Will is the one for me. Once I accepted that…everything got a hell of a lot easier.'

Violet turned to Daisy. 'What about you?'

'I thought my marriage could only ever be a show, a business deal,' Daisy reminded her. 'But Rose is right—when you know, you know. So, the question is—do you know?'

Did she? Violet wasn't even sure. 'All I know is that it hurts, not having him here,' she admitted.

Rose and Daisy exchanged a look. Violet wasn't used to being on the outside of those looks. She didn't like it.

'Hurts like a dull ache, like something's missing but you can still feel it?' Rose asked. 'Like a phantom limb?'

'Or hurts like a sharp, blinding pain. The sort that consumes you until you can't think about anything else?' Daisy added.

'Both,' Violet admitted. 'And all the time.'

Rose and Daisy grinned across at each other.

'Honey, you totally know,' Rose said as she hopped off the desk.

'Where are you going?' Violet asked, standing when Daisy stood to follow.

Daisy flashed a smile back over her shoulder. 'To look at maternity bridesmaid dresses, of course. In lavender.'

Violet sank back down into her chair. She wished she could be so confident. Maybe she would have been, before Nick and everything that followed.

She took a deep breath. Maybe she would just have to be again; maybe she could find that lost confidence—if it meant winning Tom back.

He shouldn't be here. Tom was almost one hundred per cent certain he shouldn't be here. But Rick had called and said he was playing after all, and did Tom have any suggestions for a one-off stand-in guitarist for the night…and Tom couldn't not help. Not when he knew what a difference it could make to the night he and Violet had worked so hard to put together.

Even if she didn't want him there.

'Thanks again for doing this,' he said to Owain as a wide-eyed volunteer let them through the artists' gate.

'Are you kidding? Playing with the Lemons? It's an honour, man.' Owain's smile was wide, genuine—and world-famous. Tom had met the guitarist when his band was just starting out, and he'd rapidly become one of those friends he could call on for a night out whenever they were in the same city. These days, Owain's band played sold-out arena tours and, while the frontman might be the most famous member, any true music lover knew it was Owain's guitar playing that made their songs so memorable.

It didn't hurt that he had legions of female fans either, Tom thought. That had to be a bonus for tonight.

'I guess this is where I leave you,' he said as Owain headed through to the bands area. Normally, Tom would have been in there too, mingling, chatting, lining up interviews and soaking in the atmosphere. Tonight, he couldn't take the chance of bumping into Violet.

She had to be around here somewhere, he thought, as he waved goodbye to Owain. Probably racing around, double-checking everything, keeping everything under control in a way he couldn't have imagined her doing when they'd first met.

Strange to remember how he'd thought she was a spoilt rich kid, incapable of doing anything except trade on her parents' names and her own notoriety. He was happy to admit he'd been totally wrong about her.

He just wished she'd believe she was wrong about him, too.

'Tom! You made it.' Rick Cross clapped a hand on his shoulder and Tom tried not to jump.

'Hey. Things going well?' Tom asked, since he couldn't exactly ask, *How's Violet? Where is she? Will she ever forgive me?*

'Best Benefit Concert ever,' Rick announced, then lowered his voice. 'Don't tell Rose I said that, though, yeah?'

'Wouldn't dream of it.'

'Speaking of my girls, have you seen any of them yet?' Rick asked, his tone far too nonchalant. 'Say, Violet, for instance?'

'Ah, no. I thought it was probably best if I stayed out of the way a bit tonight,' Tom said. 'I really just came to bring Owain as a favour to a mate.'

'I see.' Rick subjected him to a long assessing look. 'And here I was thinking that you were here to set things right between the two of you. Never figured you for someone who'd quit at the first hurdle.'

'I'm not…I never said I'd quit.' Tom *wasn't* a quitter. But he also knew when he wasn't wanted. 'Maybe I'm just giving Violet a little space before I make my move.'

'Or maybe you're too scared she'll never trust you.'

How did the old man do that? See right to the heart of his every worry? Tom could understand it working with his daughters, but he'd only known the man a month.

Rick flashed him a quick grin and gripped his shoulder again. 'Don't worry, son. I'm not a mind-reader. But I've been where you are. Sherry and I always say "when you know, you know" and it's true. But we got married in a hurry, and knowing it's the real thing doesn't always make it any easier when times are hard. It just means you know it's worth fighting through.'

'And fighting for,' Tom murmured, almost to himself.

'Always that,' Rick agreed. 'Go on. Go find her. I think she's backstage.'

He shouldn't. This was her big night. She'd worked damn hard for it, and he didn't want to get in her way now. But on the other hand…how could he let this awful feeling in his chest that had started the moment he'd left Huntingdon Hall grow any bigger?

'Backstage, you say.' Tom squared his shoulders, wishing this didn't feel so much like heading into battle. 'Then I guess that's where I'm going.'

CHAPTER TWENTY-ONE

THE ATMOSPHERE BACKSTAGE was incredible. How had she never experienced this before? Normally at the Benefit it would be Rose rushing about behind the scenes, while Violet, Daisy and their mum would watch from a carefully sectioned off area of the crowd.

But now Violet knew—backstage was the place to be.

The act on stage finished their last song with a resounding chord that echoed off the trees surrounding the concert area, and the audience exploded into wild applause. Violet grinned and clapped along as the band traipsed off, high-fiving each other as they came.

'Great job, guys,' she told them, and got wide smiles in return. This was what all the work had been for. To put together a spectacular night that would help raise money and awareness for a cause that really counted.

It almost didn't matter that the person she wanted to share it with wasn't there.

Almost.

'Violet?'

Her breath caught in her throat at the sound of Tom's voice behind her. Of course he was here. How could a music journo miss a night like tonight?

She turned slowly, barely registering the next act as they took to the stage, even as the singer, Sammy, called back to her, something about a shout-out. There was cheering and music and noise all around her, and all she could see or hear was Tom, standing there, solemn-faced, watching her, waiting for her to speak.

And suddenly she had to figure out what she wanted to say.

She'd thought she would have more time. That she could tackle this at her own leisurely pace. But, instead, here he was and she needed to fix things. Somehow.

This could be her last chance.

'Tom.' His name was a start, right? A very small one, but still.

He stepped closer, just one pace. 'Things seem to be going great tonight.'

'They really are.' She bit her lip. 'I wasn't sure if you'd come.'

'Neither was I. But Owain asked me to come with him.'

'That's the only reason?' She almost didn't want to ask. Just in case.

'No.' How could one word send such a flood of relief through her system?

'I'm glad you came,' Violet admitted. 'I wanted to…I never gave you a chance to explain, last time. And I think…I'll listen now. If you still want to talk.'

'I do,' Tom said, but the hesitation in his voice made Violet nervous.

'But?'

Tom shook his head. 'You have a lot going on here today. It can wait.'

'I'm not sure it can.' Violet frowned. There was something more here. Something she wasn't getting. 'What is it?'

Tom leant back against the side of the stage with a sigh, and Violet had to step closer to even hear him over the noise of the band starting up. 'I can explain everything, and I think I can probably do it well enough to make you forgive me. This time.'

'Well, good?'

'But the thing is, Violet, that's only good for this time. What happens the next time I do something you don't agree with, or the next time something reminds you that I'm a hated journalist. You kick me out without listening again?'

'So…you're saying it's not worth trying?' Her stomach dropped lower and lower as every second passed without Tom's answer.

'I'm saying it's something I want you to think about. I want to know that you can trust me because I'm *me*. Not because I can tell you that my editor got a tip from an anonymous source and those photos in a brown envelope, and gave me the story to write as a test. To prove I could. To earn my stripes. And I thought it was just a practice run, that it wouldn't go to print. I don't want you to trust me just because I swear to you I asked him not to print it, and he laughed at me and I realised Mom was right all along.' He sighed, running a hand through his hair. 'I can explain as much as you want, Vi, and I will, probably often if we decide to make a go of things. But I need to know you trust me enough to not *need* the explanation to keep loving me. Does that make sense?'

It did. It was just an awfully big ask.

She opened her mouth to respond, to promise him whatever he wanted if he'd just *stay* long enough for them to sort things out. But then she heard her name blaring out of the speakers on stage, via Sammy, the lead singer's, microphone.

'And a huge shout-out to Violet Huntingdon Cross for putting together such an epic party! Come on out here, Violet!'

'You should go,' Tom said, stepping back from her. 'I don't think she's used to being kept waiting.'

'But we need to—'

'I'll find you later,' Tom said. 'We'll talk then.'

But later would be too late; Violet knew it in her bones. Which meant it would have to be this way, instead. 'Go find Mum and Daisy and Rose. They're out front.'

Tom nodded, and was gone before Violet even stepped out onto the stage.

The lights flashed and burned her eyes and the cheers made her head pound, but nothing could dim her determination. She knew what she needed to do now. She just needed the courage to go through with it.

'Thanks, Sammy,' she said, stepping up to the microphone. She couldn't make out anything beyond the blurs of light in the crowd; she just had to trust that Tom was out there, listening. 'And thank you all for coming tonight.' She paused while the crowd cheered, and tried to ignore the way her knees were shaking. 'The Huntingdon Hall Benefit Concert is always a highlight of the year, but this is the first time I've been able to be so involved in it. You might have noticed that I've been keeping a bit of a low profile over the past few years. But that's…' she stumbled over her words for a moment and bit the inside of her cheek hard, determined to keep it together '…that's going to change.'

There were murmurs running through the crowd now, questions and speculations and probably a few off-colour jokes, too. Violet ignored all of them, looked up into the lights and said what she needed to say.

'I wanted tonight to be a memorial for my Uncle Jez, for his life, and a way of raising both money and awareness for people who find themselves in the same position and need our help.' She took a breath, drawing in courage.

'Whenever we suffer a loss—from a loss of a job, or our reputation, all the way up to a beloved family member— we have to grieve. We have to heal and we have to move on. And sometimes that can be the hardest part—letting go of the past and opening ourselves up to the possibilities of the future. It's taken me a while, but I'm finally able to do that. I am moving on. And you're going to be seeing more of me because of it. I'm going to be out there, raising awareness everywhere I can. I want to let people know that if they need help, it is out there for them. And I want to make sure they get it—because if I can spare one other family a loss like we've suffered this week, it will be worth every minute.'

The roar of the crowd's applause rumbled in her ears and the heat in her cheeks started to fade. She'd done it. She'd taken that step forward and moved on—she just hoped that Tom had seen it.

Because now she needed to find him for the next part.

Handing the microphone back to Sammy, she rushed off stage as the band started up their next song. Weaving her way through the business backstage, smiling vaguely at every clap on the back or supportive comment, she headed for where she hoped Tom would be—with her family.

The pride in his chest felt too big for his body, as if it might burst out of him at any moment. Never mind talking to the press on the phone or holding meetings with managers. Violet had put herself back out there—completely. She'd stood up in front of the crowd, the press and everyone watching on TV and declared herself part of the world again. A woman with a mission.

She wasn't ashamed any more, and it was beautiful.

'Did you *see* that?' Rose bounced up next to him, pure delight shining from her face.

'She was magnificent!' Daisy agreed.

'She most certainly was,' Sherry said, smiling with pride.

'Where is she?' Rose asked. 'I need to hug her.'

'Not until I do,' Tom murmured, and the three women turned to look at him.

Which was, of course, when Violet bounded in.

'Vi! You were brilliant!' Rose and Daisy reached for their sister, and Violet grinned—but her gaze was fixed on Tom's face. He could feel it, even as he stared back.

'Sorry, guys, but I need to talk to Tom,' Violet said.

They both ignored the knowing looks her family exchanged as they headed out of the private area, past the edge of the crowd and around through some of the smaller stalls set up on the outskirts of the concert. Tom vaguely recognised some of the women from the village manning one of the charity support stalls. As they passed them, Violet waved, then reached out to hold Tom's hand. Another sign she was done worrying about what others thought? He hoped so.

Of course, right now he was more interested in finding out exactly what *she* thought about their potential future together.

Eventually, they reached the security barriers out of the concert site, and Violet slipped them through with her pass. 'Where are we going?' Tom asked.

Violet shrugged. 'It doesn't really matter. I just…some things are still private, right?' She flashed him a quick smile and tugged him further along, until they were surrounded by trees at the edge of the wood. 'This will do.'

Tom wanted to ask what, exactly, it would do for. But Violet seemed nervous enough. For once, he'd have to curb his natural impulse to ask questions, lots of them, and let her talk in her own time.

Sometimes, he'd learnt, you got the best interviews that way.

Violet sucked in a deep breath, then let it out again. Tom stamped down on the impatience rising inside him. He had to let her take her time.

'Okay, so…I learnt something while you were gone. Or realised something, I guess. That…maybe people have never been able to move past my past, so to speak, because I've never done anything else. I need to replace those memories—those stories and those jokes—with new and better ones.'

'And that's what you were doing up there on the stage,' Tom guessed.

Violet nodded. 'Starting to, anyway. And it means moving on. Not just from that stupid sex tape, but from the last eight years of hiding, too. Of not trusting anyone and always expecting the worst.'

'Well…good.' Because that sounded positive. But he still needed to hear her say the words.

Violet looked up and met his gaze, her eyes wide and blue and totally open for the first time since he'd met her. 'My mum and dad, they always say that when you know, you know. And I think they're right.' The side of her mouth twisted up into a half smile. 'And I *did* know, deep down. It was just hard to see, behind all that doubt and fear and mistrust.'

'And now?' Tom asked, his heart thumping too hard, too loud in his chest.

'And being without you…it swept all that away. It hurt so much to be apart from you that none of the rest of it mattered any more. All that mattered was telling you that I love you. And I trust you. I do.'

'Really?' God, why couldn't he just take her words at face value?

Violet took his hand between hers. 'Enough to trust you with the rest of my life. If you'll have me.'

Tom blinked. 'You want to get married?'

Violet smiled, slow and warm. 'Why not? It seems to be all the rage this year. Besides, when you know, you know.' She reached up and kissed him once on the lips. 'And I know that whatever happens, whatever you've done or whatever you will do, I trust you to do it for us, not just for a quick story. I'm not the same person I was when that sex tape was made, and I know you're not the same person who let his editor use that story. And I'm not interested in who we were. Only who we can be together.'

And that was all he needed to know. Wrapping his arms tight around her waist, he pulled Violet close, kissing her long and deep until the sounds of the concert, the lights, even the breeze through the trees ceased to register. All that mattered was him and Violet, and their future together.

Finally, he pulled back, just enough to rest his forehead against hers. 'You did the same for me, you know,' he whispered fiercely. 'I spent so many years carrying around the guilt from that story, from my mom never knowing that I realised she was right, even if it was a little late. Meeting you…it made me face that guilt, and all my preconceptions about who you were. If you hadn't shown me that it was possible to move beyond our own pasts…I never could have come back here today. I never could have told you I love you too.'

Violet kissed him again, swift and sharp and full of feeling. But Tom wasn't done talking.

'I should get down on one knee, I know, but I don't want to move that far away from you,' he said, and Violet laughed. 'Violet Huntingdon-Cross. Will you do me the honour of becoming my wife?'

'Only if you'll do me the honour of being my husband,' Violet said, and kissed him again.

'Then it's settled. Your mum gets to plan another wedding.' He squeezed her tighter. 'What do you think? Next summer? Big celebrity bash?'

Violet laughed. 'Haven't you heard? The Huntingdon-Cross sisters don't wait that long for their happy ever afters.'

'True.' Tom smiled. 'Next month, then?'

'Sounds perfect,' Violet said. 'I'm ready to start our new lives. Together.'

EPILOGUE

THE SUMMER SUN shone down on Huntingdon Hall as crowds gathered for the fourth, and final, Huntingdon-Cross wedding celebration of the year. Violet peeked through the curtains of her bedroom, careful not to be seen, and watched the cars pulling up on the long driveway.

Somewhere out there, probably pacing with his soon-to-be brothers-in-law at his side, was her fiancé. She wondered what Tom was making of being the centre of attention for once, instead of just writing about other people's fame.

'Are you ready?' At the sound of her twin's voice, Violet let the curtain fall back into place and turned to smile at Rose.

'More ready than I thought I could ever be,' Violet said.

Stepping forward, the lavender silk of her bridesmaid's dress rustling around her, Rose hugged her sister, a feeling so warm and familiar that Violet felt love in every squeeze.

'Mum is downstairs, waiting to give final approval on the three of us before she heads out to the ceremony area,' Daisy said, her seven-months-pregnant bump appearing a moment before the rest of her came through the door. 'And Dad's just putting the finishing touches to his speech. Again.'

'"Final approval"?' Violet asked with a smile. 'Is she

worried Daisy might get jam on her dress, like she did when she was bridesmaid at Uncle Jez's second wedding?' The pang of pain at the thought of Jez was still there, but already it felt more like a loving memory than a searing loss. The hole he'd left would always be there, but they'd learn to live with it, Violet knew, to move on and make his death meaningful, at least.

'I was five!' Daisy pointed out indignantly.

'Just think, soon it will be your little bump trailing down the aisle in jam-smeared taffeta, leaving rose petals in her wake,' Rose said.

'Well, as long as it's not me, for once,' Violet said, checking her reflection one last time before they headed downstairs. 'I'm done being a bridesmaid, I think.'

'And today you're the bride.' Daisy's words came out a little watery, and Rose handed her a tissue for the inevitable tears.

'Don't start yet,' Rose said. 'We've got the whole ceremony to get through!'

'Not to mention Dad's speech,' Violet added. She wasn't sure if she was dreading or looking forward to hearing which tales of her life Rick Cross thought appropriate to share with the assembled company.

'Can't help it,' Daisy sniffed. 'Hormones.'

'Yeah, yeah,' Rose replied. 'A convenient excuse. They don't seem to be slowing you down any, though, do they? Seb was telling me all about your plans for Hawkesley Castle and his new TV series at dinner last night. It would be nauseating how much that man dotes on you if it wasn't so well deserved.'

Daisy elbowed Rose in the ribs. 'Don't tell me you didn't shed a tear or two when you were making those gorgeous rings for Violet and Tom.'

'Maybe just one,' Rose admitted. 'And they are very pretty, aren't they?'

'They're perfect,' Violet said. 'Just like everything else about today. Now, come on, let's go present ourselves for inspection.'

Violet followed her sisters out of the room, pausing to shut the door behind her. Strange to think she was leaving this place as herself, but would be returning as a married woman. Almost as impossible to believe as the thought of her getting married at all.

But here she was, with her sisters at her side, preparing to say *I do* to the last man she'd ever imagined marrying. And she couldn't be happier.

Sherry Huntingdon-Cross clapped her hands together with delight at the sight of them. 'Oh, don't you all look perfect,' she gushed before wedding planner mode took over again. 'Right, I'm going to head down and take my seat—that's the sign for the ushers to get everyone else seated. Rose, Daisy, you follow just behind me. Then Rick—where is your father, anyway?'

'Here, honey.' Rick Cross came rushing out of his studio, shoving pieces of paper into his pocket. 'Just a couple of last-minute edits. Don't worry,' he added with a wink at Violet. 'I kept the story about that time you fell in the pond at that hotel roof garden when we were on tour in Europe.'

'Oh, good,' Violet said unconvincingly.

'Right,' Sherry said again, commanding everyone's attention. 'I'm leaving. Daisy, Rose, prepare to follow.'

The wedding procession had been timed to perfection. As her father took her arm and led her out of the front door of her childhood home behind her sisters, Violet took a deep breath and followed her family down to the shady clearing, just behind the trees, where they'd set up the chairs and ceremony area. It wasn't a huge wedding—

despite Sherry's attempts—but neither was it the tiny one Violet would have insisted on even a few months ago.

She wasn't scared to share her new happiness, to let others see her moving on with her life in exciting new directions. She wasn't hiding any more.

At the front of the aisle, Tom turned, as if sensing her presence, and Violet couldn't hold back her smile at the sight of him in his perfect suit, waiting for her to join him.

'You ready for this, honey?' Rick asked as the string quartet struck up the canon.

'How could I not be?' Violet whispered back. 'After all, when you know, you know.'

* * * * *

MILLS & BOON
True Love
Romance from the Heart

Celebrate true love with tender stories of heartfelt romance, from the rush of falling in love to the joy a new baby can bring, and a focus on the emotional heart of a relationship.